I0713497

TANGLED IN TINSEL & KNOTS

A WHISPERING GROVE NOVEL

OMEGAVERSE ROMANCE

HARLEY KNIGHT

Tangled in Tinsel & Knots © Copyright 2025 Harley Knight

Cover Designer: Bookin It Designs
Editing: Outthink Editing, LLC

All rights reserved.

No part of this book may be reproduced or transmitted in any form or by any means, electronic or mechanical, including photocopying, recording, or by any information storage and retrieval system, without permission in writing of the author, except for use of brief quotations in a book review.

This is a work of fiction. Any resemblance to actual persons, living or dead, or actual events is purely coincidental.

CONTENTS

TANGLED IN TINSEL & KNOTS

A WHISPERING GROVE NOVEL

I kissed the wrong Santa. Now he wants to make my name on the naughty list permanent.

Cornered beneath the mistletoe with a creepy coworker closing in, I grabbed the nearest Santa for a quick-escape kiss.

Big mistake.

Because the man behind the fake beard wasn't the cheerful volunteer I'd thought he was. He was one of the infamous bounty hunters who live on the outskirts of Whispering Grove.

The kind who can track anyone, anywhere.

And the kiss? Way more than friendly.

It left me hot and bothered… and my coworker green with Grinch-level envy.

Now he's trying to steal the business out from under me and kicking me out of my home while he's at it.

My only shot at saving my dream? Three dangerously sexy bounty hunters who offer a deal I can't refuse. They'll help me fight back and give me a place to stay in their sprawling mansion, reindeer included.

Between late-night planning sessions, hot glances, and hands that linger a little too long, I'm starting to wonder if the real danger isn't losing my career but falling for three men who could wreck my heart as easily as they take down criminals.

I've landed on someone's naughty list.

I just never expected to like it so much.

CHAPTER ONE

CHRIS

Snow falls in fat, lazy flakes, pretty enough to lie about how cold this place really is.

Main Street is dressed up in picture-perfect Christmas bullshit. Twinkling lights strung between lampposts, wreaths on every storefront, families bundled up like they're extras in a Hallmark movie.

Too clean. Too soft.

This town forgets that monsters don't always hide under beds.

Sometimes they're out on bail.

"Remind me why we're doing this in the middle of Main Street?" I lean back in the passenger seat of our F-250, watching a mom wrangle three kids outside a toy store. The truck is warm, heater blasting, and I've got a good view of the bakery across the street. Flour & Fable Bakery, the sign says in swirly letters.

"Because Dirtbag Declan decided to show his face at

the bakery," Kane says from behind the wheel. He taps the steering wheel with two fingers like he's keeping time to music only he can hear. "And because you like money."

"His name is Declan Krail," Noel says from the back seat. He's hunched over his tablet, scrolling through the file for what has to be the dozenth time. The guy takes homework to another level. "Two counts of breaking and entering. Attempted theft. Arson. Two cabins burned. One almost killed a family. Battery on the officer who tried to bring him in the first time. Skipped court twice. Bail bondsman is offering a nice chunk of change."

I pull out my phone, scrolling to the text that came through this morning.

"Fifty grand split three ways." Kane's grin is all predator, nothing friendly about it. "That's new equipment. Maybe finally upgrade the surveillance gear."

"We don't need new gear. We need him in cuffs before he burns down half the town." I crack my knuckles, watching the bakery door. It's a habit I can't break, something that happens before every job. The familiar pop-pop-pop of joints settling.

"You think he's stupid enough to run?" Kane sits up straighter. His whole demeanor shifts, less relaxed, more coiled spring.

"Well, he's stupid enough to show up in his hometown after skipping bail twice." I roll down the window a crack. Cold air rushes in, carrying the smell of fresh snow and something sweet, cinnamon rolls maybe, or those fancy pastries rich people pay too much for. "So yeah, I think he's exactly that stupid."

Noel is already moving, checking the cuffs on his belt with practiced efficiency. No wasted motion with him. Every action deliberate.

It's been twenty minutes since we spotted Declan going in, stuffing his face like he's got nothing better to do than enjoy the holiday season. "We move quietly, no scene. Last thing we need is every phone on Main Street recording us."

"Too late for that." Kane nods toward a group of teenagers across the street, phones already out, filming something. Probably each other, but it won't take much for us to become the main attraction.

"Then we make it fast."

The bakery door swings open, and out walks Santa Claus. Or rather, Declan Krail in a Santa suit that looks like it survived several wars and lost all of them. The red velvet is shiny where the fabric has worn thin, the white fur trim is yellowing like old teeth, and the belt is creating a gut situation that has to be uncomfortable. He's got cookie crumbs in his fake beard.

"Ho ho ho!" His voice pitches up to a family with two young kids on the sidewalk, fake-cheerful in a way that makes my skin crawl. "Have you been good this year?"

A little girl, maybe six, nods so hard her whole body moves.

Kane snorts. "Nothing says 'criminal mastermind' like clearance-bin Santa."

"Let's go." I'm already opening my door, boots hitting snow-covered pavement. The cold slaps my face. I adjust my coat, which is long enough to hide the equipment on my belt.

We spread out like we've done this a hundred times before, because we have. I approach from behind, keeping my steps light despite my size. Noel peels left, hands in his jacket pockets, face blank as stone. Kane moves right, cutting off the street exit with nothing but his presence. The guy is built like he could flip a car, and people instinctively step back when they see him coming.

Declan is still performing, his back to me. "And what do you want for Christmas, sweetheart?"

"A puppy!"

"Well, we'll see what Santa can—"

I'm three feet away when he catches my reflection in the bakery window. His whole body locks up, shoulders going rigid. For a heartbeat, everything freezes—me, him, the family watching with confused smiles.

Then he runs.

"Fuck." I lunge forward, catching the back of his Santa coat. The cheap fabric tears, stitching giving way, but I've got enough to yank him backward. He stumbles, arms windmilling, and I use his momentum against him.

Kane slams into him from the side, and between the two of us, we take him down. We hit the sidewalk hard, snow cushioning the impact but not by much. I feel the concrete under the slush, unforgiving, and adjust my weight so his skull doesn't crack against it. Last thing we need is a lawsuit.

"Get off me!" Declan thrashes like a caught fish, the Santa hat flying off into a snowbank. "I didn't do anything!"

"Sure you didn't." I pin his shoulders, knees on either side of him. "That's why you ran the second you saw us."

"This is police brutality!"

Kane laughs, low and dark, and flashes him his bounty hunter identification badge. "We're not cops. We're something much worse for you." He's got Declan's legs now, controlling the thrashing. "Cops have rules. We just have a contract."

The little girl who wanted a puppy is crying now, full-on wailing into her mother's coat. The mom is staring at us with an expression that promises tomorrow's Nextdoor post will be titled something like "Violent Thugs Attack Innocent Man on Main Street."

"Keep moving, folks." Noel has appeared, using his considerable frame to block the view while I get Declan's wrists behind his back. His voice is flat, bored even, like this is the least interesting thing he'll do today. "Just removing a wanted fugitive. Everyone can go back to their shopping."

"SANTA!" Some kid in the growing crowd is screaming. "WHY ARE THEY HURTING SANTA?"

The cuffs click closed with a satisfying finality. I haul Declan to his feet, and Noel is already there, brushing snow off the guy's shoulders with mock courtesy that's somehow more threatening than if he'd left him covered.

"Declan Krail, you missed your court date. Twice." Noel is reciting facts, voice steady as a metronome. "We're here to escort you back so you can face the consequences of burning down two cabins, nearly killing a family, and assaulting an officer. You have the right to remain silent, which I strongly suggest you exercise before you say something that makes this worse."

"I'm innocent!" Declan's voice cracks, and real tears start streaming down his face, mixing with the fake beard. The guy is going for an Oscar here. "This is a mistake! I didn't burn those cabins! I was framed!"

"The evidence says otherwise." Noel pulls out his tablet, swipes through screens with one hand while keeping Declan steady with the other. "You were identified at the scene by three witnesses. Your fingerprints were on the gas can. The Smyth family, they remember you just fine. Gave a positive ID from their hospital beds."

"That was—I can explain—"

"Save it for the judge." I grab his other arm, and together, Noel and I march him toward the truck. Kane is trailing behind, running interference, keeping the crowd at bay with nothing but his size and a smile. He's good at looking friendly while radiating don't-fuck-with-me energy.

"We'll have him back in custody within the hour,"

Noel calls over his shoulder, probably for anyone filming this on their phone. "Everyone can continue enjoying their afternoon."

We're almost to the truck when the bakery door slams open hard enough to make the bells jangle violently.

"STOP!"

I turn, and there's a woman charging toward us. She's small, maybe five-five, curves packed into dark jeans and a flour-dusted apron, dark brown curls with caramel highlights escaping from a bun in about fifteen different directions. Her eyes are golden brown, bright with determination, and they're locked on Declan.

She skids to a stop right in front of us, breathing hard, and I notice flour on her cheek, powdered sugar dusting her forearms. She smells like vanilla and butter.

"What are you doing?" Her voice is sharp, accusatory. "You can't take him!"

"Ma'am—" Noel starts.

"We NEED him!" She's talking fast, words tumbling over each other in a rush. "He's supposed to be Santa today for the Winter Party for a client. My sister planned this for months. You can't just drag him away!"

"We can, actually." I shift my grip on Declan and hand him over to Noel. "We're bounty hunters. He's a fugitive who skipped bail. This is our job."

"Lily!" Declan twists toward her. His lower lip trembles. "Lily, please, tell them I'm innocent! I shouldn't be dragged away like this! I help people! I volunteer at the shelter! This is all a misunderstanding! Tell them!"

"You burned down two cabins," Kane barks.

"LIES!" Declan shouts. "All lies! The media, they twist everything!"

Noel's jaw tightens, which is his version of wanting to throttle someone.

"Look." The woman—Lily—plants herself directly in front of me, and she has to crane her neck to make eye contact. She's barely up to my chest. "I understand you're doing your job. I get it. But do you have any idea what this is going to do? The Winter Party is in an hour. My sister has been planning this for six months. There are going to be thirty families there. You're leaving them without a Santa at the biggest event of the year."

"Your sister should've done a better background check on her Santa." I try to step around her. She moves with me, blocking.

"She did! He had references!"

"From other criminals, probably," Kane mutters behind me.

"This isn't our problem." I mean it to sound final, but it comes out more tired than anything. "We're not ruining Christmas. He ruined it when he decided to commit arson, skip bail, and hide in a Santa suit instead of facing what he did."

She has her hands on her hips, staring at us, lips thinning. "Then one of *you* needs to replace him!"

The words hang in the air like smoke.

Kane's laugh is sudden, loud, bouncing off the store-fronts. "Oh, shit. Oh, this is beautiful." He's grinning now, and it's the kind of smile that means someone is about to suffer, and that someone is usually me. "Chris. You. In a Santa suit. I would pay actual money to see that happen."

"Not happening." I'm already shaking my head, but I can feel where this is going, and I hate it.

"Chris would be perfect," Kane continues, warming to the idea like it's a roaring fire. "You've got the build for it. The height. That grumpy-bastard mall-Santa energy. Kids will think you're the real deal, straight from the North Pole, here to judge their souls."

"I'll throw you into traffic."

"You'd miss me."

Noel's mouth twitches, which is as close as he gets to laughing in public. "The suit would hide most of your more alarming features. Make you almost approachable."

"I'm going to murder both of you if you don't shut up."

Lily steps closer, chin tilted up as if she's not afraid to pick a fight with me. Brave girl. "You're taking away their Santa. The least you can do is provide a replacement."

"Ma'am, I'm a bounty hunter. I track down criminals and drag them back to face justice. I don't do parties."

Her eyes narrow. She may be small, but she somehow manages to appear like she could light me on fire with sheer willpower.

"Congratulations," she snaps. "You just explained your literal job description. I didn't ask you to do that. I asked you to fix the problem you caused."

I stare. No one talks to me like this. Usually, people go all wide-eyed, shuffle back, and give me space, rarely making eye contact. Not her.

"My sister booked one Santa," she says. "And you just arrested him."

I glance around, half expecting someone to step in and pull her away, but the crowd has conveniently vanished. Cowards.

She steps even closer, invading my personal space. "Listen, Tall, Dark, and Gruff." She's not backing down, and there's something almost impressive about it. This woman who barely comes up to my chest, staring me down like she's the one with the advantage here. "You've created a very immediate crisis. If we don't find a Santa in an hour, there might be a riot. And you owe us."

"We don't owe you anything."

"You're destroying my sister's event."

"He destroyed it." I nod at Declan. "Take it up with the arsonist."

But she's not glaring at Declan. She's staring daggers at me, and her expression shifts, going softer but somehow more dangerous. "Please," she pleads, quieter now. "I don't want to be the one to tell my sister, Hannah, that her Winter Party is ruined because some bounty hunters couldn't spare a couple of hours of their time."

And there it is. The guilt trip, delivered with surgical precision.

"That's manipulation," I point out.

"Is it working?"

"No."

Kane claps me on the shoulder hard enough to rattle my teeth. "Look at her face, man. Look at those eyes. That's weaponized cuteness. You can't say no to that."

"Watch me. No."

"Besides," Noel adds, and there's amusement in his voice that makes me want to strangle him, "you've got nothing scheduled this afternoon after we drop him off. Calendar's clear. You were just going to brood at home anyway."

Lily is pulling out her phone, fingers flying across the screen. "Please. I'll text you the address. She has suits there in different sizes, and she'll find one that fits. The party starts in an hour. You just have to show up, smile, hand out some presents, and leave. That's it. Surely you can manage that much?"

"I—"

"The guests have been looking forward to this for weeks," she continues, and she's good at this, relentless. Not pleading exactly, but applying pressure in all the right places. "Hannah has worked herself half to death making sure everything's perfect. And if Santa doesn't show, that's going to break her heart. I can't let that happen."

"I'm not Santa," I emphasize.

She grins. "No, you're better. You're the emergency Santa."

God help me. I think she's serious.

I glare at Kane, who's still grinning like the devil himself. "Do you want to live with this guilt?" he says.

Noel is watching this entire situation unfold with barely concealed amusement. Declan is simply struggling in his grip.

"You two are also taking Santa away," I point out to Kane. "This isn't just me."

"Tomayto, tomahto." Kane shrugs, completely unbothered. "But you're the one with the height and the brooding aesthetic."

"Come on," Noel adds. "Take one for the team."

"I hate you both. Deeply."

Lily is still standing there, phone in hand, waiting. Behind her, the crowd starts to disperse now that the excitement is over, but there are still people watching, phones out, probably already posting to every social media platform known to man.

I stare down at Lily.

"One hour," I hear myself say, and I want to punch myself for it. "I show up, do the Santa thing, then I'm done. And you're giving me something in return."

"Free pastries," she says immediately. "A year's worth. Whatever you want."

"Brownies." The word comes out before I can stop it, and Kane makes a noise that sounds suspiciously like he's trying not to laugh.

Her face lights up. "Deal. You show up as Santa, you get brownies for a year."

She's already typing into her phone. "I'll text you now. What's your number?"

I recite it, feeling like I'm signing away my dignity with every digit. My phone buzzes seconds later.

Lily Parker: 447 Maple Ridge. Party starts at 4 p.m. Guard's name is John. I'm texting him now so he'll let you in and get you the suit. Thank you SO much. You have no idea what this means.

"Thank you," Lily says, pocketing her phone. "Just show up and be jolly."

"I don't do jolly."

"Sure you can. Ho ho ho. Merry Christmas. Joy to the world."

"I'm going to need so much alcohol after this."

"Whatever gets you through it." She's backing toward the bakery, and there's relief on her face now, bright and genuine. "Thank you. Seriously. Just suppress your anger for a bit. You'll be great!" Then she's gone, disappeared back into the bakery.

I stand there in the snow, near a criminal in a Santa suit, while my two partners look at me as if I've just provided them with entertainment for the next six months.

"Get in the truck," I growl. "All of you. Now."

Noel is already moving, shoving Declan toward the vehicle. "This is the best day of my life. I need to document this. Photos. Video. Maybe a commemorative plaque."

"Touch your phone and I'm throwing it in the river."

"Worth it."

We pile into the truck, Declan in the back seat still cuffed, me in the passenger seat radiating anger, Kane driving and barely containing his glee, and Noel in the back with our prisoner, probably already planning how to use this against me for the rest of my natural life.

The truck rumbles to life, heat blasting, and Kane pulls onto Main Street, heading for the sheriff's station on the south edge of town.

"You're really doing this," Noel says after a minute of blessed silence.

"Shut up."

"No, seriously. You. Wearing a Santa suit. This is actually happening."

"I swear to God—"

"Already texted Adelaide," Kane announces, thumbs flying across his phone screen while somehow still driving. "Your sister's going to lose her mind when she hears about this."

"If you tell anyone—"

"Too late. Already told everyone. This is going in the group chat. This is going in the Christmas card this year. This is going on your gravestone."

Noel leans forward between the seats. "For what it's worth, you're going to traumatize any kids there. Your face isn't exactly jolly."

I growl under my breath.

Kane is still laughing, the sound filling the truck cab. "Ho ho ho, motherfucker. Welcome to your nightmare."

I flip him off with both hands and stare out the window at the snow-covered streets of Whispering Grove, wondering how the hell my afternoon went from tracking down a wanted criminal to agreeing to wear a Santa suit.

"I'd better get really good brownies for this," I mutter.

"Free brownies for a year," Kane points out. "That's like, what, at least three to four hundred brownies? More?"

"Not enough. Not nearly enough."

CHAPTER TWO

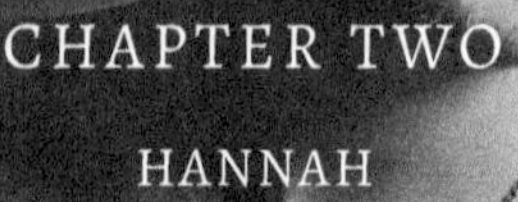

HANNAH

The Winter Party is perfect.

And I mean *perfect* in that terrifying way where you've orchestrated every single detail and now you're just waiting to see which one decides to betray you first.

Pinewood Lodge sits on the north edge of Whispering Grove, all exposed timber beams and stone, the kind of venue that photographers love and costs accordingly. I've transformed it into something out of a winter fairy tale with thousands of white lights strung across the ceiling in cascading waves, creating the illusion of stars. Garland wrapped around every beam, threaded with burgundy ribbon and silver ornaments that catch the light. The large stone fireplace on the east wall crackles with fire, stockings hung along the mantel, flames casting warm shadows across the space.

The twelve-foot Douglas fir dominates the north corner. I personally supervised the tree's installation, made sure it was positioned exactly right so it's visible from every angle. More lights, more ornaments, a gold star on top that required a very tall ladder and a prayer that I wouldn't fall to my death.

Near the tree, a string quartet plays something classical and festive.

The venue is split between function and mingling. Half the space is filled with round tables—seating for thirty families—with white tablecloths and centerpieces made of pine cones, candles, and winter greenery. The other half is standing cocktail tables scattered throughout, tall and circular, perfect for guests to gather around with drinks and appetizers. Right now people are everywhere.

On the far wall, a projection screen cycles through company photos. Team-building exercises. Office parties. Summer picnic. Cascade Tech employees looking happy and productive, the kind of corporate nostalgia that reminds everyone why they're here.

This event is everything I promised it would be.

Six months. That's how long I've been working for Confetti & Meatballs Event Planning, building this partnership with Scot Giordano, proving myself to his uncle Giuseppe, the man who owns the company outright and has the power to sell it to us if he decides we're worth the investment.

Scot's family started this business twenty years ago. His mother's side, with their Italian heritage and a dream to create magical events for their community. It grew from there, became the premier event-planning company in the mountain region. A roster of clients that reads like a who's who of the area, revenue that makes my baker's salary look like pocket change.

Giuseppe brought me on six months ago as a junior partner, provisional, nothing in writing yet. *Prove yourself first, Hannah. Show me you can bring in clients and execute at our level.*

Scot vouched for me. Convinced his uncle I was worth the risk, and so far, he has approved of my work.

The deal on the table—unofficial, handshake, the kind of thing that keeps me up at night—is that Giuseppe sells the company to both of us. Fifty-fifty partnership. Equal investment, equal ownership, equal say in everything.

But only if I prove I belong here.

This event is another one of my proofs. My client, my planning, my execution. Cascade Tech flew thirty families in from Seattle for this corporate thank-you party, and I made damn sure they'd never forget it.

I smooth down my dress, black with subtle silver threading that catches the light, fitted but professional, paired with heels that make my feet scream but photograph beautifully. My hair is in loose waves, makeup simply done.

My phone buzzes in my pocket.

I pull it out. Lily's name is on the screen, calling for what has to be the third time tonight.

I silence it and shove the phone back into my pocket. Whatever crisis my sister is having at the bakery can wait. I love Lily, but her chaos and my career-defining evening cannot collide right now.

"Hannah!" One of the waiters flags me down near the cocoa bar. "We're running low on the white chocolate peppermint. Should I bring out the backup?"

"Yes, and check the marshmallow situation. I saw a kid dumping half the bowl into his cup."

He grins and disappears toward the kitchen.

I scan the room again, mentally checking boxes. Music, perfect. Lighting, gorgeous. Food, flowing. Guests, happy. Santa is by the tree with his back to me, surrounded by children while parents snap photos. Thank God Declan showed up after my original Santa bailed for a better-paying gig.

Then I see Scot, my business partner.

He's leaning against the bar, tie loosened, jacket abandoned on a nearby chair, holding what looks like his fourth whiskey of the afternoon. His usually perfect dark blond hair is messy, falling across his forehead. He has a strong jaw, small eyes, and an athletic build from his college soccer days, but right now he mostly looks drunk.

My stomach drops.

On paper, he's exactly the kind of business partner I'd want. He knows the industry inside and out, has the family connections, the client relationships, the experience I'm still gaining. He's charismatic when he wants to be, can charm anyone into anything.

The problem is, somewhere around month three of

our partnership, he decided we should be more than business associates.

It started small. Comments about how I looked in certain outfits. Hands lingering when we carried equipment together. An invitation to dinner that felt less business meeting, more date night.

I shut it down. Firmly, professionally. We're colleagues building a company together. Nothing more. I'm not interested in anything romantic with him.

"Hannah!" Scot spots me, pushes off the bar with too much force. He stumbles, catches himself, grins wide. "There's my partner! The mastermind behind all this!"

"Scot. Maybe switch to water? We're still working," I say in a hushed tone.

"We're celebrating!" He reaches for me, arm going around my shoulders, pulling me against his side. The smell of whiskey wafts off him. "Look what you did! This is incredible! You're incredible!"

"Scot." I duck out from under his arm, creating space. "We're at a client event. Keep it together."

"I am." His hand finds my waist, fingers pressing in. "Just appreciating my beautiful, talented partner. Can't I do that?"

I step back, putting a solid three feet between us. "You're done drinking. I'm cutting you off."

His expression shifts, something ugly flickering beneath the charm. "Since when do you make the rules?"

"Come on, Scot, let's be professional." I keep my tone light, businesslike, even though I want to throttle him. "Drink water. Sober up. We've got another two hours."

I turn away before he can argue, heading toward the dessert station, where I need to coordinate bringing out the second wave of mini cheesecakes. People are demolishing them faster than expected, which is a good problem, but still a problem.

For the next thirty minutes, I'm in constant motion to ensure it all runs smoothly.

I am checking the gift list on my phone, making sure we haven't missed anyone, when Scot appears again. He's several steps away, weaving through the crowd with a lazy grin that makes my skin crawl.

He lifts his chin toward the rafters. "Look up, Hannah," he says, voice thick. "Fate's pointing upward, babe."

I hate it when he calls me that word. I have told him a dozen times, but I glance anyway, and my stomach drops.

Mistletoe. Hanging over me, the berries bright against dark wood.

Fuck.

"No," I say, pulse spiking. "Scot, don't."

He keeps coming, slow and confident, like this is something he is owed.

"You pushed me away all afternoon," he says. "All these months. Like I'm a stranger instead of your partner. But here we are. Under the mistletoe at the perfect moment. You know the rules. One kiss."

He keeps moving closer. Not running. Not rushing.

Just walking with this awful certainty that I'll let him kiss me.

If this becomes a scene, everything I worked for tonight could fall apart. "I'm working," I whisper. "This is not appropriate. Please stop."

His grin sharpens. "Just tradition. One little kiss."

Panic claws up my throat, so I take a step back. Then another. And collide with a wall.

Except it's not a wall; it's a person. Tall. Solid. Unmoving.

I glance over my shoulder.

Red velvet. White fur trim. A Santa suit. Relief hits me so fast it's dizzying. Santa, thank God. I can use this and make this work without creating a scene.

Scot is still closing in, licking his lips, and I almost gag.

My brain shifts into survival mode. I spin halfway, grab the front of Santa's coat, turn him toward me, my eyes locked on Scot. "Santa, kiss me. Christmas luck. Just a quick one."

I don't wait for permission.

I rise up on my toes, yank Santa by the coat, and move to kiss his cheek, except he's turned and our lips clash.

For half a second, nothing happens.

Then he kisses me back, slow and sure, and my entire world tilts. Warm hands cradle my hips, steady and confident, and heat rolls through me so fast I forget where I am.

My eyes fly open.

The man in front of me is not Declan, our Santa. His eyes were a muddy brown when I met him two days ago to go over party details. These eyes are moss green, sharp and steady, watching me like he already knows every secret I have ever kept.

And his scent hits me a heartbeat later. Cinnamon cake. Burnt caramel. Cedar. Rich and sharp under the sugar and pine of the party around us.

Declan smelled like the outdoors and cheap deodorant. Sweat and cold air. Nothing like this. Nothing that makes my knees go loose and my tongue forget how to move.

The thought registers somewhere in the back of my mind, distant and irrelevant, because holy hell, this man knows what he's doing. His mouth moves against mine with devastating confidence, like kissing is an art form he's perfected. One hand comes up to cup the back of my head, fingers threading through my hair, angling me exactly where he wants me. The other hand settles on my waist, broad and warm even through my dress, pulling me closer until I'm pressed against solid muscle.

I should stop this. Pull back. Say *thank you* and deal with Scot and salvage what's left of my professional reputation.

Instead, I kiss him back like my life depends on it.

My hands slide up his chest. Damn, he's built, nothing but hard planes under that ridiculous costume, and he makes a low sound in his throat that short-circuits every logical thought in my brain. Everything about him is intoxicating, and I press closer, inhale deeper, drown in his scent.

Nobody kisses like this.

His tongue sweeps against my bottom lip, question and demand all at once, and I open for him without thinking, without hesitation. The hand in my hair tightens just slightly, possessive, and I make a sound I've never made before—I purr against him.

This is insane. This is a stranger. *This is Santa Claus.*

I don't care.

I kiss him back with everything I have, weeks of stress and tension dissolving into pure sensation. His mouth is hot against mine, demanding and giving at the same time, and I'm drowning in the taste of him, something dark and slightly sweet, addictive.

When we finally break apart, I'm gasping, dizzy, my lips tingling and my brain struggling to come back online.

I stare up at him.

That's when reality crashes back in.

The Santa beard is hanging loose around his neck, forgotten, and the face above me makes my breath catch for an entirely different reason.

This is definitely, absolutely, one hundred percent not Declan.

This man is gorgeous in a way that should come with a warning label. Sharp jaw covered in dark stubble. High cheekbones. A mouth currently curved in a smirk that leaves me buzzing. And his eyes focused on me with an expression that's equal parts amused and heated.

His dark hair falls across his forehead as if he just rolled out of bed. Combined with the Santa suit straining across his shoulders, it's absurd and unfairly attractive all at once.

"You're—" My voice comes out rough, and I have to clear my throat. "You're not the Santa I hired."

His smirk deepens, and there's pure male satisfaction in those green eyes. "Definitely not Declan. Though I have to say, that's one hell of a way to say hello. You make a habit of kissing strangers like you're trying to set them on fire?"

My face goes nuclear. "I... that wasn't... I needed—"

"YOU BITCH!" Scot's voice cuts through the moment like a blade.

I spin around, and the expression on his face makes my blood run cold. Fury and humiliation twist his features into something ugly, something I've never seen before. People are staring now, conversations dying as heads turn in our direction.

"Scot." I step toward him, hands raised, trying to de-escalate. "Keep your voice down. Let's go talk in private, as we're at an event."

"I don't give a shit about the party!" He's swaying, whiskey and rage making his movements jerky, unpredictable. "You won't kiss me, but you'll kiss some random asshole you don't even know?"

My stomach hurts. "We're business partners. That's

it. I've told you that repeatedly." I reach for his arm, trying to calm him, trying to pull him away from the growing audience. "Scot, please, not here."

He shakes me off hard enough that I stumble, catching myself on a nearby table. "Business partners? I brought you into this company! I vouched for you when my uncle wanted to hire someone with actual experience! And this is how you repay me?"

Santa moves closer behind me. I sense him there, solid and protective, a physical barrier between me and Scot's escalating anger.

"Scot, you're drunk. You're making a scene."

He takes a step closer, and several guests quickly move out of his way. "You've been stringing me along for months. Making me believe we were building something together, and not just the business. And now you humiliate me?"

"I never strung you along. I've been completely clear about boundaries from day one."

"Bullshit." The word comes out slurred. "You smiled at me. You laughed at my jokes. You worked late with me. What the hell was I supposed to think?"

"That I was being professional!" My voice rises despite my best efforts. "That I was being a decent colleague! That doesn't mean I want to date you!"

"We're done." Scot is backing away now, pointing at me with the hand still holding his glass. Whiskey sloshes over the rim, spattering on the floor. "You hear me? Done. Find yourself a new business, because I'm out. My uncle is going to hear about this. You'll be finished in this town before New Year's. Mark my fucking words, Hannah. You're going to regret this."

"Scot, wait…"

But he's already turning, shouldering past confused guests who scramble out of his path, heading for the exit. I watch him leave, my partnership and my future walking out the door.

The room has gone quiet except for the music. Everyone is staring. The perfect evening I crafted is crumbling in real time, and there's nothing I can do to stop it.

My throat goes tight. My eyes start burning.

I'm going to cry. Right here, in front of everyone, at the most important event of my career.

"Hell of a first impression." The voice behind me is low, rough around the edges, unexpectedly gentle. "I feel like I just kissed my way into a soap opera."

A laugh escapes me, half sob, completely genuine. "That's one way to put it."

"You okay?"

I shake my head, not trusting my voice, and turn to face Santa.

"Come on." A hand, large, calloused, surprisingly careful, wraps around my elbow. "Let's get you out of the spotlight."

He guides me away from the main room, somehow making it look casual, like we're just moving through the party instead of fleeing the wreckage of my professional life. The crowd parts easily, people stepping aside for him without seeming to realize they're doing it.

We end up at the bar tucked in the southwest corner, partially hidden by decorative pine garland. The bartender takes one look at my face and starts making me something without being asked.

Santa positions himself between me and the rest of the room, blocking me from view, giving me space to fall apart in private.

The drink appears, hot cocoa, but when I take a sip, there's definitely whiskey in it. Maybe rum. Something strong enough to burn on the way down.

"Figured you needed it," he says.

I drain half the mug, feeling warmth spread through my chest, loosening the panic squeezing my lungs.

"Breathe," Santa says, his tone steady, like he does this all the time. "In through your nose. Hold it. Out through your mouth. Again."

I follow his instructions, dragging air into my lungs, forcing it out slowly. Once. Twice. Three times.

The hyperventilating eases.

My hands stop shaking.

"That's better. You're okay."

"Not really." My voice wavers. "I just destroyed everything. My partnership, my career, probably this entire event."

"Look at the room."

I glance past him. The party is still going. Conversations resumed, and the quartet never stopped playing. People are eating, drinking, laughing.

"Nobody cares," he says. "Ten minutes from now, they'll forget it happened. Drunk guy caused a scene, got shut down, left. That's it. The event's fine."

"Scot's not going to forget."

"He's a jackass who can't handle rejection." He says it matter-of-factly, like it's simple math. "That's his problem, not yours."

I sigh. "He's my business partner. *Was* my business partner. Now I don't know what he is." I laugh, but it comes out broken. "God, this is such a disaster. Six months of work, gone. Giuseppe is never going to sell us the company now, not after this mess. Scot will make sure of it."

Santa is watching me with those intense green eyes, and I notice for the first time how he holds himself, weight balanced, ready to move, like someone who's used to things going sideways fast. There's a stillness to him that's almost predatory, but somehow it makes me feel safer instead of scared.

"Who are you?" I finally ask. "And where the hell is Declan?"

His mouth quirks, and I catch the hint of a dimple. "Funny story, actually. Your Santa, Declan, turns out he's wanted for arson. Two cabins, nearly killed a family. Also, attempted theft, battery on a cop, and skipping bail. Twice."

I blink. Process. "What?"

"My partners and I picked him up this afternoon on Main Street. He was outside your sister's bakery in a Santa suit, eating cookies like he didn't have a care in the world." He crosses his arms, and the Santa suit pulls tight across his chest in a way that's deeply distracting. "We were hauling him into our truck to take him in when your sister... Lily, right? She came running out, panicking about the party having no Santa. She wouldn't let us leave until I agreed to fill in so it didn't ruin your event."

I stare at him.

He stares back, waiting.

"Hold on." I lift up a hand, my brain struggling to catch up. "You're telling me you're not an actor. You're not a performer. You're, what, law enforcement?"

"Bounty hunter."

"You hunt down criminals for a living?"

"Yep."

"And Lily convinced you to play Santa for me?"

"More like guilt-tripped me into it, but yeah, basically."

I stare at him. He's massive, at least six-two, probably more, with shoulders that look like they were built for tackling people. The Santa suit is straining at the seams, white fur trim looking absurd against obvious muscle. His hands—I remember how they felt, one in my hair, one on my waist—are definitely not mall-Santa hands. They're big, scarred across the knuckles, the hands of someone who works with them.

A laugh bubbles up from somewhere deep in my chest. I try to hold it back, but it's impossible. It spills out, half hysteria, half genuine amusement.

"I'm sorry," I gasp, pressing my hand to my mouth.

"It's just, you're enormous. That suit barely fits. You look like you could snap someone in half. And you…" I stop myself, but he's watching me with that smirk again.

"And I what?"

"Nothing."

"Finish the sentence."

"No."

"Come on. I want to hear it."

"Fine." The whiskey is making me bold. "You kiss like you've done it a thousand times and knew exactly what you were doing."

His smirk goes full wattage. "For the record, you kissed me first."

"I was desperate."

"You were phenomenal." He says it simply, like it's a fact. "That wasn't desperation. That was… something else entirely."

Heat crawls up my neck. "I shouldn't have done that. That was completely inappropriate. You were doing my sister a favor, and I basically attacked you—"

"I'm not complaining."

"You should be."

"Trust me, I'm not." He shifts slightly. I catch another wave of his scent, and part of me wants to press my face against his neck and inhale.

He's quiet for a beat, studying me. "Want me to talk to your business partner, Scot?"

"Talk to him how?" I ask. "Like, politely? Over cocoa? Or with your knuckles? Maybe throw him in a river? Or simply finish him and leave him tied to a pine tree?"

He actually laughs, a low sound that makes the room feel smaller. "All very viable options," he says, amusement flickering across his face. "But I find subtlety usually works best."

I picture a bounty hunter whispering and smiling politely while Scot clutches his pearls. "Right. Like a Hallmark special in which the handsome stranger gently explains boundaries."

His grin goes predatory and very sincere. "Except I'm not in the business of gentle explanations. I'm in the business of results."

My stomach does that stupid flutter thing. "How bad are we talking? One to ten?"

He leans in, eyes flat and serious for a second. "Depends on how stupid he gets. Solid eight. Maybe nine if he insists on being dramatic."

I snort. It comes out like a laugh. "He gets very dramatic when he drinks. He's a ten at karaoke and a nine at terrible decisions."

"Then definitely nine," he says. "I prefer efficiency."

"Same thing," I say.

He tilts his head, amused. "Fair point."

We both grin, and for a second, the panic lifts. He makes it feel likely that I can survive Scot.

But I should walk away and go hide in the kitchen until I stop vibrating.

His gaze slides over me, steady and unhurried. There is nothing soft in his eyes. He looks at people the way a wolf looks for exits. And somehow I feel safer standing next to him than I have all night.

"I know men like Scot," he explains. "If you need help, you can contact me anytime," he offers.

I study him, this stranger who just derailed my entire evening in the best and worst possible ways. There's something about him that doesn't quite fit the Santa costume, something rough and competent underneath the red velvet.

"Thanks. I'm Hannah Parker, by the way," I finally say. "Though we're way past introductions at this point."

His laugh is rough, surprised. "Chris Merrick, from Evernight Retrieval Agency. And yeah, we definitely skipped a few steps."

"That's one way to put it."

"So," he says, voice dropping low, intimate enough that I feel it under my ribs. "Any chance we get out of here? Real drinks instead of spiked cocoa."

My pulse jumps.

Part of me, the responsible part, knows this is a terrible idea. I just met him. My career is currently smoldering in a dumpster behind the venue. This is absolutely not the moment to leave with a beautiful stranger who kisses like sin and smells like everything I did not know I wanted.

The other part of me, the part still trembling from that kiss, the part that is exhausted from holding everything together, screams yes.

"I can't." I check my watch because looking at him is too tempting. "This is my event. I need to stay until the end and make sure everything shuts down properly. Especially after causing that disaster."

"That wasn't you."

"Semantics." I glance back at him and immediately regret it. Those green eyes leave my stomach fluttering. "I have another ninety minutes before breakdown."

"And you have to be here the whole time?" he asks.

"Unfortunately." My throat tightens. "Please don't leave. Not yet. I need a Santa for the gift-giving part."

Something in him shifts. Not soft exactly... but focused. Like I just became a priority.

"Yeah," he says quietly, the corner of his mouth lifting upward. "I'll stay."

"Really?"

"Santa sticks around until the party ends." He cracks his knuckles. "Besides, someone needs to make sure that jackass doesn't return."

Heat moves through me in a slow wave. I should tell him I can handle it. That I don't need protection and this is wildly inappropriate.

None of the words show up. All I can manage is "Thank you."

His attention settles on me again, heavy and unhurried. He studies me like he's deciding how far he's willing to go. And the terrifying part is... I want to know the answer.

"Come on." Chris nods toward the crowd. "Let's get you back to work before people start wondering if Santa kidnapped the event planner."

I huff a laugh, shaky. "That would make a hell of a headline."

Without thinking, I touch his arm. Solid muscle under cheap felt. My fingers tingle. I drop my hand fast and pray he didn't notice.

He did. His eyes cut to where I touched him, then back to my face, like he's adding that detail to a list.

We move toward the main room. I try to pull my thoughts together before I drown in them. "I should get back," I say. "Pretend everything is fine."

He stares down at me. "I'll be right here. If anything comes for you, it comes through me first."

My breath stutters. That should scare me. Instead, it settles low in my stomach like heat curling under my ribs. I nod and force myself away, then weave through guests, smiling, adjusting decorations, checking on vendors.

At least on the outside.

Inside, everything is fraying.

Scot had been furious. I saw it in his eyes before he disappeared. If Scot tells his uncle lies about me, I will lose the partnership, the funding, trust in the industry. Everything I worked for.

I straighten a stack of brochures with shaking hands.

I kissed a stranger. One reckless move and every-thing is at risk.

There is no universe where this ends well.

I glance back across the room. Chris is still there. Watching me through the crowd, arms folded, like he already decided I belong under his protection.

I tell myself to look away. Focus. Work. Fix this. Make tonight flawless so the client has nothing to complain about. But my pulse won't settle, and the truth slips in like a whisper I can't silence.

I don't know who he really is.

And worse… a dangerous, stupid part of me wants to find out.

CHAPTER THREE

HANNAH

Flour & Fable Bakery at eight o'clock in the evening smells like heaven having a love affair with Christmas.

Even from the sidewalk, I hear laughter and the hum of voices, book-club night keeping the lights bright and the ovens working overtime.

I push the door open, bells jingling overhead. Warmth and sugar hit me at the same time. Cinnamon. Chocolate. The lemon-vanilla candle Lily always burns that smells divine. The bakery only has a few customers, unlike the book café, which is packed.

Then Chris follows me inside.

Which makes the room feel even smaller.

He's out of the Santa suit now. Instead, he wears black jeans that look lived-in and a dark button-up shirt that fits too well across his chest and forearms. Tattoos disappear under the sleeves, and his hair is damp like he washed the party out of it. He appears more dangerous like this. Less funny. More... real.

I tell myself not to stare. It doesn't work.

"I'm coming in for brownies," he murmurs, voice low as he scans the room. "And maybe to make sure you didn't sneak home to have a breakdown alone."

"That's not my style," I say. "I prefer to have breakdowns in public restrooms like a lady."

He laughs.

Lily spots us, eyes narrowing like she's assessing who I brought along. She wipes her hands on her apron and marches over. "You," she says, pointing at Chris. "I hope you did an amazing job being Santa."

He chuckles louder. "I didn't exactly have a choice, but I'm glad I did." He glances over at me, and Lily is staring at us both.

"Okay, what did I miss?"

"I'll tell you later. Anyway, you look like you survived a tornado made of glitter sugar and nonsense," I say.

"I had a late night. The twins, Sage and Blake, just turned five months, and they aren't sleeping great. They've been keeping us up all night. Then it's been nonstop all day, and the book club is blowing up." She nods toward the book café room connected to the bakery, where a crowd has filled every available seat. Archer, one of Lily's lovers, stands at the front, holding a massive hardcover like it's sacred scripture. He talks with one hand, animated and utterly in his element. The few straggling customers in the bakery have all gone to join them.

People hang on his every word.

Since he started the club, foot traffic has nearly doubled. It definitely doesn't hurt that Archer is stupidly attractive, all velvet voice and librarian-kink vibes. Half the room is staring at him like he's about to read them love poetry instead of Gothic poetry.

I'm honestly shocked that Lily hasn't clawed anyone's eyes out. She looks surprisingly calm for a woman watching other females openly ogle her man.

Chris leans on the counter, and I become distressingly aware of my heart doing cardio. He fits here too easily. Like he belongs.

"So," Lily says, eyebrows lifting, "are you feeding the bounty hunter or just admiring him like a Christmas decoration?"

My cheeks are on fire while Chris winks at me, loving the attention.

I am *absolutely* admiring.

He gives me that almost smile again, the one that feels like he's peeling back layers without even trying. "I'm here for brownies. And to keep her out of trouble."

I hate how easy this feels. How warm he looks in the glow of fairy lights wrapped around the pastry case. How every cell of my body is tuned to him when I should be focusing on salvaging my career.

My stomach twists, but Chris shifts closer, just enough that his heat leaps over to me. He's not touching me, but close enough.

Lily snorts. "Wasting no time for your payment for playing Santa, hey." She glances my way. "I'm paying in brownies because they are that good." She smirks as she rifles beneath the counter. "You sure you don't want something stronger? You look frazzled. How did the Winter Party go?"

I gasp out loud. "The event was worse than I thought. I think Scot is kicking me out of the partnership. I texted him about twenty times and got nothing. So he's either avoiding me or dead in a ditch, and honestly, I'm not sure which option gives me more peace."

"Dead in a ditch is very dramatic," Chris says.

Lily flicks flour off her wrist and gives me that forensic stare of hers. "Very *episode eight cliffhanger* of you."

"I've been studying your true crime binges." I lean against the counter. "If he's dead in a ditch, think I could stage it to look accidental?"

"Easily," Lily says. "I've seen at least six cases that would translate." She rolls another rum ball in coconut behind the counter. "You'd need an alibi. I'd volunteer, but I crumble under questioning."

"You lied straight to my face three days ago about not eating the last croissant," I say.

"That was different. I was starving."

I snort.

It's only then that I notice Chris watching us with that dark, unreadable gaze. "Want me to pretend I didn't hear the murder planning?" he asks.

I flick him a look. "You're a bounty hunter. Pretty sure murder talk is just… Tuesday for you."

His mouth curves, sharp as a blade. "I mean, if you need it done…"

Lily perks up. "Well, we already know you accept baked goods for payment."

"I've been paid in worse," he adds.

I lift a brow. "Like what?"

"Goat," he says without blinking. "Once."

I choke on my coffee. "You got a goat as payment for a job?"

"And it tried to kill me," he corrects.

"That feels personal," I say.

"It was." He tilts his head slightly. "Point is, if your business partner turns up dead, I'll try not to look too impressed."

Lily nods approvingly. "See? Reasonable."

I rub my forehead. "I love that none of you are talking me out of this."

"Weighing pros and cons," Chris replies. "Your pros are winning."

James steps out from the café kitchen, tall, dark copper hair, black T-shirt, forearms to die for. His presence shifts the air, heavier, protective. James is another of Lily's three Alphas. I've seen the way people look at him, like they're not sure whether to flirt or run. The guy did spend some time in prison, so he has this rough edge to him. Reminds me slightly of Chris.

"Hannah."

"James," I reply. "Making coffee or plotting a coup? Hard to tell with that face."

A ghost of a smile. "Why limit myself?"

I glance at Lily. "How do you live with a man who could intimidate a brick wall?"

"Brick walls are cowards," James says.

Lily laughs and moves to him without thinking. He presses a kiss to her temple, one hand sliding briefly to her waist before he goes to plate pastries. Casual. Intimate. Like breathing.

I admire the way her men *adore* her. All three of them. No question, no hesitation. I remember when I was terrified to tell Lily I wanted to leave the bakery for event planning, so I kept it a secret for a long time. I thought she'd hate me. Instead, she hugged me, shoved a box of cookies at me, and said she was proud.

And now…

Now I'm on the verge of losing everything before it has even started. Because Scot sucks. Because maybe I wasn't firm enough. Because I thought he was a friend.

Lily looks up suddenly.

"Oh—James, this is Chris. He's the guy who arrested Declan today. And then took his place as Santa at Hannah's party."

James pauses, eyes flicking over Chris, evaluating, measuring.

"That so?"

Chris shrugs. "Seemed like she needed a Santa."

"Actually," Lily cuts in loudly, "he only did it because

I bribed him with brownies for a year after arresting the first Santa."

I choke. "A year? Lily, that's—"

"Standard rate for heroics," she says solemnly. "And I did it for you."

My heart melts.

Chris smirks. "I would've done it for six months' worth, but she negotiates like a demon."

"A demon with an apron," James agrees, kissing the top of her head again before setting a tray of pastries on the counter.

I shake my head, laughing despite the dumpster fire my life is becoming.

"Well, you got a great deal, because her brownies are basically currency," I add.

"Good," Chris says, quiet and rough. "I could use a little sweetness."

And he looks at me when he says it.

Not at the pastries.

At me.

Warmth spreads through my chest. I shouldn't like the way he stares at me, but God help me… I really, really do.

"Anyway." Lily reaches under the counter, pulls out her phone. "Speaking of Santa, I tried calling you about fifty times today. What if it was an emergency?"

"Was it?" I grab a snowflake cookie from the display plate on the counter, taking a bite and offering one to Chris, who takes it. Butter and vanilla and just the right amount of crunch. Perfect, like everything Lily makes. "I was in concentration management mode."

"You're always in that mode." She swipes through her phone, turns it to show me, coming around from behind the counter where James is. Fifteen missed calls. Twenty-three texts. All from her.

I scan the texts quickly.

Lily: COPS ARRESTED SANTA!

Lily: Okay, not cops, bounty hunters.

Lily: Declan's a CRIMINAL!

Lily: Arson!!! He burned down cabins!!!

Lily: Got a replacement but he's TERRIFYING.

Lily: Also hot, but that's not the point.

Lily: HANNAH, ANSWER YOUR PHONE!

"Okay, that would've made more sense." I'm still giggling as I hand Chris the phone so he can read Lily's deranged message thread. He looks entirely too pleased with himself.

He sets the phone down, gaze cutting to me. "Would it have mattered? If you *had* seen the messages? Would you still have kissed me?"

The room goes quiet.

Lily's eyebrows shoot up. "Wait—*you kissed him?*"

My face heats so fast I'm surprised the frosting on the cookies doesn't melt. "It wasn't... I didn't..." I gesture helplessly. "Scot was coming at me under the mistletoe, and I thought Chris was Declan, okay? It was supposed to be a quick cheek kiss. A diversion. And then..." I swallow. "Well. Things escalated."

James glances at Chris over Lily's head. A single, male, acknowledging nod.

Traitor.

Chris's mouth curves, slow and satisfied.

"Oh, sweetheart. That wasn't a diversion." His voice dips, low enough to vibrate in places I don't want to think about. "You kissed me like you were trying to drag me under. Like you wanted to see if I'd drown with you."

Fire climbs up my neck and cheeks.

Lily practically wheezes. "HANNAH!"

"Shut. Up," I hiss.

Chris only leans back against the counter like he didn't just verbally body-slam me into next week. "For the record, I've been hit harder than that, but never by anyone who tasted that good."

"I'm moving to Alaska. Don't contact me."

"No," Lily says, delighted. "We are living here forever. In this moment. I'm framing it."

James slides a fresh latte toward her as she goes back behind the counter with him. He leans forward, presses a kiss to her temple, and murmurs something that has her grinning. Watching them together is bliss.

"Can you pack half a dozen brownies in a box for Chris?" she asks James, who grins and goes to work.

Twenty-six years old, and I haven't gotten within a mile of finding my pack. Meanwhile, my little sister has three Alphas who look at her like she hung the damn moon.

I'm genuinely happy for her.

I just wish I believed I could ever have something like that. Then I'm staring at Chris, who hasn't stopped watching me. Sure, we had a fun kiss, but men like him don't want Omegas like me. Especially extremely handsome men who can have any girl they want. He looks like he just stepped out of a photo shoot for *Rugged Mountain Men Monthly.*

Which was why, last month, I had made an appointment with that matchmaker downtown, Evelyn... something, the Omega who supposedly has a sixth sense for compatible packs. Showed up at her office, sat in the waiting room for twenty minutes, then fled before she could call my name.

Because what if she can't find anyone for me? What if I'm one of those Omegas who just... don't match? And I'm meant to be alone?

James is handing Chris the brownies when my phone chimes with a notification. I click it open and notice that it's from Scot. My insides twist until they hurt.

"What's wrong?" Lily asks immediately. "You've gone pale as snow."

I swallow hard and lift my gaze. "Just got an email from Scot."

"And?"

"Haven't read it yet."

Lily is at my side. "Let me do it." She takes the phone, and I try to shrink away, knowing it's not going to be good.

Chris is at my other side, rubbing my arm. "It's going to be okay."

"Effective immediately, I'm dissolving our partnership agreement," she reads aloud. "You're no longer affiliated with Confetti and Meatballs Event Planning. All client relationships revert to me. Any attempt to contact the company's existing clients will be considered interference." She glances up. "That fucker! But there's more," Lily says. "He copied someone called Giuseppe in on the email. Lawyer?"

"That's his uncle." I suddenly feel sick to my stomach and take the phone back, needing to read what else he says. "And apparently he spent the last few hours sending emails to his existing clients, telling them I'm no longer with the company and he'll be handling all future events personally."

"Can he do that?" Lily is outraged.

"I don't know. Maybe. We never formalized the partnership in writing, so his uncle still owns the company. I have nothing in writing." My throat tightens. "It was all handshake agreements, verbal promises. Scot's uncle said we'd work together for six months, prove ourselves, and then he'd sell us the company fifty-fifty."

"That's bad," James says quietly.

"That's catastrophic." I grab another cookie, a Christmas tree this time, and take a bite. "My reputation, probably gone by the time Scot finishes spinning his story."

Chris is still looking at the email over my shoulder.

"He mentions an upcoming event that you're responsible for. So you still have the ones you sourced, right?"

I scroll down the long email. "I've got a Christmas petting zoo event in two days. I found the event, booked it, planned everything. But Scot has already told the animal vendors—the entire petting zoo component—that I'm gone and not to deal with me, as I'll cause drama. Asshole." I'm trembling. "I'm a nobody who thought she could play event planner."

"Hey." Chris's voice cuts through my spiral, sharp and firm. "Don't do that. Don't diminish what you've built."

"I haven't built anything. I've been borrowing someone else's company and pretending it was mine."

"You brought in new clients," Lily adds. "You proved yourself."

Chris leans forward, one hand propped on the counter. "This jackass is threatened by you because you're good at what you do. That's not nothing."

Lily squeezes my arm. "He's right. You're incredible at this. Scot knows it. That's why he's panicking."

"Panicking or not, he's winning." I grab another cookie and devour it in three bites. "I'm about to face a client empty-handed with no animals for a petting zoo party. That's not exactly a strong position."

I stand there, frozen, while my entire world crumbles around me. Then I reach for another cookie, but Lily drags the tray away from me.

"You're stress-eating," she observes out loud.

"I need to drown in cookies."

"No more cookies. You're going to make yourself sick."

I walk across the room and slump into a chair at a table near the window, head in my hands. "I'll be black-listed before Christmas."

"Maybe I can help." Chris's voice cuts clean through the rising static of my panic as he strolls over to join me.

I look up and immediately regret it.

He's sitting across from me, forearms braced on the table, looking entirely too composed for a man who spent the evening playing a vigilante Santa. The shirt he changed into clings to broad shoulders and arms marked with faint scars, hints of a life that should terrify me far more than it does.

I hate that he's seeing me like this, all frazzled, anxious, one meltdown away from screaming. I wanted to be confident and put together tonight. Not... this puddle of professional failure.

But he doesn't look put off. He appears interested. Which somehow makes everything worse.

"Unless you know someone with a mobile zoo," I manage, trying to sound casual, "I'm screwed."

His mouth curves, slow and sure. "I might. I know people with animals." He leans back in his chair, casual, like he's discussing the weather. "Small farms. Hobby ranches. And..." He pauses, and his mouth quirks. "I have reindeer."

Silence.

I stare at him.

Lily stares at him.

James makes a choked sound that might be surprise.

"You what?" I finally manage.

"We have reindeer."

He says it so calmly that I momentarily think I hallucinated it.

I blink. "You're a bounty hunter… who owns reindeer."

"That's what I'm telling you."

I stare. "You keep saying that like it's a normal sentence."

"Technically," he says, "I'm a bounty hunter who *inherited* reindeer. Noel's grandmother left them to him. We tried to find them a new home, but…" He shrugs. Broad shoulders. Unfair. "They grew on us."

"Who's Noel?" I ask.

"One of my pack. We take down bad guys together," Chris says with another shrug.

Lily is practically vibrating as she rushes closer to our table. "Wait, you have reindeer."

"Yep. Eight of them."

"Like… living on your property."

"In the back pasture. Barn, fencing, the works."

A laugh bursts out of me, too sharp, too tired, too delighted. "Do they have names?" I don't know why that's the thing I ask. My brain is melting.

"Yep. Noel named most of them after chess pieces. Rook, Bishop, Knight… whatever. Kane wanted to name one Sparkles. We vetoed that."

"RIP Sparkles." I press a hand to my chest. "Gone before his time."

His mouth kicks up, and damn, it shouldn't look that good on him. He's been watching me like this all night.

"This is perfect," Lily blurts out. "You need animals. Chris has animals. The universe is saying, *Here, dumbass, take the reindeer.*"

"Look, I can make it work," Chris adds. "The reindeer, plus I can reach out to some contacts who run small farms—goats, sheep, maybe a pony or two. Build you a proper petting zoo in forty-eight hours."

I stare at him, trying to process. "Would you really do that? I'll pay you, of course."

"I'd do it for you, Hannah. And because Scot's a jackass who deserves to fail. And you need a shot at proving yourself."

"Chris—"

"Call it a favor. Lily gave me free brownies for a year. I'm giving you reindeer and some animals for a weekend." His grin goes wicked. "Seems fair."

Lily is squeezing my arm so hard it hurts. "Say yes, Hannah. For the love of God, say yes."

I look at the brownie container on the table in front of Chris. At my sister. At James, who's nodding slightly like this makes perfect sense. At Chris, who's sitting there offering to save one of my jobs. And I'm laughing at how bizarre the night is.

"Of course I'll accept help," I hear myself say. "Let's talk details."

Chris's smile turns heated and infinitely dangerous. "Thought you'd never ask."

Lily squeals again, and James is definitely laughing now. I'm sitting in my sister's bakery, planning a petting zoo with a man I kissed while my career hangs in the balance.

This is either the best decision I've ever made or the worst.

Given my track record, probably both.

CHAPTER FOUR

KANE

The reindeer are staging a rebellion this morning.

I'm standing in the back pasture with a bucket of grain, watching our herd decide collectively that breakfast can wait while they fuck around in the fresh snow. Bishop, one of our older males who lost his antlers three weeks ago, is headbutting Knight over absolutely nothing. Rook is off by himself near the tree line, staring into the woods like he's contemplating an escape plan. Queen is digging through snow, looking for whatever vegetation she thinks is hiding underneath, antlers still firmly attached because she's female and gets to keep hers until spring.

"Come on, assholes," I call out. "It's eight in the morning. I'm freezing. You're getting fed whether you cooperate or not."

Bishop ignores me completely, continuing his headbutting campaign. The rest of the reindeer don't seem to be obeying me either.

"They're not going to listen to you," Noel says from behind me. He's hauling another bucket of grain, long hair tied back, breath misting in the cold air. "They never listen to you."

"They do when I have food."

"That's a basic survival instinct."

I dump grain into the first feeder, and immediately Pawn trots over. She's the youngest female at three and a half years old. She's got her antlers too, and she hasn't learned to be an asshole yet. My favorite, if I'm being honest, though I'd never admit it to the others.

She nudges my arm with her nose, warm breath against my jacket.

"Yeah, yeah, I know." I scratch behind her ears, and she leans into it. "You're starving. Totally neglected. Haven't eaten in twelve whole hours."

Pawn makes a soft noise, content, and starts eating.

The rest of the herd finally decides food is more important than whatever drama they were manufacturing. Even Castle, our most standoffish female, deigns to approach the second feeder Noel is filling.

We've got eight total. Four males, four females. Inherited from Noel's grandmother when she passed three years ago, and we were going to rehome them until we realized they'd kind of grown on us. Now they're permanent residents, eating our money and taking up five acres of prime pasture land.

Worth it, though. They're good company. Better than most people.

The land stretches out behind our property, fenced with serious hardware. Ten feet high, reinforced posts, electric wire running along the top. It's not just for keeping the reindeer in. When you spend your days hunting down bail jumpers and dragging them back to face charges, you make enemies. The fence keeps those enemies out, should they track us down.

Beyond the pasture, thick woods climb into mountains, snow-covered and pristine. Beautiful country, even if it's cold enough to freeze your balls off six months out of the year.

The house sits about a hundred yards in front of it. Three stories of stone and timber, screaming old money and ranch life. Noel's grandfather built it back when he was running cattle and making serious profit. Now it's ours, and we've added our own touches. Security cameras on every corner. Reinforced doors.

Chris emerges from the house and strolls over to join us. Must have just woken up, seeing as he told us jack shit last night and went right to his room once he got home. Now, he leans against the fence, coffee mug in hand, and he's got that look on his face. The one that means something happened and he's deciding how to tell us.

"So." I finish pouring grain, watching Pawn eat with single-minded focus. "You going to tell us what's got you grinning like that, or are we playing twenty questions?"

Chris takes a long sip of coffee, deliberate. "Santa gig went sideways but in the best fucking way."

"Go on." Noel has moved to the water troughs, checking for ice. "Did you scare children? Tell me you terrified at least one."

Chris's grin widens. "Event was boring as fuck for the first hour or so. Did the ho-ho-ho bullshit, smiled for photos. Standard mall-Santa crap."

"Sounds thrilling."

"It wasn't. Until the hottest woman I've ever seen dragged me under the mistletoe and kissed me like she wanted me to strip her down and lick every inch of her body right there in front of at least a hundred people."

I pause mid-pour.

Noel straightens, turns around slowly.

Chris just grins wider, waiting.

"Lucky bastard," I finally say, because honestly, good for him. "How hot are we talking?"

"Dark hair down to here." Chris gestures to his lower back. "Curves that have me hard as a fucking rock. Waist small and fit my hands so well when I grabbed her. Softest breasts against me. Her mouth…" He stops, runs a hand through his hair. "Fuck, her mouth should come with a warning label."

"And she just kissed you?" Noel is skeptical. "Out of nowhere?"

"She was trying to avoid some drunk asshole who was her business partner and wouldn't leave her alone. Saw the mistletoe, saw me, made a decision." Chris's expression shifts, goes heated. "No hesitation."

Chris sets his mug on the fence post. "I swear to God I almost dragged her out of that party right then."

"But you didn't."

"I'm not a fucking animal. There were kids around." He pauses. "Barely restrained myself, though."

Noel is watching Chris with that assessing look he gets when he's reading someone. "Who was she?"

"The event planner, Hannah Parker. Lily's sister." Chris says her name like it matters, and I file that away for later. "She planned that entire event herself. Every detail perfect, ran it like a general commanding troops. Smart, competent, takes zero shit from anyone."

"Sounds like your type," I observe, dumping the last of the grain.

"Fuck yeah, she is. The type I didn't know existed until last night."

I exchange glances with Noel. Chris doesn't talk like this. Chris is the steady one, the grounded one, the guy who hooks up and moves on without getting attached. This is new territory.

"And after the kiss?" I ask.

"That drunk jackass, her business partner, lost his shit. Made a scene, yelled at her in front of everyone, stormed off threatening to destroy her career." Chris's voice goes hard. "She was shaking after he left. I got her away from the crowd, talked her down from a panic attack."

"White-knight routine," Noel says. "Classic."

"Fuck off. She needed help."

"I'm not criticizing."

Chris ignores him. "Point is, I got close. Real close. Had my hands on her, my mouth on hers, breathed her in while we were kissing, and…" He stops, and something in his expression shifts. Goes serious. "I think she's my scent match."

The words hang in the cold morning air. I wait for the punch line.

It doesn't come.

"You're serious," I finally say.

"Fuck yeah."

Noel's jaw tightens. "Chris. Two months ago, you were convinced that Omega in Seattle was your scent match. Spent three weeks tracking her down, making plans, then realized she just wore the same perfume as someone you hooked up with in college."

"That was a mistake."

"A big one."

"This isn't like that." Chris's voice turns firm. "I know what I felt. Her scent was like lightning. Made every instinct I have scream that she's mine. I've been hard since it happened, can't stop thinking about her, can't focus on anything else."

I study him. He's not joking. Not exaggerating, as he really believes this.

"You seeing her again?" I ask, trying not to sound like I'm prying.

Chris's mouth curves like he's been waiting for the question. "Day after tomorrow. Her bastard business partner, Scot, stole her animal vendors for some holiday petting zoo. She's desperate, career is on the line."

I pause. "Is that so?" The words come out deceptively flat, but inside, something coils tight. Chris is soft under all that muscle and bad attitude. Always has been. A pretty Omega with trouble in her eyes… yeah, that's exactly the sort of trap he'd walk into smiling. He thinks with his loyalty first and his brain later. I've seen him get burned for it, and damn if I won't break someone's kneecaps if he gets hurt.

"Our reindeer," he repeats like it's already a signed contract. "We'll bring them to her event. Plus whatever extras we can scrounge up."

Noel leans on the pasture fence, arms folded. "You offered livestock to a woman you just met?"

"Yep."

"Well," Noel says slowly, rolling his shoulders, "if she can handle them, she can borrow them." He shrugs. "They like people. Mostly. If someone loses a glove, not my problem."

"That's the spirit," Chris says. "We'll do great."

Noel gives him a look. "Wait, you volunteered us?"

Chris's grin is pure sin. "Kinda figured that's where you two come in."

I snort. "Oh, absolutely. Because we didn't just survive a two-hour car ride with eight antlered assholes in the trailer last month. Let's do it again but with screaming toddlers."

"Think of the joy," Chris says. "If anyone dies, Noel can write the eulogy. He's poetic when he's depressed."

"Fuck you," Noel says mildly.

I laugh under my breath. This is the problem with

us. We'll do just about anything if someone asks nicely. Or if Chris asks at all.

"And," Chris adds, pointing at us, "you both owe me."

"For what?" I ask.

He levels me with a look. "You made me wear that goddamn Santa suit. In public. With children. One of them bit me."

"Natural consequences," Noel offers with a chuckle.

Chris spreads his arms. "Now it's your turn. Help me haul reindeer to a party and make sure Hannah doesn't get steamrolled by her dickhead partner. Easy."

"Famous last words," I mutter.

Noel scrubs a hand through his long hair. "If this is a scam, Kane's going to murder you. And then me."

"Relax," Chris states. "She's not like that."

I narrow my eyes. There it is. That quiet, certain note in his voice that tells me he's already attached. Fuck. He meets my stare head-on, steady, stubborn.

"She's... good," he says simply. "Bad day. Wrong people. Could use a win."

It hits something old in me, that feeling of wanting to be the guy who shows up when no one else does. I sigh. "Fine. I'm in."

Chris brightens like a damn sunrise.

Noel groans. "You're both idiots."

"Then you're volunteering too," I say.

He flips me off but doesn't argue.

Because we're the type of fools who crawl into the dark for strangers.

Chris claps his hands together. "Great! I'll text some friends about borrowing their animals."

I point a finger at him. "But if one of those reindeer takes a dump in my truck again, you're cleaning it with your toothbrush."

Chris just grins. "Worth it."

Noel sighs. "This is going to be fun."

"Probably," I agree, feeling a reluctant spark of interest for this mysterious Omega. But beneath all the teasing, my thoughts settle into something sharper, protective.

If she's trouble and hurts him, I'll end it.

But if she's worthy? God help her. Because when Chris chooses someone, he never lets go. And neither do I.

We finish up with the reindeer, making sure everyone is fed and watered. Bishop is back to headbutting Knight, but it's half-hearted now, more habit than actual aggression. Rook has found a spot in the sun and parked himself there. Castle is already heading toward the barn, done with outdoor time.

"All right, everyone inside." I secure the gate, double-check the lock. The barn is open if they want to go inside. It's heated, insulated, plenty of space for all eight plus equipment. We rebuilt it two years ago specifically for them, made sure it was solid enough to handle mountain winters. "We've got that skip trace job tomorrow morning."

We head back toward the house. "The bail jumper

from last week who thought moving away from Idaho and to the mountains would solve his problems."

"Right." Chris cracks his knuckles. "We leave at five, should have him in custody by noon if the intel is good."

We reach the house, stomping snow off our boots on the back porch. The security panel blinks green, no alerts, no attempts to breach the perimeter overnight. Inside, it's warm, smells like the coffee Noel made at dawn.

"Adelaide is coming home for Christmas, right?" I ask Chris as we head into the kitchen.

"I think so, as she hasn't gotten back to me to confirm." He grabs a fresh mug, pours coffee.

"Hope she can make it. It's been a while since she's visited."

"Me too." There's affection in his voice. "She'll probably show up with some stray animal she rescued or a new business idea that requires funding."

"Or a new boyfriend," Noel suggests.

"Fuck, I hope not. The last one was an ass."

I snort. Then we settle around the kitchen table, and Chris starts making calls while Noel pulls up maps on his laptop. I grab my own laptop, start researching petting zoo regulations and insurance requirements, because someone has to think about the boring practical shit.

We've been doing this for years, the three of us, working together, backing each other up. Started as kids, as we went to the same school and found each other there. Turned into a pack that works like a well-oiled machine. Bounty hunting pays the bills, gives us purpose, lets us do some actual good in the world.

And now we're adding petting zoo operators to our résumés.

Though, I'm curious to find out more about this Omega Chris is already infatuated with.

CHAPTER FIVE

HANNAH

"Are you sure you should go there alone?" Lily's voice crackles through my car's speakers, concerned and slightly judgmental, which is her default setting when I'm doing something she thinks is questionable.

"Yes, it'll be fine." I adjust my grip on the steering wheel, watching Main Street scroll past through intermittent snowflakes. "I just need to verify that he actually has reindeer. That's all."

"You could've asked him to send a photo."

"A photo can be faked. I need to see them with my own eyes." I pause at a red light, watching a family cross the street, bundled in matching scarves. "After Scot, I can't… I can't afford to so easily trust again. I need to know this is real before tomorrow." I also googled him, but there's almost nothing on him online.

There's a beat of silence on the other end. "Okay. Fair. And good idea to bring the brownies as an excuse."

"Obviously. Perfect cover story. Just dropping by with baked goods to thank him for helping, totally casual, definitely not stalking to verify his livestock claims."

"That's only slightly creepy."

The light turns green, and I ease forward. "Besides, he won't mind. Right? I mean, who turns away brownies brought to their home?"

"Someone with a restraining order against you, maybe."

"Not helpful, Lily."

She laughs, and I can picture her in the bakery, probably elbow-deep in cookie dough, phone wedged between her shoulder and ear. "Fine. But I want all the updates."

"You watch too many murder documentaries."

"And you're about to drive to an isolated property to confront a bounty hunter you barely know. One of us is being sensible here."

"One of us is being paranoid."

I'm driving through the heart of Whispering Grove now, and even mid-morning on a Friday, the town is packed. Tourists everywhere, families window-shopping, couples sipping coffee on heated patios, kids pressing their faces against bakery windows.

Over the phone, I hear Lily working. We are often on the phone where we don't say anything, and it's like having each other close when we go somewhere alone.

Around me, the entire town looks like a Christmas card magically came to life. Garland wrapped around every lamppost, lights strung between buildings, wreaths on every door. Store windows display elaborate holiday scenes of Santa's workshop at the toy store, a winter wonderland at the boutique, gingerbread villages at competing bakeries trying to outdo each other.

Speakers mounted on poles, and a group of carolers in Victorian costumes stands outside the bookstore, singing something classical and beautiful.

Despite everything, despite Scot, despite my imploding career and anxiety churning in my gut, I love this vibe. I love Christmas in Whispering Grove. The energy, the magic, the way the whole town transforms into something out of a snow globe.

Fat flakes stick to my windshield before the wipers sweep them away. It's the perfect postcard weather, picturesque without being dangerous.

"I'm heading out of town now," I tell Lily as I turn onto Mountain Pass Road. "Leaving civilization behind. If I don't come back, tell everyone I died doing something brave."

"Like verifying reindeer ownership?"

"Exactly. Very noble. Put it on my tombstone."

"Here lies Hannah Parker, killed by suspicious livestock verification. Has a nice ring to it."

I snort, navigating the curve that takes me away from Main Street and toward the mountain range. The road narrows, trees pressing in on both sides, snow heavier here where the plows haven't reached yet.

"So how'd you even get the address?" Lily asks.

"Mr. Walsh. At the post office."

"The guy who's been running that place since dinosaurs roamed the earth?"

"He's not that old. Maybe seventy?" I slow down for a patch of ice. "I was there this morning mailing Christmas cards, because I'm an adult who does things on time, and I asked if he knew anyone in town who owned reindeer."

"And he just… told you?"

"He said there used to be a couple. Greg and Mary Saxon. They ran a small hobby farm on their property, kept reindeer. But they both passed a few years ago, and the reindeer went to someone else. Family, maybe? He wasn't sure. But he had the address because he still delivers mail there."

"So you're driving to a dead couple's property to find reindeer that may or may not exist."

"When you say it like that, it sounds bad."

"Because it is bad, Hannah."

"It's fine. It's research. Due diligence." I take another turn, and the road gets even narrower, climbing now.

"Or you're about to trespass on private property owned by armed bounty hunters."

"You really need to stop watching those murder shows."

"And you really need to start watching them. They're educational."

The trees thin out slightly, revealing glimpses of the valley below. Whispering Grove spreads out like a toy town, all those Christmas lights twinkling even in daylight. Beyond it, mountains rise in every direction, snow-capped and dramatic.

It's beautiful. Isolated as hell, but stunning.

"Okay, I think I'm getting close." I check the GPS on my phone. "Mr. Walsh said it's about twelve miles out from town center, private drive on the left marked with a stone pillar."

"Marked how? With *Trespassers Will Be Shot* signs?"

"You're not helping my anxiety here."

"I'm preparing you for reality."

"Your version of reality involves me getting murdered by reindeer-owning bounty hunters."

"Stranger things have happened."

I spot the turn, a stone pillar about four feet tall with the words "Saxon Estate" carved into it, partially obscured by snow. The driveway curves off into the trees, disappearing from view.

"Found it." I slow down, then signal even though there's no one behind me. "I'm turning in."

"If anything feels wrong, leave. Don't be polite. Don't worry about being rude. Just leave."

"I will. Promise."

"I'm serious."

"So am I." I turn onto the private drive, tires crunching on gravel under snow. "But I'll be fine. What's the worst that could happen?"

"Do you want the list alphabetically or by likelihood?"

"Goodbye, Lily."

"Stay on the phone!"

"Fine." I keep her on speaker as I drive, following the winding driveway through dense trees. "But if this turns into a three-hour conversation about your true crime theories, I'm hanging up."

"Deal."

The driveway goes on forever, or at least a quarter mile, which feels like forever when you're driving toward potential disaster. Trees press in on both sides, thick and dark, branches heavy with snow. It's quiet here, peaceful in a way that's either serene or ominous, depending on your perspective.

Currently leaning toward ominous.

Then the trees break, and I see it. "Holy shit," I breathe.

"What? What's 'holy shit'? Hannah, what do you see?"

"The gate." I've stopped the car about twenty feet away, staring. "There's a gate. A serious gate. It's massive, maybe ten feet tall, made of thick metal bars." The bars curve at the top, decorative but definitely designed to keep people out. On either side, stone fencing extends in both directions, at least seven feet high, with metal spikes running along the top.

Not just spikes. Actual fortified metal deterrents that look sharp enough to do damage.

"Well, that's not creepy at all," Lily mutters.

"That's what I'm saying." I inch the car closer, trying to see past the gate. "I can see a driveway continuing on the other side. Open land. Looks well kept but no sign of reindeer. There's a house in the distance, huge, like a mansion, and to the left, a large barn."

"Maybe the reindeer are in the barn?"

"Perhaps." I pull up to the gate, put the car in park. "Okay, I'm getting out. Moment of truth."

"Be careful."

"Always am."

I grab my jacket from the passenger seat, shove my phone into my pocket, still connected to Lily, and climb out into the cold. Snow immediately sticks to my hair, my shoulders, and I pull my jacket tighter.

The gate has a call box mounted on a stone pillar. I walk over, press the button.

Nothing.

I wait ten seconds, then press it again.

Still nothing.

"Hello?" I call out, feeling ridiculous. "Anyone home?"

Silence.

I peer through the bars of the gate. The driveway continues for at least another hundred yards before reaching the house. The property looks vast, with acres of fenced land and what might be gardens or pastures buried under snow.

And no sign of anyone.

"No one's answering," I tell Lily.

"Then come home. You tried."

But I'm staring at the gate, and something reckless bubbles up in my chest. The fence is tall, yeah, but it's not impossible. The metal bars have decorative curls and patterns with plenty of places for footholds. And the spikes at the top look intimidating, but there's space between them.

"Hannah," Lily says, and her voice has gone suspicious. "Are you in the car already?"

"I'm just… assessing."

"Assessing what?"

"Whether I could climb this."

"HANNAH."

"Just for a quick look!" I'm already walking along the fence, examining it. "I'll climb over, walk up to the barn, verify that the reindeer exist, then leave. Five minutes, max."

"That's breaking and entering!"

"It's borrowing their driveway without permission. Totally different."

"It's a felony!"

"Only if I get caught." I find a good spot—the decorative metalwork is particularly elaborate here, lots of handholds on the gate. "Besides, what's the harm? I'll take one look, confirm that Chris wasn't lying, and be on my way before anyone even knows I was here."

"This is how people end up on the news. And what if they have a major Cujo dog?"

"It would have heard me by now and come running." I grab the lowest bar, test my weight. Solid. "I'm doing this."

"God, be careful."

I start climbing. It's easier than I expected, and my boots find purchase on the curves and swirls. Up I go, hand over hand, trying not to think about how insane this is.

Halfway up, I pause. "You still there, Lily?"

"Unfortunately."

"Just making sure you haven't abandoned me in my time of need."

"I'm documenting your poor life choices so I can tell the police exactly how stupid you were."

"That's the sister I know and love."

I reach the top, carefully navigating between the metal spikes. They're decorative but sharp, and I don't want to explain to an ER nurse how I impaled myself breaking into a bounty hunter's property.

Just as I'm straddling the top, trying to figure out the best way down, the entire gate lurches.

I yelp, grabbing on to the nearest spike to keep from falling.

The gate is moving. Opening. Someone activated it.

"Oh, shit," I gasp.

"What? What's 'oh, shit'?"

"The gate's opening. Someone's home. Someone saw me."

"GET DOWN!"

"I'm trying!" But the gate is still moving, and I'm still perched on top of it, and this is officially the most embarrassing moment of my entire life.

I scramble down, my boots slipping on metal, my

hands scraping, and I definitely tear my jacket on something sharp. But I make it to the ground, landing in snow with an ungraceful thump.

"Did you die?" Lily asks.

"Not yet." I'm breathing hard, face burning with humiliation. "But someone definitely saw me."

"Then RUN."

"I can't! I've come this far." I brush snow off my jeans, trying to look casual. Like I always climb gates and get caught. Totally normal activity. "I'm just going to… go get my car and drive through like I was invited."

"You're insane."

"Probably."

I jog back to my Honda, climb in, and drive through the now-open gate like I own the place. Fake it till you make it, right?

The driveway continues through more open land, definitely pastures under all that snow. The house gets bigger as I approach, and oh my God, it's enormous. Three stories, stone and timber construction, the kind of place that belongs on a ranch for wealthy people who want to pretend they're rugged while still having heated floors.

I pull up to the front, put the car in park, and sit there for a second.

"Okay," I tell Lily, my phone in my hand now. "I'm here. Someone clearly knows I'm here, because they opened the gate. So I'm going to go knock on the door, explain myself, and hope they don't shoot me."

"Please be careful."

"I'll do my best. If you don't hear from me in an hour, call the cops."

"That's not even funny."

"Come on, murder doc girl. I thought you'd love the dramatic setup."

"I love it when it happens to other people, not my sister."

"Fair point." I'm walking toward the front door now, boots crunching in snow. "Okay, I'm knocking. Wish me luck."

"Good luck not getting arrested."

"Your confidence is inspiring. Okay, gotta go and do this. Call you later."

"You'd better."

I disconnect the call before she can argue some more, shove my phone into my pocket, and knock on the wooden front door.

Nothing.

I wait, knock again.

Still nothing.

The house looks closed up, windows shut, no lights visible, no movement. But someone opened that gate.

I glance back at the driveway. The gate is still open behind me, like an invitation. Or a trap.

"Hello?" I call out, knocking one more time. "Chris? Anyone home?"

Silence.

Okay. This is weird.

I turn away from the house, surveying the property,

and move to its side. The barn is to my left, maybe fifty yards away. I can't see any reindeer in the visible pastures, but there's a large fenced pen behind the barn, and what looks like a vegetable garden buried under snow.

Maybe they're in the barn?

I head that way, trudging through snow, my breath misting in the cold air. The barn is huge, easily big enough for multiple animals, with a solid structure that looks recently rebuilt. There's a wooden beam across the door, keeping it shut.

And I can hear noises inside. Movement. Animals.

My heart rate picks up, so I reach for the wooden beam, lift it, and push the barn door open.

A reindeer suddenly charges out.

I shriek, stumbling backward, landing hard on my ass in the snow as a blur of brown fur and flailing legs barrels past me.

"What the—"

More reindeer are inside. At least seven of them, all staring at me from the dim interior of the barn with expressions that clearly say "Who the hell are you?"

Oh my God. He was telling the truth. Chris actually has reindeer.

Relief floods through me, immediately followed by panic. Because one of them is now loose, and I broke into his property.

"Shit, shit, shit." I scramble to my feet, slam the barn door shut before any others escape. "Come back here! You can't just—where are you going?"

The reindeer, smaller than the others, definitely younger, no antlers, which means either very young or female, is trotting away from me toward the house.

"Hey! Stop!"

It doesn't listen.

I chase after it, my boots slipping in the snow. "Come back! Please come back! I'm sorry I let you out!"

The reindeer ignores me, heading straight for a pile of chopped wood stacked near the side of the house. Behind the woodpile, a large evergreen tree leans against the house, probably waiting to be set up somewhere for Christmas, still wrapped partially in netting.

The reindeer scrambles up the woodpile with surprising agility.

"No. No, no, no, don't you dare—"

It reaches the top of the woodpile, uses the leaning tree as a ramp, and suddenly it's on the roof.

I stare up at it, dumbfounded.

The reindeer stares back down at me, looking entirely too pleased with itself.

"Are you kidding me right now?" I yell. "That's not even… How did you… Get down here!"

It blinks at me, unconcerned.

"I'm serious! You're going to hurt yourself!" I'm pacing now, hands in my hair. "Or fall through the roof! Or get stuck up there and die, and then Chris will kill me for killing his reindeer!"

The animal sits down in a gentle pose on the roof, getting comfortable.

"Oh, you've got to be joking."

This is a disaster. This is a catastrophic failure of judgment that I'm going to have to explain to three bounty hunters who are probably watching me on camera right now, laughing at the crazy woman who broke into their property and released their livestock.

I pat my pockets like a nervous rabbit. Nothing but phone, keys, and lint. No emergency scone. My brain panics for exactly two seconds before I remember where I left the goods—the car.

"Stay," I tell the reindeer as if it understands English and common sense. It stares at me, unimpressed, chewing on the air. "Okay." I take off, skittering across the frosted lawn toward the driveway. Cold hits my cheeks so hard my nose stings. I fling open the car door, dive in, and aim for the open platter of brownies and carrot cake muffins. I break off a small piece of a muffin, as reindeer like carrots, right?

Then I sprint back. The reindeer is still on the roof, because of course it is.

I wave the goodie like a flag. "Hey, you," I call, breathless. "Down here, Rudolph. Yes, you. Do you think you're one of Santa's reindeer or something? Because I am not leaving until you come down and behave."

It snorts and flicks an ear. I offer a piece of the muffin on both palms like some kind of pastry priestess. "Look at me. This is fresh from this morning. Not the sad, stale kind, but Lily's signature. You will regret refusing this."

The wind shifts, and the scent must reach the reindeer full on. Its nostrils flare. Hope lights in its eyes, which is ridiculous because this is a beast, not a golden retriever. It edges down the tree with the same agility it used to climb up, hooves hitting the woodpile next, and leaps down to the ground with terrifying grace. That's when I notice an axe embedded in one of the logs, and my heart stops for a second, but the reindeer lands clear, unhurt, and trots straight toward me.

I practically weep with relief. "Yes! Good Rudolph. That's it. Come get it."

It bounds forward and snuffles the piece of carrot muffin out of my hands with a sound that could be mistaken for a purr if you are professionally delusional. Crumbs coat my fingers. I laugh, wiping them on my jeans. "You massive pastry thief."

The reindeer chews solemnly. I stroke its muzzle because now feels like a good time to establish a friend-ship. But it headbutts me, gentler this time, like it's playing.

"Okay, no. We're not playing. We're going back to the barn." I grab for what I think might be a collar around its neck, but it's just fur, and the reindeer dances away from me. "Come here!"

It bolts toward the pasture instead.

"No! Wrong direction!"

I chase after it, and we end up in a muddy patch where snow has melted into slush. My boots sink, and I'm slipping, and the reindeer is having the time of its life running circles around me.

"Please," I gasp, making another grab. "Please just cooperate for five seconds."

This time I manage to get a grip on the fur of its neck. It tries to pull away, I hold on, and we both slip in the mud.

I go down hard, knees first, mud splashing everywhere. It's cold and wet and disgusting, and I can feel it soaking through my jeans.

"This is your fault," I tell the reindeer, who's now calmly standing next to me like nothing happened. "You know that, right? This is entirely your fault."

It blinks at me with those big, innocent eyes.

"Don't give me that look. You're a menace." I struggle to my feet, mud everywhere, on my jeans, my jacket, my hands. I can feel it on my face. "And you're coming with me to the barn right now before—"

"What are you doing to Corn Dog?" A low, male voice comes from behind me.

I freeze and turn slowly, and there's a man standing about ten feet away, half hidden by the corner of the house.

And oh my God, he's gorgeous.

Tall, definitely six-four, with long light brown hair, falling past his shoulders. He's wearing all black—tactical pants, boots, some kind of vest that might be Kevlar. Blue eyes that are currently studying me.

This must be one of Chris's partners. Has to be. No one else would be on this property, right?

"Do I know you?" His voice is calm. "What are you doing here?"

I try to find words. Any words. But my brain is struggling to process the fact that I'm covered in mud, holding on to a reindeer named Corn Dog, and facing down a man who looks like he just walked out of the woods after wrestling a bear with his bare hands and winning.

"I just—Chris—reindeer—I wanted to check—" I'm stammering, gesturing uselessly. "I thought he was home. I didn't mean to—the gate opened and I—my name's Hannah."

Corn Dog chooses this moment to escape my grip, bolting toward the pasture again.

"Dammit!" I lunge after him, but the man moves faster, cutting off Corn Dog's escape route. Between the two of us, we manage to corner the reindeer and herd him toward the fenced pen behind the barn.

The man opens the gate, and Corn Dog trots inside like he planned this whole escape just to torment me. The gate shuts with a solid click.

I exhale, leaning against the fence. "Oh my God. That reindeer is exhausting."

"They're all exhausting." The man is watching me, and there's definitely amusement in his eyes now. "But especially him."

"Why's he named Corn Dog?"

"That's a long story." He crosses his arms, and the movement makes his vest shift, revealing more tactical gear underneath. "Let me guess. You're the event planner who kissed Chris yesterday."

Heat floods my face. "Oh. He told you about that."

The man's smirk widens. "I'm Noel Saxon, by the way, and this is my home."

Saxon. Like the original owners. "You're related to Greg and Mary?"

"My grandparents." He tilts his head, studying me. "How'd you know about them?"

"Mr. Walsh at the post office. I asked who owned reindeer in town." I try to wipe mud off my face, but my hands are also muddy, so I'm probably just making it worse. "I'm really sorry for breaking into your property. I just needed to verify that Chris actually had reindeer before tomorrow's event."

"By breaking in." Noel's voice is dry. "That's one way to do it."

"In my defense, no one answered the call box out front."

"Because I was watching you on my phone." He pulls out his phone, shows me the screen. Security camera footage. Of me. Climbing the fence. "I opened the gate when I saw you dangling because I was worried you'd fall and sue us."

Oh my God. He watched the whole thing.

"You couldn't have given a girl a warning?" I mutter, trying not to drown in humiliation.

"I'm not used to people breaking into my property. Usually, they just knock and wait."

"Usually, I do too. Today has been an exception." It's deeply unfair how attractive he is. And how he's just standing there, emotionless, while I'm mentally melting across from him.

His scent drifts over on the breeze. Crushed pine needles and dark chocolate. It's divine, which is bad. Very bad. I cannot be attracted to Chris's friend as well. That's a recipe for disaster.

But damn, the mountain air must do something to men out here, because both of them look like they were carved by very generous gods.

"Look." I try to gather my composure, which is difficult when I'm covered in mud and probably have it in my hair. "I'll come clean. I've had some trust issues lately. My business partner screwed me over, and I needed to know that Chris wasn't lying about the reindeer before I showed up tomorrow with no backup plan."

Noel's expression softens slightly. "That's fair, actually. Trust is important." He studies me, and I'm acutely aware of how disgusting I must look. "But you're filthy. Come inside, clean up. I've got some clothes that'll be too big, but better than wearing mud."

"I can't. I'm a mess. I'll ruin your house."

"The house has been through worse." He's already walking toward the front door. "Come on. Unless you want to drive home while covered in mud?"

He has a point.

I follow him, leaving my muddy boots outside on the porch. The door opens into a huge entryway, and I stop dead, staring.

This place is incredible.

The entrance opens into a huge great room with vaulted ceilings and exposed timber beams. A massive stone fireplace dominates one wall. The furniture is all dark leather and wood, oversized couches arranged around the fireplace, a bar setup in one corner with expensive-looking bottles on display.

Animal skins hang on the walls—elk, deer, what might be a bear. There's a huge flat-screen TV mounted above the bar. Bookshelves line another wall.

The kitchen connects through an open archway, all stainless steel and granite counters, professional-grade appliances.

To the right, a wide staircase curves up to the second floor. Multiple hallways branch off in different directions, suggesting the house goes on forever.

This isn't a house. This is a lodge. A very masculine, very expensive lodge.

"Holy shit," I breathe.

Noel glances back at me. "Yeah, Grandfather had a thing for grand gestures. This way."

He leads me up the stairs, which are wide enough for three people to walk side by side, and down a hallway with multiple doors. He opens one, gestures me inside.

"Guest bathroom. Shower's through there. Towels are clean. Take your time."

"Thank you. I really appreciate this."

"No problem." He pauses in the doorway. "I'll grab those clothes for you. When you're done, come downstairs."

Then he's gone, and I'm alone in a bathroom that's bigger than my bedroom.

I shower quickly, scrubbing mud out of my hair, off

my skin, watching brown water swirl down the drain. Even my underwear has mud on it, so I rinse everything in the shower, wringing it out as best I can.

When I emerge wrapped in a towel, plush and expensive, I crack the door open and find a neat stack of clothes on the floor outside. Sweatpants, a T-shirt.

I grab them and change quickly, rolling the sweatpants at the ankles, tying the drawstring tight so they don't fall off. The shirt hangs to mid-thigh, so I knot it at my hip, creating some semblance of a shape. It's baggy and ridiculous, but it's clean and dry, so I'll take it.

I stuff my wet, muddy clothes into the plastic bag Noel left.

Craziest day ever. But on the bright side, I now know Chris wasn't lying. The reindeer are real. This is all real.

I head downstairs barefoot, following the sound of voices.

There are three men in the great room. Noel, Chris, and a third man. They're standing by the fireplace that's now roaring to life.

The third man is huge, six-five at least, broad and muscled, wearing the same tactical black gear as Noel. Dark blond hair, hazel-green eyes, a grin that suggests he finds everything hilarious.

They're laughing when I emerge, and they all turn to look at me.

I freeze at the bottom of the stairs.

Three gorgeous, dangerous-looking Alphas, all

staring at me while I'm wearing borrowed clothes and no shoes and probably still have mud somewhere I missed.

My body wants to sway toward them, a sudden, unexpected heat building low in my belly, which is troubling.

"Clothes," I blurt out, because apparently that's the only word my brain can produce.

Noel's grin widens. "They suit you."

"Sure. If the look I'm going for is 'drowning in fabric.'" I walk farther into the room, aware of their gazes on me. "I'm Hannah, by the way. Since I haven't officially met all of you properly."

"Kane Reed," the third man says and walks over to me with a bottle of water in his hand, which he offers me. I take it gratefully, gulping half of it down. "Chris told us about you, but good to finally meet you."

Chris is smiling now, leaning against the fireplace with his arms crossed. "Good to see you again, Hannah. Though I have to say, I'm impressed. You tracked down where I live and broke into the property. That's dedication."

"It's creepy, right?" My face is burning. "But in my defense, I just needed to verify that the reindeer existed. I wasn't stalking you."

"She was definitely stalking you," Noel says. "Wait till I show you the footage of her dealing with Corn Dog." Noel is already chuckling, and I'm narrowing my gaze at him.

"Nothing exciting," I say, but they're already nodding at Noel. Just wonderful—I've now become a clown.

All three of them are still grinning, and I make the mistake of stepping closer instead of farther away.

Instant regret.

Kane's scent is new to me—gingerbread, campfire smoke, and orange zest—and it's mixing with the scents from Chris and Noel, smothering me at once. Heat races under my skin, and my pulse skips hard enough that I feel it in my tongue. My knees don't go weak, but there's a sudden, ridiculous awareness of my own breathing, my own body, like every inch of me has woken up.

I don't do this around Alphas. Ever. Certainly not around three at the same time. My body clearly didn't get the memo. I force my face into something normal. Businesslike. Adult-in-control-ish.

"So." I down the rest of the water like it might drown the problem. "We're set for tomorrow? The event?"

Chris nods. "Yeah. We've got the reindeer, plus goats, sheep, and a miniature horse. Along with some chickens and bunnies. Transport is squared away. We'll show up early and handle the setup."

"Thank you so much. That's... perfect. Let me text you the details of where to go." I hand him my phone, he types in his number, and then I send him a message with all the details. The next thing I do is take a deliberate step back. Then another. Distance helps. Not much, but enough to breathe. "I should go. You all look busy, probably need to, I don't know... reorganize evidence boards or whatever bounty hunters do after catching criminals."

They exchange looks, definitely entertained.

I am face-planting in my own dignity. "Thanks for letting me clean up," I add, still edging toward the door. "And your house is incredible. Really beautiful. Very… lumberjack spa." *Shut up.* I need to shut up. "Oh!" I blurt. "I brought brownies. They're in my car. For Chris. As a thank-you."

"Brownies?" Kane perks up. "What kind?"

"Dark chocolate. Lily's recipe. The good ones."

"I'm already in love with your sister."

"You and everyone else." I shake my head, amused despite myself.

All three walk me outside, and I jam my feet back into my still-muddy boots and freeze.

There's a reindeer in my front seat, and my door is open. I must have forgotten to shut it when I retrieved a piece of the muffin earlier.

"Corn Dog," Chris barks behind me, voice dropping into a warning.

The reindeer lifts its head. Its entire muzzle is smeared with crumbs. It blinks at us, unbothered, then casually dips its head back down.

"No. No, no, no—ARE YOU KIDDING ME?" I shout.

That gets everyone moving.

"What the hell—" Kane jogs forward just as Corn Dog snuffles deeply on the tray of goodies.

Noel and Kane don't say a word; they just move. Fast. Accurate.

They are at the reindeer's side in seconds, one big hand on Corn Dog's withers, guiding him back out with the kind of authority that somehow works.

"Buddy," Kane tells the reindeer, hands braced around his neck, "those weren't for you. And you can't eat them in her Honda. Where are your manners?"

Corn Dog snorts crumbs at him.

I step back, mortified, watching these men wrangle a reindeer who clearly has zero shame and a new addiction.

The tray sits crooked in the passenger seat, the carrot cake muffins half devoured, every top bitten clean off. The brownies right beside them are untouched. But they might have been slobbered over.

Chris takes one look at the carnage and sighs with the genuine heartbreak of a man who just lost something he loved.

Noel and Kane wrangle Corn Dog back toward the barn, still laughing, and I'm left standing by my car, feeling mortified, with Chris. "God, I'm so sorry. I'll bring you fresh brownies."

"Hey, it's not your fault. No one can control Corn Dog." Despite everything, he's laughing.

"Anyway, I'm curious. Why do you call him Corn Dog? I asked Noel, but he didn't tell me."

Chris grins. "He got into our kitchen as a baby. Found a plate of corn dogs that Noel was planning to deep-fry for a barbecue. Ate about a dozen before we caught him."

"Oh, shit."

"His stomach swelled up like a balloon," he adds. "Thought he was going to die. Emergency vet visit, whole dramatic ordeal. But he survived, and the vet started calling him Corn Dog, and it stuck."

I'm laughing now. I can't help it. "That's the best origin story I've ever heard."

"He's a menace," Chris says. "But he's family."

I turn to Chris, and the laughter fades. "Look. I'm sorry for breaking in, for letting him escape, for all of this. For not trusting you." I pout.

"Hey." His voice softens. "I get it. I do background checks before working with anyone new. You needed proof. That's smart."

"I should've just asked."

"Honestly? I respect the commitment."

"You're not mad?"

"I'm entertained, and I can't wait to watch the footage."

Relief washes through me while I'm partly mortified. "Okay. Good. That's good." I climb into my driver's seat, which smells like reindeer now, and start the engine. "I should go. Before I cause any more trouble."

"See you tomorrow," Chris says.

"Tomorrow. Right. The event. Where I will be professional and not break any laws."

"Setting the bar high."

"I'm an overachiever."

I'm pulling away when my phone rings. Lily. I answer. "I'm alive."

"Oh, thank God. I was about to call the police. What happened? Tell me everything."

I glance in my rearview mirror. All three men are standing in front of the house, watching me drive away.

"I have so much to tell you," I say.

"Then spill."

And I do…

CHAPTER SIX

NOEL

$\mathcal{I}$'ve tracked fugitives through three states, tackled armed suspects in dark alleys, and once spent eighteen hours in a freezing surveillance van waiting for a bail jumper to surface.

None of that prepared me for standing in a petting zoo.

The festival grounds are packed, with families everywhere, kids running between food stalls selling kettle corn and funnel cakes, and bounce castles inflated and busy in the distance. Christmas music blares from speakers, competing with the general roar of happy chatter. The kind of scene I normally avoid. Too many people, too much noise, too many variables I can't control. When you spend your days hunting criminals, you learn to prefer quiet spaces where you can see threats coming.

But somehow, I'm here.

And surprisingly, it's not as bad as I expected.

Maybe because I can't stop watching Hannah.

She's everywhere at once, checking the fence line around the petting zoo, adjusting the hand-painted signs we hung this morning, talking to the teenager manning the ticket booth. She's wearing dark jeans that fit her perfectly and a cream-colored sweater. Her hair is pulled back in a ponytail, a few dark strands escaping to frame her face.

Every time she moves, I catch a hint of her scent on the breeze. Sweet sugar-cookies, coffee, and marshmallow, faint but unmistakable. Delicious enough to eat.

It's been driving me insane since yesterday.

The petting zoo itself appears decent. We set it up at dawn with a large shared pen with five-foot fences, reinforced gates for controlled entry and exit, all the animals in one place. Two reindeer are in the back corner for now, already drawing stares from people passing by. Our goats are all over the place, the sheep we borrowed are huddled together looking nervous, and that miniature horse Kane insisted on bringing is living its best life near the entrance. Then the chickens and bunnies are having the time of their lives going everywhere. While the fair is running, the petting zoo doors haven't opened yet.

"Noel!" Hannah is waving at me from the entrance to the small building attached to the petting zoo, the makeshift office. "Can you guys come inside for a sec before we open up?"

I catch Chris's attention—he's double-checking water troughs—and jerk my head toward the building.

Kane is already heading that way, abandoning his goat supervision.

The structure looks absurd from the outside. Someone painted it to resemble a cartoon elf house, complete with oversized candy cane decorations flanking the door and a shingled roof. There's a wreath on the door with bells that jingle when Hannah pushes it open.

Inside is better.

One large room, maybe fifteen by twenty feet, with wooden walls painted white and an exposed-beam ceiling. There's a folding table covered in supplies against the far wall—first aid kit, bottled water, extra animal feed, clipboards with paperwork. A few folding chairs are scattered around, and it's warm. Someone hung a mirror on the wall, probably for costume checks or last-minute appearance fixes.

It's functional. Cozy, even.

And the second the door shuts behind us, Hannah's scent floods me in full force. I have to lock my jaw to keep from inhaling deeply like some kind of creep.

I've spent years learning to control my reactions. Bounty hunting requires it. You can't let suspects see you rattled, can't let fear or attraction or anger show on your face when you're trying to talk someone into custody.

But this is different. I force myself to focus on her face instead of drowning in her scent.

"Okay." Hannah turns to face us, clasping her hands together. "First, thank you to all three of you. I know this isn't your usual gig, and you're doing it for free, which is—I can't even express how much that means to me."

"It's no problem," Chris says, leaning against the wall, all nonchalant. "We're happy to help."

I'm still on the fence about this.

"Still. I owe you. Big-time." She's nervous. The way she's twisting her hands together, the slight tremor in her voice. "So I have one more favor to ask. And I completely understand if you say no, but I figured I'd at least try because—"

"What do you need?" Kane interrupts gently.

She takes a deep breath, then reaches under the table and pulls out a bundle of what appear to be clothes.

Oh, no.

"The client loved the idea of themed staff for the petting zoo," Hannah says quickly, words tumbling out. "And I thought it would be fun and festive, you know." She unfolds the bundle, revealing a Santa suit as she stares at Chris.

He groans. "You're kidding."

"What's another one for the team?" Kane adds with a smirk.

"You were perfect as Santa at the Winter Party! The kids loved you!" Hannah is practically pleading now. "And the client is advertising your presence on all the signage around the festival."

Yet Chris is already reaching for the suit, resignation clear on his face. "Fine. I'm getting used to this gig anyway."

I've never been more grateful that Chris volunteered to be Santa, because that means Kane and I don't have to.

Then Hannah pulls out two bundles, smirking at Kane and me.

Elf costumes. Green tunics with zigzag hems. Red tights. Pointed hats with bells sewn onto the tips.

"Absolutely not," I say immediately.

"Not happening," Kane agrees, and I'm glad we're on the same page about this.

"Come on!" Hannah holds up a smaller version of the costume. "I'm wearing one too! The whole petting zoo staff needs to match. It's part of the theme!"

"It's humiliating," I add.

"It's festive!"

"Those are very different things."

She's staring at us with those wide chocolate eyes, and I can feel my resistance starting to crumble. Which is infuriating. I don't do costumes. I track criminals and drag them back to face justice, and I wear dark colors so blood doesn't show.

This is so far outside my comfort zone that it's in a different time zone.

"Please?" Hannah's voice dips. "I promise you'll look great. And I really need this to be perfect. Scot is probably lurking around somewhere, waiting for something to go wrong so he can report back to his uncle that I can't handle events on my own."

That does it. The thought of that prick trying to sabotage her kick-starts my protective instincts.

"Fine," I hear myself say. "But if anyone I know sees me in this, I'm blaming you."

"So that's a yes!" Hannah actually bounces on her toes, excited, and my gaze drops to her chest before I can stop myself. Not fair. That's completely not fair. She's going to win every argument if she keeps doing that.

"We'll do it," Kane says, sounding resigned. "But I'm not happy about it."

"You don't have to be happy. You just have to look adorable." She's shoving costumes at us, grinning wide. "Get changed! I'll be back in five minutes!"

Then she's gone, door swinging shut behind her, bells jingling, and I'm left holding green felt and red tights.

There's a moment of silence.

"Fuck! We're really doing this?" Kane barks, staring at his costume like it might bite him.

"Apparently." I set mine on the table, start stripping out of my jacket.

Chris is already pulling on the Santa pants, shaking his head. "Could be worse. She mentioned yesterday that she had a backup reindeer costume. Full bodysuit. Antlers. Tail."

I pause mid-shirt removal. "No way."

"Yep."

"I'm burning that costume the second I find it," Kane says.

"Get in line," I add.

I finish undressing down to my boxers and T-shirt,

eyeing the elf costume with deep suspicion. The tunic looks big—Hannah must have ordered sizes for large men—but this is going to be snug.

I pull it on. It fits, barely. The fabric stretches across my shoulders, the hem hitting mid-thigh. The tights are worse, being thin red material that leaves absolutely nothing to the imagination.

I catch sight of myself in the mirror and seriously consider just walking out and dealing with the consequences.

Kane is struggling with his own costume, muttering curses under his breath. "How do people wear this stuff voluntarily? This is torture."

"Someone invented these costumes specifically to punish large men."

"I'm filing a complaint."

"With who?"

"Santa. He started this whole mess."

Chris snorts from across the room. He's fully dressed now, red suit, black boots, white beard adjusted perfectly. "You two look ridiculous."

"You're literally dressed as Santa Claus," I say.

"I look fantastic. There's a difference."

I pull on the pointed hat, bells jingling with every movement, and catch Kane's eye. He's looking just as absurd as I feel.

"Hey." I keep my voice low. "You get close enough to scent her yet?"

Kane goes still, his expression shifting. "What?"

"Don't bullshit me," I say. "Yesterday, when she was

cleaning up. And now, stuffed in this broom closet of a room with her. You scented her, yeah?"

Kane's jaw locks so hard I can hear his molars complain. "I wasn't gonna say anything."

I bark a laugh. "Why the hell not?"

His gaze cuts to mine, sharp, uneasy in a way he never admits to. "Because if I'm right, if she's actually what I think she is, that changes everything."

Chris stops pretending he isn't listening and drags a palm over his beard, smug bastard that he is. His grin is slow, wolfish, like he's picturing her pressed under him already. "Told you she's my scent match. Knew the second she kissed me."

I swear my spine tightens. "You two are way too fucking calm about this."

Kane starts pacing—well, as much pacing as one can do in a room the size of a coffin. "All three of us scenting the same Omega? Meaning she's ours."

"So what's the move?" I ask.

"We figure out if she feels it too," Chris says, leaning back like he's working through a bar tab, not our entire damn futures. "Then we court her. Show her we're worth the mess."

I pinch the bridge of my nose. "She's drowning in career shit and trust issues. You think she's gonna hear three bounty-hunting Alphas say 'You're ours' and clap her hands like it's Christmas?"

Chris shrugs. Kane half chuckles.

I want to hit them both.

"I think biology is gonna make the call before her

brain gets there," Kane adds. He crosses his arms, a tank of a man, blocking the only exit. "Her heat will show sooner or later. Better she's with us than alone. Or worse, handled by some random asshole who doesn't know what the fuck he's doing."

The image punches every rational thought straight out of my skull. Some unknown Alpha's hands on her. Her in heat. My teeth grind loudly enough that Chris raises a brow.

"Easy," he drawls, fighting a grin. "Thought you were the patient one."

"Since when?" Kane shoots back.

"Since," I say, adjusting the stupid hat, bells jingling like a damn mockery, "I realized scaring her off would be the dumbest shit we could do. She's skittish. One wrong move and she'll run."

Kane nods. "So we play it careful. Get close. Let her settle. Wait for the right moment."

I hate how reasonable that sounds. "Exactly," I admit out loud. Though, inside, every instinct is clawing at me, telling me to find her, put my scent on her, make sure the whole damn world knows she's not fair game.

Chris shoots a look between us.

"So... careful?"

I shrug. "Careful-ish. She's an Omega, not a porcelain figurine. But yeah. Slow enough that she doesn't think we're hunting her."

Kane's mouth kicks up like he's already ruining the plan. "We *are* hunters."

"Yeah," I say. "But not for her. Not unless she asks real nice."

Chris whistles low. "Fuck, she's gonna kill us."

"Probably," I mutter. "And I'll still hold her fucking hand while she does it."

Kane snorts out a laugh, the tension easing just a little. But under it, beneath the jokes, the pacing, the swearing, we're all thinking the same thing: If she's ours... we're making her ours.

The door opens, and Hannah strolls in, all smiles. Every thought in my head evaporates.

She's wearing the elf costume, and she has no idea how good it fits her.

The dress is green, fitted from a sweetheart neckline that showcases her breasts, that impossibly small waist. It flares at the hips, the skirt hitting mid-thigh and showing off legs covered in red-and-white-striped tights. Little boots with bells complete the look.

Her dark hair is down, waves falling past her shoulders, and she put glitter on her cheeks. She looks like every fantasy I didn't know I had wrapped up in festive packaging.

I'm staring. We're all gawking.

"Well?" She does a little spin, bells jingling, and the skirt flares enough to show more thigh. "What do you think?"

None of us can answer.

My mouth is hanging open. My brain is completely offline. Every instinct I have is screaming at me to cross the room and—

"That good, huh?" Her laugh is nervous, and she's blushing now, that pretty pink climbing her cheeks. "Come on, we need to get out there. The client is about to open the gates."

She takes a quick glance at Chris in his Santa suit, then at Kane and me in our elf costumes. Her eyes linger down our bodies, widen slightly, and then jerk away.

She loves what she sees. I grin widely.

"Let's go," Hannah calls from the doorway, grinning back at us. "Time to spread Christmas cheer."

We file out into the petting zoo area, and immediately chaos erupts.

"SANTA!"

"LOOK, ELVES!"

"ARE THOSE REAL REINDEER?"

Kids are screaming, parents are laughing, and everyone is trying to get through the gates at once. Hannah is managing the flow, directing families to different areas, explaining the rules about gentle touching and supervised feeding.

I'm stationed near the reindeer section. My job is to make sure overexcited kids don't pull tails or try to climb on backs. Rook and Bishop are tolerating the attention, probably because Hannah snuck them extra treats earlier.

The next two hours pass in a blur of explaining reindeer facts, preventing disasters, and trying not to think about how ridiculous I look in this costume.

A little boy tugs on my tunic. "Mr. Elf, are these Santa's reindeer?"

I crouch down to his level. "They're in training."

His eyes go huge. "For pulling the sleigh?"

"Exactly. Very intensive training program. They have to pass several tests."

"Like what?"

Shit. I'm in too deep now. "Flying. Navigation. Cookie taste-testing."

"Cookies?"

"How else do you think Santa knows which cookies are worth eating? The reindeer test them first."

He runs off to tell his parents, and I notice Kane watching me from the goat section, grinning.

Around noon, I spot the demographic shift in visitors.

Fewer kids are coming through the gates. More women in their twenties and thirties, traveling in groups, giggling and pointing.

At us.

One approaches me while I'm refilling a water trough for the reindeer. "Hi! Can I get a photo with you?"

I straighten. "Sorry, no photos."

"Why not?"

"Elf union rules." The lie comes easily. "We can't have our images posted online. Ruins the magic."

"Oh." She looks disappointed. "That's too bad. You're really hot."

"Thanks?" I step back, creating distance. "Enjoy the reindeer."

She lingers for another minute, clearly hoping I'll change my mind, then moves on when I don't.

This happens four more times in the next hour.

Chris is getting swarmed near the miniature horse, women lining up to sit on Santa's lap. Kane is surrounded by them, and they are ostensibly interested in the goats but keep finding excuses to touch his arms and ask about his workout routine.

I catch Hannah watching from across the pen, and I swear there's jealousy in her expression. Possessiveness.

I like it.

A lot.

She moves past me to check the goats, pretending she isn't paying attention, but her gaze keeps drifting my way like she's tracking a threat she hasn't decided whether to run from or tackle. I lean in just enough to brush her space. "You keep looking at me," I murmur. "I'm flattered, but you're gonna hurt yourself if you stare that hard."

Her cheeks warm immediately, which tells me everything. "Relax," she says, lifting her clipboard like it's a shield. "I was making sure you weren't losing any children."

"Pretty confident that's not what you were noticing," I say, smiling because she's cute when she tries to play it cool.

She exhales like I'm exhausting, then mutters, "It's a small pen. You're loud. My eyes had nowhere else to go."

"They could've gone anywhere, sweetheart. They picked me." I wink, and she gives me the look women give men right before either kissing them or threatening bodily harm. For her, these might not be mutually exclusive. She shakes her head and walks away, hips stiff, like she's too aware that I'm watching.

Two hours later, I crouch to help a kid who dropped his feed cup. The moment I bend, I feel the fabric of my tights strain, then it gives with the kind of catastrophic rip that doesn't ask permission. It detonates.

I freeze. Wind everywhere wind should not be.

I stand slowly, spine straight, fully aware that the back of my pants is now a crime scene. Several heads turn. A mother gasps and covers her child's eyes like I've summoned Satan.

Somewhere behind me, Hannah makes a sound like she just bit her fist to keep from laughing. I hear a choked "Oh, no," but she's absolutely delighted.

Chris, operating as Santa against his will, loses every ounce of composure. His laugh bursts out like he's been shot. "Noel—holy—" He can't finish. He's doubled over. Bells jingling. Beard shaking. Useless.

I can't move. I'm a statue of humiliation. This is how I die, ass out, surrounded by livestock and children with sticky hands. Not chasing a fugitive off a roof. Not wrestling a wanted criminal from a moving car. No. Exposed in a petting zoo while wearing elf tights.

A chicken stares at me like it's judging me.

Hannah finally rushes over, stepping in behind me as if she's shielding a VIP from sniper fire, though I'm pretty sure she's laughing behind her hand. "Okay. Inside. Before someone livestreams this."

I mutter, "Pretty sure they already did," and she steers me toward the elf house.

"Just walk," she says, her voice a little breathless. She's trying to be professional, but she's pink in the cheeks and biting her lip, and for a moment, I'm not sure if she's flustered or two seconds from laughing herself unconscious.

"I don't suppose you've got a spare pair of pants tucked in your bag of holiday miracles."

"I've got a sewing kit," she says. "That's the best you're getting."

"I'd rather bleed out."

"You'll survive," she says, guiding me through the door. "But if you don't hurry, I'm going to lose it laughing, and then you'll be on your own."

I don't doubt it.

The elf house door swings shut just as Chris calls after me, "Good news, your underwear is festive!"

I flip him off behind the door. I'm ninety percent sure he got a picture.

We duck inside, and the blessed quiet after all that crazy outside is almost as good as the air on my overheated face. Then I take off the elf tights.

Hannah digs through her backpack like she's defusing a bomb. "Needle... thread... miracle patch kit —yes. Knew I packed you." She turns toward me and freezes.

Her gaze drops to my underwear. Then a strangled

noise escapes, somewhere between a laugh and a tiny death. "So..." she says, eyes sparkling, "festive briefs, huh?"

"They were the only clean pair," I mutter.

"They have *candy canes* on them." She tries to keep a straight face and fails as she smiles. "This is... not the vibe I expected from a dangerous bounty hunter."

"What vibe did you expect?" I pass her the tights.

"I don't know. Something grim. Black. Maybe 'I lift motorcycles to relax.' Not... holiday-themed." She sits, threading her needle, cheeks pink.

I'm immune to nothing. Not her blush. Not the way she bites back her smile. Not the fact that she's sewing this stupid costume like it's a sacred mission.

"So," I say casually, "what's your underwear style?"

"Normal."

"That's not an answer."

"It is."

"Absolutely not. 'Normal' could mean anything. Polka dots. Flowers. Dinosaurs."

Her lips twitch. "I'm not telling you."

I lean a little closer, just enough to make her breath hitch. "C'mon. Professional curiosity."

"Yeah, right," she states with a cheeky grin.

"I'm a dedicated researcher." I gesture vaguely. "I investigate... patterns."

She tries not to laugh and fails. "You're ridiculous."

"And you're avoiding the question."

"Because it's none of your business."

"That sounds like a yes to dinosaurs."

She stabs the needle through the fabric with unnecessary force. "It's not dinosaurs."

"Unicorns?"

She tightens her lips like she's trying not to smile. "Are you finished?"

"Not even close."

She hands me the tights, brushing my fingers accidentally, though it feels intentional enough to unleash something hungry under my ribs.

"There," she says. "Patch is visible, but it'll do." She stands, dusting imaginary lint from her elf dress. "Try not to rip them again."

"No promises."

Her gaze meets mine, a flick of mischief. "Didn't think so."

And just like that, the room feels too small. Too warm. Because she's still close, smelling like sin, and I suddenly want to know every ridiculous, adorable secret she has, including what she's wearing under that dress.

I take the tights from her, pull them back on. The fabric is snug, but the repair holds when I test it by doing several squats.

When I turn back around, Hannah is standing, and the space between us is maybe eighteen inches. Close enough that I can see every spot of glitter on her cheeks in detail, smell her scent even stronger now that we're alone.

Her eyes travel up from my torso to my chest, and I watch her pupils dilate slightly.

"You know," I say quietly, "those D and D people were really onto something with the whole elf-fantasy thing."

She blinks, refocusing on my face. "Perhaps."

I step closer, and she doesn't back away. It takes everything I have not to close the remaining distance and kiss her. "Hannah. Did you ever think you'd find your scent match at a petting zoo?"

Her eyes go wide, her breath hiccupping.

"Ah." I keep my voice gentle, nonthreatening. "You sense it too, then."

She's blinking rapidly, and I can practically see her mind working through the implications. "I—that's not—look, I need to focus on this event right now. Not complicate it with… whatever this is."

"It's not a complication."

"I beg to differ." She moves toward the door, but I step sideways, not blocking, just delaying, and rest my hand against the wood.

She glances up at me, and I can spot her trembling slightly. Fear? Attraction? Both?

"I won't do anything you don't want," I say quietly. "But I need you to be honest with yourself. You feel it. The pull. The recognition. You know what we are to you."

She swallows hard. "I'll think about it."

The words surprise a laugh out of me. "Okay, then."

"Noel, I'm just dealing with the disaster to my career with Scot. I can't pile pack dynamics and scent matches and whatever else comes with this on top of everything else. Not right now."

"You don't have to decide today, but sometimes the universe doesn't wait." I move my hand from the door, giving her space to leave if she wants. "I can be patient. Think about it. We'll talk later."

She darts out the door before I can say anything else, and I'm left standing alone in the small room, my heart racing, my entire body still humming with her presence. I give myself ten seconds to calm down, then head back outside.

Kane appears at my elbow immediately. "What were you two doing in there for so long?"

"I told her she's our scent match."

His shoulders stiffen. "You just—you straight up told her?"

"Someone had to. She knows we know. And yep, she feels it too. We just have to wait for her to accept it."

"Chris is going to be insufferable when he finds out."

We're both watching Hannah now, and there's something different in how she moves, more aware of where we are in the space, glancing over at us more frequently.

A goat wanders over to her while she's talking to a family with two kids. It starts chewing on the hem of her dress.

She doesn't notice.

Kane and I exchange looks. "Should we tell her?" Kane asks, keeping his voice low.

"Where's the fun in that?" The goat keeps chewing,

fabric unraveling, and Hannah is still completely oblivious, focused on explaining the proper way to pet another goat to a very serious five-year-old.

"She's going to lose that dress," Kane observes.

"Probably."

"And you're not going to warn her."

"Not yet."

We watch as the goat keeps going. Another seam on the side starts to give, threads popping one by one.

Hannah is gesturing animatedly, describing something about wool production, completely unaware that her costume is slowly being destroyed.

"We're terrible people," Kane mutters.

"The worst."

But neither of us moves to help.

Then Chris appears, sees what's happening, and immediately shoos the goat away from Hannah.

Kane and I both glare at him.

He catches our expressions and grins, completely unrepentant.

Traitor.

Hannah finally notices the goat situation, examines the damage to her dress, and gasps at the mess. Then she stares up at us from across the pen, catching the two of us watching, fully aware we've been enjoying the spectacle. The goat bleats, stretching toward her hem again as Chris holds it back, and she mutters that she's going to grab a bucket of grain.

I should look away and get back to work. Give her distance. But my body refuses. My instincts have already decided that she's the center of my map now. Even if she's not ready.

I've lived with enough empty places to know what it feels like when something fills the quiet. Too many rescues came too late. Too many names I could not save. I have carried the weight of that since I was young, and I told myself I would never fail again.

So when she walked into my life smelling like fate, I refused to look away. I can't. This is a gift I never thought I'd be trusted with. Someone who might choose me back. Someone I could protect and worship like the sky at midnight. I have lost enough. I will not lose her.

CHAPTER SEVEN

The petting zoo event was perfect.

Which is great. Fantastic. Exactly what I needed to prove I can handle events without the Confetti & Meatballs name attached.

So then why do I feel like I'm about to throw up?

I'm gripping the steering wheel of my Honda like it might escape if I let go, navigating Main Street at seven in the morning while my brain replays the same conversation on a loop.

Did you ever think you'd find your scent match at a petting zoo?

Noel's voice. Those intense blue eyes. The way he said it like it was already decided, like my biology had made the choice before my brain could catch up.

Three gorgeous, dangerous, competent Alphas who smell like everything I've been craving without knowing it. And my life is a goddamn dumpster fire.

I just left Scot's uncle Giuseppe's house, desperate to

talk to him. His car wasn't there. Lights off. No answer when I knocked. Phone goes straight to voicemail.

Scot got to him. I know he did. Probably spun some story about me being unstable, unprofessional, a liability to the business. And Giuseppe, whom I've been trying to impress for six months, is ghosting me like I'm a telemarketer selling timeshares.

My phone rings through the car's Bluetooth, and Dad's name flashes on the screen. I answer. "Hey, Dad."

"Morning, sweetheart. Just calling to remind you about tomorrow night."

My mind goes blank. "Hmm. Remind me again."

"Your mother's family's Christmas dinner." His voice is gentle, patient, like he's talking to a child. "We discussed this last month, remember?"

Oh, shit. Oh, no. The annual gathering at my aunt's Victorian nightmare, where Mom's family pretends they care about us for exactly three hours before going back to ignoring our existence for another year.

"Dad, I really don't think I can make it. Work's been crazy, and there's so much I need to figure out with—"

"This is something we do for your mom. You know this."

The guilt trip. The one I can never argue with because he's right. A memory surfaces, sharp and painful. I'm standing on a stool in our kitchen, watching Mom frost sugar cookies shaped like stars. She's humming "Silent Night," dark hair pulled back in the same ponytail I always wear, flour dusting her red apron.

"Why do we go to Great-Aunt Martha's if she's always mean to us?" I'd asked, watching her create perfect frosting swirls.

Mom had smiled. "Because family is important, baby. Even when they make it hard. Sometimes showing up is the most loving thing we can do."

That was our last Christmas with her.

I was fourteen when cancer took her. Six months from diagnosis to gone, and she spent those final weeks teaching Lily and me everything she knew about the bakery. All those little tricks that made Flour & Fable special, passed down like sacred knowledge.

Dad worked himself half to death after that. Double shifts at the local diner, trying to keep us fed and housed while juggling two grieving daughters. I watched him age ten years in one, watched him choose between paying the electric bill and buying groceries, watched him cry in the bathroom when he thought we couldn't hear.

We survived. Barely.

And now, every December, we drive to Great-Aunt Martha's mansion, where Mom's relatives ask when I'm going to find an Alpha, make passive-aggressive comments about the quaint little bakery, and pretend they've been supportive all along.

They didn't visit when Mom was dying. Didn't help when we were drowning. Didn't call, didn't care, didn't do a damn thing.

But Mom loved them anyway. So we go.

"Fine," I hear myself say, throat tight. "I'll be there."

"Good girl. Lily can't make it this year, so it'll just be us two."

I nearly drive through a red light. "Wait, what? Lily is bailing?"

"She's got some wedding out of town for one of her Alphas' friends, and they're taking their babies. Left me a message this morning."

"If she gets to skip, I should get to skip!"

Dad chuckles. "Life's not fair, kiddo."

"I hate this."

"I know. Pick me up at five tomorrow? Don't be late. Love you."

"Love you too, Dad."

He hangs up, and I'm left stewing in frustration and dread.

Just great. An evening with relatives who think I'm a failure, asking invasive questions about my nonexistent love life.

This will be fun.

I pull up to Flour & Fable Bakery. Lily has already turned on the Christmas lights framing the windows, illuminating displays of gingerbread houses and elaborate frosted cookies that probably took her hours.

The place looks warm. Inviting. Safe.

I park on the street, grab my purse, and push through the front door. Bells jingle overhead, and the scent of fresh bread and cinnamon wraps around me.

God, I love this place.

It will always feel like home. Mom's recipes, Mom's dream.

The display cases are packed with holiday specials. Gingerbread cookies with intricate icing. Sugar cookies shaped like snowflakes and bells. Cranberry orange scones. Those little spiced apple tarts that sell out by noon. Peppermint bark brownies. Lemon raspberry macarons with edible gold leaf because Lily likes to get fancy sometimes.

Everything is gorgeous. Professional. Exactly the kind of quality that makes this bakery the most popular in three counties.

Lily is behind the counter in a red sweater with a reindeer on it that's so aggressively festive it should require a permit. Her curls are piled on her head in a messy bun, and she's packing cookies into small paper boxes.

She spots me and grins. "Hey, you. How'd yesterday go? Did anyone get trampled?"

I collapse against the counter, dropping my purse on the floor. "Coffee first. Crisis processing second."

"You look like someone kicked your puppy." She's already moving to the espresso machine, a beautiful Italian beast that makes coffee so good it's basically drugs. "What happened?"

Within moments, she sets a perfect latte in front of me, foam decorated with a little swan that's almost too pretty to drink. "Now spill about yesterday before I die of curiosity."

I take a sip, perfect temperature, perfect flavor, liquid salvation in a cup. "The event was flawless. Every detail worked. The reindeer were a huge hit, kids loved the goats, parents raved about the setup. I got three emails this morning from people who attended asking if I'm available for their events."

"That's amazing!"

"Well, I've decided if I can't keep running Confetti and Meatballs, I'll start my own event-planning business. Doesn't look too hard to set up online. I just need a name, a logo, and a little shameless self-promotion."

Lily grins. "That's the spirit. You don't need a fortune, just Wi-Fi, caffeine, and that scary level of determination you get when you've been wronged."

"I prefer to call it entrepreneurial vengeance." I take another sip of coffee, already feeling the spark of energy. "Now I just need a name that screams 'professional.'"

"Okay, shoot." She leans on the counter, all in. "What've you got so far?"

I tap my chin. "If I'm doing this, I want something clean and businesslike. Something people won't laugh at."

Lily immediately ruins that. "What about *Chaos and Champagne?*"

"No."

"*Party Like A Mother?*"

"Absolutely not."

"Okay, okay..." She pretends to think deeply. "*Hannah-Saves-Your-Ass Events.* Very honest branding."

I glare at her through my coffee steam. "I'm trying to look legitimate, not like I host interventions."

She grins, utterly unhelpful. "Fine. *Evergreen Events. Hannah Parker Events*—ooh, that one actually slaps."

I pause. "That… doesn't suck."

"Thank you. My genius is underappreciated. Now, tell me how the bounty hunter beefcakes behaved at the petting zoo. And if the answer isn't 'shirtless,' I will be personally offended."

I laugh. "No shirts came off."

"Tragic."

"But," I continue, "everything went perfectly. The animals behaved. Nobody cried. And Noel—" I start laughing before I can finish. "Completely blew out the seam of his pants."

Lily gasps, delighted. "No."

"Oh, yes. Right in front of Santa's chair. Full exposure. Kane nearly choked trying not to laugh, and I think the reindeer judged him harder than the parents did."

She's howling now. "You're kidding. You brought them to one event, and they already gave you viral content." Then she pulls out a plate, carefully arranging three perfect macarons. "But you're still giving me info about the bounty hunters while you eat. I want all the details."

The café portion is empty right now, too early for most customers, so it's just us standing at the counter, Lily on her side, me on mine, with expensive cookies and good coffee between us.

"They were great," I say, taking a bite of a macaron. Tart lemon, sweet raspberry, the crunch of the shell giving way to soft filling. Heaven. "Really professional. Handled everything perfectly."

"And?" Lily prompts, grinning.

"And what?"

"What else happened? You're leaving something out. I can tell."

I take another bite, avoiding her eyes. "Noel told me we're scent matches."

Lily drops the towel she was holding. It hits the floor, and she's staring at me with her mouth open, eyes wide. "That's huge."

"Said I'm their scent match. All three." I shove the rest of the macaron in my mouth, suddenly needing something to do with my hands. "Just said it straight out. No preamble. Just 'Did you ever think you'd find your scent match at a petting zoo?'"

Lily is around the counter in a flash, grabbing my shoulders. "That's incredible! That's amazing! Do you know how much that means—"

"I know."

"Then why do you look like someone died?"

I set down my coffee, suddenly exhausted. "Because my life is imploding, Lily. My career is destroyed, my partnership is over, Scot is actively sabotaging me, and now three Alphas I barely know are claiming that we're destined mates? The timing couldn't be worse."

"Or it couldn't be better." She's moved back to her side of the counter. "Maybe this is exactly when you need them. When everything else is chaos. To balance things out."

"I don't want them to see me failing."

"They've already seen that, and they're still here." She picks up her towel. "Hannah, you can't control when you meet your mates. Biology doesn't care about your five-year plan."

"Well, biology has shit timing."

"Biology always has shit timing. That's kind of its thing." She's grinning now. "But seriously. What are you going to do?"

"Avoid thinking about it until my brain stops screaming."

"Solid plan."

"Thank you."

"That was sarcasm."

"I know."

I take a sip of my latte, desperate to redirect the conversation before Lily starts rewriting my entire life again. "Oh, speaking of disasters, I talked to Dad this morning. He said you bailed on Great-Aunt Martha's Christmas dinner tomorrow."

Lily freezes, lowers her gaze.

I level a betrayed stare at her. "How could you leave me alone at their mercy? At least when it's both of us, the interrogation gets split fifty-fifty. Now it's just me. Solo. Unarmed. Walking straight into a firing squad."

She winces. "Yeah… about that. James's friend has a wedding out of town, and we can't get out of it. Sorry."

"You're abandoning me," I accuse, pointing a macaron at her like it's evidence in court. Then I devour the dessert.

"In my defense," she says slowly, "I have a very real allergy to Great-Aunt Martha's casserole, and her personality."

She's quiet for a moment, and I can practically see the wheels turning in her head. That's never good.

"I have an idea," she finally says. "You might think it's insane, but hear me out."

"Your ideas are always dangerous." I grab another macaron. "Does it involve me doing something stupid?"

"It involves you being smart." She's got that look now, the meddler's glint, pure sin distilled into human form. "Take one of those hot bounty hunters to the family Christmas dinner tomorrow."

I choke on my macaron. "Are you crazy? I need distance from the Alphas to work out my own feelings, not spend more time with them. I have to figure out what I want before I dive into their pack dynamics and scent matching and all that complicated stuff."

"Or..." Lily is scrolling through her phone now, and I recognize that look. She's plotting something. "You use this as an opportunity to get to know one of them better. Low stakes, supervised by Dad, plenty of distractions. See if he can handle our terrible relatives."

"That's not a selling point."

"It absolutely is. If he can survive our family, he can survive anything."

I'm about to argue more when she hits a button on her phone, and suddenly it's ringing on speaker.

My stomach drops. "What are you doing?" I'm

reaching for the phone, but she dances back, keeping it out of range.

"Solving your problem."

"Lily, I swear to God—"

"Hey, Lily!" Chris's voice comes through the speaker, and my entire body reacts. Heat floods my face, pools low in my belly, makes my pulse kick up like I've been running.

Damn it.

"Morning!" Lily is way too cheerful. "So, Hannah's in a bit of a situation. She needs a date, or a fake date, if you prefer, to a family Christmas party tomorrow night. Any chance you're free?"

"Lily!" I hiss, lunging for the phone again over the counter.

She spins away, still grinning.

There's a pause. Then Chris laughs, low and warm and amused. "Fuck me, I wish. But Kane and I are chasing a target two states over tomorrow. Won't be back until super late."

Disappointment crashes through me, which is stupid because I didn't want him to come anyway. This is good. This is what I wanted.

So why does it feel like losing?

"Damn." Lily sounds genuinely disappointed. "That's too bad."

"Yeah. I'm gonna need a rain check on that, though." Chris's voice shifts, goes quieter. Intimate. "Missing a chance to spend time with Hannah? That's killing me right now."

My face is on fire. My entire body is on fire.

"But," Chris continues, "Noel's free tomorrow. He'd be perfect for this. And between you and me, he's been looking for an excuse to get more time with your sister."

Noel. Who told me we're scent matches and looked at me like he could see straight through every wall I've built.

I'm making frantic gestures at Lily, mouthing, *Say no* and *Hang up*, but she's ignoring me completely.

"Perfect!" Lily is practically bouncing. "Noel's great. Count it as a date. Though, fair warning, family gatherings usually involve interrogations. He might get grilled."

"Oh, he's great at improvising and making up shit on the spot. He'll be fine."

"I like his style," Lily adds.

"So is Hannah there with you, listening?" he asks.

I freeze.

Lily looks directly at me, eyes sparkling. "Oh, yeah. She's right here, practically hyperventilating from embarrassment and excitement."

"Lily!" I'm going to kill her. Actually murder her.

"Hannah." Chris's voice drops lower, and suddenly it feels like he's in the room instead of on the phone. "I know you're scared. I know your life's a mess right now and you don't think you need complications. But here's the thing, sweetheart. You're a revelation. I can't stop thinking about you for five seconds. So stop running. Let Noel take you to this party. Let us show you what it's like to have Alphas who actually give a shit."

My knees are weak. My brain is offline. My entire body is screaming at me to say yes, to give in, to stop fighting what apparently everyone but me knows is inevitable.

I can't find my voice.

"Tomorrow night," Chris continues. "Noel will pick you up, Hannah."

Before I can even form a protest, Lily pops in with "Oh, I'll text you the details. Dad's going with them too."

Chris lets out a low chuckle, the kind that rumbles like he's actually amused. "An escort. Nice. Should he dress formally for the occasion?"

Lily waves a hand even though Chris can't see the gesture. "Please. Dad is the least of Noel's problems. My father is zen. A nap. A warm beverage. Great-Aunt Martha is the final boss."

Chris snorts under his breath. "Sounds… fun."

"Oh, you have no idea."

"Okay, speak later, then." The line goes dead.

I glare at Lily.

She stares back, grinning like the cat who ate the canary and then the entire dairy section.

"I hate you," I whisper.

"You love me."

"I'm reconsidering that position."

"Too late. You're stuck with me." She's already making herself a coffee, totally unbothered by the crisis she just unleashed. "This is perfect. You get to show your family you're not some sad, single Omega, and you get quality time with one of your Alphas. Win-win."

"He's not my Alpha."

"Yet."

"We're not dating."

"You are after tomorrow night."

"This is under Dad's supervision!"

Lily leans her hip against the counter, eyes sparkling with unholy glee. "Just imagine their faces when you walk into the house with him. Tall. Muscles. Tattoos. That whole broody storm-cloud thing he's got going on. I swear Cousin Patty might pass out. Or worse, try to touch him."

"Lily." I pinch the bridge of my nose. "You're having way too much fun with this."

"Oh, absolutely."

"You're forgetting the part where he knows nothing about me and they're going to interrogate him like a firing squad."

She grins wider, dangerously, gleefully. "Don't worry. I have a plan for that. Leave everything to me."

"That's what worries me," I mutter. I open my mouth to argue further, but the bells over the bakery door jingle.

Scot walks in.

My entire body goes cold. Lily stiffens beside me, and the warm, safe atmosphere of the bakery evaporates.

He's wearing dark jeans and a black leather jacket. His blond hair is styled perfectly, and there's a smug expression on his face that makes me want to throw my coffee at him.

Actually, forget the coffee. I want to throw the espresso machine.

"Thought I'd find you here." He's looking at me like I'm dog shit he stepped in. "You always run to your little bakery when things get tough."

"What do you want, Scot?"

"Just came to deliver some news." He's leaning against the doorframe now, completely relaxed. Like he owns the place. "Packed up all your stuff from the apartment above the business. You're not living there anymore."

The words take a second to land. Then they hit me as though I ran into a mountain. "You did what?"

"Packed your shit. You can't live in my building anymore." His smile is cruel, satisfied. "The apartment is for Confetti and Meatballs employees only. You're not an employee. So you're not living there. Locks are already changed." He steps back from the door and glances outside on the sidewalk.

Lily is already moving toward the door, and I follow her out on legs that feel numb. Outside, in front of the bakery, are my belongings. Garbage bags. Cardboard boxes. My entire life, dumped on the street like trash.

I can't breathe.

"What the fuck, Scot?" My voice is shaking. "You went through my stuff? You had no right—"

"It's my building." Arms crossed, he looks so fucking pleased with himself. I want to murder him. "Don't worry. You didn't have much. Nothing interesting."

"You're a real piece of shit, you know that?" Lily's voice is ice. "A pathetic, vindictive piece of shit."

"I'm practical." Scot is backing toward his car—a sleek black BMW parked at the curb. "This is what happens when you make stupid choices, Hannah. Actions have consequences. Maybe next time, you'll think twice before embarrassing someone who tried to help you."

I'm shaking now, rage bubbling up. "You tried to force yourself on me! You got drunk and made a scene! You're the one who destroyed everything!"

His grin widens. "Enjoy being homeless and jobless."

He climbs into his BMW and drives off, and I'm left standing on the sidewalk, staring at my life scattered in the snow.

I feel violated. Exposed. Like Scot reached into my chest and ripped everything out. "That fucking asshole."

Lily's arms are around me, pulling me close. From anger or shock or both, I can't tell.

"Hey. It's okay. You can stay with us." Her voice is fierce. "We've got a spare room at the house. It's yours. For as long as you need. I mean, I would offer you the apartment upstairs here, but I've got tenants in there already."

"This is too much." My voice cracks.

She pulls back, hands on my shoulders, forcing me to look at her. "Fuck Scot. Fuck his uncle. Fuck everyone who doubted you. You're going to prove them all wrong."

Something shifts in my chest. The fear and humiliation start hardening into something sharper.

Rage.

Pure, focused, burning rage.

"You're right," I say quietly. "This is war now. And I'm going to find a way to destroy him."

"That's my sister." Lily is grinning. "Now let's get your stuff inside before it's completely ruined."

We start hauling boxes and bags, and I'm seething the entire time. Every soaked cardboard box, every ripped garbage bag, every item of clothing covered in slush, it all feeds the fury building inside me.

Scot thinks he's won.

He has no idea what's coming.

CHAPTER EIGHT

NOEL

I'm driving my truck with Hannah in my passenger seat and her father in the back, and I've never been more determined to make a good impression in my entire life.

Chris briefed me yesterday. Family dinner. Dysfunctional relatives who make Hannah feel like shit. She needs to show up with a hot boyfriend on her arm to shut everyone up.

Fuck yeah. I can do that.

I went all out tonight. Hair down, falling past my shoulders instead of being tied back like I usually wear it for work. Didn't shave this morning—figured the shadow would make me look more intimidating. People find beards scary, and I want to look just dangerous enough that her relatives think twice before asking invasive questions. Dark button-up shirt over a black tee, sleeves rolled to my elbows to show off the tattoos running down both forearms. Jeans that fit right. Boots.

And the beaded bracelets I picked up in Bali last year, because I like how they look against my skin.

At six-four, I'm going to stand out. That's the entire point.

Hannah keeps stealing glances at me. Quick looks when she thinks I'm not paying attention, her eyes traveling from my hands on the wheel to my arms to my face.

I love it. Love that she's watching. Love that she's trying to be subtle and failing completely.

Lily's plan was simple but brilliant. She rigged me up with an earpiece connected to her phone so she can feed me information all night. Tell me things about Hannah, their relationship, details that'll make me look like I've been dating her for months instead of pretending for one evening. She was insistent that this would work, talking a mile a minute about how she'd be my inside source and ensure I didn't get caught in any lies.

I grin, thinking about what a firecracker she is. Hannah's sister doesn't do anything halfway.

The earpiece crackles to life. "Testing, testing. Can you hear me?"

"Loud and clear," I murmur.

Hannah glances at me. "What?"

"Just confirming something with Lily."

"Oh God, I can't believe you let her rope you into that!"

"Insurance." I tap my ear. "She's feeding me intel all night so I don't accidentally contradict your life story."

Hannah groans. "This is going to be a disaster."

"It's going to be perfect," her father says from the back seat. "So, Noel." Her father leans forward slightly. "Hannah mentioned you're a bounty hunter. That's dangerous work."

"Yes, sir." I keep my voice calm, respectful. First impressions matter with fathers, and I learned that the hard way with my own. "That's why I work in a team of three. We've got each other's backs, do extensive research on every target before we move. One of our rules is to never go in blind. No surprises."

"Smart approach. Very smart." He settles back. "I was actually caught up in a bank robbery once. Scared the hell out of me."

Hannah twists in her seat, eyes wide. "Dad, what? You were in a bank robbery? You never told us this!"

"Oh my God, Dad was in a bank robbery?" Lily's voice comes through the earpiece, excited and loud. "Tell him I want to know everything when I see him next!"

I chuckle. "Lily wants the full story later."

"Of course she does." Hannah is smiling despite herself. "She's probably already planning to use it in one of her murder documentary theories."

Their dad laughs. "Didn't want to scare you girls. This was before you and Lily were born, back when I was working at the credit union downtown. Three guys came in with guns, whole hostage situation. But there was a bounty hunter who got caught up in it, and he took the main guy down. Just tackled him like he was made of steel. Big guy, about Noel's size. Very impressive."

"That's insane," I add.

"Well, the cousins are definitely going to lose their minds when they see you, Noel," Hannah mutters. "Mission accomplished."

Her father chuckles. "They need something to talk about besides your love life. Or lack thereof, according to them."

"Dad!"

"What? I'm just repeating what they say."

"Anyway," Lily continues in my ear, "we're arriving at the wedding, so I might be quiet during the ceremony. But I'll be back for the main event."

"Sounds good," I say quietly.

Hannah turns to her father. "So you know the deal, right? Noel is helping me out tonight. He's my boyfriend for the evening. Just for show."

I grin, catching her father's gaze in the rearview mirror, and wink. "Yep. Fake boyfriend. Playing the part. We all know the drill."

Hannah stares at me. "Noel."

Her father laughs. "Don't worry so much, sweetheart. Just be yourself. Both of you." He pauses. "So, where did you two actually meet? For real?"

"In a roundabout way, through a bounty hunt," I admit. "But it all worked out."

"It's a long story," Hannah adds quickly. "I'll tell you later."

Her father's smile turns soft as he watches Hannah.

"Your mother would've loved this. The chaos, the absurdity. She always said the best stories came from the strangest circumstances."

Hannah's expression shifts, the corner of her mouth lifting. "Yeah. She would've."

We're climbing higher into the mountains now, Whispering Grove fading behind us, replaced by dense forest and winding roads. The snow is heavier up here, coating everything in white.

I'm watching Hannah and her father banter, and I feel something twist in my chest. Something that's not quite envy but close to it. I never had this with my parents. Every conversation ended in arguments, slammed doors, them telling me I was throwing my life away with bad choices and worse friends. I brought cops home more times than I could count as a teenager, from fights, stupid shit I did because I was angry and didn't know how else to be.

When I left at eighteen, they were relieved. I saw it in their faces. And they've never reached out since. No calls. No messages. Nothing.

Chris and Kane became my family. The only family that matters.

But watching Hannah with her father, seeing this easy affection, I can't help wanting that. Wishing I'd had it.

"Your mom would be proud," her father says quietly. "That we keep the tradition alive. That we still show up even when it's hard."

Hannah reaches over to take his hand. "She always

said showing up was an act of love."

"She had more patience than all of us combined." He grins and clears his throat. "You two got my stubbornness, unfortunately."

The road curves, and suddenly houses start appearing through the trees. Big houses. The kind with circular driveways and landscaping that requires a full-time staff.

Then number thirteen comes into view. Martha's house sits at the end of a long driveway, and I actually slow down to process what I'm seeing.

The house itself is a Victorian mansion, three stories of white-painted wood with green shutters and a wraparound porch. But that's not what catches my attention.

It's the decorations.

Every single window glows with colored lights that make the house resemble a stained-glass cathedral. The gutters drip with icicle lights, thousands of them, bright enough that I'm surprised passing planes don't mistake it for a landing strip. The lawn is covered with inflatables, but these aren't normal snowmen. These are life-sized carolers with moving mouths and blinking eyes, arranged in perfect choir formation.

"Oh, geez." Hannah's voice is strangled. "She's upgraded since last year."

The neighboring houses are visible through the trees, equally large, equally expensive, but their decorations look almost restrained in comparison. Tasteful wreaths. Simple white lights.

"Did she hire a theme park crew?" I ask jokingly.

Hannah's father chuckles loudly from the back seat. "I think she became one."

"I'm counting eight—no, ten—new animatronic reindeer." Hannah sounds genuinely disturbed. "And is that a nativity scene made of holograms?"

I park behind a row of luxury cars. Mercedes, BMW, Porsche, all of them pristine.

Her father whistles low. "She put a projector on the roof."

It kicks on as if on cue, casting a twenty-foot glowing Santa waving across the yard. Music blares from the speakers with "Jingle Bell Rock" at a volume that could damage hearing.

"Is that a snow machine?" Hannah is still staring, transfixed by the show.

Her father sighs. "Welcome to the family, Noel."

We climb out of the truck, and I immediately move to Hannah's side. She's wearing a dark green dress that hugs every curve, hits just above her knees, paired with black tights and heeled boots. Her hair is down in waves, and she looks gorgeous and nervous and like she'd rather be anywhere else.

I take her hand, threading our fingers together.

She resists slightly, trying to pull away. "Noel—"

"Relax," I murmur. "We've got this."

Her father reaches the door first, knocking, and a woman in her mid-thirties answers. She's wearing a knitted dress covered in snowflakes, and her mouth literally drops open when she sees me.

"Hi, Patty." Hannah's father moves forward, carrying his baked casserole. "Good to see you again."

Patty doesn't respond. She's staring at me, eyes wide, taking in my size, my tattoos, the entire package.

I step forward, keeping Hannah's hand in mine, and lean down slightly. "Hey. I'm Noel. Hannah's boyfriend."

Patty makes a squeaking sound.

Hannah opens her mouth, probably to add something diplomatic, but I lean closer to her, press a soft kiss near her temple, and say loudly enough for Patty to hear, "Actually, I'm her scent match. Her Alpha."

Hannah looks up at me, whispering urgently, "Don't need to say that part."

I smirk down at her. "Oh, I do."

Patty stumbles backward, bumps into someone behind her, and suddenly the narrow entryway is packed with people. The hallway stretches back toward what looks like a dining room, hardwood floors gleaming, walls painted cream and decorated with family photos in expensive frames. There are maybe fifteen people crowded in here now, all turning to stare at us.

Perfect entrance.

I let go of Hannah's hand, slide my palm across her lower back, drawing her against my side. "Hey, every-one. I'm Noel, Hannah's main squeeze." I let my voice carry, making sure everyone hears. "She's my scent match."

"Oh my God!" Lily is practically screaming in my ear. "You'd better be memorizing their faces! I can tell from the silence that they're all shocked! Tell me they're shocked!"

I lift my hand, the one with the microphone glued to one of my wooden bracelets, and whisper toward it, "You'd love to see this."

"I knew it! I'm missing everything!"

Hannah's father is already pushing through the crowd, completely unbothered by the shock. "All right, everyone, let's get started. I brought a pasta bake." He holds up a casserole dish and heads toward the dining room.

Hannah tugs me forward, and immediately we're swarmed. People pressing closer, reaching out to touch my arms, my shoulders, like I'm some kind of exhibit.

"He's real," someone murmurs.

"Look at those tattoos!"

"Is his hair naturally that color?"

An older woman approaches, and Hannah immediately steps forward. "Great-Aunt Martha! So good to see you!"

So this is the infamous Martha. She's wearing a red dress that screams "I'm in charge here" with a pearl necklace. Her gray hair is styled in perfect waves.

"Hannah, darling!" She pulls Hannah into a hug that looks more possessive than affectionate, then turns her attention to me. "And who is this?"

"Let me introduce you to Noel," Hannah says. "My boyfriend."

Martha pulls me into the same aggressive hug-and-kiss routine, then reaches out to squeeze my bicep.

Hard. "Oh, Hannah, you finally snagged yourself a good one!" Her voice carries across the room. "How on earth did you manage this? Your cousins could use some tips."

"Actually, I chased her." I speak before Hannah can respond, keeping my tone easy but firm. "Hannah is the real catch here. And it's not just me. My two friends are claiming her also."

Silence. Complete, total silence.

Hannah is glaring at me.

"Oh, this is beautiful," Lily whispers in my ear. "I can feel their shock from here."

"We're a pack," I clarify, which somehow makes their stares worse.

Mouths are literally hanging open. Then everyone starts talking at once, and we're being herded toward an oversized dining table.

Dark wood polished to a shine, set with china. Crystal glasses at every place setting. Cloth napkins folded into elaborate shapes. The walls are painted a deep burgundy, and there's a chandelier overhead that's dripping with crystals.

Hannah and I end up squeezed together in the middle of one side of the table, her father directly across from us, and suddenly everyone is fighting for the seats nearby. Women, mostly.

Hannah leans close, voice low. "You're doing amazing, but let's keep things simple. We're not staying long."

"Whatever you want, sweetheart."

Her father is already deep in conversation with an

older man, reminiscing about something, while younger family members start bringing food to the table.

There's a huge turkey, golden and perfect. Ham glazed with something that smells incredible. Mashed potatoes. Green bean casserole. Cranberry sauce. Rolls. Sweet potato casserole with marshmallows. Three different types of pie visible on a side table. And yes, what has to be Martha's infamous meatloaf, based on the conversation in the car—gray and gelatinous and somehow still steaming despite looking like it died weeks ago.

At least twenty people squeeze around the table, and I'm hyperaware of how close Hannah is, our arms bumping every time one of us moves.

I fucking love it. Love being this close to her, feeling the heat of her body, catching hints of her scent even with all the food smells competing for attention.

Martha stands at the head of the table, tapping her wineglass with a fork until everyone quiets down.

"Welcome, everyone! I'm so thrilled we could all gather for another Christmas together. It's wonderful to see Hannah and her father join us as well." Her smile tightens slightly. "Though we're disappointed Lily couldn't make it this year."

"She's got better places to be," Lily mutters in my ear, and I fight to keep my expression neutral.

"Let's take a moment to remember those who can't be with us." Martha's voice softens. "Especially Hannah and Lily's mother, Olivia, who loved these gatherings so much."

Hannah has gone tense beside me, and I slide my hand under the table, rest it on her thigh. She doesn't pull away. If anything, she leans slightly into the touch.

"Now!" Martha's voice brightens artificially. "Let's eat and celebrate this blessed Christmas season!"

"Oh, good, the torture begins," Lily says. "Try not to eat the meatloaf. Seriously. Three years ago, someone needed their stomach pumped."

People start serving themselves, passing dishes in both directions, and I notice how everyone keeps glancing our way. Some of the women are staring at me with expressions I recognize—interest, speculation, the kind of look that says they're wondering what Hannah has that they don't.

Then a woman in her forties leans forward from three seats down, blonde hair in perfect waves, makeup flawless. "So, you two must tell us how you met! I'm dying to know."

"That's Sasha," Lily says immediately. "Total bitch. She once—"

But I'm already answering. "We met through Hannah's sister, Lily. I helped with an event she was planning, and we hit it off."

"What kind of event?" Sasha presses, leaning forward even more. She's wearing a low-cut blouse, and the move is deliberate.

Hannah jumps in smoothly. "A petting zoo. Holiday-themed. Noel brought actual reindeer, which was incredible and saved the entire event."

"You own reindeer?" asks a woman in her late twenties who is practically bouncing in her seat. "That's so unique! Where does someone even find a man like you?" She laughs, but there's an edge to it. "I mean, if Hannah could catch you, there must be hope for the rest of us single Omegas, right?"

"That's Rachel," Lily supplies. "*Desperate* doesn't even begin to cover it."

Hannah stiffens beside me, and I can feel her bristling at the implication.

"Hannah didn't catch me," I say, keeping my tone light but letting some steel show through. "I pursued her. Relentlessly. She's brilliant, creative, capable of running circles around most people I know. I'm the lucky one, because she gave me a chance."

Rachel deflates visibly.

"And what do you do for work, Noel? You look very… physical," Sasha asks, the whole table watching.

"I'm a bounty hunter."

That gets attention. Multiple people lean forward, suddenly interested.

"That sounds deadly!" Martha says from the head of the table.

"It can be." I take a bite of turkey, which is actually good. "But it's satisfying work. Bringing people to justice who thought they could escape consequences."

"Have you ever been shot?" a man in his fifties asks, genuinely curious.

"Twice. Vest caught both rounds."

"Terrifying," Hannah murmurs, and her hand finds my thigh under the table.

"What's the scariest situation you've been in?" Sasha again, persistent.

I think for a moment. "Probably the time we tracked someone to an abandoned warehouse. Intel said he was alone. He wasn't. Had three friends with him, all armed. Turned into a standoff that lasted four hours before backup arrived."

"How did you stay calm?" another woman asks.

"Training. And trusting my partners. Kane and Chris had my back the entire time."

"Those Hannah's other lovers?" an older woman asks. "The ones you mentioned earlier?"

Hannah clears her throat.

"Yes, ma'am. We've been working together for years. They're family."

Hannah squeezes my hand under the table, and I squeeze back.

"So how long have you and Hannah been together?" Sasha isn't giving up, eyes sharp enough to cut glass.

I glance at Hannah, letting her take the lead. "A few months," she says smoothly. "But it feels longer. Like we've known each other forever."

"That's the scent-match bond," I add. "When you meet your mate, time doesn't really matter. You just know."

"How romantic," Martha says in the exact tone someone would use to describe mold.

Before I can respond, Lily's voice fills my ear. "Translation: She thinks you're lying. She always thinks people are lying. It's her spiritual gift."

I hide a smirk with my glass.

"Where did you grow up, Noel?" Rachel tries again.

"Here in the mountains."

"What do you do for fun?" another aunt asks.

Before I can think, Lily chirps in my ear, "Say, 'Hiking. And chopping wood shirtless.' They'll eat that up."

I blink. "I… hike. And work outdoors a lot."

Lily adds, "Trust me, they think chopping wood is a form of character development."

"What did Hannah tell you about our family before tonight?" Martha asks, folding her hands like she's about to conduct an interrogation.

Lily is already cackling in my ear. "Oh, I've got this. Say, 'She told me you're all very… enthusiastic hosts. And very opinionated. Especially about other people's lives.'"

I repeat it carefully. "She told me you're enthusiastic hosts. And… very opinionated."

Hannah's eyes go wide. Her father coughs into his hand to hide a laugh.

"Opinionated," Rachel huffs. "We're involved."

"Same thing," Lily mutters.

"And what kind of pack are you part of, Noel?" someone else asks. "What values do you have?"

Lily jumps in instantly. "Say, 'Loyalty, honesty, and minding our own damn business.' But soften that last part. Maybe."

"I value loyalty," I say aloud. "Honesty. And giving people space to live their own lives without judgment."

Hannah's father is definitely laughing now. He tries to disguise it with a sip of wine. Fails.

An older aunt leans forward, eyes narrowing like she smells blood in the water. "And children? Do you want children, Noel?"

"Eventually," I say honestly. "When the time is right."

"And you, Hannah?" she continues mercilessly. "You're not getting any younger, dear."

Hannah goes rigid beside me. "I'm twenty-six."

"Exactly. Your mother had you at twenty-two."

Before Hannah detonates, I step in. "Hannah is building a career right now. She's talented. Driven. And I'm not rushing her into anything."

The aunt's lips thin. "Biology waits for no one."

Lily mutters in my ear, "Say, 'Then biology can book an appointment and wait outside.'"

I don't go that far, but close. "Hannah's not here to follow deadlines designed by other people."

Silence. Tight. Sharp.

Then Hannah's father clears his throat. "Hannah and Lily are both very free-spirited, just like their mother."

But he's smiling. And under the table, Hannah's fingers brush mine—the smallest thank-you.

Silence drops over our section of the table.

"How about we focus on the food? This turkey is excellent, Martha," Hannah's father says.

The conversation shifts, thank God, fragmenting into smaller groups.

"That was perfect," Lily whispers in my ear. "You just made half of those women fall in love with you, and the other half hate Hannah even more. Mission accomplished."

I'm fielding questions from a couple of the men now about bounty-hunting techniques while Martha is interrogating Hannah's father about the bakery. I keep my hand on Hannah's thigh the entire time, a constant reassuring pressure that reminds her I'm here.

After what feels like an hour but is probably only thirty minutes, Hannah pushes back her chair. "Excuse me. I need to use the restroom."

I'm on my feet immediately. "I'll come with you."

"To the bathroom?" Sasha raises an eyebrow.

"To make sure she doesn't get cornered," I say bluntly.

Hannah leads me through the house, past family photos that chronicle decades of gatherings, past a living room that's decorated within an inch of its life, down a hallway that's quieter, darker.

She pushes open a door to what looks like an old study with dark wood paneling, floor-to-ceiling bookshelves, and leather furniture that's probably older than I am.

I follow her inside, shut the door behind us. "So this is the hiding room," I observe.

She moves toward the bookshelves, running her fingers along the spines without really seeing them. "God, I hate this. The questions, the judgment, the constant pressure."

"Your family is intense," I murmur.

In my ear, Lily snorts. "Intense? Try emotionally weaponized."

Hannah huffs out a soft laugh. "That's a polite word for it." She rubs her temples. "Thanks for defending me about the children thing. I was two seconds away from stabbing a dinner roll."

"I meant it," I say. "You get to decide your timeline. Not Aunt—"

Lily cuts in. "Aunt Reproductive Regret."

I choke on a laugh, covering it with a cough.

Hannah narrows her eyes. "What was that?"

"Nothing," I say too quickly. "Just… swallowed wrong."

Her eyes stay suspicious.

We step farther into the study, the sanctuary of the moment. "My mom had me young," she says quietly. "I think they expect me to follow the tradition. But I'm not ready. I don't even know if I want kids. Is that terrible?"

"It's honest," I tell her. "Nothing wrong with knowing yourself."

Lily pipes up: "Tell her she's the most put-together person in that house, which, low bar, but still."

I shake my head slightly. "Your sister thinks you're amazing and perfect just as you are."

Hannah's brows lift. "Did she say that?"

Lily: "No, I didn't, but sure, go with it."

I smile. "She implied it."

Hannah snorts, but her shoulders relax.

"This is where Lily and I always hide," she says,

moving toward the bookshelves. "To breathe. And avoid awkward questions. And avoid everything."

I take a breath, steadying myself. "You look gorgeous, by the way."

She blushes instantly. "And you," she says, eyes flicking over my hair, "look like a dangerous lumberjack someone recruited for a runway show."

Lily: "Okay, accurate."

"That's a new one," I say. "But I'll take it."

"OH MY GOD! SOMEONE JUST FELL INTO THE WEDDING ARCH. I REPEAT—WE HAVE A MAN DOWN!" Lily's voice explodes in my ear.

"I think we're good now, Lily," I say. "Enjoy the wedding. And I'm out."

"Have fun," she says.

I sigh, reach up, and pluck the earpiece out, then drop it into my pocket and look at Hannah.

Her smile is slow.

We stand in the warm quiet of the study, muffled laughter drifting through the walls.

"So," I say, voice softer. "Have you... thought about the scent-match thing? About us?"

"Constantly," she admits.

"And?"

"And I'm terrified." Her hands twist. "What if it goes badly? What if you all realize I'm not worth the trouble and leave? I can't take more rejection, Noel. I'm... hanging on by a thread."

My chest cracks open. "I think," I say gently, stepping closer, "you don't give yourself nearly enough credit."

Her breath catches.

"And we're not going anywhere," I add. "Not now. Not later. Not ever. Let us be the ones who hold you up when you're tired."

She looks at me like she's seconds from either crying or kissing me. Maybe both. Her breathing picks up, and fuck, I smell her scent growing stronger, wrapping around me, tightening everything low in my gut until I can hardly think straight.

I close the distance between us in two steps, and suddenly Hannah is backed against the bookshelf, eyes wide, pulse visible in her throat.

"I can barely hold back right now," I murmur, and my cock is already responding, hardening in my jeans. "Your scent is driving me fucking insane. It's got a grip on my balls and won't let go."

"Sounds like a *you* problem." Her voice is breathless, but there's challenge in it.

"It's about to be an *us* problem."

She slips past me and darts toward the door, but I'm faster. I meet her there, and my hand hits the wood above her head, blocking her escape, and she spins to face me.

We're close now. "So you feel nothing?" I lean down, inhaling deeply. "Because your scent is screaming at me, gorgeous. Telling me exactly how much you want this."

"I don't—"

"You have no idea how hungry I am for you. How

much I want to make you mine, show you everything you've been missing. But if you need me to stop, I will. Just tell me."

She's blushing, but she tilts her head back, meets my eyes directly. "Maybe I'm not missing anything. Maybe you're just desperate because you can't control what's in your pants."

Then she lowers her hand between us, wraps her fingers around my cock through my jeans.

Her eyes grow huge, shocked and pleased. She clearly wasn't expecting that size. She pulls her hand away quickly, but the damage is done. My control is about to collapse.

"You shouldn't have done that," I whisper.

Wildness roars through me, every instinct screaming to claim, to take, to mark. I know I should back up, give her space, be the patient Alpha I promised to be. But I'm so far gone that I'm leaning in, capturing her mouth with mine.

She doesn't resist. She kisses me back like a fucking lioness, fierce and demanding and absolutely fearless. Her mouth opens under mine, and she's pulling me closer by my shirt. I groan against her lips.

This is everything. This is what I've been craving since I first scented her.

I deepen the kiss, one hand sliding into her hair, the other gripping her hip, and she moans, a sound that goes straight to my cock. My tongue sweeps against hers.

Her body is on fire against mine, every curve

pressed to my chest, and she's trembling. But it's arousal, raw and undeniable, her scent spiking until I'm drowning in it.

I break the kiss, trail my mouth down her neck, and she gasps.

"I need to taste you," I growl against her skin, letting my teeth graze slightly. "Need to get on my knees and lick your sweet pussy until you're screaming my name and begging me not to stop."

She shudders, and I can scent how wet she is, how much she wants this despite her stiffness. But then she's pushing at my chest, and I let her move me, confused.

Until she spins us, puts my back to the door, and slowly sinks to her knees.

Holy fuck.

"I love this side of you," I breathe, watching her hands go to my belt.

She's glancing up at me, eyes dark with desire, and starts working the buckle. Gets it open. Pops the button on my jeans. Lowers the zipper with agonizing slowness.

"Hannah—"

"Quiet," she murmurs and pulls me free.

Her eyes are full as she stares down at me. I'm big—I know I'm big—and watching her study me, watching her lick her lips, is the hottest thing I've ever experienced.

"Like what you see?" I manage with a grin.

She doesn't answer with words. She leans forward, runs her tongue along my length, and I nearly black out.

Then she slips her lips over the tip of my cock, drawing me into her mouth, and I have to brace my hands against the door to stay upright.

Wet heat. Tight suction. Her tongue is working magic. Every nerve ending in my body is screaming.

"Fuck," I hiss. "Hannah, you feel so fucking incredible."

She takes me deeper, and I'm fighting every instinct to thrust, to take control, to fuck that beautiful mouth. But this is her show, and I'm going to let her run it.

She's working me with her tongue, taking me deeper, her hand cupping my balls, and I'm right on the edge, barely holding on. Watching her mouth wide and full of me is insatiable. She keeps sucking, licking under my shaft until the tip hits the back of her throat. I moan, my hips grinding against her. She stares up at me with tears in her eyes but never stops, and I fucking love her already.

Then someone knocks on the door.

We both freeze.

Her mouth is bulging full of me, her eyes huge and startled, and I'm using every ounce of willpower not to move.

"Busy," I call out, voice strained. "Come back later." I reach back blindly, manage to find the lock, and twist it.

She grins around me, actually fucking grins, and keeps going.

The knock comes again. "I need to get something from there!" Patty's voice, loud and insistent. "What are you doing? Why is the door locked?"

Hannah is using the distraction to tease me, her tongue tickling my cock, and my vision blurs, my legs shake.

"We're organizing," I gasp. "The books. Very important alphabetizing happening right now."

"What?" Patty sounds confused and suspicious.

Hannah fondles my balls, sucks harder, and I groan. Fuck me.

"Open up!"

Of all the times.

"Critical organizational work!" I call out, voice cracking as Hannah takes me deeper. "Very delicate! Can't be interrupted! Come back in thirty minutes!"

Hannah's pace picks up.

Another set of knocks, sharper, angrier. "No one organizes anything that loudly!"

I slap a hand over my mouth because I'm one second away from groaning loudly enough to be heard across the valley.

Hannah makes a low, obscene sound around me on purpose.

I grit my teeth. "For the love of—Hannah—sweetheart—mercy—" I'm gone. Absolutely done for. I come and burst in her mouth with a force that damn near folds me in half, my hand flying back to brace on the door, knees shaking.

She swallows all of it, every last drop, like the perfect Omega she is, throat working to take it. I'm panting, sweating, trying to remember basic physics.

Knock, knock, knock. "THIS IS HIGHLY SUSPICIOUS!"

Hannah finally pulls back, licks me clean, and then has the audacity to grin up at me like she didn't just almost send me into cardiac arrest.

I stare at her, weak. "Were you trying to kill me?"

"Maybe." She licks her lips primly.

Knock. "I can *hear* whispering! What's happening in there?!"

"We'll let you know when we're finished organizing, Patty!" Hannah says.

"That's not how organizing works!"

Hannah takes my hand, letting me pull her up.

"Now you're just being ridiculous!" Patty barks, footsteps stomping away.

I tuck myself back in very carefully while Hannah watches like she's waiting for an encore.

"Think she knew what we were doing?" she asks.

I blink at her. "I was screaming about delicate organizational work while you had my cock in your mouth. Patty thinks we're alphabetizing porn magazines at best."

She snorts so hard she nearly doubles over. "We should get back before they try to break down the door," she says, turning for the door.

"Or..." I catch her wrist, pull her flush against me, my mouth brushing her ear. "I could return the favor right now. Get on my knees. Taste you. Make you come so hard you forget your own name."

Her breath stutters, which is music to my ears.

"It's tempting," she whispers, heat blooming under her skin. "But we really do need to go."

"Fine." I let her turn… then reel her back in again, my voice dropping, dark and possessive. "Just know something, Hannah."

She swallows.

"You can run all you want. But you're my scent match. Which makes you mine. And I always claim what's mine." My lips brush her throat. "It's only a matter of time before you stop fighting it… and let me take you apart."

She shivers, her entire body lighting up, her arousal spiking, sweet and sharp. "We'll see," she breathes, trying—and failing—to sound steady.

I press a slow kiss to her pulse. "No running, Hannah. Not from me."

She doesn't pull away.

And I know, with blinding certainty, this Omega is about to wreck my entire world, in the best possible way.

CHAPTER NINE

HANNAH

We just dropped Dad off at his house, and now Noel's truck is idling in the dark street, engine running but neither of us moving.

The silence stretches between us. I can hear the heater blowing, the occasional pop of the engine settling. My hands are twisted in my lap, and I'm staring at them like they hold all the answers.

"So," Noel finally says, turning slightly in the driver's seat to face me. "Do I take you all the way back to Lily's place? That's over an hour from here. Or you could crash at mine tonight."

My immediate reaction is to say no. To politely decline, make up some excuse about not wanting to impose, maintain the boundaries I've been desperately trying to keep between us.

But I'm exhausted. The party drained every ounce of energy I had, and the thought of that long drive, followed by trying to sleep in Lily's spare room and not making too much noise to wake up her little ones, sounds overwhelming.

"I couldn't—"

"Look." Noel cuts me off, and his voice is gentle, but there's steel underneath. "Lily already told me what happened with Scot. About him packing up your stuff, changing the locks, kicking you out of your own apartment."

His admission freezes me in my seat. Of course she told him. My face burns up and I turn away, staring out the passenger window at absolutely nothing, just needing to not look at him right now.

He knows. They all know that I got kicked out, that I'm so pathetic I couldn't even keep a job.

The shame is suffocating.

"I don't need your pity," I manage, and my voice comes out sharper than I intended.

"Good." Noel's response is immediate. "Because I'm not giving you any."

That has me turning toward him.

He's watching me and he's right; his expression isn't pitying. It's... understanding. Maybe even angry on my behalf.

"But you don't have to be so stubborn," he continues. "Or hide when you need help. That's not weakness, Hannah. That's just being human."

My throat tightens. I want to argue, to insist that I'm fine, that I don't need anyone. But I'm so tired of lying.

"What's going on?" he asks quietly. "Talk to me."

I take a breath. Hold it until my lungs burn. Let it out slowly.

"This is really hard for me," I finally say, and my voice cracks on the words. "I've always been the strong one. Always. When Mom died, I was fourteen, and suddenly I had to be the adult for Lily. I took care of her while Dad worked doubles at the diner—made sure we ate and helped her with her homework and didn't fall apart. I held the bakery together when we had no idea what we were doing. I kept everything running so Dad didn't have to worry, so he could just focus on keeping us fed and housed."

Noel doesn't interrupt. Just listens, his hand resting on the console between us.

"And I was good at it," I continue. "Being strong and the one who had all the answers. Making sure everyone else was okay." My hands are trembling. "But now it's all falling apart, and I don't know how to not be that person. I don't know how to ask for help or to admit I'm falling apart."

"You just did," Noel says softly.

I glance at him, and there's something in his expression that leaves me smiling.

He reaches over, places his hand on my thigh. His palm is warm, grounding, real. He squeezes gently. "You're allowed to need people, Hannah. That doesn't make you weak. It makes you brave for admitting it."

"Doesn't feel brave."

"The bravest thing you can do is let someone help carry the weight." His thumb strokes small circles against my leg, and the simple touch is almost too much. "You've been holding up everyone around you for years. Let someone hold you up for a change."

No words come.

"Besides," Noel continues, "it makes more sense for you to stay somewhere in Whispering Grove rather than out of town if you're building your business. Lily lives over an hour outside of town, in the mountains. You'd be driving constantly, wasting time and gas and energy. Staying with us, you're ten minutes from downtown. From clients. From everything you need to succeed."

I stare at him, and my brain is already running through the logistics despite my emotional resistance. He's right. It's completely, frustratingly logical.

Lily's house is beautiful but isolated. Every client meeting, every site visit, every supplier consultation would require driving over two hours round trip. I'd be exhausted before I even started working.

"Is that really a good idea?" I ask slowly. "An unmated Omega living with three Alphas under one roof?"

The question hangs in the air between us.

"We're all well behaved." His grin flashes in the darkness, but there's sincerity underneath. "Can't speak for Corn Dog, but the rest of us have self-control. We've got a nest room, fully stocked, completely private. We'll never enter without your explicit invitation. You'd have your own space, your own sanctuary."

A nest room? Very modern of them. Very progressive. Which makes me wonder—are they planning to find an Omega for their pack? Is that why they built it? Have they been searching, and I'm just convenient timing?

My stomach twists uncomfortably.

"What have you got to lose?" Noel asks.

Everything, my brain whispers. My control. My independence. My carefully constructed walls that keep me safe from being hurt.

But out loud I say, "I'll think about it."

"Fair enough." He nods, accepting. "But tonight, stay over. Save yourself the drive. Plus, I just bought this incredible imported ice cream, Italian, aged in bourbon barrels, costs more than it should, and I'm breaking into it tonight. You can help me demolish it."

Despite everything, the emotional exhaustion and fear and confusion, I smile. "Tempting me with ice cream?"

"Solid strategy, right?"

I look at this huge Alpha who spent the evening defending me to my terrible relatives, who stayed close when I was drowning, who sees me struggling and doesn't run away.

"Thank you," I say quietly. "For tonight. For everything. I'll think about moving in. I promise." I twist my hands together. "But I want to visit Scot's uncle in the morning. Super early so I can catch him. I don't have my car here, and I need to see him before he's fully poisoned against me. Last chance to convince him to sell me the business instead of his nephew."

"I'll drive you," Noel answers. "And I'll come with you. Feel better about you having backup in case Scot shows up. Chris told us what a jackass he is."

Warmth spreads through my chest, unfurling like sunlight. "That might be nice, actually."

"Perfect." He starts the truck, and the engine rumbles to life. "Ice cream awaits. And trust me, it's worth staying for."

We pull away from the curb, and I'm watching him as he drives. The streetlights play across his face, highlighting his cheekbones, the strong line of his jaw, the way his hair falls past his shoulders.

He's so different from anyone I've ever known. Dangerous and gentle all at once.

"So," I say, needing to fill the silence. "Have you always wanted to be a bounty hunter?"

His jaw tightens slightly, just a small tell. "No. Actually almost quit early on."

"What happened?"

He's quiet for a moment, and I watch him gather his thoughts. "One of my first jobs. I was twenty-one, stupid, thought I could handle anything alone. Went after a target who seemed low-risk, small-time fraud, nothing violent in his history. Should've been easy."

"But it wasn't."

His hands grip the wheel tighter, knuckles going white. "I found him at a gas station outside Denver. Thought I'd just walk up, explain the situation, bring him in peacefully. But he panicked. Pulled a gun I didn't know he had. Started shooting."

My stomach drops. "Oh, shit."

"There was a clerk working the night shift. Woman, maybe forty-five. She was restocking cigarettes behind the counter." His voice goes flat, emotionless in a way that means he's likely feeling too much. "He shot her. Three times. She died before the ambulance arrived, and I blamed myself for years. Thought if I'd waited for backup, if I'd approached differently, if I'd been better at my job, she'd still be alive."

Without thinking, I reach over and place my hand on his thigh. The muscle flexes under my touch, solid and warm and real. "That's not your fault," I say firmly. "You didn't pull the trigger. You didn't make him bring a gun. You didn't force him to shoot."

"Took me a long time to believe that." He glances at me, and there's old pain in his eyes, scars that haven't fully healed. "Kane finally talked me down. We'd already started working together, and he spent weeks drilling it into my head that I can't control what other people do. I can only control my own actions, my own choices. I can't take responsibility for someone else's decision to kill."

"It sounds like Kane saved you."

"He did. He and Chris both." The tension in his shoulders eases slightly as he talks. "They convinced me not to walk away. Told me I could either quit and let the guilt win, or I could channel it into something better. Use it as motivation to save as many people as possible. Honor her death by preventing others."

"It's good you stayed," I say.

"Yeah. We changed everything about how we work, always go in teams now, never take unnecessary risks, plan every detail before moving. And in the last few years, we've brought back over two hundred targets. Helped put away some really dangerous people. Made the world safer, even if it's just a little bit."

"That's incredible." I squeeze his thigh gently, wanting him to feel supported the way he's been supporting me. "You should be proud of what you've built."

"I am. Mostly." He covers my hand with his, threading our fingers together, and the simple gesture has my heart stuttering. "But I still think about her sometimes. Wonder what her life would've been like. If she had kids, grandkids, dreams she never got to live."

"That's what makes you good at what you do," I say. "You care. You remember. You don't treat people like statistics."

We're quiet for a moment, just the sound of the truck and the heater running, our hands linked on his leg.

"So when did ice cream become your rebellion?" I ask, trying to lighten the mood.

He laughs. "I was never allowed to have it as a kid. My parents were strict. So the first time I had my own money, my own place, I went to the store and bought six different flavors. Ate myself sick. Best decision I ever made."

"Very rebellious."

"I'm full of surprises."

"Clearly. Frozen dairy as an act of defiance."

"You mock now, but wait until you try this stuff. It's going to change your life."

I find myself staring at those powerful forearms covered in tattoos, dark ink swirling across muscle and tendon. The way his hands grip the wheel. There's something about men's forearms that makes my brain short-circuit. The visible strength, the way they flex with every small movement.

"What are you thinking about?" he asks, catching me staring.

"Your arms," I admit.

"Yeah?"

"They're very distracting."

His grin goes wicked. "Should I cover them? Don't want to be a hazard."

"Too late. Already distracted."

"I'll take that as a compliment."

"You should." I'm blushing now, but I don't look away. "Very effective arms."

"Effective for what?"

"Things."

"Very specific," he teases. "Care to elaborate?"

"Nope. Remaining mysterious."

"You're being adorable."

"That's the goal."

We're approaching the mansion now, and he pulls out his phone, taps something into it. The massive metal gates swing open smoothly, and we drive through onto the long driveway.

"Very high-tech," I observe.

"Necessary when you make enemies for a living." He pockets his phone as we navigate the curve through trees. The house comes into view through the trees, stone and timber lit from within, warm and inviting instead of intimidating.

My brain should be screaming warnings. Should be second-guessing this entire decision.

But all I can think about is the kiss earlier. The way having him in my mouth felt almost calming, like my body recognized something it needed. I feel drawn to him in ways that terrify me because I don't know how to trust this pull.

But maybe I can be professional. Keep boundaries. Enjoy ice cream and conversation and nothing more. Sure. That's definitely going to work.

We park in front of the house, and I follow him inside. I kick off my heels at the door, and the relief is immediate. My feet are screaming gratitude.

"It's almost ten," Noel says, glancing around the quiet house. "Chris and Kane are probably in their rooms if they're back from the night's job."

The house is peaceful, most lights off except in the kitchen. The stone fireplace in the great room is blazing, flames dancing and crackling, casting moving shadows across the leather furniture. Makes me wonder if the other two guys are home since their fireplace is on.

Though, I would kill to have a home like this.

It's everything I've ever wanted, cozy and warm and

safe. Sometimes when I can't sleep, I play YouTube videos of those fantasy cabins with fireplaces roaring while rain pounds outside on the window. This could be one of those places. The kind of home I've been dreaming about my entire life.

I set my wallet and Lily's spare house key on a side table and sink into the enormous couch facing the fire. My feet don't touch the floor, so I curl my legs beneath me.

The heat from the fire washes over me, and I close my eyes for just a second, letting the tension drain from my shoulders.

"Don't fall asleep yet," Noel says. "Ice cream first. Then sleep."

I open my eyes to find him returning from the kitchen, and my breath catches. He's shed his button-up shirt, now wearing just jeans and a tight black tee that shows off every line of muscle, every defined plane. His boots are gone, feet bare on the hardwood, and there's something intimate about seeing him comfortable, relaxed, at home.

And he's holding a black container of ice cream with two spoons sticking out like flags.

The firelight dances across his face, all shadows and angles, and for a few seconds, I let myself imagine this being real. Coming home to the three of them every night. Building a life here. Saying yes to being their Omega and trusting that they wouldn't break my heart.

My pulse thunders so hard I can feel it everywhere—throat, wrists, between my legs.

He sits next to me, close enough that our legs touch, and leans in with a grin that's pure sin. "Choose your weapon."

I select a spoon.

The ice cream is beautiful—swirls of cream, flecks of what might be real vanilla bean, threads of caramel running through everything.

I take a bite. Oh my God. Rich. Creamy. The bourbon adds depth without overwhelming, and the caramel is perfectly balanced between sweet and salty, with little pockets of crunchy hazelnut adding texture. "This is incredible," I moan and immediately take another scoop.

"Right?" He's grinning, watching me with obvious satisfaction. "We're going to eat the whole thing tonight."

"I'm not even sorry."

"Good. Because I have two more in the freezer."

I laugh. "Two more? Why do you need three containers?"

"When you find something good, you stock up. Avoid future regret." He takes another mouthful, and a little bit of caramel sticks to his lower lip.

Without thinking, I lean forward and swipe it with my thumb.

He catches my wrist before I can pull back, brings my thumb to his mouth, and sucks the caramel off slowly.

Heat floods through me, my heart racing.

"That's cheating," I whisper.

"All's fair in ice cream and war."

We're both reaching for the container at the same time, spoons colliding, and I try to get the better angle, but he blocks me. We're play-fighting like children, laughing and jostling, and somehow I end up half in his lap, our faces close enough that I can feel his breath.

He runs his nose along mine, a gentle motion that's sweet and ridiculous, and I'm smiling madly despite the heat building between us. I try to return the gesture, but he's faster, and suddenly he's leaning in, capturing my mouth with his.

I taste ice cream and bourbon and the salt-sweet of caramel, and I moan against his lips without meaning to.

"You taste amazing with ice cream," he murmurs when we break apart.

"You're not playing fair."

"Never said I would."

I reach for more ice cream, determined to regain some control, but he's already scooping up a dollop and putting it directly on his lips, grinning at me with a challenge in his eyes.

Then he's kissing me again, and I'm laughing against his mouth, trying to push him back, but he's got me pinned now. Half on top of me on the couch, one hand braced against the cushions, the other cupping my face.

The kiss deepens. His tongue sweeps against mine, tasting of promises I shouldn't believe but want to. Something cold hits my chest. I gasp, pulling back, and there's melted ice cream sliding down into my cleavage, leaving a sticky trail.

"Oh, no," I start to say.

"I got it," Noel says, and his voice dips. He sets the tub on the side table, and then his mouth is on my chest, licking up the trail of melted ice cream, moving lower and lower toward the edge of my dress. His tongue is hot against the top of my breasts, and I'm so turned on I can barely breathe.

My panties are soaking wet. My body is on fire. Every nerve ending is screaming for more, and I know exactly where this is heading.

Which is why I panic. I wriggle out from under him, breathing hard, my hands shaking as I push against his shoulders.

He lets me go immediately, sitting back, giving me space.

He's sprawled on the couch now, still clutching his spoon. He licks his lips slowly, deliberately.

"You should probably show me my room," I blurt out, grabbing my wallet and keys from the side table. "I'm exhausted. Long day. Need sleep."

He blinks, and I watch him process the abrupt shift. "Oh. Already?"

"Yeah. Sorry. Thanks for the ice cream. It was amazing."

He doesn't push. Just nods, sets the container on the coffee table, and stands. "Sure. Come on."

I follow him upstairs. The second floor is quiet.

Noel leads me to a room at the end of the hall and

opens the door. Moonlight streams through large windows, bathing everything in silvery blue light. The bed is enormous, easily big enough for five people, with gauzy netting draped overhead, mounds of pillows and cushions in every shade of blue and gray and cream.

It's a sanctuary. A nest.

"This is your room," Noel says quietly from the doorway. "No one enters without your explicit consent. Ever. It's yours if you want it."

I step inside, and the urge to dive into that bed is almost overwhelming. Noel stands in the doorway, hands gripping the frame so tightly his knuckles are white. His chest is pressed forward slightly, and he looks like a wolf watching prey—patient but hungry.

I can still taste him. Ice cream and bourbon and skin. It takes everything I have not to drag him inside and lose myself completely in whatever this is between us.

"Good night, then," I manage, my voice barely steady.

He stares at me for a long moment, and I watch the war play out in his expression, want versus respect, desire versus restraint.

"I'm just down the hall." He points left. "If you need anything at all, and I mean anything, you come find me. Understand?"

I nod, not trusting my voice.

"Good night, Hannah." He pulls back into the hallway.

"Good night, Noel. Thank you for everything

tonight." I push the door shut before I do something reckless. The latch clicks, and suddenly I'm alone.

The room spins with how hot I feel. My skin is too tight. My nipples are hard and sensitive, pressing against my bra. My entire body feels like it's vibrating at a frequency only I can hear. So, I jump onto the bed, sinking into ridiculous softness. Pillows and cushions cradle me from every side, and under different circumstances, this would be heaven.

But I can't stop thinking about Noel. About his kiss. His hands. His mouth on my chest. His cock, God, his cock, so big and thick and perfect in my mouth earlier. How much better it would feel between my thighs, filling me, stretching me, sating this impossible ache building in my core.

My pulse is racing everywhere, but especially between my legs.

The heat consuming me intensifies with every passing second. I lift my dress, shimmy out of my stockings and panties, and kick them off the side of the bed onto the floor.

The cool air helps. For about thirty seconds. Then the ache returns, worse than before. I reach down between my thighs and find myself absolutely soaking. A single touch and I'm moaning in the quiet room. I have to bite my lip to keep from making more noise.

This is more than arousal. This is deeper, an ache in my core that I recognize from pre-heat. That desperate, clawing need that's almost impossible to satisfy without heat suppressants or an Alpha's touch.

Was I too quick to send Noel away? He was clearly ready. More than ready. I could've invited him in, let him take care of this, let him—

No. This isn't my heat. My cycle isn't due for weeks. This is just me being horny because I kissed an attractive Alpha and my body is overreacting. Except it feels like I'm drowning.

I strip off my dress and bra, then turn on the ceiling fan. Cool air washes over my burning skin, teasing my sensitive nipples, and I gasp at the sensation. It helps for maybe a minute before the ache intensifies again, burning hotter.

I try lying on my side in bed. My back. My stomach. Nothing is comfortable. Every position deepens the ache, makes me more aware of how empty I feel, how much I need to be filled.

This is exactly why Omegas shouldn't live with unmated Alphas. Our bodies betray us, needing what we can't have, demanding what we shouldn't want. I'm soaked between my thighs, and I stumble toward the bathroom, thinking maybe cold water will shock my system into submission.

But halfway there, pain curls sharp and deep around my core, and I moan, gripping the doorframe to stay upright. I'm shuddering with arousal.

In that moment, I know what I have to do. I snatch one of the sheets off the bed, wrap it around my naked body. The fabric is soft against my oversensitized skin, and even that simple touch has me moaning.

I know I'm desperate and I'll probably regret this in

the morning. But I can't bring myself to stop. My feet carry me to the door, and I pull it open without letting myself think, without letting doubt creep in.

The hallway outside my room is dark and quiet. Everyone is asleep.

I pad barefoot down the hallway, and I don't let myself hesitate with only Noel on the brain.

CHAPTER TEN

HANNAH

I'm sneaking down the hallway like a criminal, clutching a sheet around my naked body, and every logical part of my brain is screaming that this is a terrible idea. But the logical parts of my brain stopped being in charge about ten minutes ago when the ache between my thighs became so intense that I couldn't think about anything else.

My skin is on fire. Every nerve ending is screaming for touch, for friction, for an Alpha's body against mine. My inner thighs are slick with arousal, and I'm pretty sure I'm leaving a trail of scent behind me that would make any Alpha in a one-mile radius lose his mind.

This is insane. Desperate. Exactly the kind of behavior I'd lecture someone else about, and yet here I am, padding barefoot down a dark hallway toward Noel's room because my body has decided it needs him right now or it's going to spontaneously combust.

The first door I cross is slightly ajar. That has to be it.

My heart is pounding so hard. My entire body is trembling with need. Pure, primal, overwhelming need. Not want. Not desire. *Need.*

I've never felt anything like this before. Never been this out of control and desperate for touch.

Nothing insane about showing up naked in someone's room because your body has decided it's going to die without them.

I reach for the handle and stumble, catching myself against the frame. The wood is cool under my palm, grounding me for half a second before the heat surges back.

"Calm down," I whisper to myself. *Just... ask for help. He offered. You're just taking him up on it.*

My voice sounds strange in the quiet hallway. Breathless. Desperate.

I push the door open slowly, wincing at the small creak of hinges.

A strange scent finds me immediately, and I nearly moan out loud. Pine. Rich and clean and grounding. It's coming from a small ceramic diffuser on the bedside table, white vapor curling up from it in delicate wisps. The room is dim, lit only by moonlight filtering through curtains and that small warm glow from the diffuser.

I can barely make out details. Dark furniture. Minimal decoration. Very masculine. Very Noel.

And there, on the massive bed, Noel is shrouded in night.

He's sprawled on his back, one arm thrown over his face, the other stretched above his head. His legs extend from under the blanket, and even in the shadows, I can tell he's huge. The size is right. The build is right.

My body recognizes him on some instinctive level.

I stand at the end of the bed, frozen between rationality and desperation. The ache intensifies, cramping low in my belly, and I bite my lip to keep from whimpering.

The sheet around me slips from my fingers. It pools silently at my feet, and I'm completely naked in Noel's bedroom, and this should feel wrong, but all I feel is burning need.

I climb onto the bed as carefully as I can, trying not to jostle him awake yet. The mattress dips under my weight, and I freeze, but he doesn't stir. Just keeps breathing deep and even.

I need to be under the blanket, then I don't have to face him when he wakes up. Don't have to see his expression. Can just focus on the relief, on making this ache go away.

I pull the blanket up and slide underneath.

It's stifling under here. The musky heat from his body combines with my own overheated smell. I'm sweating within seconds. The pine scent is everywhere, infused into the sheets, but there's also something else. Multiple scents layering over each other. My brain is too fuzzy to analyze it properly.

Doesn't matter. What matters is that I'm here, and he's here, and I'm going to get what I need. I'm positioned between his spread legs, and I reach out in the darkness, finding him by touch.

His cock is soft. But large even in this state. Impressive.

The moment my fingers wrap around him, he throbs. Comes to life in my hand, hardening so fast it's startling. A grin spreads across my face despite my desperation. So responsive. So perfect.

I'm already rocking my hips without meaning to, trying to get friction, trying to ease the ache. My thighs are soaking wet. Arousal slides down my legs.

He groans low in his throat, a sound that buzzes through the bed and straight to my core. His erection is rock-hard in my hand as I slowly work him up and down.

"I'm all yours," I whisper into the darkness. I move to straddle him, but the thought of facing him, even in the dark, leaves me spinning with anxiety.

I can't look at him. Can't watch his face. Too vulnerable. Too exposed.

So I pivot awkwardly, moving to straddle him in reverse. Facing away from his head, toward his feet. The blanket slides down my back as I position myself, and cool air hits my overheated skin. Better. Slightly better.

I rub myself over his hardness experimentally, testing the angle.

The friction is everything. I'm purring like some

kind of satisfied cat, and I do it again and again, harder this time.

Fuck... I'm shuddering with excitement from his touch alone.

I lift my hips, positioning myself, and his hand is suddenly there. Supporting his cock. Holding it steady for me.

Heat floods my face even though he can't see me blushing in the dark. "Hope this is okay," I breathe.

He makes a sound of approval, a grunt, rough and affirming, and that's all I need.

I sink down slowly and gasp. He's so thick. Stretching me even though I'm soaking wet, even though my body is begging for this. I work myself down gradually, taking more and more, and it's so tight I can barely breathe.

He groans behind me, hands finding my hips, gripping hard enough to leave marks.

"You're so big," I gasp. "I can barely—"

His hands guide me down the rest of the way, and suddenly he's fully seated inside me, and I'm trembling from the intensity of it. Just having him fully embedded in me calms the ache, the desperation... I could stay like this all night and be satisfied.

In truth, I've never been this full. It borders on too much, but in the best possible way.

His hands push me up slightly, then pull me back down, setting a rhythm. I catch on quickly, using my thighs to lift and lower myself.

My toes curl.

The slide of him inside me. The fullness. The way he hits something deep inside. Before I know it, I'm riding him, sweating, loving every damn moment. I'm moaning uncontrollably now. Can't help it. Can't stop the sounds spilling from my throat.

My hands brace on his thighs as I lean forward slightly, changing the angle, and that's even better. Perfect. Exactly right.

I bounce harder, faster, chasing the release that's building.

He's grunting beneath me, hips driving up to meet every roll of my body, each thrust hitting a place that has my breath scattering. The bed rocks beneath us, the frame releasing a low groan that sounds like it might give out before either of us does.

His hand slides from my hip to my ass, fingers gripping, guiding, encouraging me to move exactly how he likes. The pressure is perfect, grounding and filthy at the same time. Then his fingers glide between my cheeks, slow and deliberate, teasing a place I have never let anyone touch.

I tense for a second. The sensation is new and strange and wicked. It shoots through me like a spark jumping between live wires. He circles there with lazy patience, and my thighs tremble.

He strokes again, a little more firmly. My breath stutters. My body leans into it without asking my permission. He does it again, and the pleasure ripples through me in a way I can't hide. I am already shaking, trying to ride him and hold myself together at the same time.

He murmurs something low that I can't make out. Then he presses a finger inside my ass, slowly and carefully, giving me time to take the stretch.

The shock of it punches a sound out of me. Hot. Deep. Impossible to ignore.

He holds still for a moment, letting my body adjust, letting me breathe through the intensity. Then he begins to move his finger in a rhythm that syncs perfectly with his thrusts. The sensation builds fast, too fast, stealing every coherent thought I have. My muscles flutter around him. My vision blurs.

I close my eyes and let myself get lost in sensation. The pleasure coils and tightens until I feel like I am rolling straight toward the edge with no way to stop myself.

My orgasm hits hard. It floods through me in waves, each one sharper than the last. My body clamps around him, my hips jerking, my voice breaking open. Heat pulses through every inch of me. He holds me tightly through it, gripping my waist, keeping me moving while the climax tears through me again and again.

"Noel!" His name rips from my throat.

By the time it finally loosens its hold, I am shaking and gasping, while aftershocks twitch through my thighs. He is still inside me, thick and hot and throbbing, and I can feel his restraint like a tightly held thread.

I breathe heavily, still trembling, knowing I am nowhere near done with him.

In that moment of bliss, my eyes flutter open. And I see him.

Noel. Standing in the doorway, wearing nothing but boxer briefs with an erection so obvious it's obscene. He's startled, with huge eyes.

My brain stutters. Wait!

If Noel is standing there…

Then who…?

I twist my head to look over my shoulder.

Kane is lying beneath me, grinning like he just won the lottery.

"No." The word comes out strangled. "Oh, hell."

I scramble off him, his huge cock and his finger slipping out of me, and panic floods through the post-orgasmic haze. My legs barely hold me as I lunge for the sheet at the end of the bed.

"Kane, I'm so sorry! Shit, I thought… I…" I'm babbling now, clutching the sheet to my chest. "I thought you were Noel! The door was open and I didn't —I couldn't—I'm so sorry!"

Kane is still grinning, propped up on his elbows, his cock erect like a flagpole, glistening with my juices, looking entirely too satisfied. "No apology necessary, my sexy girl. That was hands down the best wake-up call I've ever had. Though I gotta say, I'm a little disappointed you thought I was someone else the whole time."

"Disappointed?" Noel's voice from the doorway is strained. "That was supposed to be me, you bastard."

"You snooze, you lose." Kane's grin widens. "Or in this case, you sleep, I reap the benefits."

I'm going to die. Right here. Right now. Just cease to exist from sheer mortification. My mouth opens, but no sound comes out.

I did not just have sex with the wrong Alpha.

I did not just scream Noel's name while riding Kane.

This is a nightmare. I push past Noel, who's still frozen in the doorway like a statue, and run down the hall. My feet are slapping against the hardwood. The sheet tangles around my legs.

Behind me, I hear laughter. Both of them, chuckling.

I slam into my room and lock the door behind me. Then I dive onto the bed, bury my face in the pillows, and pray for death. "This is how I die. Not from heat or embarrassment or anything normal. From this. This exact moment."

I replay everything in my head and want to scream.

Climbing into his bed. Touching him. Taking him inside me. Coming all over him while screaming another man's name.

And Noel. Standing there. Watching.

I can never face them again. Never. I'll have to leave. Move to another state. Change my name. Become a hermit. But worse than the embarrassment is the creeping horror.

Kane was asleep. He couldn't consent. And I just... I just...

Did I assault him?

The thought makes bile rise in my throat.

He was sleeping. I climbed into his bed. I initiated everything without asking, without making sure he was awake and willing.

What have I done?

There's a knock at my door.

"Hannah?" Noel's voice, muffled but clear. "You okay in there? Want to talk?"

"Go away!" I yell into the pillow.

A low chuckle. "If it's any consolation, Kane is thrilled. Says it was the best sex he's had in years. Though he's a little bitter that you wouldn't let him finish."

"That's not funny!" I'm never leaving this room. Never. "That's not—I can't—just go away!"

"Hannah—"

"Noel, please." My voice cracks. "I need to die of embarrassment in private."

"You're being dramatic."

"I just had sex with your packmate, thinking he was you! How is that not the most mortifying thing that's ever happened to anyone?"

"To be fair, we do all use the same diffuser oil. Easy mistake."

"That doesn't make it better!"

There's a pause. "You didn't do anything wrong. Kane's not upset. Hell, he's probably the happiest he's been in months. And I'm..." Another pause. "Well, I'm jealous as hell, but that's not your fault."

I press my face harder into the pillow, wishing I could suffocate myself.

"You're going to have to face us eventually."

"Then I'll leave. First thing tomorrow. Go back to Lily's. This was a mistake."

"Hannah—"

"Please." I'm begging now, and I don't care about pride. "Just give me tonight. Let me process this. We can talk tomorrow. Or never. Preferably never."

A long silence.

"Okay. But you're not leaving. We'll figure this out. And, Hannah? You're welcome here. Always. No matter what."

His footsteps retreat from my room, and I'm alone with my humiliation.

I burrow deeper into the pillows, pulling the comforter over my head, creating a cocoon of shame.

Somewhere down the hall, I hear muffled voices. Laughter. They're definitely talking about me. About the crazy Omega who can't tell one Alpha from another. I groan into the pillow and pull the blanket tighter.

Tomorrow. I'll deal with this tomorrow.

Tonight, I'm just going to lie here and wait for the sweet relief of unconsciousness.

Or death.

Whichever comes first.

It's eight in the morning, and I'm already showered, dressed in last night's green dress, and contemplating whether I can escape this mansion without facing anyone.

The shower helped. Sort of. At least the crushing heat from last night is gone, my skin doesn't feel like it's on fire anymore, my pulse has returned to something approaching normal, and I can think in complete sentences again instead of just primal need.

But the mortification? That's alive and well.

I pace my temporary room, barefoot, chewing my thumbnail until it hurts.

What if being around three Alphas is triggering my heat early? What if last night wasn't a one-time thing but the start of my cycle going completely haywire? I need heat suppressants and a plan. Plus, to not accidentally throw myself at another Alpha while thinking he's someone else.

Maybe I can just sneak out. Call an Uber. Pretend last night never happened. Move to a different country where no one knows I screamed the wrong name during sex.

Perfect plan.

I crack open my door, listening hard.

Silence. Blessed silence.

I tiptoe down the hallway, wincing at every small creak of the floorboards. The house is so quiet I can hear my own heartbeat. Down the stairs, moving as carefully as possible, praying that everyone is still asleep or at least locked in their rooms.

My shoes are by the front door. If I can just get to them and slip out, I'm home free.

I reach the bottom of the stairs and freeze.

Kane is standing in the living room, leaning against the back of the couch with his legs stretched out in front of him, one ankle crossed over the other. Hands in his pockets. Smirking at me like he's been waiting for hours.

He's wearing dark jeans that hug his thighs, a green flannel shirt with the sleeves rolled up to his elbows, exposing thick, muscled forearms dusted with dark blond hair. His boots look worn. And those hazel-green eyes are tracking my every movement like a predator watching prey.

He's built like someone who could throw me over his shoulder without breaking a sweat. Broad shoulders, chest pressing against the flannel, arms that seem to call to me.

My gaze drops to his package before I can stop myself, and my brain helpfully supplies exactly what he's packing because I know firsthand now.

My nipples tighten in immediate response.

Traitors.

"Oh," I manage, voice strangled, gaze shooting back to his face.

His smirk widens into a full grin. "Were you expecting Noel?"

Heat floods my face. Last night crashes back in vivid, horrifying detail.

"Look." The word tumbles out in a rush. "I'm so sorry about last night. It's just that I'd shared ice cream with Noel, we kissed, and I figured he could help me with some pre-heat issues, and I really hope you don't think I meant to break into your room and assault you because I would never intentionally—"

He bursts into laughter, head thrown back, shoulders shaking, the sound rich and genuine and filling the entire room.

"Baby girl." His voice when he speaks again is warm, amused, but underneath there's something darker. "You think that's what happened? Because that's not what I experienced. I was blessed by a sex goddess who climbed into my bed and offered herself to me. The same goddess I've been fantasizing about since the moment I first met you."

My mouth opens, but no sound comes out.

"Your scent woke me up," he continues, moving closer with slow, deliberate steps. "Rich and sweet and desperate. Told me exactly what you needed. And as your Alpha, it's my responsibility—my privilege—to be there for you. However you need me. Whenever you need me. Even if I'm asleep and you think I'm someone else." His grin turns wicked. "Though I'll admit, hearing you moan Noel's name while riding my cock was a bit of a blow to the ego."

"Kane—"

"But you came apart so beautifully, squeezing me so tight I could barely think, and I figured I could forgive you for the name mix-up." He's standing right in front of me now, close enough that his scent of warm gingerbread, campfire smoke, and orange zest wraps around me. "Between you and me? I'm yours to use however you want. Rub up against me at three in the morning, climb into my bed when you're burning up, scratch whatever itch needs scratching. Don't ever think it's anything else. Don't doubt for a second that I didn't enjoy every fucking moment of having you."

My heart is racing so hard I feel dizzy. The way he's watching me like I'm something precious and sexy and exactly what he wants weakens my knees.

"I just..." I don't know what to say. "I thought I—"

"I was very much a willing participant in everything that happened." His voice drops lower, intimate. "Best wake-up call of my entire life. Next time, though, maybe get my name right? Do wonders for my self-esteem."

Despite everything, I laugh. It comes out slightly hysterical, but it's genuine.

We stand there in charged silence, his scent curling around me, making my body remember exactly how he felt inside me. I turn toward the door before I do something stupid. "Well, I should go, then."

I slip into my heels, and he's suddenly there, opening the front door with exaggerated courtesy.

I step outside into the crisp morning air. Fresh snow covers everything, the driveway already cleared in clean lines. Trees surrounding the property are frosted white, branches heavy with snow, and birds chirp somewhere in the distance. It's beautiful. Peaceful.

And Kane is right there.

"So where are we going?" His tone is cheerful, like we're about to embark on a grand adventure.

I turn to face him, glancing up at him. "I'm going to visit Scot's uncle. You're staying here."

He laughs, not quite mocking but close. "I'm coming with you. This way to my truck."

"That's not necessary—"

"Noel told me everything this morning." He's walking toward the garage, and I'm following because what else can I do? "About the party, about Scot being a dick, about you moving in with us—"

"Temporarily," I jump in quickly.

He shoots me a look over his shoulder that says he doesn't believe me for a second. "Right. Anyway, Chris, Noel, and I had a chat at dawn. We all agree that with your pre-heat scent being so strong and your needs potentially spiking without warning, it makes sense for you to have one of us with you at all times."

I stop walking. "I don't think that's necessary. I have work to do, clients to see. I don't need a babysitter."

He clicks a button on his keys, and the garage door lifts smoothly. "A partner. Someone to have your back. Someone to help when your body decides it needs an Alpha's touch."

"Look, last night was one thing, but I have a heat clinic I can go to if—"

"And now you have three Alphas living with you who will take care of you." His voice is firm. "We're your scent matches, Hannah. That means we're supposed to be there for you."

"Why are you so infuriating?"

"I'm just being logical." He grins.

I laugh, slightly hysterical but real. "Logical. Sure. My life spiraling into chaos is totally logical."

"Give it time. You'll see." He gestures toward the garage. "But first, let me drive you to see Scot's uncle. Make sure that asshole doesn't show up and cause problems."

"Fine." I throw my hands up. "You can come with me today because I need a ride. But then you drop me at Lily's so I can get my car and go back to some semblance of normal—"

"And then come back here where you have a home until you sort out your next steps," he finishes for me. "You think we're going to let our scent-match Omega wander around town, potentially slip into heat somewhere without us nearby? You need to understand something about us. We're possessive. Overprotective.

And when we claim something as ours, we don't let go." His eyes lock with mine. "And you, Hannah, are ours."

He disappears into the garage before I can formulate a response. My brain is still processing his words. The casual possessiveness. The absolute certainty. The way he said *ours* like it's already decided, like I don't get a vote. I should be angry. Should be pushing back against this Alpha nonsense. But instead, I'm standing here swooning like some romance novel heroine, and I hate how much I like hearing him claim me.

An engine roars to life, and an electric-blue pickup truck emerges from the garage.

It's gorgeous, all sleek with dark tinted windows, chrome accents catching the morning sun, mag wheels that look custom and expensive. The paint job is flawless, almost metallic in the light.

Kane pulls up alongside me and rolls down the window. He's grinning, one arm draped over the steering wheel, and the sight of him like this, confident, relaxed, sexy as hell, has me swooning on the spot, and I have to grip the door to not fall over.

"Want to climb in, baby girl?"

Well, when he puts it like that...

I open the passenger door and haul myself up into the truck. The interior is just as impressive—black leather seats, blue ambient lighting running along the dash and doors, everything clean and modern and smelling like fresh leather mixed with Kane's scent.

"So where's Noel?" I buckle up as Kane heads down

the driveway. "He promised to come with me this morning."

"Noel thought it might be better if I took you." The gates are opening automatically. "He mentioned you might try to sneak out of the house at dawn, never face us again, possibly move to another country. And best to deal with me instead of hiding from the obvious."

I cut him a sideways look and half laugh. "As if I would do that."

He chuckles like he knows exactly what I was planning.

"I need the address for Scot's uncle's place," he says.

I grab my phone, find my notes where I've saved every important address and contact, and punch Giuseppe's information into the GPS mounted on his dashboard.

"You know," Kane adds as we pull away from their property, "I've never had sex with someone I haven't kissed first. So I think you owe me a proper kiss."

I laugh despite myself. "I don't think so." Yet, I can't help staring at his mouth. Full lips that curve easily into smiles, and I know deep in my bones that he'd be an incredible kisser. Probably the kind who takes his time, who knows exactly how to make you melt.

My brain unhelpfully supplies images of last night. How he gripped my hips with those huge hands, so solid and powerful. The way he drove me up and down over his cock, plunging into me over and over, controlling my movements like he knew exactly what I needed before I did.

My body trembles just remembering.

Stop thinking about that.

"So tell me about you," I say, desperate to change the subject. "What made you become a bounty hunter? That seems like an unusual career choice."

"Dropped out of college." He says it easily, no shame. "Engineering program. Hated every second of it. Spent a year working construction, had no real plan for my life. I knew Chris and Noel from school, and then one day, they showed up on a job site and took me in, trained me, gave me purpose."

"That's really sweet."

"They're my family. Only family that matters." He glances at me, and there's something soft in his expression. "Well, until now. Now we've got you too."

Something warm unfurls in my chest, spreading through my ribs, making it hard to breathe properly.

"What about you?" he asks. "Always wanted to be an event planner?"

"Since I was a kid." I settle back in the seat, relaxing into the conversation. "I used to plan elaborate birthday parties for my stuffed animals. Had spreadsheets, time-lines, budget breakdowns. My dad thought I was insane."

Kane laughs. "You made spreadsheets as a child?"

"I was very organized. Still am, actually. Can't help it."

He's grinning now, clearly enjoying teasing me. "So what's your dream event? If money and logistics were no object, what would you create?"

I think about it, letting myself sink into the fantasy I've been building for years. "New Year's Eve masquerade ball in a castle. Somewhere in Europe, maybe Scotland. Ice sculptures throughout the venue, live orchestra playing classical music and modern covers. Champagne fountain in the center of the ballroom. Everyone in formal wear with elaborate masks, the kind that are works of art. And at midnight, we'd have synchronized fireworks visible through massive windows, while guests unmask and toast to new beginnings."

When I glance at Kane, he's watching me, admiring.

"What?" I ask.

"Nothing. Just love watching you talk about your passion. Your whole face lights up. It's beautiful."

Heat floods my cheeks. "You're just trying to flatter me."

"I'm being honest." His hand finds mine on the console, squeezing gently. "And we're going to make that event happen someday. I promise."

"You can't promise that."

"Watch me."

We're driving through town now, and a comfortable silence stretches between us. I'm very aware of his hand still holding mine, thumb stroking against my skin. This feels natural. Easy. Like we've known each other for years instead of days.

"Oh!" Kane sits up straighter. "I taught Corn Dog a trick."

I grin. "What kind?"

"He can bow on command now. Took me weeks, but if I say, 'Corn Dog, show some respect,' he drops his head and bends his front legs like he's bowing to royalty."

"That's actually adorable."

"It's strategic. I can bring him to events, have him bow to important guests. Instant charm offensive."

I burst out laughing just as we pull up to Giuseppe's house, and my stomach immediately ties itself in knots.

The house sits back from the street behind a low stone wall and ornamental iron gates that sit open. It's a two-story contemporary design with lots of glass and clean lines, cedar siding weathered to a beautiful gray, a flat roof with what looks like a rooftop garden barely visible. The landscaping is immaculate even under the snow, with sculpted evergreens and winter-blooming plants adding color.

This house screams money, but in a tasteful way.

We get out, and Kane's hand immediately finds the small of my back as we walk to the front door.

I knock, half expecting no answer after days of radio silence.

But the door opens almost immediately.

Giuseppe stands there, and my first thought is that he looks unwell. He's in his sixties, thin in a way that suggests recent illness rather than genetics. His face is pale, eyes tired but still sharp. He's wearing expensive wool slacks and a cashmere sweater in a deep burgundy that hangs slightly loose on his frame.

"Giuseppe," I say quickly, before he can shut the

door. "I know Scot might have told you things, but I'd love the chance to talk to you. Tell you my side. Please."

"Of course, Hannah." His voice is raspy, like he's been coughing. "I was in the hospital. Pneumonia and a chest infection. Gave everyone quite a scare. But Scot did come visit, which was thoughtful." He glances at Kane, eyebrows rising slightly. "How rude of me. Come inside, please."

"This is Kane," I say. "My… boyfriend."

Kane extends his hand, and when Giuseppe takes it, Kane says, "Actually, I'm her Alpha. Part of her pack."

I roll my eyes. Just like Noel last night, marking his territory.

Giuseppe's eyebrows rise higher, but he just nods. "Well. Come in, come in."

We follow him inside, and I try not to gawk. The entryway opens into a sprawling open-concept space. Polished concrete floors with radiant heating. Exposed wooden beams crossing the ceiling. Abstract art on white walls. Everything minimal but clearly expensive.

"I tried calling you several times," I say as we walk. "And messaging. I was worried when you didn't respond."

"Really?" Giuseppe pulls out his phone, frowning at the screen. "I don't see any messages from you. Not a single one."

I show him my phone, the unanswered texts, the call log showing multiple attempts.

"That's very strange," he mutters, squinting at his screen.

"Actually," Kane says, "this could happen if her number is blocked on your phone. I know because it happened to me once. Ex-girlfriend who didn't want to hear from me anymore."

I glance at him sharply. Ex-girlfriend?

He catches my look and winks.

I'm not jealous. Why would I be jealous of some random woman from Kane's past? Except there's a spike of it anyway, sharp and unwelcome, and I push it away forcefully.

Giuseppe is fiddling with his phone, tapping through menus. "You're absolutely right, Kane. Hannah's number was blocked. But I would never…" He looks up, confusion and dawning anger mixing on his face. "Scot was handling my phone in the hospital. I was too out of it to notice."

He keeps walking, leading us deeper into the house. I'm shaking my head that Scot would stoop so low, yet I'm not surprised. Asshole.

The living room has me pausing. An entire wall of floor-to-ceiling windows overlooks a terrace and a pool, currently covered with a blue tarp and buried in snow, but I can imagine how incredible it must be in summer. A stone fireplace dominates one wall, fire crackling and throwing warmth into the space. Modern furniture in grays and whites. And in the corner, taking up a ridiculous amount of space, stands the biggest white Christmas tree I've ever seen.

It has to be twelve feet tall, perfectly shaped, decorated exclusively in shades of blue and silver. Delicate glass birds with real feathers perch on branches. Over-sized baubles catch and reflect the firelight. Ribbons in shimmering silver cascade down in elegant swirls. There are what look like hand-blown glass icicles, each one unique. The tree topper is a massive silver star.

It's the kind of tree you see in magazines. The kind people hire professional decorators to create.

I'm staring, unable to help myself.

Giuseppe notices and smiles slightly. "My late wife loved Christmas. This was her design. I keep it the same every year in her memory."

"It's beautiful," I say softly.

Giuseppe gestures for us to sit, and I sink onto a plush gray couch. Kane sits beside me, close enough that his arm goes naturally around my back, his hand resting on my hip.

The touch settles something anxious in my chest. Like his presence alone can ground me when I'm spiraling, so I don't push him away.

Giuseppe paces in front of the fireplace. "I'm too old and too sick to deal with the childish games Scot sometimes plays. The business..." He sighs heavily. "I don't want to see it fall apart because of family drama."

He lowers himself onto the couch across from us, moving carefully like everything hurts.

"When Scot came to see me in the hospital," Giuseppe continues, "he told me you two had a falling out. Said you weren't trustworthy, that you were using the business for your own gain, that I should sell to him immediately before you destroyed everything we'd built."

I take a breath, choosing my words carefully. "Scot has been trying to pursue me romantically. Beyond business partners. When I made it clear I wasn't interested, he became angry. Aggressive. He told me the partnership was over, packed up my belongings without permission, kicked me out of my apartment, and changed the locks."

Giuseppe's expression darkens.

"I don't want to cause drama," I continue. "I'm not trying to turn you against your nephew. But I want a fair chance to prove I'm dedicated to running Confetti and Meatballs. I care about that business, about the clients, the events, the reputation you've spent decades building. I want to honor that legacy, not destroy it."

This is my last shot. Working with an established business, all those clients already on the books, the reputation already built, it would be so much easier than starting from scratch.

Kane leans closer, his breath warm against my ear. "You're doing amazing, baby girl."

The way he says it, low and intimate and full of confidence in me, sends heat spiraling through my body. His voice, the huskiness of it, the casual touch, the pet name that should annoy me but doesn't. How did these Alphas start affecting me this fast?

Giuseppe picks up his phone from the coffee table, taps the screen, and sets it down on speaker.

It rings twice before connecting.

"Uncle Giuseppe!" Scot's voice comes through, warm and solicitous. "How are you feeling? I was going to come by later to check on you."

"You're on speaker, Scot. I have Hannah here with me."

Silence. Then Scot's tone shifts, goes cold. "I told you to be careful with her."

"Just listen," Giuseppe adds, then coughs, hard, wet coughs that make him wince.

"Uncle, are you—"

"Let me finish." Giuseppe's voice is firm despite the obvious pain. "I'm too old to keep running my business, too old to deal with drama and accusations flying back and forth. I thought you could handle taking over, Scot. But now I have serious doubts."

"Uncle, what—"

"There's been a development with the Whispering Grove council," Giuseppe says, cutting across whatever Scot was about to launch into. "They've hired Confetti and Meatballs for this year's Whispering Grove Christmas Tree Lighting celebrations. Carols, markets, everything for the night."

My heart stalls, then takes off at a sprint. Oh. "That's... huge," I breathe.

"It is," Giuseppe agrees. "The council committee has made it clear that if this year goes off without a hitch, they'll lock in Confetti and Meatballs to run the event for the next five years. It's a massive contract. Good money, good profile. Exactly the kind of thing that can secure the future of this business."

Five years. My brain starts doing frantic math: income, stability, the kind of portfolio piece other councils drool over.

"Perfect," Scot says smoothly. "I'll start drafting a proposal for the program, and—"

"No," Giuseppe cuts in, voice suddenly sharp. "You won't."

Silence crackles down the line.

Kane's hand finds the small of my back, warm and steady, as if he senses my spine trying to liquefy.

"What do you mean, *no?*" Scot's tone tightens. "Uncle, this is exactly what I've been waiting for. You know how hard I've worked for this business. I've always been here for you."

"I'm very aware of who my family is," Giuseppe replies, and there's an edge there I've never heard before. "I'm also aware that profits have been sliding for the last few years. Bookings down. Costs up. Reputation… tired."

My stomach twists. I know those numbers. I've seen the spreadsheets. Lived in those late-night panic emails.

"And in the last six months?" Giuseppe continues. "Since Hannah came on board? Profits are finally going *up* again. New clients. Better reviews. People talking about Confetti and Meatballs like it's exciting again. That's not an accident."

My cheeks heat, and I stare at the floorboards. Compliments feel strange when they're wrapped in this much pressure.

Scot scoffs. "With respect, Uncle, she's been here five

minutes. You're really going to rewrite the entire future of the company based on a couple of decent months and some social media hype?"

Anger flares low and sharp under my ribs. "Pretty sure the social media hype includes the three council members who personally emailed asking for a quote," I say before I can stop myself. "But sure, let's pretend that had nothing to do with landing the event." I just hadn't known that Giuseppe had been personally meeting with the council.

Anyway, the words taste reckless the second they're out. I clamp my lips shut, immediately regretting that I've stooped to sniping.

Kane's thumb moves in a slow, grounding stroke along my spine. *Breathe*, his touch seems to say.

"You fucking bi—"

"Enough." Giuseppe's voice cracks like a whip, loud enough that even Kane startles.

Silence hums.

"My decision is made," Giuseppe says. "The contract is ours *this year*. After that, it depends on how we deliver. So here is what's going to happen. Hannah will be leading the entire Whispering Grove Christmas Celebration for Confetti and Meatballs."

The room tilts.

"What?" My voice comes out thin. "Giuseppe, that's—"

"You'll have full control," he pushes on, as if I haven't spoken. "Budgets, schedules, vendor coordination, client meetings. Everything goes through you."

My mouth goes dry. Full control. Over such a huge event and whether this business has a future or whether I lose everything I've just started to build.

"And me?" Scot demands. "Where exactly do I fit in this little fantasy?"

"You'll *not* be involved in this one, Scot," Giuseppe says. "You're sitting the celebration out. Completely. No client emails, no vendor calls, no advice. I need to see what Confetti and Meatballs can do with Hannah at the wheel and no interference from you."

I almost choke. Scot banned from the biggest event of the year? That's like telling a shark it has to watch someone else swim in its feeding grounds.

"You're kidding," Scot says flatly. "Tell me you're kidding."

"I'm not." Giuseppe lets out a breath that crackles with tired disappointment. "I've watched you, Scot. You work hard, but you don't listen. You don't adapt. You ignore advice that doesn't come from your own head, and you've treated Hannah like a temporary problem instead of an asset."

A small, petty part of me wants to fist-pump. The rest of me is too busy panicking because if he's taking Scot off the board, that means all eyes are on me.

"But I *am* giving you something," Giuseppe continues. "In fact, I'm giving you more than you deserve. Because this is not just about the celebration. It's about the business."

Kane's fingers curl slightly against my back. I can feel the tension rolling off him.

"What does that mean?" I manage, though my voice wobbles.

"It means," Giuseppe says, "that this is your one chance, Hannah. If you pull off the Whispering Grove Christmas Tree Lighting celebrations and if it runs smoothly, the council is happy, the town is happy, and there are no major disasters, then I'll be drawing up papers to make you the owner of Confetti and Meatballs."

My breath punches out of me. That's... that's everything. Security. Control. Finally being more than the temp he could cut loose. My throat tightens.

Silence hums on the line, sharp as broken glass.

"And if she fails," Scot says at last, voice suddenly very calm. Too calm. "If she can't make it work... it comes to me?"

A cold shiver slides down my spine. I already know I'm not going to like this.

"If there are serious problems because of Hannah," Giuseppe says slowly, as if he hates the words even as he says them, "if she fails to deliver and we lose the five-year contract because of that, then the business goes to you, Scot. All of it. I sign over my shares, and you take full control of Confetti and Meatballs."

The world narrows to the sound of my own heartbeat.

So if I succeed, I finally get a real place here. If I fail, I hand everything to the man who would happily shove me into traffic.

"Let me be sure I understand," Scot says, every word

clipped. "I'm forced to sit out the biggest job we've ever had, and if she screws it up, the entire business comes to me?"

"That's right," Giuseppe replies.

Kane's hand tightens on my back, fingers digging in just enough that it almost hurts. It anchors me to my body instead of the roaring fear trying to drag me out of it.

This is insane. This is—this is—

Kane shifts closer, shoulder brushing mine, silent and solid.

Scot is breathing hard enough that I can hear it over the speaker.

"So that's it?" he grits out. "You're gambling the entire company you built on her? On an Omega you barely know? I can run this celebration and ensure we get it for another five years!"

Giuseppe's sigh crackles down the line. "We'll also be having a very serious talk about how you speak about the people who work for you," he says. "And about the fact that you blocked Hannah's number on my phone. I know you did it, Scot. We'll discuss that later."

Silence.

"Good luck, Hannah. You'll need it," Scot says finally, the words tight and poisonous.

The line goes dead.

I realize I'm on my feet as Kane rises beside me, moving with that smooth, contained energy that always makes me feel like he's ready to catch me if I fall.

"You shouldn't have done that," I whisper, the words

directed at no one and everyone. At Giuseppe. At myself. At the universe for thinking this is a fun game.

Because this isn't just pressure. It's an open invitation for Scot to root for my failure, and if he can't touch the celebration directly, he'll look for other ways to knock things sideways for me to fail. Accidentally-on-purpose vendor issues. Misplaced invoices. A rumor here, a concerned query there.

"Hannah," Giuseppe says quietly. I glance up. He's pushing himself to stand, one hand on the armrest for balance. The effort puts new lines around his eyes, and guilt spears through my panic. He appears exhausted. Older than he did a year ago. "This isn't a gift. It's a test. I'm putting my faith in you, and I'm putting the business on the line. Don't make me regret it."

"I... I understand." Do I? I'm not sure I do. All I can really grasp is that one wrong move and everything I've worked for slides straight into Scot's hands.

And I *know* he heard the conditions like a challenge, not a warning.

Kane's fingers lace through mine, squeezing hard enough that it jolts me out of the spiral.

"I won't disappoint you," I say, even though my pulse is doing backflips. "I promise I'll do everything I can to make the celebration perfect."

Giuseppe studies me for a long heartbeat, then nods once. "Good," he adds. "Because if you can pull this off with Scot sulking on the sidelines, there won't be much this town, or anyone else, can throw at you that you can't handle."

No pressure. And I read between the lines easily. He wants me to win. Prefers me over Scot. But he can't just cut his nephew out and hand me the crown without a reason. He has to be able to point at the celebration and say the event decided it, not him.

We're outside moments later, walking back to Kane's truck, and I exhale so hard my breath clouds in the cold air.

"God, that was intense. Not how I expected it to go at all."

"You were incredible," Kane assures me, opening my door for me. "So strong. Watching you stand up for yourself, fight for what you want, fuck, Hannah. That was sexy as hell."

I climb into the truck, and he's in the driver's seat in no time, starting the engine.

"I'll help you with anything you need to pull this off," he adds as we drive away from Giuseppe's house. "Research, planning, stalking Scot, late-night sex, whatever you need. I'm yours."

My heart does a weird little flip. Everything blurs for a moment under the heat of his promise.

Maybe I really *can* do this.

Assuming Scot doesn't blow up my world first.

"And it's another excellent reason for you to stay living with us. You'll probably need to meet with council members, do site visits, all kinds of things that are easier when you're based in town instead of an hour away in the mountains."

That's… actually a valid point. I nibble my lower lip, thinking through logistics.

Kane is staring at my mouth again like he might pull over and kiss me senseless.

"Let's go get your stuff from Lily's," he says, voice rough. "Bring it all home where it belongs."

Home.

The word settles warmly in my chest, spreading like hot chocolate on a cold day.

I should probably be panicking more about how fast this is moving. About how I barely know these men and I'm already considering living with them permanently.

But sitting here in Kane's truck, his scent wrapped around me, his confidence in me making me feel capable and strong, I start to think that maybe things might actually work out.

CHAPTER TWELVE

HANNAH

It's past midday, and I'm sitting cross-legged on my bed in what's apparently my new room, surrounded by boxes and bags and the scattered pieces of my life.

Kane helped me haul everything up from Lily's place about an hour ago. Boxes of clothes, my laptop and charger, stacks of event planning books and magazines I've collected over the years, the few kitchen gadgets I'd accumulated, framed photos of Mom and Lily and Dad. Along with new baby photos of Sage and Blake that Lily framed for me. It all looks pathetically small spread out in this enormous space with its Omega-size bed and walk-in closet and attached bathroom.

I just got off the phone with Lily, who, instead of freaking out like a normal person, kept insisting that I'm doing the right thing.

"If you feel like they're your scent matches, Hannah, you need to give this a real chance. You can't run from biology forever. And from everything I've seen, those guys are obsessed with you. Like, completely gone for you. Don't throw it away because you're scared."

"I'm not afraid."

"You're terrified. I can hear it in your voice. But you're also excited, and that's what matters."

Now I'm changed into comfortable jeans and a soft blue sweater that's seen better days but feels like a hug. I'm barefoot on the plush carpet, trying to convince myself I haven't made a massive mistake.

And I'm pretty sure there are still crumbs from the pork roll *banh mi* we grabbed for lunch down my bra. Kane took me to this tiny Vietnamese place tucked in a strip mall between a laundromat and a nail salon, and the sandwich was so amazing—crispy bread, savory pork, pickled vegetables, cilantro, jalapeños—that I devoured it without caring about being ladylike. Crumbs everywhere.

A knock sounds at my door.

"It's open," I call.

The door swings wide, and there stands Chris, all six feet, three inches of pure muscle and deliciousness filling the doorway, with that devastating smirk on his face that I adore.

"Welcome home," he says, smiling warmly.

I'm staring. Can't help it. Can't even pretend I'm not.

He's wearing blue jeans and a gray long-sleeved thermal shirt that clings to every defined muscle of his chest and arms. His deep brown hair is slightly tousled like he's been running his hands through it.

That smirk. God, I remember from the Santa incident, from our kiss that's been replaying in my head on a loop since it happened.

"You have no idea how excited I am that you're here," he says, one shoulder propped against the frame.

My heart does a stupid little stutter.

"Careful," I say, lifting my chin. "Say things like that and I might start thinking you like having me under your roof."

One corner of his mouth kicks up, slow and wicked. "I do." His gaze drags over my room, then back to me, deliberate enough that my skin prickles. "Safer for you. Easier for me to keep an eye on you."

There it is again. That possessive edge under the easy charm that I pretend I don't notice.

"Now, put on warm clothes and boots. We're heading out."

I blink. "Where?"

"We're going to get a Christmas tree."

I laugh, because I genuinely cannot picture it. "You're joking. You three are going shopping for a tree? I thought you had one, propped up against the back of the house."

His eyes spark. "That one's for donating and too small for us. Plus, Kane said you were disappointed that we didn't have one up yet."

I grin, remembering the gorgeous white tree at Giuseppe's place. "I guess he could have construed my words that way."

"So we fix it. Today. All four of us. You get your tree, and I get to saw in front of you. Everybody wins."

My pulse thuds between my ribs with excitement about getting a tree. "Sure, why not?"

"Five minutes," he says. "Boots, coat, downstairs." He winks, then walks away from my room, broad shoulders disappearing down the hall, and I stand there clutching the hem of my sweater, trying to remember how to breathe, let alone say no to an Alpha who wants to chop down a Christmas tree just because I asked why theirs wasn't up yet.

I grab thick wool socks, my heaviest cable-knit sweater over a thermal layer, and my winter coat. By the time I'm bundled up and heading downstairs in my snow boots, I'm sweating slightly, but at least I won't turn into a popsicle.

All three of them are waiting in the living room, and the sight stops me on the bottom step like I've walked into a wall.

They're geared up for serious outdoor winter activity, and they look like they stepped out of some kind of rugged-Alpha catalog.

Kane is in a forest-green jacket that makes his hazel eyes pop, worn jeans, heavy boots laced tight. His dark blond hair is slightly wind-tousled, and he's grinning at me like we're about to commit a heist instead of cutting down a tree.

Noel is wearing all black that showcases every line of muscle, heavy-duty boots, his long hair tied back in a way that emphasizes his strong jaw. He looks dangerous. Competent. Like he could track someone through a blizzard and enjoy every second.

Chris has added a dark jacket over his shirt and is holding what looks like professional-grade rope coiled over one shoulder.

"There she is," Kane says, his grin widening. "Ready for an adventure, baby girl?"

"I mean, there's a great tree shop on the edge of town," I offer, descending the last step. "They've got pre-cut trees, totally reasonable prices, and you don't risk losing fingers to frostbite."

All three of them laugh like I've told the funniest joke they've ever heard.

"We're doing this ourselves," Noel says.

"The way it's meant to be done," Chris adds, moving toward me. He reaches out, tugs my coat zipper up the last few inches. "Can't have you freezing on us."

"Old-school lumberjack style it is," I say, trying to sound casual instead of completely flustered by his proximity.

I follow them outside into the crisp afternoon air. Kane's blue truck is parked and running, the exhaust puffing white clouds.

Kane pops into the garage and soon emerges carrying a professional-grade saw, the kind with serious teeth that mean business.

Chris is checking the rope, testing its strength with pulls that make his forearm muscles flex. Noel is cracking his knuckles.

"Okay, definitely old school," I admit, climbing into the back seat of the truck.

Kane and Noel take the front seats, Chris sliding in beside me.

Kane backs down the driveway, and I'm trying very hard not to stare at Chris at my side.

"So what kind of decorations do you usually use?" Kane asks once we're on a dirt road, heading deeper into the mountains.

"Everything," I admit, relaxing into the seat. "I'm completely excessive about Christmas. Ornaments from every year of my life, including the truly hideous ones I made in elementary school. Tinsel, so much tinsel. Lights in multiple colors. Candy canes. Glass balls. Homemade ornaments. Popcorn strings if I'm feeling ambitious."

"We keep ours pretty minimal, a tradition my grandparents used to carry out back in their day. I used to spend lots of time here growing up to not deal with my parents," Noel says from the front. "And they taught me how to hang walnuts that are spray-painted gold, bake apples on the night we put up the tree, add hand-wrapped chocolates in brown paper tied with twine, and include candy canes."

"It's keeping the old traditions alive," Kane adds.

"Is that right, Candy Kane?" Chris adds.

Kane groans dramatically. "I will murder you and make it look like an accident."

"He loves to be licked," Chris adds, completely ignoring the threat. "It's basically his favorite activity."

I'm laughing. I can't help it. "Very clever wordplay."

Snow covers everything in pristine white, trees heavy with it, the world looking like someone shook a giant snow globe and let everything settle perfectly.

"So how does this actually work?" I ask, desperate to think about something other than Kane's mouth each time he glances back at me over his shoulder. "Can you just chop down any random tree, or is that, like, super illegal?"

"There's public land where the forest service allows it with permits, and where the best trees grow," Chris explains, nudging me with his shoulder, moving in closer to my space.

"We do it every year," Kane adds.

We pull off onto another dirt road that's been partially plowed, parking in a small lot that's empty except for one other truck in the distance.

The cold hits immediately when we climb out and burns my lungs in the most invigorating way. Everything is quiet except for the crunch of our boots in the snow and the distant calls of birds.

"Most common Christmas trees around here are various pines," Noel details out loud as we start walking into the forest, following a trail that's been packed down by previous visitors. "We prefer white pine since the needles are long and soft. They don't stab you like other pine varieties do when you're decorating."

"The most common wild-growing fir in this area is balsam," Kane adds, stepping over a fallen log and then turning to offer me his hand. "Makes a beautiful

Christmas tree. Smells incredible. Holds its needles well."

"You guys really know your trees," I observe, slightly breathless.

"We take Christmas seriously," Chris says from behind me.

We spread out slightly, each of us scanning the trees around us. The forest here is sparse enough to walk comfortably, the snow pristine except for animal tracks crisscrossing everywhere. I'm not exactly sure what I should be searching for, as they all look gorgeous to me.

"What about this one?" Kane calls, pointing to a tree that's maybe five feet tall and perfectly shaped.

"Too small!" Noel calls back. "We need something that makes a statement!"

"This one?" Chris gestures to a massive specimen that would require a crane to move.

"Unless you're planning to cut a hole in the ceiling and turn it into a two-story-tree situation!" Kane replies.

"Don't tempt me," Chris says. "I love a challenge."

Noel pulls a thermos from his pack pocket. "Hot chocolate break?"

"We've barely started," Kane says.

"I'm up for a hot drink." I'm already heading toward him like he's holding the Holy Grail, the cold seeping through my clothes.

"Spiked with vanilla schnapps," he admits, unscrewing the top and pouring into small collapsible cups he produces from another pocket and hands them out.

We stand in a loose circle, warming our hands on the cups. The hot chocolate is perfect, rich and creamy with real chocolate and just enough schnapps to create a pleasant burn in my chest.

"Look over there," Chris says quietly, voice dropping to barely a whisper. He's pointing, and I follow his gaze to see two rabbits hopping through the snow about thirty feet away. Their fur is pure white, nearly invisible against the background, and they're moving in that distinctive stop-and-go pattern.

"They're adorable," I breathe, not wanting to scare them.

We watch in silence until they disappear into the underbrush, and there's something peaceful about the moment, the four of us standing together in the quiet forest, snow falling gently around us, the world reduced to just this.

Kane bends down, scooping up a handful of snow and packing it into a ball, and he lifts his gaze to me.

"Don't you dare," I warn, recognizing that look, backing away.

He throws it anyway, but at Chris, who dodges with surprising agility and immediately retaliates with his own perfectly aimed snowball that catches Kane in the chest.

Within seconds, it's absolute war.

I'm laughing so hard I can barely make snowballs fast enough to defend myself. I'm outnumbered, outmatched, and they're clearly all way more experienced at snowball combat than I am. Snow hits my shoulder, my back, and somehow gets down the collar of my coat, making me shriek.

"Truce!" I gasp, hands up in surrender. "Truce! I'm defenseless here!"

"Winner picks the tree," Kane declares, brushing snow from his jacket.

"That's completely unfair! You all ganged up on me! That's cheating!"

"All's fair in snowball warfare," Chris says, grinning unrepentantly. "So we get to choose the tree."

But Noel walks over, his large hands gentle as he brushes snow off my shoulders and back. "I'll support whatever tree you choose. Even the odds."

"My hero," I say.

His blue eyes hold mine for a moment, something intense passing between us, before he steps back. We keep walking deeper into the forest, debating the merits of various trees we pass. Too sparse. Too short. Too lopsided. Wrong needle color. Branches too weak to hold ornaments.

Then we round a thick cluster of pines, and there it is.

A balsam fir, maybe eight or nine feet tall, perfectly symmetrical, with that classic Christmas tree silhouette. The needles are a gorgeous blue green that almost appears frosted, branches strong and evenly spaced, the whole thing looking like it grew specifically to be someone's Christmas tree.

"That one," we both say simultaneously, just as Kane and Chris say the same thing, standing several feet away.

The guys share looks, then all three start laughing.

"Unanimous decision," Kane says, shaking his head. "That's got to be fate or something."

"Or we all just have excellent taste," I counter.

They get to work immediately, and I step back to watch because there's no way I'm getting in the way of three large Alphas wielding sharp implements.

Chris and Noel clear snow from around the base, using their boots to push it away, revealing the trunk. Kane positions himself with the saw, testing his grip, adjusting his stance.

And, okay, I'm definitely enjoying the show way more than I should be.

Kane grips the long-handled saw with Noel on the other end, boots planted in the snow as they line it up against the trunk, thick as my thigh. The first drag of the blade bites in with a harsh rasp, metal teeth chewing into wood. Kane's shoulders bunch beneath his jacket, his whole body working with the motion like he's done this every winter since before he could drive.

They fall into a steady push-and-pull, breath fogging the cold air, the saw singing through the tree in rough strokes. It doesn't take forever, but it takes long enough. Noel adjusts his grip, jaw set, as he leans into the next pull, boots sliding just a fraction before he steadies.

By the time the blade is almost through, my fingers are numb, but the rest of me is embarrassingly warm.

With a final, brutal pull, the trunk gives. The tree cracks, a sharp, splintering sound, and the whole thing tips away from where I'm standing. The guys are already moving, hands braced, guiding it down so it falls cleanly into the snow without crushing the lower branches. It lands with a soft, muffled thud, sending up a puff of white, and just like that, our Christmas tree is down.

"You three sure you weren't lumberjacks in a past life?" I call as they start hauling the tree toward the trail, and I turn, staring at the tip of the tree leaving a neat groove through the snow.

A snowball nails me square between the shoulder blades.

I yelp, spinning around. All three of them freeze mid-step, identical innocent expressions pasted on like they rehearsed it.

"Cowards," I accuse. "Own your crimes."

Kane shrugs, completely unbothered. "You started it. You throw around compliments like that, we're gonna get cocky."

"You were already cocky," I mutter.

Chris's mouth curves. "She's not wrong."

They drag the tree back to the truck together. I've got one hand on a branch, more for moral support than actual help, but no one calls me on it. Every time I stumble, one of them steadies me with a hand at my elbow or the small of my back, and my dignity slowly dies a festive, glittery death.

At the truck, they hoist the tree up to the roof rack

in one smooth surge of muscle that makes my stomach go warm. Chris tosses the rope over, then sets to work tying it down. The knots he makes look complicated, the rope cinching tight around the trunk.

"Show-offs," I say under my breath, but I can't stop smiling.

"You love it," Kane tosses back, not even looking up.

He's not wrong.

"Don't worry," Noel adds, glancing at me from under his lashes as he checks the last strap. "We'll teach you to tie knots eventually. Hands-on lesson."

Heat pricks the back of my neck. "I can tie knots."

Chris's gaze drops to my mouth for a beat too long. "We'll test that theory another time."

We pile into the truck. A blast of hot air hits, and I groan in relief. My cheeks are numb. My fingers ache as they thaw.

"That was incredible," I admit, peeling off my gloves and shoving my hands as close to the vents as I can. "I've never cut down a tree before. Never even thought about it. I feel like I've committed a very specific form of Christmas crime, and I like it."

"First of many traditions," Kane says from the front.

The drive back feels faster. Maybe because we're all buzzing from having successfully wrestled a tree out of the forest.

Back at the house, they manhandle the tree inside with the same unbothered strength they used in the forest. "Hold up," Noel states, and they pause on the porch to shake off the snow. Needles rain down in a fragrant green shower, the scent of pine punching through the cold air.

Then comes the doorway. They angle the trunk, tilt, shuffle, reverse, try again. Noel walks backward, one hand on the bark, calling out directions, while Kane and Chris do most of the lifting.

"Watch the top," Noel warns.

"I *am* watching the top," Kane grunts. "The top is fine. The doorway is the problem."

"Try not to remodel the house with the tree," I offer helpfully, hugging my arms around myself.

Three heads swivel toward me at once. For a heartbeat, they all just… look. Snow in their hair, cheeks flushed from the cold, big bodies filling the entryway like this is the most natural thing in the world, like I belong here, standing in their foyer, bossing them around about Christmas décor.

Something tightens in my chest.

"Eyes on the tree, sweetheart," Chris says, but his gaze lingers a little longer on me before he turns back.

They finally get it positioned over the heavy-duty stand waiting in front of the massive windows in the corner of the room.

Noel braces the trunk upright, both hands wrapped around the bark, forearms flexing. Kane crouches to adjust the screws at the base, jaw working as he tightens each one. Chris steps back, circling, squinting at the angle like he's personally offended by the concept of it being slightly crooked.

"Left a bit," Chris instructs.

"That's what *you* said last night," Kane mutters.

I choke on absolutely nothing. Noel snorts, trying and failing to hide a grin. Chris goes still for a beat, then very deliberately doesn't look at me, which only makes it worse because now I'm imagining what he's not saying.

"Up," Chris says, voice a little rougher. "Just a hair."

"That's what—" Kane starts.

"Noel," Chris cuts in, deadpan. "Please hit him for me."

Noel obliges with a sharp elbow to Kane's ribs. "Behave. There's a lady present."

My face is blazing. "Pretty sure that ship sailed the second someone started making *knot* jokes."

Kane flashes me a wicked smile but lifts his hands in mock surrender. "Hey, you're the one who said we were good with wood."

"I did *not* say that."

"You were *thinking* it," Noel adds mildly.

I absolutely was.

Eventually, Chris straightens, gives the trunk one last assessing look, and then nods. They all step back. The top of the tree stretches for the ceiling, leaving enough space for a star.

"God, it's huge," I breathe, staring up at it.

Silence.

I can *feel* the way all three sets of eyes land on me in unison. The air charges, something electric and shameless crackling between us.

Kane is the first to crack. "That's what you said last

night," he blurts, this time with zero shame, and looks unreasonably pleased with himself.

Noel groans. Chris finally looks at me, heat and humor tangled in his gaze, like he's picturing the same things I am.

My stomach swoops. I roll my eyes, desperately trying to claw back some dignity. "You know, at some point, one of you is going to say something that doesn't sound like it belongs on late-night cable."

"Doubtful," Noel says.

"Not when you keep setting us up like that," Kane adds.

Chris's mouth tilts, that slow, dangerous smile that grabs my attention. "Careful, Hannah. Keep talking about how big it is, and we're going to start thinking you're flirting."

I stare at the tree instead of them, heart racing, ridiculously aware of every inch between us, and every place I suddenly wish there *weren't* distance at all.

They disappear into what I assume is storage, returning with multiple boxes stacked in their arms. I watch them unpack strings of white lights still in their packaging, wooden ornaments that look handmade, dried orange slices that smell like Christmas, cinnamon sticks tied together with twine, those hand-wrapped chocolates Noel mentioned, candy canes still in their wrappers.

Chris moves to a sound system I hadn't noticed, and music fills the room, classic Christmas songs, Bing

Crosby and Nat King Cole, the kind that makes everything feel warm and nostalgic.

Then he disappears into the kitchen, and soon the smell of baking apples fills the entire house, sweet and spiced with cinnamon and maybe nutmeg, making my mouth water.

We all start decorating the tree, beginning with lights. Then we hang ornaments of wooden reindeer, carved snowflakes, some that look like they might be from their childhood based on the worn edges and faded paint.

Chris vanishes down the hall again and returns with a massive ball of twine, a smug look on his face like he's just saved Christmas. "Emergency sugar rations," he says, dropping it on the coffee table beside a mountain of candy canes and wrapped chocolates. "We decorate; we snack. Win-win."

We start tying little loops and hanging them on the branches, and somewhere between the first candy cane and the sixth chocolate, the space around me... shrinks.

Kane steps in close behind me to reach a higher branch, his chest brushing my shoulder. One big hand settles on my waist, steadying me like he's worried I might topple over from the sheer weight of existing.

"Easy there," he murmurs, breath warm against my ear. "Can't have you face-planting into the tree. Bad for the ornaments."

"I am perfectly stable," I say, even as my pulse kicks up. "You're the one crowding."

His thumb strokes once across the curve of my hip before he lets go.

Noel moves in on my other side with a string of tinsel. He ducks under my arm, his shoulder sliding along mine as he reaches past. Knuckles skim down my spine by accident, leaving a trail of sparks in their wake.

"Hold this?" he asks, looping the strand into my hands without waiting for an answer.

I lift my arms, and he steps in behind me to adjust the angle, his chest pressing against my back, voice low by my ear. "Just like that. Don't move."

"As if I could," I mutter. My heart is pounding so loudly I'm terrified someone will comment on it.

A moment later, my hair slips forward over my shoulder. Chris is suddenly in front of me, close enough that I can see the darker ring around his irises.

"Hang on," he says softly.

His fingers slide into my hair, tucking the strand back behind my ear with unnecessary care. His knuckles brush my cheekbone, warm and rough, and instead of pulling away, he lets his hand linger along my jaw for a heartbeat. Maybe two.

"You're going to get sap all over it if you're not careful," he adds, his thumb grazing the corner of my mouth like he's checking for smudges.

"I am *very* careful," I say, a little too breathless. "You're all the ones behaving like unsupervised teenagers in a tinsel factory."

"All I'm hearing," Kane says from somewhere to my left, "is that you volunteered to supervise us."

I should feel boxed in. Three big men bracketing me, reaching around me, close enough that every breath brings a different mix of cedar, cold air, and something purely them. Instead, I find myself leaning in. Testing it. When I step to the side, I accidentally bump into Noel's chest. His hand slides to my hip instantly, steady and sure. When I reach for a higher branch, Kane is suddenly there, palm flat against the small of my back, holding me like I'm something precious and breakable. Chris passes me another candy cane, our fingers tangling for a second longer than necessary.

My brain keeps whispering, *Too much, too close, too fast.*

My body keeps whispering, *More.*

"Hand me that star?" Noel asks eventually, nodding toward the wooden star, dark-stained and smooth, like someone loved it enough to wear the edges down over time.

I pass it to him, and he heads for the ladder they've set up beside the tree. He climbs, the muscles in his thighs flexing under worn denim, jacket stretching over his back with every step. I try—*really* try—not to stare.

I fail immediately.

He reaches the top, bracing one hand on the ceiling while squeezing it up there. The movement pulls his shirt tight over his stomach, and I swear I see God for a second. He is bulging...

When he climbs back down, I drag my gaze up way too late. He catches it; of course he does. That slow, knowing grin spreads across his face.

"See something you like, sweetheart?" he drawls.

Caught.

"Maybe. Possibly," I say, lifting my chin. "I'm not admitting anything without a lawyer present."

Kane barks out a laugh. "Your face is admitting plenty."

"It's fine," Noel says, unbothered. "Equal opportunity. She can objectify all of us. I vote in favor."

Chris returns with more tinsel. "Focus," he says mildly, though there's amusement tugging at his mouth. "Horny later. Sparkly now."

Kane produces a red fabric tree skirt from a closet, thick and soft, and we crouch together to spread it around the base, shoulders bumping, knees brushing. Every small touch feels intentional now. Every glance lingers a second too long.

Finally, we step back in a line, shoulder to shoulder, facing the tree.

Outside, the world beyond the glass is falling snow growing heavier. Inside, it's just us and the soft glow of lamps and the sharp scent of pine.

"Oh, wow," I breathe. "That's… that's absolutely spectacular."

"Moment of truth," Noel says, moving to the wall.

He flips a switch.

The tree explodes into light. White bulbs wink to life between branches, catching on tinsel, bouncing off glass ornaments and foil-wrapped chocolates. The wooden star glows softly at the top, haloed by tiny points of light.

It's… perfect. Warm and wild and a bit over the top. *Theirs.* And somehow, looking at it, it feels a little like *mine* too.

We drift toward the couches without anyone having to say it. Kane and Chris take the bigger sofa, spreading out like they own it. Noel and I drop onto the smaller one. Before I can overthink it, his arm slides around my shoulders, firm and easy, pulling me in against his side as though I belong there.

The worst part? I do. My body just slots in, my head finding the space beneath his jaw as if it's done this a hundred times.

Across the room, Kane sprawls back, his ankle hooked over one knee, gaze flicking from the tree to me and back again, like he's not sure which he likes looking at more. Chris leans forward, forearms on his thighs, eyes on the lights but attention clearly not *on* the lights, if the way it keeps drifting to me is any indication.

"I feel like this might be our best Christmas yet," Chris says eventually. "Like we're finally… I don't know. Complete." His gaze lifts to mine and holds. "Like a real family."

Something in my chest squeezes. Hard. It feels like an invitation.

I don't say anything because I don't trust my voice not to crack, but part of me desperately wants it to be real. Wants to believe I deserve this happiness, this warmth, these men who look at me like I'm something precious.

Chris heads into the kitchen and returns with bowls of the baked apples that are soft and caramelized, swimming in custard that's rich and vanilla scented and still warm. He hands them out, and we eat in comfortable silence, just the crackling of the fire Kane started and the soft Christmas music still playing.

The apples are incredible. "I absolutely love this," I say finally, setting my empty bowl on the coffee table. "I'm not sure how I got so lucky to experience this. To be here with you three."

"It's simple," Noel says, his deep voice rumbling through his chest where I'm leaning against him. "You're ours. We're yours. You just need to accept that truth as we slowly convince you."

"We're patient when it matters," Chris adds, his grin softer than usual.

I glance around at these three dangerous Alphas who hunt criminals for a living, who could probably break someone in half without trying, who've somehow made space for me in their lives, their home, their pack.

It's too good. Too perfect. Too much like every fantasy I've had but never believed could be real.

And in my experience, when something seems too good to be true, it usually is. Something always goes wrong. Someone always leaves. Happiness like this doesn't last.

But sitting here, full of apples and warmth and belonging, surrounded by the smell of cinnamon and pine and them, watching the tree lights twinkle while it snows outside and the fire crackles, maybe I can let myself hope.

Just for today.

CHAPTER THIRTEEN

CHRIS

*H*annah has been holed up in that room for the last hour, planning the town celebrations for her event, and I'm down here trying to give her space when every instinct I have is screaming at me to go check on her.

This is fucking torture.

Kane and Noel are out running errands, picking up supplies, checking in with a contact about an upcoming target. We agreed one of us would always be around her, especially after what happened the other night when she climbed into Kane's bed thinking it was Noel's. Her pre-heat is making her needy. The memory makes me grin despite the ache in my cock. Wish it had been my bed she'd stumbled into, my cock she'd ridden until she screamed.

But knowing she came apart on Kane while moaning Noel's name? That's its own brand of torture and the hottest thing I've ever heard about.

Since I kissed her as Santa, she has fucking haunted me. Can't sleep properly or focus on anything but the phantom taste of her mouth, the way she pressed against me, soft and warm and perfect.

Last night I barely slept. Just lay there staring at my ceiling, fighting the urge to walk down the hall and stop by her room. See if she was awake. See if she needed anything.

Ask if she'd let me touch her the way I've been fantasizing about since the moment I scented her.

It's not much better this morning.

So I'm making breakfast. Pancakes from scratch because the boxed shit is an insult to food. The first batch is already plated and waiting on the dining table. Now I'm chopping strawberries and bananas into perfect slices. Whipping cream with the mixer is done and in a bowl because I want this to be perfect for her.

The whole house smells like vanilla and butter and maple syrup, and if this doesn't coax her downstairs, nothing will.

I'm working on the second batch, watching bubbles form on the surface before flipping, when I hear her burst out laughing from the living room.

"Corn Dog! Should you be in here?"

Fuck, no! That goddamn reindeer got inside again?

I drop the spatula and sprint out of the kitchen, rounding the corner to find a complete disaster.

Corn Dog is up on his hind legs, front hooves braced against our Christmas tree, stretching his neck to try to catch a walnut ornament with his mouth. The nut keeps swinging away from him, and he's making these frustrated huffing sounds that would be funny if I weren't so annoyed.

Around the base of the tree, candy cane wrappers lie torn, open, and scattered everywhere, baubles knocked off branches and rolling across the floor, walnuts that have fallen and been partially chewed.

On the dining table, one corner of the tablecloth is bunched up where he clearly tried to climb up, and there's half a pancake on the floor with teeth marks, the rest sitting on the table looking violated.

"Corn Dog!" I bark, noticing the front door now swinging open. Did I forget to latch it?

The reindeer pauses, peers at me over his shoulder with those big brown eyes like he's saying *Oh, you said something?*, and then immediately goes back to trying to catch the walnut.

I shake my head, already moving to shut the door properly, when I spot Hannah stepping down the final step from upstairs.

And fuck me, she's gorgeous.

She's wearing jeans, these soft-looking denim ones that sit perfectly on her hips, not tight but draping over her curves in a way that makes my imagination run wild. Her shirt is a long-sleeved thermal in a deep burgundy that skims her body, loose enough to be comfortable but clinging in places that make my hands itch. The neckline dips just low enough to show her collarbones, and the way the fabric moves when she breathes is mesmerizing.

My gaze drops to her breasts. I can't help it, not even going to pretend I'm trying, and the way they press against the fabric with each breath has me captive.

"Morning," I manage, forcing my eyes up to her face, where she's fighting a smile. Then I march toward Corn Dog again and swing an arm under his belly, wrenching him off the floor and tucking him under my arm like a very large, very indignant football.

He makes outraged reindeer noises, bleating and grunting, and starts thrashing his legs.

The bastard isn't light. He's got to be a hundred pounds of muscle and attitude, and I need my second arm to keep him from squirming free as I haul him toward the back door.

"Yeah, yeah, express your feelings," I mutter as he tries to headbutt me. "You're still in trouble."

I manage to get the door open one-handed and carry him out to the pen, which is swinging wide because this escape artist has figured out how to work the latch.

"Get in there, troublemaker." I release him, and he immediately rushes toward the snowman we built this morning when we fed him. And proceeds to absolutely demolish it.

He's headbutting it, stomping on it with his front hooves, destroying our work with obvious glee. Snow explodes everywhere.

"You have serious aggression problems," I tell him, pulling out the padlock from the side gate we bought specifically for this purpose. "You know that? Might want to talk to a professional about all that pent-up rage."

Corn Dog knocks the snowman's head clean off, sending it rolling.

The other reindeer are just standing there watching him like they can't believe they're related to this maniac.

I secure the lock, testing it twice. "Try getting out now, Houdini."

He's too busy stomping on snow chunks to care about my threats.

When I head back inside, Hannah has already cleaned up the mess around the tree and the table—wrappers in the trash, ornaments rehung, tablecloth straightened, and munched-on food removed.

She's sitting at the table now, eyeing the pancakes that survived Corn Dog's rampage.

"This smells divine," she says, gesturing toward the kitchen, where I still smell the second batch cooking. "Clearly worked too well—got me downstairs and broke Corn Dog into the house."

I laugh, heading back to the kitchen to finish the fresh batch. "He's got a nose for good food. Can't blame him for having taste," I call out.

I plate the new pancakes, golden and perfect, still steaming, and grab fresh plates since Corn Dog contaminated the others. Load up a tray with the pancakes, the bowl of whipped cream I made, fresh fruit arranged in a separate bowl, maple syrup squeeze bottle, and clean forks and knives.

When I bring it all out and set it on the table, her eyes light up like I'm presenting her with treasure.

"You made all this?" She sounds genuinely amazed.

"Someone had to learn their way around a kitchen." I sit next to her—close enough that our knees brush under the table—and start serving her. "Can't hunt criminals on empty stomachs."

Her scent curls around me as she leans forward, and it's fucking intoxicating. My mouth waters for her.

I stack three pancakes on her plate, top them with sliced strawberries and bananas, and add a dollop of whipped cream that I know is perfect because I made it myself.

She takes a bite, and the sound she makes is low in her throat, her eyes closing, and it goes straight to my cock.

"These are incredible," she says, already going for another bite. "Like, legitimately the best pancakes I've ever had. Where did you learn to cook like this?"

"Taught myself. Got tired of eating microwaved food." I'm watching the way her tongue darts out to catch a drop of syrup on her bottom lip, and my jeans are getting uncomfortable.

I rip off a piece of pancake with my fingers, dip it in syrup, and hold it up to her mouth. "Open."

She hesitates for half a second, then parts her lips.

I feed her slowly, watching her mouth close around my fingers, and when her tongue slides along my skin to catch the syrup, my control nearly shatters.

"Again," I say, my voice coming out rough. This time

when I feed her, she licks my fingers deliberately, slowly, thoroughly, maintaining eye contact, and I'm barely holding it together.

My cock is so hard it's painful, straining against my jeans, and all I think about is those lips wrapped around something else entirely. She's going to destroy me. Absolutely fucking wreck me, and I'm going to let her.

I feed her another bite, and when she swallows quickly, she licks my fingers again—taking her time, her tongue warm and soft—and I break.

I lean in and lick her lips, tasting maple syrup and her.

Then we're kissing. Her mouth opens under mine immediately, her tongue meeting mine, and she tastes like everything I've been craving. Sweet and warm and perfect. I angle my head to deepen the kiss, my hand coming up to cup the back of her neck, fingers threading through her hair.

She half gasps, half moans.

I immediately draw her onto my lap without breaking our kiss, and she straddles me easily, her thighs bracketing mine, and starts rocking against me. The friction is incredible, torture and pleasure all at once, and I grip her hips to guide her movements.

Fuck, she's perfect like this. Small in my arms but strong, soft yet with muscle underneath, and so fucking sexy I can't think straight. Her weight is just right, her body fitting against mine like we were designed for this.

I reach up and squeeze her breasts through her shirt, loving how she fills my hands, how she moans against my mouth when I find her nipples through the fabric and roll them between my fingers.

"You taste so sweet," I growl against her lips. "But I need more of you."

She tries to respond but purrs instead, an actual Omega purr that vibrates through her chest, and her eyes go wide. "Oh, that's new," she breathes, sounding shocked.

I chuckle, dark and pleased, my hands sliding up under her shirt to touch bare skin. "That's your body reacting to mine. Calling to me. Telling me exactly what you need."

"Is that so?" She's teasing now, rolling her hips deliberately, grinding against my erection.

"Absolutely."

We're kissing again, harder this time, more desperate. I'm drowning in her scent that's heavy with arousal. She's growing wet, I know it, and the knowledge turns me feral. In one motion, I sweep everything on the table aside—plates clattering together, silverware scattering —and lift her onto the surface.

She gasps, laughing breathlessly, but then we're kissing again, and there's nothing funny about it anymore.

Her scent is everywhere now, fogging my thoughts, reducing me to base instincts. This is what it's supposed to be like with scent matches—overwhelming, consuming, impossible to resist.

I break the kiss, breathing hard, my forehead pressed to hers. "I'm going to taste you now. Every inch.

Make you come on my tongue until you forget how to speak."

My hands are already at her jeans, fingers working the button open.

She bites her lip, but she's smiling, giving me permission without words, and lifts her hips. I take my time sliding the denim down her legs, letting my hands drag along her thighs, learning the shape of her. Her panties are simple cotton, dark purple, and already damp at the center.

Fuck yes.

I hook my fingers in the waistband and pull them down too, slowly and deliberately, watching her face the whole time.

She kicks them off completely, leaving her in just that burgundy shirt and socks. The image is going to be burned into my brain forever.

Her thighs are soft, unmarked, and when I spread them wider, I see she's completely bare, smooth and absolutely perfect.

"Lie back," I instruct. "Time for me to really feast."

She leans back on her elbows, legs dangling off the edge of the table, and giggles softly, nervous but excited.

I lift her legs and place them over my shoulders, then I just stare at her offering for a long moment. Her lips are pink and swollen, already slick with arousal.

So I grab the squeeze bottle of maple syrup from where it rolled, and her eyes go wide when she realizes what I'm planning.

"Chris..."

I squeeze, and the syrup drips between her legs in a slow stream. She laughs out loud and squirms. It slides over her outer lips, pools between them.

"It's cold!"

I use my fingers to pry her open and squeeze more syrup directly onto her, coating her inner lips, letting it drip over her. Then I lean in and lick.

One long stroke from bottom to top, and I moan at the taste. "Fuck," I growl against her. "Perfect fucking combination." Then I go wild on her.

Licking and sucking, devouring her like she's the best meal I've ever had, because she is. The maple syrup mixed with her natural taste is addictive, sweet and earthy and uniquely her, and I can't get enough.

She's squirming and gasping, her hips jerking every time my tongue hits her clit, and the sounds she's making are better than any music.

I slide my hands under her ass, lifting her slightly off the table for better access, and work her with every-thing I have. My tongue circles her clit, flicks over it, then I'm sucking it into my mouth while my fingers dig into the soft flesh of her ass.

Her gasps turn to moans, then into cries, and her thighs start trembling against my shoulders.

"Chris," she gasps, one hand fisting in my hair. "Chris, I'm—"

She doesn't finish because she's coming, screaming so loud I'm glad we don't have close neighbors. She releases her hold of me and is completely on her back, shuddering.

Her whole body arches off the table, thighs clamping around my head, and I don't let up. I keep licking, keep sucking her clit, drawing out her orgasm until she's thrashing and begging incoherently.

Wave after wave crashes through her, and I wish I were inside her right now, fucking her.

When she finally goes limp, collapsed on the table and panting, I release her clit and glance up, licking my lips slowly.

She's completely undone, hair messy and spread across the table, shirt rucked up, showing her stomach, chest heaving, eyes glazed and unfocused.

"Fuck, I love seeing you like this," I murmur. "Could look at you wrecked and satisfied all damn day and never get bored."

She tries to sit up, her movements uncoordinated and shaky. "That was… something else. But now I'm all sticky."

I grin, standing and helping steady her. "Oh, you definitely are. Stay right there." So I head to the bathroom, grabbing a clean towel and running it under warm water. I grab a dry one too and bring them both back.

She's watching me with a grin as I gently wipe between her legs and her inner thighs, cleaning away the syrup and her arousal, then dry her carefully with the second towel.

"You often clean up after yourself?" She sounds amazed.

"Every Alpha should treat his Omega like a queen.

That's basic fucking respect." I hand her the jeans and panties she kicked off earlier. "Any man who doesn't take care of you after isn't worth your time."

"Chris, you keep making me blush." She's covering her face with her hands. "I'm going to be permanently red around you three."

"Good. Love seeing you flustered."

She dresses quickly, fingers fumbling slightly with the button of her jeans. When she's done, she stares at me, and I see the question forming behind her eyes. Before she asks it, I pull her into my arms, holding her close.

"You have no idea how lucky we are to have you here," I whisper against her hair, breathing in her scent. "Resisting rutting you, knotting you, claiming you completely, it's close to impossible. But we're going to try until you're ready for all of us. Deal?"

"Sounds fair," she whispers, her arms coming around my waist.

I pull back to study her, and her cheeks are pink. I'm so fucking gone for this woman that it's not even funny.

She wriggles out of my embrace, smoothing down her shirt. "Okay, then, let's clean up this mess." She starts gathering scattered silverware while I pick up the plates. She carries them to the kitchen, and I follow with the rest, planning to wash the tablecloth too.

She grabs juice from the fridge, pouring herself a glass while I load the dishwasher.

"So I have a job tomorrow night," she says, leaning against the counter. "I need to check today that it's all ready to go. Should be straightforward and nothing Scot can sabotage since it's already booked and confirmed. Fingers crossed it stays that way."

"Tomorrow night?" I glance at her while rinsing a plate. "We've got targets to track down tomorrow. Maybe two of us handle that and one comes with you?"

"What? No." She waves me off. "I have a friend helping out. I booked her venue for the event, and she has her Alphas around if anything goes wrong. Plus, I have my Honda to take me into town."

I grin, shutting off the water. "That Honda is getting pretty old. Might be time for an upgrade."

"It runs perfectly fine, thank you very much." She's feigning offense, pointing her juice glass at me. "Not all of us have mansions and fancy trucks."

"Yet," I say. "Give it time, gorgeous."

She rolls her eyes, but she's smiling, and I'm licking my lips, still tasting maple syrup and her sweet pussy. Best fucking morning I've had in years.

CHAPTER FOURTEEN

HANNAH

I'm standing inside the Winterscape Bar, pressed against the exposed brick wall where the lighting is dim enough that no one in the bachelorette party crowd notices me, and I'm buzzing with excitement.

Tonight is going to be perfect.

The venue looks incredible. Ruby really came through for me, transforming her industrial-chic bar into something special. The usual tables and chairs have been cleared away, replaced by rows of seating facing a makeshift stage connected to a room we're using as a backstage. String lights crisscross the exposed-beam ceiling, casting warm amber glows that compete with the rotating colored spotlights she installed just for tonight. Silver and pink balloons cluster in corners, tied with matching ribbons. There's a glittery banner across the back wall that reads SARAH'S LAST NIGHT OF FREEDOM in huge letters, and smaller decorations of champagne bottles and wedding rings scattered throughout.

The bar itself is closed during this event. The brick walls are decorated with more balloons and streamers, and there are high-top tables scattered around the perimeter for women who want drinks but still want to see the stage.

I owe Ruby big-time for this. She let me hire out her entire venue, and she gave me a fair price while helping set up everything.

Fifty women are packed into the rows of chairs facing the stage, already rowdy and excited. Bachelorette sashes, tiaras, and veils are scattered throughout the crowd. They're drinking, laughing, the energy already high before the show even begins.

This is exactly what I wanted. What I planned for.

The music starts, a strong beat pumping through the speakers that Ruby's team positioned on either side of the stage. The lights dim except for the spotlights focusing on the stage.

Three male dancers emerge from the back, and the crowd erupts in cheers.

They're dressed as construction workers, complete with plastic hard hats, reflective vests, and tool belts. The lead dancer takes center stage while the other two flank him from behind, holding fake stop signs.

I watch as they start moving to the music.

The lead guy is gyrating his hips, turning, flexing. His movements are fine. Serviceable. He's hitting the beats, doing the basic moves you'd expect, but it's not anything incredible.

Ruby sidles up next to me, and I'm grateful for the company.

She's stunning as always, about my height at five-four, but built curvier. Her reddish-blonde hair frames her face, and she's wearing leather pants with a chunky cream sweater that hangs off one shoulder, and combat boots.

"They're okay," Ruby says, watching the dancers.

"Yeah," I agree, but I'm studying them more critically now.

The lead dancer spins, and it's a bit clumsy. Not terrible, but not smooth either. His movements are mechanical, like he's going through motions he's memorized rather than feeling the music.

"Actually," Ruby leans closer, lowering her voice. "Is it me, or are they lacking something?"

I've been thinking the same thing. "It's not just you. They're fine, but they're not great, you know? Like they know the moves but they're not really selling it."

"Right?" Ruby is fidgeting with her snowflake pendant. "And they're not exactly hugely built either. I mean, they're fit, but I've seen strippers before. These guys are just sort of average."

She's right. The dancers are in decent shape, but they're not the chiseled specimens their website photos promised. More like guys who go to the gym occasionally rather than live there.

"Maybe I'm being too critical," I whisper. "The crowd seems into it."

We watch as the dancers strip off their reflective vests with no buildup or tease. Just pull them off and toss them aside.

"Eh, the women are drunk and happy," Ruby says diplomatically. "But yeah, these guys aren't exactly setting the stage on fire."

"I'm paying them a lot," I admit quietly. "Like, a lot. They came highly recommended. Their website had all these professional photos and glowing reviews."

"Well, they might have oversold themselves a bit." Ruby grimaces sympathetically. "But hey, the bride seems happy."

I search the front row for Sarah, the bride-to-be. She's wearing a white veil with pink netting and a sash that says *Bride* in rhinestones, and she's laughing and clapping along with her friends.

Okay. Maybe it's fine. Maybe I'm overthinking this because I want everything to be perfect.

The dancers finish their number to decent applause, and they exit backstage. The music keeps playing between sets, and women are chatting, getting refills at the bar.

"They're fine," I tell Ruby, trying to convince myself. "Not amazing, but fine."

"Sure," Ruby agrees, but she doesn't sound convinced either.

The second song starts, and the dancers emerge in different costumes now. Old-school prisoner outfits with black-and-white horizontal stripes, fake ball-and-chain accessories.

This should be better, right? Fresh energy, new look.

They're shuffling around the stage, doing the same basic moves as before. One of them is stripping off his striped shirt.

"Okay, these guys definitely oversold themselves," Ruby mutters.

"Yeah." My stomach is sinking slightly. Not a disaster, but definitely not the high-energy, professional show I was promised. "I'm definitely asking for some money back after this."

Heavy boots thunder across the stage from the back entrance, and I stare at the side of the stage, wondering what's going on.

Three massive figures burst onto the stage, dressed head to toe in black tactical gear. They move fast, coordinated, charging straight for the dancers with purpose.

The music is still blaring, and for a few seconds, no one processes what's happening. I am clueless.

The dancers freeze, confusion crossing their faces.

Then one of the figures grabs the lead dancer, spinning him around and wrenching his arms behind his back.

The dancer yelps, trying to twist away. "What the fuck? Get off me!"

The second and third figures move on the other two dancers simultaneously. One dancer tries to run, but he's tackled from behind, hitting the stage floor hard.

The third dancer swings wildly, trying to fight back, but he's outmatched.

My heart stops as the stage lights illuminate their faces.

Noel. Chris. Kane.

Oh my God.

Noel has the lead dancer in a submission hold, zip-tying his wrists together while reciting something to him. The dancer is struggling, kicking, trying to break free.

Chris has the runner pinned facedown on the stage, one knee in his back, while he secures the zip ties. Kane is grappling with the one who tried to fight, and the dancer is not going quietly. He's throwing elbows, trying to headbutt Kane, but Kane's too strong. He gets the guy's arms behind his back and clicks the zip tie into place.

The crowd is dead silent, staring.

Then someone in the third row starts clapping.

Others join in.

Suddenly, the entire venue erupts in wild cheering and applause, women jumping to their feet.

"Take it off! Take it off! Take it off!" they start chanting, clearly thinking this is part of the show.

I'm rooted in place, dread pooling in my stomach like ice water. This is not part of the show. "Oh, fuck," I breathe.

Ruby turns to me, eyes wide. "Is this the act? Because holy shit, those three are gorgeous. Where did you find them? I would watch them strip any day of the week."

"No," I manage. "I need to deal with this. Can you stall the audience?"

"For sure."

I'm already moving, pushing through the side door that leads backstage.

The room is cramped with the six men now crowding it. My three Alphas are hauling the still-struggling dancers toward the rear exit that leads to the alley.

"You can't just arrest us! We have rights!" one of the dancers growls.

"You lost those rights when you skipped your court date," Chris says calmly, grip firm on his guy's arm.

"This is bullshit!" the lead dancer spits. "Let us go and we'll finish the show. We won't even charge the lady. Just let us go!"

"Not happening," Noel says.

"Hey!" I shout, and all of them turn.

Kane does a double take, his hazel eyes going wide. "Hannah? What are you doing here?"

"This is my event!" I'm trying not to yell, but it's close. "What are you doing here?"

"Your event! Oh, shit!" Chris's eyebrows rise. "You didn't mention it was a bachelorette party with strippers."

"Horrible timing," Noel adds, but his voice is matter of fact, like this is just mildly inconvenient. "But these guys are our targets for the night."

The dancers are still struggling against the zip ties, grumbling. "We did nothing wrong!" one shouts.

"Yeah, we're innocent!" another adds.

"Shut up," I snap at them, and they actually go quiet. My head is spinning. This is my event, my paid entertainers. And my Alphas just arrested them in front of fifty drunk women who think it's performance art.

"This will ruin everything," I say, starting to pace because I need to move or I'll scream. "Why does this crazy stuff keep happening to me?"

"We can't release them," Chris mentions gently, and his moss-green eyes are sympathetic. "You know that, gorgeous. They're wanted criminals. We have a legal obligation to bring them in."

"Yeah, how do I keep hiring wanted men?" I throw my hands up. "What are the actual odds? This is just my spectacular luck."

The dancers are struggling. "Please," one of them whines. "This is all a misunderstanding."

"Do I need to gag you?" Kane grunts. "Because I will."

They shut up.

I'm staring at my three Alphas now, really studying them in their tactical gear. Black cargo pants, fitted black shirts that showcase every muscle, boots, utility belts. They're huge, intimidating, exactly what you'd picture dangerous bounty hunters to look like.

The crowd went absolutely wild when they appeared onstage. And an insane idea forms in my head.

"Maybe you guys can take their spots," I say.

Silence.

Then all three start laughing like I've told the funniest joke they've ever heard.

"I'm serious!" I move closer, craning my neck to meet their eyes. "You take my entertainment, you need to step in and replace it. That's only fair."

"Oh, we only strip for you," Noel says, but he's grinning.

"Look, I know this is insane." I'm pleading now, and I don't care. "But I'm completely stuck here. I need your help. My reputation is on the line, as is my business—everything I'm trying to build with this event-planning career. So if I don't deliver entertainment, my client will be furious, word will spread, and I'll be done before I even start."

Chris studies me for a long moment. Then he sighs. "Okay, it's doable. I'll take these assholes to lockup and process them. You two take one for the team, just like I did with Santa." He's pointing at Noel and Kane.

"What? No!" Kane's eyes enlarge, something close to panic flashing across his face. "Absolutely not. No way."

"Hell no," Noel adds, shaking his head. "I'm not a stripper, Chris. I hunt criminals, not dance for drunk women."

"Come on," Chris says, already hauling one of the dancers toward the exit. "For Hannah. She needs this."

"I don't dance," Kane protests. "I can't dance. I'll look like an idiot up there."

"You won't," I promise. "You just have to move to the music. Be sexy. The women will eat it up."

"Be sexy," Kane repeats flatly. "That's your professional advice?"

"Yes," I say firmly.

Noel and Kane are looking at each other, having some kind of silent conversation.

"You'd be helping her out," Chris says slowly.

"We'd be making fools of ourselves," Kane counters.

"She needs us," Noel adds, surprising me with his changing tune.

"She's asking us to strip," Kane states.

"In front of fifty women," Noel says. "Who are very drunk and will probably throw things."

"Guys," I interrupt their back-and-forth. "Please. I'm begging you. I'll owe you anything. Name it. Whatever you want."

Kane's eyes darken at that. "Anything?"

"Within reason," I amend quickly.

Noel is grinning now. "Fine. But you owe us big-time."

"Thank you!" I could kiss them both. Actually, I want to kiss all three, but there's no time.

Chris is wrestling the three dancers toward the door. "Come help me get these assholes into the truck first. Then you two can play stripper."

"Fuck off," one of the dancers spits.

"Keep talking," Chris says pleasantly. "I love it when they resist. Makes the paperwork more fun."

Noel and Kane move to help, each grabbing a criminal. The six of them disappear out the back door into the alley, where I assume their truck is parked.

Ruby pops her head around the corner. "Safe to enter? What's happening? Everyone's getting antsy out there."

"Small change of plans," I say quickly as she joins me. "We have bounty hunter strippers now."

Ruby's eyes light up. "Those three massive guys who just tackled your dancers? They're stripping?"

"Two of them. The third is taking the criminals in to process."

"Holy shit." Ruby is laughing now, her whole face lighting up. "Who are they? Like, professionally? Friends of yours?"

"Actually…" I bite my lip. "They're my scent matches. All three of them. We're still figuring things out. It's new and complicated, but yeah. Those initial strippers? They were actual wanted criminals. So that was a real arrest you just witnessed."

Ruby gasps. "Are you serious? That was real?"

"Completely. That's been my life lately. Just absolute chaos."

"That's insane!" But she's grinning. "Your scent matches are bounty hunters who just arrested your strippers, and now they're going to strip instead?"

"Yep. That's exactly what's happening."

"Best bachelorette party ever," Ruby declares.

The back door opens, and Noel and Kane return, both looking slightly winded.

"Criminals secured," Noel announces. "Chris is driving them to lockup. He says to stall as long as possible because he wants to get back in time to see this."

Kane is already loosening up, rolling his shoulders.

"Fuck, which boxers am I wearing today?" He checks his waistband, then chuckles. "Oh, these'll work."

"Same," Noel says, grinning as he checks his own. He glances my way. "Not telling you, though. You'll have to wait and see."

"Okay, so here's the plan," I say, forcing my brain into event coordinator mode. "You're going in as bounty hunters who just caught the bad guys. Keep the tactical look for now, strip down to your boxers. Do some moves, hip thrusts, run your hands over your chests, flirt with the audience. Make them feel special."

Both men are staring at me.

"That's it?" Kane asks. "Just thrust and flex?"

"Basically, yeah, but also dance. The women will go wild. Trust me."

Noel is already warming up, doing practice hip rolls that are surprisingly fluid. "I'm going to rock this for you."

Kane turns pale. "My body isn't made for this. Give me a tree to chop to music, and I'll do it. This? Not my specialty."

"You'll be fine," I assure him. "Just follow Noel's lead, as he looks ready."

"I have an idea for a joint routine," Noel explains.

Kane groans. "Please tell me it's not *Dirty Dancing*. I'm not lifting you above my head."

Noel chuckles. "Nope, but the other night, I watched *Magic Mike*."

"Of course you did," Kane mutters.

"We're going to grind that floor," Noel continues. "Watch the women go wild for us. It'll be fun."

Ruby and I exchange glances. "This could flop spectacularly," I whisper to her.

"Or it could be legendary," Ruby counters. "Either way, it's going to be entertaining."

"I need a drink," Kane says.

"After," I tell him firmly. "You two practice. I'm going to calm the crowd and introduce you."

I head back out front with Ruby, my heart pounding. The women are getting restless, some standing and stretching, others at the bar getting refills. The energy is flagging. I encourage everyone to get their last drinks as the next act is about to start, so they all rush to the bar, buying us some time.

Once they're all back in their seats, Ruby's DJ, who also runs the lights, dims them, and I grab the microphone from where it's resting on a small table near the DJ booth set up in the corner, away from the stage.

The DJ looks at me, and I go over to him and ask for something high-beat but sexy. He ponders it, and finally he nods. So with a deep breath, I step up onto the stage and lift the microphone to my mouth.

"Ladies!" I call out, and gradually conversations die down. "Are you having a good time?"

Cheers and whistles.

"Those bad boys who crashed our stage? They're ready to take down their next targets. Could that be you?"

More cheers, and screams of "Me!"

"Well, they're ready to give you a performance you'll never forget!" I'm selling this hard, hoping I'm not over-selling. "Just remember, no touching unless invited! Let's hear it for The Bounty Hunters!"

The crowd erupts. Women are on their feet.

I hand the microphone back to Ruby, and we retreat to our spot by the brick wall.

"I have no idea what to expect," she whispers.

"Me either. But here goes nothing."

The DJ kills all the lights except for two blue spot-lights that suddenly illuminate the back of the stage.

Noel and Kane are standing there, perfectly still, and even from here, I see the tension in their bodies.

The music starts with a heavy bass beat that I don't just hear but also feel vibrate through my chest. It's layered with something sultry underneath, a rhythm that makes my hips want to move.

The guys remain still for several long seconds, and panic flutters in my chest. *Please don't freeze. Don't have stage fright.*

Then they move. In perfect synchronization, they take slow, deliberate strides forward. Their boots hit the stage in pattern with the beat, and the sound echoes through the venue.

The women scream.

I smile, butterflies erupting in my stomach.

Noel reaches the front of the stage first, and he drops into a crouch so smoothly it looks choreo-graphed. His hands run slowly down his chest, over his abs, down his thighs. Every movement is deliberate, sensual.

Kane mirrors him on the other side, and they're feeding off each other's energy.

They rise together, circling each other like predators, and then Noel drops to the floor in a perfect push-up position. He does a slow, grinding thrust that has me burning up, his muscles taut behind his clothes.

The crowd loses their minds.

Kane follows suit, their bodies moving in waves.

They roll onto their backs, then flip over again with this fluid grace I didn't know they possessed, and spring to their feet.

"Holy shit," I breathe. "When did they practice that?"

Ruby is fanning herself with her hand. "They're incredible. My Alphas need to take lessons for my private sessions. This is professional-level."

We're both transfixed.

They start peeling off their tactical vests now, slowly, teasingly. They turn their backs to the audience and look over their shoulders with a wink before pulling their vests off and tossing them toward the back of the stage, where they land with a loud clunking noise.

The long-sleeved compression shirts come next. Noel grabs the hem and pulls it over his head in one smooth motion, and the reveal of his body makes me forget how to breathe.

Muscles everywhere. His chest is sculpted, abs defined in perfect ridges, shoulders broad and powerful.

The stage lights make his skin glow, highlighting every line and curve.

Kane's shirt comes off next, and I'm drooling. Maybe even more so with how his muscles ripple as he moves.

Women are throwing things onto the stage now—money, definitely, but I also see what looks like a bra land near Kane's feet.

Noel turns and does this slow ass-wiggle thing that should be ridiculous but somehow isn't. Kane drops low, grinding against the floor, showcasing the strength in his arms and chest as he rolls back up.

They're moving around each other, doing body rolls that highlight every muscle. Noel's rhythm is perfect, hitting every beat. Kane's style is different, more power-based, but it works.

They toe off their boots, kicking them to the back of the stage, and they're barefoot now in those low-hanging tactical pants.

Noel does something I've only seen in videos—the worm move, where his entire body undulates in waves across the stage floor. It's mesmerizing, and the way his muscles contract and release is hypnotic.

Kane drops into a one-armed push-up position and lowers himself slowly, his bicep flexing, then pushes back up and spins on his back.

My pulse is racing everywhere, but especially between my thighs.

The music builds to a thundering crescendo, bass vibrating through the floor, and they spin around in unison to face away from the crowd.

Hands go to zippers.

The entire auditorium holds its breath.

They shove their tactical pants down at the same time, bending at the waist to step out of them and unknowingly giving the audience a front-row view of two very unfair asses. The crowd *detonates*.

Women are on their feet, shrieking, drinks sloshing. The chant starts up again, louder, wilder. "More! More! Take it all off!"

They kick the pants away and turn around in their boxer briefs. Tight. Clinging. Completely, devastatingly unhelpful.

Kane's are bright green with tiny gingerbread men printed all over them—and every single cookie is frowning with its little iced arms crossed and the words *Bite Me* stamped across the waistband.

Noel's are deep red, covered in cartoon snowmen wearing sunglasses and Santa hats. Across the front, in glittery gold script, it says *Jingle All The Way*.

I slap a hand over my mouth, a laugh bursting out of me anyway. Oh, they are never living this down.

The audience, however, eats it up like it's the best thing they've seen all year, cheering.

"Bite that cookie, baby!" someone screams from the front row, pointing at Kane's briefs.

"I wanna jingle your bells!" another woman yells at Noel, and her friends absolutely lose it.

"Get on the naughty list!"

"Gingerbread, over here!"

"Jingle-boy, turn around again!"

It's ridiculous and festive and somehow makes them ten times hotter.

They're big men, broad, solid, and those stupid novelty briefs do nothing to hide it. The fabric is stretched just enough that a few women in the front start fanning themselves, one of them nearly dropping her drink when she leans too far forward.

Someone in the middle section actually swoons and sits down, her friends clutching her shoulders while laughing so hard they're crying.

"Oh my God!" a voice screeches from somewhere behind me. "The *Bite Me* one is mine. I call dibs!"

Kane shoots a murderous look toward us, like he's already planning revenge on me for convincing him this was a good idea. Noel just tips his head back and laughs, running a hand over the glittering slogan on his waistband like he's fully prepared to lean into the bit.

And the crowd is ready to worship at the altar of terrible Christmas underwear.

The front rows explode in shrieks.

The woman Noel has been crawling toward almost falls off her chair laughing and screaming at the same time. I can't stop laughing. He winks at her, blows a kiss, and she screams like her soul left her body.

Kane is still playing coy, shoulders hunched, one hand covering the writing on his waistband like he's trying to be modest and failing spectacularly. He peeks out between the fingers of his other hand, and the crowd goes mad, shouting that he's perfect, that he's beautiful, that he should never wear pants again. When he finally drops his hands and flashes a giant grin, the noise hits a new level.

They're working opposite ends of the stage now, making sure no one feels left out. Noel is all swagger and precision, milking every beat for maximum effect. Kane is a weaponized mix of power and boyish charm.

The song builds toward the final chorus, and they gravitate back to the center, drawn together like magnets. They move perfectly and end up with Noel on one knee, flexed and smirking, Kane behind him with his arms crossed and his head tipped like a challenge.

The music cuts.

The venue erupts.

It's not just noise; it's a wall of sound. Women are screaming, laughing, howling their appreciation. Money starts flying like confetti, twenties and fifties fluttering onto the stage.

"They did good," Ruby murmurs.

"They might have missed their calling," I say.

Onstage, Noel and Kane straighten, then bow. Then they jog off toward the back, disappearing behind the curtain.

The crowd does not calm. If anything, they get worse. *Feral* is the only word for it. They're chanting for more, stomping their feet, demanding an encore.

"That was… I don't even have the words," Ruby says. "That was the hottest thing I've ever seen, and I'm mated."

"I need to check on them," I manage. My voice

comes out a little breathless, like I was the one up there grinding to the beat in novelty briefs.

She grins as I hurry toward the side of the stage.

As the door swings shut behind me, muffling the roar of the bar, the noise drops away. It's just the hum of backstage lights, the faint echo of the music still playing out front.

Both men are leaning against the wall, chests heaving, covered in a sheen of sweat that leaves their muscles glistening.

"Fuck me," I blurt out before my brain catches up to my mouth. "I might have just had an orgasm watching you both."

They stare at me with identical expressions of hunger.

Kane and Noel are both still in their Christmas briefs. There's a sheen of sweat along Noel's throat, a drop sliding down between his pecs, and I have to physically lock my knees to stop from swaying.

"Where did you learn those moves?" I ask, shamelessly staring. I can't help it. I'm drinking in every line of muscle, every bead of sweat, every flex and stretch. "Because I might need some private shows. Like, soon. Very soon."

Noel laughs, still catching his breath, hands braced on his thighs. "That was more exhausting than tracking down criminals," he says. "Who knew dancing could be such a workout?"

The way his stomach tightens when he laughs is so unfair.

"I didn't think I'd like it so much," Kane admits. He drags his forearm across his forehead, smearing sweat and leaving his hair even more of a chaotic mess. My gaze tracks the movement, the way the muscles in his arm tighten, the way a glistening trail runs from his chest down over his abs and disappears into that stupid green waistband. "But hearing them scream like that?" He huffs out a breath, still wired. "Kind of addictive."

He appears lit from the inside, eyes bright with left-over adrenaline. It does dangerous things to my heart rate.

"So what persona are you doing next?" I ask, trying very hard to focus on the logistics of the event and not on how badly I want to lick a line up his chest. "There are more costumes to select from behind you on the desk, as the guys left them here."

"Wait." Kane's eyes almost bulge out. "We're doing more than one performance? I gave everything I had. All my moves."

I blink. "Well, yeah. I don't have any other entertainment lined up. You two are it for the rest of the night. Maybe two or three more songs?"

Noel straightens, rolling his shoulders back like he's settling a mantle over them. "Okay, leave it to us," he says, already striding toward the pile of costumes the original dancers abandoned. "We've got this."

He passes close enough that the heat from his body brushes mine, and the scent of him punches straight through me. My fingers twitch with the urge to touch him, to see if he's as hot under my palm as he appears.

Kane moves in on my other side, slower, staying right in my space. He's close enough that the fine hairs on my arm stand up, that I can hear the rough drag of his breath. I try not to stare. I fail spectacularly.

There's a flush along his throat, color high in his cheeks. He appears wild. Untamed. Like if I told him I wanted him right now, he'd put his hands on me and forget there was a room, a bar, a world beyond us.

"You know," he murmurs, leaning down until his mouth is right at my ear. His breath is hot against my skin, and my stomach drops like I've missed a step. "If you want your own personal dance, we have conditions."

The way he says *we* sends a bolt of heat straight through me. I giggle. "Oh yeah? Like what?"

He smiles, slow and satisfied, like I've given him exactly the answer he wanted. His fingers find my hip, just the tips pressing in through my clothes, not quite a grab, but not quite innocent either.

"We go all the way," he says, voice dropping, each word a deliberate stroke. "Everything off. And you have to watch us. Completely naked too. Only fair, right?"

My face burns up, and the heat doesn't stop there. It rushes through my chest, my belly, lower, leaving me lightheaded. I swallow, my mind trying to picture it and immediately shorting out.

"Yeah, I don't think so," I manage. "None of you would be able to concentrate on your moves if I were watching naked."

His thumb flexes against my hip in a tiny, possessive squeeze, like he's imagining it too.

"Oh, we would," Noel calls from the costume heap without even turning around. He's bent over a box, briefs stretched obscenely tight, and I lose my train of thought for a second. "We'd be very motivated to perform our absolute best."

The word *perform* does not feel safe in this conversation.

"Focus on your next performance first," I say, the words a little breathier than I'd like. "Then we can discuss… private shows."

Kane's gaze drops to my mouth, then back up. There's something hungry there now, layered over the amusement.

"Careful what you promise, Hannah," he murmurs. "We take our commitments very seriously."

Across the room, Noel straightens, holding up a new costume piece. "Good news," he says. "Round two is going to blow their minds."

Kane doesn't look away from me. "Yeah," he says softly. "Pretty sure that's becoming a theme tonight."

Before I can turn away, Kane hooks two fingers in the waistband of my jeans and tugs.

I stumble a half step, and then his mouth is on mine.

There's no hesitation, no testing the waters, just a hard, hungry press that steals the air from my lungs. He tastes like sugar and salt and faint beer, his lips hot and a little rough, and my hands go to his bare chest on instinct.

He's slick with sweat, heat rolling off him in waves. My fingers drag over the solid plane of muscle, finding the curve of his shoulder, the heavy beat of his heart under my palm. He makes a sound low in his throat, half groan, half growl, and the hand at my hip tightens, dragging me flush against him.

The world drops away in a rush. There's no bar, no roaring crowd. Just the thud of bass through the wall, his mouth moving against mine, his breath mixing with mine as he deepens the kiss.

He tilts his head, angling for more, and I open for him without even thinking about it. Heat roars through me, sharp and bright. My knees soften. He's the only thing holding me upright, fingers digging into me, thumb pressing just under the waistband of my jeans like he wants more skin.

I slide one hand up, up, until my fingers brush the back of his neck. Damp hair, hot skin, the flex of tendon. He kisses like he dances, committed, all in, nothing held back, and every second of it feels like a bad idea I never want to stop having.

When I finally tear my mouth away, I'm breathing hard, my lips tingling, my whole body buzzing like I've been plugged into a socket.

My gaze drops before I can stop it.

Yeah. That's… not subtle.

His cock is straining against those ridiculous green boxer briefs, the fabric pulled tight over gingerbread men and the "Bite Me" slogan now sitting at a very distracting angle.

Heat slams low in my belly.

"Maybe we shouldn't be doing this right now," I whisper, though I don't step back. I can't. My fingers are still curled against his chest, feeling every rapid breath.

His eyes are darker than I've ever seen them. "Pretty sure that ship sailed the second you promised us private shows," he murmurs.

From across the room, Noel laughs, the sound rich and amused. "The women are going to lose their minds," he calls, not even looking up from the costume pile. "Authenticity in performance and all that."

The reminder hits like a splash of cold water. Fifty drunk, feral women. A schedule. An event I am technically responsible for.

"I'll stall as long as I can," I tell them, forcing my hand to flatten once more against Kane's chest before I peel myself away. He lets me go, but his fingers trail along my waist as I step back, reluctant to lose contact. "Take your time. Make it good."

"Oh, we will," Noel says, finally glancing over with a wicked grin. "Wouldn't want to disappoint your audience."

My audience.

My men.

The thought is reckless and dangerous and does awful, wonderful things to my pulse.

I slip back out front. The noise swallows me instantly. Ruby is already onstage with the microphone, working the room like the pro she is, getting them to shout, to cheer, to keep the energy high.

My head is spinning.

That pulse of arousal I felt when I took Noel into my mouth, how I crawled into Kane's bed? The same tight, breathless need from breakfast with Chris yesterday? It's slamming into me again, harder this time. Meaner.

Waves of heat that have nothing to do with the temperature in the bar roll through me, leaving my skin too tight. There's a heavy ache building between my thighs, persistent and insistent, and every time I blink, I see Kane's mouth, Noel's grin, the way they moved onstage in those stupid briefs.

Not sure moving in with them and being this close all the time is doing my pre-heat situation any favors.

I need suppressants. Soon. Very soon.

Before I do something even more reckless than letting them strip for fifty drunk women…

Like asking for that private show and not stopping at a kiss with all three.

We stumble through the front door, and the blast of warmth from inside is so welcome I could cry. My face is numb from the cold, my fingers stiff.

Kane is already kneeling by the fireplace, arranging logs. "Just got a text from Chris. He's still at the station processing those idiots. Says it's a busy night down there, but he'll be home when he can. And apparently he has something to tell us."

"Probably pissed that he missed our amazing performance," Noel says, shrugging out of his jacket and hanging it by the door. "We were legendary tonight."

I laugh, toeing off my boots and lining them up neatly. "You two were incredible. Saved my entire event, after almost destroying it first," I tease.

Flames catch and start licking up the wood in the fireplace. "So really, we just evened out the damage."

Noel pulls on his jacket again, zipping it up. "I'm

heading out to feed the reindeer and get them into the barn for the night. Going to be a cold one. That snow is really coming down now."

He disappears back outside, and Kane follows him out to help, leaving me alone in the entryway.

I head upstairs to change into black leggings that are so soft they're basically pajamas, and an oversized pink T-shirt. I have on a black tank top underneath because the one thing I refuse to do is wear a bra in this house after hours.

The bra comes off the second I get home. Always has, always will. But living with three very attentive Alphas means I can't just fling it off the moment I step through the door like I used to at my old place. Hence the tank top compromise.

I wash my face in the attached bathroom, brush my teeth, pull my hair into a messy ponytail, and head back downstairs in my thick wool socks.

The living room has transformed into something from a magazine spread. The fire Kane started is blazing now in the stone fireplace, flames dancing and crackling, casting warm light across the room. The Christmas tree lights are on, twinkling softly in whites and golds. The overhead lights are dimmed to that perfect level where you can see, but everything has this cozy, intimate glow.

Through the windows, snow is falling harder now. Big, fat flakes that are accumulating fast on the ground, on the trees, covering everything in pristine white.

I hope Chris gets home soon. The roads are going to be dangerous.

The guys still aren't back from the barn, so I stroll into the kitchen and grab a glass from the cabinet, filling it with cold water from the dispenser and downing half immediately. My throat is raw from talking over loud music all night, from stress, from everything.

Then I remember the chocolate chip cookies I spotted in the pantry a few days ago when I was exploring. The good kind that's soft-baked with huge chunks of chocolate and tastes like heaven. I grab them and a can of Dr Pepper from the fridge.

Back in the living room, I sink into the plush couch and set my drink on the side table. The cookie package fights me, the plastic refusing to tear where it's supposed to, and I end up using my teeth to rip it open. The crinkling sound is loud in the quiet room, competing with the crackle and pop of the fire.

I pull out a cookie and take a huge bite. Pure bliss. Soft and chewy with melted chocolate. I love having a fireplace. This whole house, actually. The high ceilings, the exposed beams, the windows that let in so much natural light during the day. It's starting to feel like home in a way that scares me because I'm supposed to be here temporarily. Just until I sort things out.

Except I'm not sorting anything out. I'm settling in, getting comfortable, and letting myself imagine staying.

I finish the first cookie and immediately reach for a

second one because tonight was stressful and I deserve carbs and sugar.

Then I look up.

Kane and Noel are standing near the fireplace, facing me.

They're still in their clothes from tonight, jeans and long-sleeved shirts, barefoot now with their boots left by the door. But there's something about the way they're positioned, lit by the fire, that makes them look unreal.

Kane with his dark blond hair slightly messy from the cold outside, hazel-green eyes locked on me. God, his body, all broad shoulders and defined muscles visible even through his shirt. That crooked grin on his face that's equal parts trouble and charm.

Noel next to him, shorter by an inch, his long brown hair pulled back in a low knot that emphasizes his strong jaw and those piercing eyes. The shirt he's wearing clings to every line of muscle in his chest and arms.

How do I keep myself in check around them? How do I function like a normal human being when they look like that? And there's music playing suddenly, something with a slow, sultry beat that definitely wasn't on a second ago.

I burst out laughing, cookie crumbs falling onto my shirt. "Oh, so my private show? Excellent timing, boys." I tuck my legs under me, getting comfortable, and take another bite of my cookie.

They're staring at me with identical expressions,

amused but also hungry in a way that has nothing to do with food.

"You forget the deal, baby girl?" Kane asks, crossing his arms over his chest in a way that makes his biceps bulge even more against the fabric.

My body reacts immediately. Fire burning deep in my gut.

"How about we just focus on you both dancing for me?" I suggest around my mouthful of cookie. "I'm exhausted, and you both still have that post-performance energy going."

They exchange a glance, some silent communication passing between them. Then suddenly they're both on me.

The cookie is ripped from my grasp, Kane taking it, and they're hauling me to my feet. Fingers dig into my sides, finding every ticklish spot, and I'm shrieking with laughter.

"Hey!" I'm gasping for air, trying to squirm away. "Stop! That's my cookie!"

"You want to see our best work?" Kane says between my giggles, his fingers relentless. "We need payment."

They're already tugging at my oversized shirt, trying to pull it up, and I'm batting their hands away weakly while laughing so hard tears are forming.

"Hey, I never agreed to that!"

They release me immediately, stepping back with matching grins that are pure mischief. Kane brings my stolen cookie to his mouth and takes a huge bite, maintaining eye contact the whole time.

"Then no show," Noel says simply, turning away with exaggerated disappointment.

"Oh, come on!" I pout at their backs. "That's not fair at all!"

"Then clothes off," Kane says, finishing my cookie in one more bite.

"But it's freezing!"

They shrug in unison and start to walk away, heading toward the stairs like they're actually going to leave.

I should let them go. This is already treading into dangerous territory, and I'm supposed to be taking things slow. Building trust. Not jumping into bed, or couch, when I already made enough of those accidents.

They glance back at me. The heat in their eyes. The way their bodies are practically vibrating with the need to touch me, to perform for me, to give me this.

They want more. I know they do. So eager to do this, and clearly excited about the prospect of dancing just for me, that I can't resist.

They did me a huge favor tonight. And part of me—the part that's been aching and burning since I moved in with them—desperately wants to see them naked. Wants their hands on me and to stop fighting this pull between us.

"Fine," I hear myself say. "But just down to my panties and tank top. That's the deal."

They turn back immediately, and the smiles on their faces unleash the butterflies in my stomach. "Deal," Noel says, his voice dropping lower.

They move closer, predatory and purposeful, and Kane reaches out to tug on the hem of my shirt. "So do it."

"Can't I do it after you start dancing?" I'm stalling because my hands are shaking slightly and I'm not sure if it's from nerves or anticipation.

"Fine," Noel says. "But if you don't strip by the end of the first song, we'll be doing it for you."

Heat floods through me at the threat, and my body responds immediately—nipples tightening, wetness pooling between my thighs. My pre-heat is definitely ramping up because this level of instant arousal isn't normal for me.

"Okay, fine," I manage, retreating back to the couch on shaky legs and grabbing another cookie just to have something to do with my hands.

The music grows louder, filling the room. Not the upbeat strip club music from the bar, but something slower. More intimate. A deep bass line that I don't just hear but also feel sink into my bones, with a melody layered over it that's pure seduction.

They position themselves between the fireplace and the couch, giving me a perfect view. The fire creates this halo effect, light and shadow playing across their features, highlighting every angle and plane of their faces and bodies.

I drag the blanket from the back of the couch over my lap, preparing to keep my word about stripping, and settle in to watch.

Kane moves first.

He rolls his shoulders back, stretches his neck side to side like he's loosening up, and then his hips start moving to the beat. Slow, sensual rolls that are completely different from the energetic performance at the bar. This is intimate. Personal. Just for me.

My breath catches.

Noel joins in, his movements fluid and graceful, complementing Kane's power perfectly. Where Kane's motions are strong and deliberate, Noel's are as smooth as water, and together they create this hypnotic rhythm.

They're not rushing but taking their time. Building anticipation with every sway of their hips, every flex of muscle.

Kane runs his hands down his own chest, over his abs, fingers hooking into his waistband but not pulling down. Just teasing. Promising. Noel turns, throwing me a look over his shoulder that's pure sex, then slowly starts drawing up his shirt, revealing inches of skin with agonizing slowness.

I forget how to breathe properly.

The shirt reveals his abs and chest, and he tugs it off. It falls to the floor behind him, forgotten. His body is ridiculous. Abs cut in perfect definition, chest broad and sculpted, shoulders that could carry the world. The firelight creates shadows in all the dips and valleys of his muscles, and I want to trace every line with my tongue.

Kane's shirt is next. He grabs the hem and pulls it over his head in one smooth motion, and now I'm staring openly, cookie frozen halfway to my mouth.

He's just as built as Noel but in a slightly different way. Where Noel is lean muscle, Kane is pure power. Thicker through the chest and shoulders, arms corded with muscle that flexes with every movement.

They're both shirtless now, skin gleaming in the firelight, moving to the music with their eyes locked on me.

Heat is building through me. That ache from before, the one that's been simmering since I moved in, is roaring back to life—my pre-heat making everything more intense, more desperate, more impossible to ignore.

God, maybe this wasn't such a good idea. I should take off my shirt. That was the deal.

I set down my cookie with trembling fingers and grab the hem of my oversized shirt, pulling it up and over my head slowly. The tank top underneath is thin and black, clinging to my breasts, and I don't bother covering up even though every instinct is screaming at me to do so.

Both their gazes drop immediately to my chest. Kane stumbles slightly in his next move, still staring at my breasts, and Noel makes this low sound in his throat that goes straight between my thighs.

I pull the blanket up to my waist, suddenly hyper-aware of how exposed I am, how vulnerable.

But they keep dancing, and I can't look away.

Kane's hands go to his belt, unbuckling it with deliberate slowness. The leather slides free of the loops with a whisper of sound, and he drops it on the floor beside him. Noel does the same, and now they're both working their buttons and zippers in sync.

Pants slide down muscular thighs—God, their thighs —and they step out of them, kicking them aside. They're in tight boxer briefs now, and I nearly swallow my tongue.

My turn.

I shift under the blanket, my hands shaking now for real. I hook my thumbs into the waistband of my leggings and shimmy them down my hips. It's awkward doing it while sitting, and I have to lift my hips, the blanket slipping down to my thighs, revealing my legs and the edge of my purple cotton panties.

Kane's eyes lock on to the exposed skin, and he actually trips over his own feet mid-move.

We all burst out laughing, the tension breaking for just a second.

"Smooth," Noel teases, but his voice is strained.

"Shut up," Kane mutters, but he's grinning even as his eyes stay glued to my thighs.

I manage to get my leggings off completely, and I adjust the blanket to cover me from my waist down, legs folded under me.

But my body is burning up. That ache between my thighs is pulsing in time with my heartbeat. This is pre-heat, has to be, because I've never felt this needy, this desperate, this out of control before.

They're moving closer now, swaying to the music, and their hands go to the waistbands of their boxer briefs.

Wait, they're actually going to do this?

My heart is hammering against my ribs. Every nerve ending is on fire. Their combined scents are wrapping around me, and together they smell like everything I've ever wanted.

I watch, transfixed, as they push the boxer briefs down simultaneously.

Hip bones appear. That defined V cutting down. Dark hair at the base, then they bend forward, drawing them down all the way.

I should look away. Should close my eyes or focus on literally anything else in the room. But they're staring at me with such intensity that I'm frozen.

They step out of the underwear and kick them aside. Then they stand up straight, completely shameless.

My eyes drop to their groins without my permission. And I see their cocks covered in long white tube socks. Ridiculous athletic socks pulled up over their erections like some kind of absurd modesty covering.

I burst out laughing so hard I actually snort, which makes me laugh even harder. "You guys!" I'm gasping for air, clutching my stomach. "You put socks on your dicks?"

"Gotta maintain some mystery," Kane adds, flexing slightly and making the sock bounce.

I'm dying. Tears are streaming down my face from laughing.

Then suddenly they're on either side of me, crowding onto the couch. I shuffle over automatically to make room, and they press in close, their naked bodies warm and solid against me.

Their mouths descend on me simultaneously.

Kane kisses me first, and it's not gentle. His lips are demanding, his tongue sweeping into my mouth and stealing whatever breath I have left. Then Noel's mouth is on my neck, sucking and licking, and my head spins.

I'm drowning in them. In their scents mixing together and filling my lungs. In the heat of their skin pressed against mine. In the way they're touching me everywhere at once.

I'm kissing them both, turning my head to catch Noel's mouth while Kane's lips trail fire down my throat to my collarbone, then switching back to kiss Kane while Noel sucks a mark into my shoulder.

The blanket is yanked away and tossed somewhere, and their sock-covered erections are pressing against my thighs as they crowd closer.

I'm giggling breathlessly but also gasping because their hands are everywhere—in my hair, on my waist, sliding under my tank top.

"Fuck, you taste incredible," Kane murmurs against my pulse point, and I whimper.

"Been thinking about this all night," Noel adds, his hand cupping my breast through the thin fabric of my tank top, and I arch into his touch, his thumb brushing over my nipple.

Their voices are wrapping around me, low and dark and full of promise, and I'm losing the ability to think coherently. Before I fully process what's happening, they're pulling my tank top up. I lift my arms automatically, and it's gone, tossed behind the couch.

I'm bare from the waist up, and for a second, I'm self-conscious, but then both their mouths descend on my breasts, and conscious thought evaporates.

Kane takes my left breast, his mouth hot and wet and perfect. His tongue swirls around my nipple before he sucks it between his lips, and the sensation shoots straight to my core. Noel mirrors him on my right breast, and having both of them sucking and licking and worshipping me simultaneously leaves me crying out.

My hands thread through their hair, holding them to me, and I'm arching into their mouths shamelessly.

My body is humming. Every nerve ending is alive and singing. That deep ache from before is consuming me now. It settles deep between my thighs, pulsing and demanding attention. It's only when the Alphas touch me that it eases even slightly, and right now it's screaming for more. I can't think about anything except them. Their mouths. Their hands. Their bodies pressed against mine.

"I love how you both feel against me," I breathe, barely recognizing my own voice, which is wrecked and needy.

They release my breasts but only to kiss every inch of skin they can reach, working their way across my chest, up my throat, along my collarbones.

"Do you have any idea how smitten we are with you?" Noel asks against my sternum, his voice rough.

"Completely obsessed," Kane agrees, kissing up to my jaw. "Can't think straight when you're around."

Then Noel's hand is sliding into the elastic of my panties from one side, and Kane's hand joins from the other.

They're both kissing me again as they work my panties down together. I'm so needy right now I could scream. So hungry for their touch that I'm trembling. My body is pleading for them, demanding relief from this ache, and I know exactly where this is heading, but I can't make myself stop it.

Don't want to stop it.

They need me, sure. But I need them a hundred times more right now. Need their hands on me, their mouths on me, their anything on me before I combust.

They pull my panties off completely. As they kiss me breathless, they gently spread my legs.

They remain sitting on either side of me on the couch, and their hands trail down my body simultaneously. Kane's fingers find my clit, while Noel's fingers explore lower, circling my entrance teasingly. And I'm arching into them, moaning.

"So wet already," Noel murmurs appreciatively against my lips.

"Soaking for us," Kane adds, increasing the pressure on my clit slightly.

I'm writhing between them, my hips moving involuntarily, seeking more friction, more pressure, more everything. Noel pushes two fingers inside me, and I nearly come off the couch. The stretch is perfect, and

I'm gasping into Kane's mouth as he swallows my sounds.

My orgasm builds fast and unexpectedly, cresting like a wave, and when it crashes over me, I'm crying out their names, my body clenching hard around Noel's fingers, pleasure radiating through every nerve ending.

"Fuck, that was beautiful," Kane says, sounding awed.

"Let's see how many more we can pull from you," Noel suggests, and there's a wicked edge to his voice.

Kane leans over to the side table and grabs two candy canes from the decorative bowl. He unwraps them both, the crinkling sound loud in the quiet room, and for a second, I think he's about to eat them.

Then he holds both candy canes up to my mouth. "Open."

I part my lips obediently, and he slides both candy canes into my mouth. I taste peppermint, sharp and sweet and cool.

"Sweet tooth?" Noel jokes, watching with amusement.

Kane grins, then pulls the candy canes from my mouth, now slick, and trails them down my body.

Between my breasts. Over my stomach. Lower.

"Oh," I breathe, realizing his intention, and my thighs instinctively try to close.

But Noel's hand is there, keeping my legs spread. "Let us play, sweetheart."

Kane rubs the candy canes over me, the curved handles slick and smooth against my oversensitized flesh, and I'm squirming at the sensation. Cool and hard and so different from fingers.

Then he pushes both the pointy ends inside me slowly, carefully, and I gasp at the strange feeling.

Noel hooks one of my legs over his thigh while Kane does the same with my other leg, spreading me wide open for them.

The curly handles of the candy canes stick out obscenely, facing upward, and both men are staring down between my thighs like they've created a masterpiece.

"This is our new festive tradition," Noel declares.

"Best Christmas decoration ever," Kane agrees.

They each grasp one of the handles and pull the candy canes out slowly. Then, before I can process what they're doing, they put them in their own mouths.

Both of them moan around the peppermint sticks.

"Holy hell." Kane's eyes roll back slightly. "Best candy cane I've ever tasted in my entire life."

"Fuck yeah," Noel groans.

They put the candy canes back inside me, and I'm gasping and writhing as they work them in and out, using them to tease me while their free hands roam my body, squeezing my breasts, stroking my thighs, touching everywhere they can reach.

Building me up again. Slowly this time, drawing it out, making me beg silently for release.

My body is on fire. Every touch sends electricity through me. I'm moaning constantly now, unable to stay quiet, my hips moving as I watch them dip those candy canes into me and then suck them.

That's when I notice movement through my pleasure-hazed vision.

Cold air rushes through the house, and all three of us freeze, turning our heads toward the kitchen entrance.

Corn Dog trots through the living room like he owns the place, completely unconcerned with the scene he's interrupting. He plods over to the fireplace with heavy steps and plonks himself down directly in front of it, releasing a contented sigh.

We all burst out laughing, the absurdity of the moment cutting through the sexual tension.

I grab for the blanket and yank it over my naked body, pushing away the guys and their candy canes with giggles. "We can't do anything with him right there. He's literally watching us."

"Corn Dog, you need to leave," Kane states firmly, but there's no real authority in his voice because he's still laughing.

"But he's cold," I protest, my earlier arousal fading slightly in the face of having an audience. "Look at him by the fire. He's comfortable. We can't kick him out into the freezing barn now."

"He's cock-blocking us," Noel says flatly, standing up and adjusting the sock still covering his erection.

I'm laughing so hard my stomach hurts.

Noel stalks toward the kitchen, muttering about the doggie door his grandfather installed years ago that

Corn Dog keeps breaking through, and I hear him securing it properly.

I find my panties tangled in the blanket and pull them on quickly, then my leggings, while Kane watches with obvious disappointment.

"This doesn't end here," Kane says, his voice still rough with arousal. "We're taking this upstairs to finish properly."

But that's when the front door opens with a blast of cold air, and Chris's voice carries through.

"What the hell now?" Kane moans.

"Fuck, you guys will not believe what I just discovered about Scot," Chris calls out.

I'm scrambling now, dragging on my tank top and oversized shirt, trying to look like I wasn't just being pleasured with candy canes thirty seconds ago.

Chris's eyes immediately widen at the scene before him.

Noel returns from securing the kitchen door, wearing absolutely nothing except a white tube sock over his very obvious erection. Kane is in the same state.

Chris scents the air deeply, his nostrils flaring, and I watch his pupils dilate. "You couldn't wait for me before starting?"

"We were warming her up for you," Kane says with zero shame, that cocky grin firmly in place.

"So, what did you find out about Scot?" I ask quickly, trying to redirect before Chris decides to join whatever this situation is.

He toes off his boots by the door and drops his keys in the ceramic bowl on the entry table. Then his gaze lands on the fireplace. "Why is Corn Dog in the house?"

"He was cold," I say defensively, pulling the blanket tighter around myself even though I'm fully dressed now. "And he's currently sleeping peacefully."

The other two guys shrug at Chris with matching expressions of *We tried.* "We didn't want to say no to her," Noel explains.

"Clearly," Chris mutters, but there's amusement dancing in his moss-green eyes despite his words.

Chris crosses to me and takes my hand, bringing it to his lips and kissing my knuckles with such unexpected gentleness that my heart does this complicated flutter thing in my chest. The gesture is so tender, so different from the rough passion of moments ago, that I'm momentarily speechless.

"Well, I found some very interesting information about Scot tonight," Chris explains, his expression shifting to something more serious as he releases my hand. "Not sure what to make of it yet, but something's definitely wrong there."

"What is it?" I ask, sitting up straighter.

Noel and Kane have pulled their pants back on, though they're still shirtless, and they're moving closer, curiosity written across their faces.

"When I was driving those dancing criminals to the station, they were whispering in the back seat," Chris explains, running a hand through his hair. "I couldn't make out most of it over the engine and the radio, but I swear I heard them mention the name Scot multiple times."

"Oh?" I say slowly, my mind already trying to make connections. "I mean, there are probably other Scots in town besides the one I know."

"Right, that's what I thought initially," Chris agrees out loud. "But we always keep the back of our transport vehicle bugged with a microphone. We've caught a lot of valuable intel that way when criminals think they're having private conversations back there.

"I listened to the full recording after I finished processing them downtown," Chris continues. "And they were definitely talking about someone named Scot who hired them and promised to pay them extremely well. They were debating back and forth about whether this Scot would still honor the payment, considering they got arrested for their outstanding warrants and didn't actually finish performing the strip show."

My stomach drops.

"It gets weirder," Chris continues. "One of them mentioned something about Scot wanting to make sure the event didn't go too well, but not so badly that it would be obvious it was sabotaged."

I'm on my feet now, the blanket falling away. "That has to be my Scot. That asshole. And I don't get the payment thing, as I paid them already in advance for tonight. Why would Scot be paying them too?"

"Where did you even find their contact information?" Noel asks.

I press my lips together, thinking back. "It was over a

month ago when I was first booking everything for this event. But now that I'm thinking about it, the contact came directly from Scot. He recommended them specifically, said they were the best in the area."

"So he deliberately steered you toward criminals who could give a mediocre performance back when you were both still partners?" Chris says. "That seems odd."

I shrug helplessly. "It feels strange because we were still on good terms when I booked them. We hadn't had our falling out yet. But..." I trail off, a horrible thought occurring to me. "What if he was setting me up to fail for weeks or even months? But I don't get it. He never showed signs of that."

Chris shakes his head, his jaw tight with anger. "I'd bet my left nut that Scot is involved in some shady shit way beyond just being a dick to his business partner. The question is, what's his endgame here?"

"Problem is those dancers aren't getting out anytime soon," Noel adds. "They'll be held at least until their court date, maybe longer, depending on their bail situation and the severity of their charges. So we can't exactly track them."

My mind is spiraling, thinking about Scot and everything that's at stake.

"Only one solution," Kane says firmly. "We start tracking Scot's movements around town. See exactly what he's up to and who he's meeting with."

I nod automatically, but the thought of Scot possibly orchestrating something from weeks ago has completely deflated me. I feel tired suddenly, a bone-deep exhaustion.

I sigh heavily. "I think I'm going to head to my room. Process all of this." I get to my feet and start toward the stairs.

"Absolutely not," Noel says immediately, and there's steel in his voice.

I turn to find both him and Kane moving toward me. "After that news, we're all watching a movie together," Noel continues, and it's not a suggestion. "Something to get your mind out of that spiral I can already see happening behind your eyes. You're not going to let that asshole get into your head and ruin what was a perfectly good evening."

"But—" I start to protest.

"No buts," Kane interrupts, and they're literally each taking one of my arms and guiding me back to the couch. "You're staying down here with us."

I notice the candy canes still sitting on the side table, sticky and slightly melted now.

"Let me get changed into something more comfortable," Chris says, already heading for the stairs. "I'll be right back."

I glance over at Corn Dog, who's still snoozing peacefully by the fire, completely oblivious to the craziness around him. He opens one eye as if sensing my attention, and I swear there's something knowing in that look.

Like even he understands that these three Alphas won't let me withdraw into my worry and anxiety. That they're going to surround me with their presence until I have no choice but to relax.

And despite the troubling news about Scot, and everything hanging over my head, I sink back into the couch cushions between Kane and Noel.

Their body heat surrounds me immediately, and their scents wrap around me like a security blanket.

For tonight, at least, I'm exactly where I need to be.

Safe. Protected. Cared for.

Even if I'm still figuring out how to accept it.

CHAPTER SIXTEEN

KANE

I've been sitting in this truck since dawn, and my ass is completely numb.

Chris is behind the wheel, both of us bundled in jackets because it's freezing out here and we can't run the heat constantly without drawing attention. We're parked down the street from Confetti & Meatballs, tucked between two other vehicles where we've got a clear view of the building's entrance but aren't obvious about surveillance, if there is any.

The sun has been up for three hours now, weak winter light doing absolutely nothing to warm the frigid air, and that asshole still hasn't shown his face.

Not once. Of course, we're grasping at straws that he's moved into this building, but we were hoping at the most that he'd show up for work here. Except, he's been a no-show all morning.

No lights coming on in the building. No car pulling up. No sign of life whatsoever.

"That fucker," Chris mutters, taking another sip from his travel mug of coffee that's definitely cold by now. "I know he's up to something big. I'd love to take him down. Squish his fucking arrogant head between my hands until his eyes pop out like grapes."

"Jesus Christ, dude. Chill." I shift in my seat, trying to get blood flow back to my legs. My knees are stiff from being bent too long. "If he's doing shady shit, we'll catch him eventually. We always do."

"Yeah, I know." Chris sets his mug in the cup holder with more force than necessary. "It just pisses me off beyond reason how much crap he's pulled with Hannah. All the manipulation, the gaslighting, kicking her out of her own apartment. And even now, I don't trust that bastard not to try ruining her town parade event weekend or the upcoming tree lighting celebration."

"You don't have to tell me." I cross my arms over my chest, trying to trap some body heat. "I was there when Giuseppe called him, remember? Listened to every single word through the phone. His threat was crystal clear—he wants that business for himself, and he'll do whatever it takes to make sure Hannah doesn't get it first."

Chris drums his fingers on the steering wheel in an agitated rhythm, staring at the dark building. "Speaking of Hannah, her heat is getting closer. I can scent it on her every morning when she comes downstairs. Getting stronger, more concentrated, more intense."

"I know." Just thinking about it causes my body to react, cock stirring in my jeans despite the cold. "Trust me, I fucking know. And she's still denying that we're a real pack. Still acting like living with us is some temporary arrangement until she figures out her next move, and resisting us when it's clear her body craves an Alpha's touch."

"What are we going to do about that?" Chris asks, glancing my way. "Because she's ours. We all know it deep in our bones. She knows it too, somewhere beneath all that fear and self-protection. But she's fighting it hard."

I blow out a long breath, watching it fog in the cold air inside the truck's cab. "Keep showing her we're there for her no matter what. Helping with whatever she needs—business stuff, personal stuff, everything in between. Bending over backwards to prove we're not going anywhere and we're not like the assholes from her past. She's scared. You see it in her eyes sometimes when she thinks we're not watching. Like she's waiting for us to disappoint her or leave or turn into controlling dicks like Scot."

Chris shifts in his seat, leather creaking, nodding.

"So we need to let her set the pace. Not make her think we're controlling her life or trying to take over every aspect of her existence."

Chris laughs, the sound filling the truck's cab. "Hard to do when we literally moved her into our house within days of meeting her, and now we're attached to her every fucking second of the day like possessive stalkers."

I snort. "Not exactly subtle about wanting her

around constantly. Noel practically shoved me out of the way this morning to volunteer to go with her into town today for the parade prep."

"He's got it so bad for her."

"Fuck, man, we all do." Chris runs a hand through his hair, messing it up further. "Last night when I got home from processing those criminals and realized I'd missed out on what you two were doing with her on the couch…" He shakes his head. "I was so fucking jealous I could barely see straight because I'm craving her that badly."

"In our defense, things escalated quickly. One minute we're dancing for her, next minute candy canes were involved. It was spontaneous."

"I'm sure it was very spontaneous and not at all premeditated," Chris says dryly. We both laugh. "Never thought I'd say this about anyone," Chris admits. "But she's the one. Forever. The endgame. I knew it the moment I kissed her in that Santa suit and she melted against me."

"I knew it when I woke up with her riding me thinking I was Noel," I say with a laugh. "Best mistaken identity of my entire life."

"Lucky bastard."

We fall into comfortable silence, both of us watching the building. It's two stories. Downstairs is the business, I assume, with the company name in large gold lettering above the door: Confetti & Meatballs Event Planning. Professional-looking signage, clean windows, but everything is dark inside. Upstairs, the blinds are shut tight on what must be the apartment where Hannah used to live before Scot kicked her out.

The thought has me simmering with anger.

Another car drives past slowly, the driver clearly lost, and we both tense until it keeps going.

"We've been sitting here for hours," I finally say. "He's clearly not coming. Place looks abandoned."

"Agreed." Chris stretches as much as the truck cab allows. "I think we should head inside. Check it out properly. See what we can find."

I perk up immediately. "Thought you'd never ask."

We climb out of the truck, and the cold smothers me. I zip my jacket up to my chin and pull my gloves on tighter. Chris does the same. We stick to the shadows and the tree line as we approach the building, moving with the kind of casual purpose that doesn't attract attention. Just two guys out for a walk in the freezing cold because we're idiots.

The driveway leads around to the back of the building, and that's where we head, completely out of sight from the street and any neighboring buildings. Perfect for what we need to do.

Chris peers through the back window first, cupping his hands around his face to block the glare from the weak sunlight. "Dark. No movement inside that I can see. No computers on, no lights, nothing."

"Let's do this, then."

Chris pulls out his lock pick set from his jacket pocket, something we all carry for situations exactly like this, and gets to work on the back door. I keep watch on the surrounding area.

It takes him maybe thirty seconds before I hear the satisfying click of the lock disengaging. "Got it," he mutters.

The door swings open silently, and we slip inside quickly, closing it behind us.

I move immediately to locate the security panel, knowing exactly what to look for and how to disable it without triggering any alarms. We've done this enough times that it's second nature now. But when I find the panel on the wall just inside the back entrance, the system isn't even armed.

The display shows "Disarmed" in green letters, and when I check the log, it hasn't been armed in over a week.

"Security's completely off," I tell Chris quietly. "They're not protecting anything valuable here. Or they don't care anymore."

"That's either really stupid or really telling," Chris observes.

"My money's on telling."

We split up to search the main floor. I take the front area while Chris handles the back offices.

The reception area is basic and impersonal—a desk with an outdated computer that probably runs on Windows XP, some filing cabinets that have seen better days, and a printer. The walls are bare except for a few generic motivational posters about teamwork and success. I go through the papers on the table, and there's nothing interesting.

"This place feels completely abandoned," Chris calls from wherever he is in the back.

"Yeah, I'm getting the same vibe. Like no one's actually worked here since Hannah left."

We regroup near the stairs that lead up to the second floor.

"Ready to check out the upstairs?" Chris asks.

I nod, and we start to climb the narrow staircase, our boots making soft sounds on the worn wood despite our attempts at stealth. The door at the top is unlocked.

When we push the door open, it's immediately obvious that nobody lives here. So much for our theory that he might have moved in, but it was a guess.

Basic furniture and nothing else really, so we head back downstairs.

Chris already drifts toward the filing cabinets, tugging them open and going through them.

I go through the desk drawers in case I missed anything. Most of what we find is boring business stuff, old contracts with vendors for events, agreements that have expired, tax documents from three and four years back. Nothing recent. Nothing that tells us anything useful.

"This is coming up clean," Chris mutters after twenty minutes of searching, flipping through yet another stack of useless papers.

I'm working my way through the bottom drawer,

finding more of the same useless crap, when my hand closes on something that feels different, glossy photo paper tucked way in the back behind some hanging folders.

I pull it out and stare at what I'm seeing.

My brain takes a second to process it.

"Fuck, look at this." I straighten up, holding the photograph so Chris can see it clearly. "I swear this is one of the strippers we arrested the other night at Hannah's event, right? And that's definitely Declan, the Santa dude we busted downtown. Why the fuck are they with Scot?"

Chris crosses the room in three long strides and practically rips the photo from my grasp to examine it more closely, holding it up to the weak light coming through the window.

"Holy shit," he breathes. "That's definitely one of the strippers. I'd recognize that smug face anywhere."

In the photograph, Scot stands in the center with his arm slung around their shoulders like they're old friends. All three of them are grinning at the camera as if they don't have a care in the world. Behind them is what looks like an old cabin, rustic wood siding, weathered and aged, with a covered porch. Mountains are visible in the background, snow-capped peaks rising against a blue sky, and what might be a thin waterfall cutting down the mountainside in the distance.

"Those fucking weasels," Chris says, his voice going hard and dangerous. "What is he up to? This isn't just being a dick to his ex-business partner. This is organized. He knows these guys personally…"

We both stare at the photo.

"So he's putting his friends in jobs at the events… that's not illegal," I say.

"Except both of his friends so far have been criminals. He's involved in something," Chris agrees. "And we're going to uncover exactly what the fuck he's doing. I refuse to believe it's as simple as him getting his buddies some jobs."

Chris pulls out his phone and takes several pictures of the photograph from different angles, making sure to capture every detail. We carefully tuck the original photograph back exactly where I found it.

Then we slip back out the way we came.

Chris relocks the door from the inside, pulling it shut with a soft click. We're jogging back toward the truck within seconds.

A squirrel suddenly jumps out from behind a tree directly in our path, and Chris actually yelps, a high-pitched sound I've never heard come out of his mouth in the entire time I've known him.

I burst out laughing so hard that I have to stop moving for a second. "Did you just scream?"

"Fuck off. It startled me." But he's looking around to make sure no one else heard that embarrassing sound.

"You hunt dangerous criminals for a living," I manage between laughs, "and a tiny squirrel makes you scream?"

"It came out of nowhere!"

The squirrel in question sits on its haunches near the tree, staring at us with those beady black eyes like it's judging Chris's masculinity. Then it flicks its tail dismissively and scampers up the tree trunk, disappearing into the branches.

"That was the best thing that's happened all morning."

"I'm going to punch you."

We're both laughing now as we reach the truck. Once we're safely inside the truck with the doors closed and locked, Chris starts the engine and cranks the heat to maximum. We both hold our hands up to the vents, trying to get feeling back in our frozen fingers.

I pull out my phone and text Hannah while we're waiting for the truck to warm up.

Me: Do you know where Scot lives, by any chance?

The response comes back almost immediately, which makes me smile because of course she's got her phone on her.

Hannah: Not a clue. Never wanted to know, so never asked him. Why?

Me: Just trying to track him down. No worries.

I pocket my phone and glance at Chris, who's studying the photographs he took on his phone, zooming in and examining details.

"She doesn't know where he lives," I report.

Chris zooms in on the background of the photo, focusing on the mountains and the waterfall. "We need to figure out where this cabin is. Those mountains, that waterfall, it's somewhere in this area."

"This is our bread and butter—finding fuckers who think they can hide in plain sight."

CHAPTER SEVENTEEN

HANNAH

The familiar scent of vanilla and cinnamon wraps around me the moment I step into Flour & Fable's back kitchen, and despite everything weighing on my mind, I immediately relax a fraction.

Lily is at the industrial mixer, wearing her usual flour-dusted apron over jeans and a sweater, her dark hair pulled back. She glances up when I enter, and her face breaks into a huge grin.

"There's my sister! I was starting to think you'd forgotten about our coffee date."

"Never," I say. "Just running behind because everything in my life is currently insane. Noel has been my shadow for the last couple of days for all my meetings and catching up with all things parade related."

"The parade is tomorrow, right?" Lily asks. "It's later this year."

"Yeah, the council wanted to draw in more tourists, so they scheduled it closer to Christmas. For the same reason, they pushed the tree lighting ceremony to just days before Christmas. So it's tomorrow, and the event is all ready to go. Though, I'm terrified something's going to go terribly wrong."

"Why? You've triple-checked everything, haven't you?"

"Yes, but..." I sigh and pace around the kitchen. "All my recent events have had issues. The Santa was a criminal who was arrested. The strippers were wanted criminals, also arrested. What if things go haywire for this too?" I rub my temples where a headache is starting to form. "Two days ago, the guys found a photo of Scot with those criminals. Together. Like they know each other. And he recommended them to me months ago to book. It's a huge coincidence that both turned out to be wanted criminals."

"Hannah..."

"And then there's the guys themselves." The words tumble out before I think them through. "They're this huge, amazing, overwhelming distraction that I'm loving way too much, and I shouldn't be because I have a business to build and a reputation to establish and—"

"Whoa, slow down." Lily dusts her hands and comes closer to me. "What's wrong with having amazing Alphas who support you and make you happy?"

"Nothing, in theory. But can I pursue my career when I have scent matches, when my body falls apart around them and forgets everything else? Yet, at the same time, I'm terrified I'm going to mess it up somehow. Or that they'll realize I'm not worth the trouble and... Gosh, I don't know. My head is pulling me in several directions."

"Stop." Lily draws me into a hug, and it calms me down. "You're spiraling."

I take a shaky breath and pull back. "I just feel so overwhelmed."

And that's not even touching the other issue. The one I haven't admitted to anyone. My pre-heat is out of control. Not the usual restless buzz in my veins. This is deeper. Lower. Heavier. My body is shifting in ways I can't logic my way out of anymore.

I keep catching myself thinking of the Omega room in their house like it's calling me when I'm not there. The bed. The blankets. The ridiculous soft lighting. Crawling onto it, curling into the center, and letting them—any of them, all of them—stand guard around me. My instincts practically purr at the thought.

God. What is wrong with me?

My temperature spikes at random. One second, I'm fine. The next, I'm flushed and trembling, thighs clench-ing, pulse racing so fast it feels like I'm about to combust. There's this deep, molten ache between my legs, a steady throb that won't let me think straight. Every instinct sharpened, every nerve exposed.

And it only gets better, easier, when I'm near them.

Except it's not going to pass. Not this time.

My body is choosing for me.

And I am not ready.

This shouldn't be happening yet. But living with three Alphas who are my scent matches is clearly accelerating everything. And I'm trying so hard to control it, to push through it, to stay focused on work. But it's getting harder every single day.

"How are things really going with the guys?" Lily asks gently, studying my face. "And don't give me the surface answer. I want the real answer."

I blow out a long breath. "They're... incredible. Supportive, protective, funny, sexy as hell. They help with my events, they make me dinner, they make me laugh until I cry. Living with them feels natural in this scary way."

"Scary how?"

"It's working so well that I'm hesitant to trust it." I finally meet her eyes. "What if I let myself fully fall and then it all rips apart? My career is already crumbling. I can't keep losing things. What if they realize I'm too much work or too damaged or too—"

"Hannah, stop." Lily squeezes my hand. "Those men are obsessed with you. Anyone with working eyeballs can see it."

"I know, but—"

"But nothing. You're scared. That's normal." Lily pauses.

"And I think my heat is coming early," I finally admit quietly. "Being around them is accelerating it. The ache is constant now, and it only stops when they're touching me. Which is a problem because I have work to do and I can't just spend all day draped over them like some needy—"

"Why not?" Lily interrupts.

I blink.

"Why can't you let them take care of you during your pre-heat? Why are you fighting it so hard?"

"Because I have a business to build! You have the bakery, and I really wanted to make event planning work, but it's just not going to plan. I'm trying to prove I can do this on my own, that I'm not some helpless Omega who needs to be coddled. Scot already tried to make me feel incompetent and dependent. I won't let anyone else—"

"Your Alphas aren't Scot," Lily says firmly. "Not even close. And accepting help and support during your heat cycle doesn't make you weak or dependent. It makes you smart enough to recognize when you need your pack."

I want to argue, but the words stick in my throat.

"How did you do it?" I ask instead. "With your guys? I know you told me about getting snowed in at that cabin, but… how did you finally let them in? How did you trust them enough to be vulnerable during your heat?"

Lily smiles, and there's something soft and nostalgic in her expression. "Oh, those were some crazy times. Being trapped in that cabin with three Alphas I barely knew while a blizzard raged outside and my heat hit unexpectedly? *Terrifying* doesn't begin to cover it."

"But you got through it."

"*We* got through it," she corrects. "Not me alone. We, together. And in truth, they were patient with me. They didn't push, didn't demand anything I wasn't ready to give. They were just there, helping me through the pain, keeping me safe, making sure I ate and stayed hydrated even when all I wanted was to lock myself in a room alone."

"That's what my guys are doing," I realize out loud. "Being patient. Being there."

"Exactly." Lily turns on her stool to face me fully. "Your men are doing the same thing mine did. They're showing you that they'll support you no matter what. And, Hannah? You need to stop stressing about it so much. Your work is important, they know that, and they support it completely. But don't put your career before your personal health and needs."

"I know that logically," I say, frustration tightening my throat. "But there's this voice in my head saying that if I give in, if I let myself fully depend on them during my heat, I'll lose myself somehow. And I've always been the one to take care of everything since we lost Mom."

"Oh, Hannah." Lily pulls me into her arms, and I sag into her because she's the one person who's seen every version of me—strong, exhausted, terrified, hopeful.

She squeezes me tighter. "You carried so much after Mom died. You shouldn't have had to, but you did. You held me together. You kept Dad sane. You made sure this bakery survived long enough for me to grow into it. You did all of that." Her voice softens, warm and full of pride. "But you don't have to carry everyone anymore. It's your turn now to be cared for. Let someone else hold you up."

My chest aches. I swallow hard, blinking fast. "Lily…"

She cups my cheeks, thumbs brushing away nothing, but they might as well be catching tears. "You deserve tenderness, sis, to be loved so loudly it drowns out everything else. So let those guys adore you. Just for once, let someone show up for you."

Something in me cracks. Just a little. Enough to let her words in.

"Thanks," I whisper. "I really needed to vent. And to hear that. And… just everything." I huff a shaky laugh. "I love you."

"I know." She smirks, bumping my shoulder. "I'm very lovable."

"You're impossible."

"Also true."

I exhale, steadying myself. "I should go. I've got a hundred things to do before tomorrow."

"Just be kinder to yourself," Lily says. "Promise me."

"I'll try." My voice wobbles, but I mean it. "Really."

She nods, satisfied, then brightens as she heads for the industrial refrigerator. "Before you go, don't forget the brownies for Chris. And take two trays. That man could eat his weight in chocolate."

A laugh finally escapes me, soft and real. "Yeah. I noticed."

And just like that, breathing feels a little easier again.

She takes out a container of brownies, the fudgy ones with chunks of dark chocolate that Chris is obsessed with. "Made extras for Chris. Tell him he'd better savor these because I'm not making another batch until next month."

I laugh. "You spoil him."

"I had a deal with him, and I keep my word," Lily says, handing me the container. She walks me toward the back door. "Your Alphas are good men, Hannah. Don't sabotage something beautiful because you're scared."

I hug her tightly. "Love you."

"Love you too. Now go home to your men and stop stressing about tomorrow. It's going to be perfect."

I leave through the back entrance, clutching the container of brownies, and head toward the truck where Noel parked. He had to pick up a few things, so I used the time to catch up with Lily.

Maybe she's right and I do need to stop fighting this so much. I need to just let go and see what happens.

But even as I think it, my stomach tightens with anxiety.

Because I know exactly where letting go will lead— with me in their beds every second of the day and night, bonded and knotted and completely claimed. With my life intertwined with theirs in ways I can't take back.

And as much as I want that—fuck, I desire it so badly it physically hurts—the anxiety is still there. Maybe if I can just get through tomorrow without anything going catastrophically wrong, perhaps then I can think about everything else.

The outdoor ice rink in the town square is packed tonight, and I'm trying desperately not to think about work.

Lily's advice keeps echoing in my head—stop putting work before my personal needs. So for tonight, I'm attempting to do exactly that. No thinking about the parade tomorrow and what might go wrong.

Just me and my three Alphas, ice-skating under the stars with dozens of other people.

Easier said than done when the enormous Christmas tree looms in the distance, dark and waiting. That's my responsibility next week—the tree lighting ceremony for the council celebrations.

Just looking at it tightens my chest.

So many things to coordinate.

"Hey," Kane says, appearing at my elbow with a concerned look. "You're doing that thing again where you're physically here but mentally running through work checklists." He taps my forehead gently. "Turn off the brain for a few hours. Doctor's orders."

Despite everything, I laugh. We've been skating for almost an hour now, and I'm continually amazed by how good all three of them are on the ice. They glide effortlessly, turning and stopping and moving backward like they've been doing this their entire lives.

Meanwhile, I'm clinging to whoever is nearest like a baby deer learning to walk.

The rink is alive with soft instrumental music playing over the speakers, fairy lights strung overhead, creating a canopy of twinkling stars, and the buzzy warmth of a winter crowd despite the freezing temperature. Breath clouds the air in little white bursts with every exhale. The cold bites my cheeks, turning them pink, and my nose is probably red, but I don't care.

This is actually nice.

I'm between Chris and Noel at the rail, taking a rest, and I'm aware of how close they're standing. Like they orbit instinctively around me, creating a protective bubble. Their scents wrap around me despite the cold air and thread beneath my skin, warming me from the inside out.

I shift slightly, trying to ease the pressure, and Chris's eyes immediately track the movement.

"You okay?" he asks quietly.

"Fine. Just cold." It's a lie, and from the way his nostrils flare slightly, he knows it.

Soon enough, we step back onto the ice again, and I try to laugh off my clumsiness, teasing them about how I haven't skated since I was twelve and even then I was terrible.

I wobble almost immediately, my ankles refusing to cooperate.

Chris catches my waist with one large hand, his fingers firm and warm even through my jacket. "Easy," he murmurs close to my ear, his breath ghosting across my skin. "Let me lead."

The ache between my thighs intensifies, and I bite back a whimper. I try again to glide forward, pushing off with one foot like I've seen everyone else doing effortlessly. But my balance wavers dangerously, my arms windmilling, and for one terrifying second, I'm falling backward.

Before my ass hits the ice, Noel materializes on my other side, his large hands bracketing my elbows and hauling me upright. Chris slides in front of me, his chest brushing my shoulder, and suddenly all three of them are forming a tight, protective circle around me.

My breath stutters in my lungs while my pulse skitters wildly.

If they keep touching me like this, steady hands on my waist, my elbows, my back, I might actually melt right down into a puddle on this ice.

When I finally steady on my skates, I reach for sarcasm because it's my favorite shield against overwhelming feelings. "Okay, so maybe I'm not going to be an Olympic figure skater. That dream is officially dead."

"I've got you," Chris murmurs, winking my way.

Kane tips his chin at Noel, mischief already written all over his face. "Race you around the rink."

Noel huffs. "You will eat ice."

"Big talk for someone who almost wiped out getting off the rail."

"That kid ran into me."

"He was five."

Their bickering pulls a laugh out of me. They push off at the same time, cutting across the rink in long, sure strokes, shoulders brushing as they pick up speed. A couple of people whistle when Noel spins at the far end and glides backward. Kane copies the move, adding a cocky little flourish that nearly sends him into the wall. I snort, warmth curling in my chest as they circle each other, still arguing.

Chris stays beside me, one hand light on my waist as we move in a slow loop near the edge. "Ignore them," he says. "They are genetically incapable of not showing off."

"I noticed," I reply, smiling. "It is a little impressive, though."

"They will be insufferable if you tell them that."

Chris's fingers suddenly tighten at my waist, just enough that I feel it. His shoulders roll back. His head lifts. His gaze is locked on something over my shoulder, jaw grinding. I follow his line of sight.

Two beefy men have just stepped onto the ice, at the far exit.

Heavy jackets. Beanies. Gloves. They appear like everyone else here. Except they have no skates on. They cut through the entry crowd without even pretending to adjust. Skaters yank themselves out of the way as the pair strides forward, eyes fixed ahead.

On us.

On Chris.

I feel him curse more than I hear it, a low vibration

through his chest and arm. "Stay behind me, Hannah." The words are calm. The tone is not.

"Who are they?" My voice comes out thinner than I want.

"Couple of assholes we brought in about six months ago." His jaw is tight, his weight shifting, ready to move in any direction. "Guess the system decided to give them another chance."

The men are closer now, shoving past a teenage couple, ignoring the glare they get in return. One of them lifts his chin in a small, ugly greeting. The other points, lips curling when he sees me standing with Chris.

He adjusts his stance, skating backward a few smooth inches so that his body is fully between me and them. His hand spreads wider at my waist, pulling me in until I can feel the hard line of his spine through his jacket. "Do not move from behind me," he says, low and steady. "Understand?"

I nod even though he can't see it and bunch my fingers into the fabric at his back, hanging on as the ice between us and the two men grows shorter with every breath.

The stockier man with a scraggly beard and mean eyes finds Chris immediately. His mouth twists into something nasty, and then his gaze slides over Chris's shoulder, looking for me. When he finds even the hint of my outline behind Chris's body, his grin widens.

"Well, look at that," he drawls. "Didn't know you'd upgraded your company."

My stomach drops. Ice pools low in my spine.

Chris doesn't move, but something in him sharpens. His stance shifts by inches, but the air around him changes completely.

The second man, tall, wiry, scar splitting his eyebrow, lets out a low whistle as he drifts a little closer. "Cute," he says, tone lined with something oily. "Didn't think you were the type to bring an Omega out in public. Brave of you." His eyes cut toward me again, deliberate. "Or stupid."

Heat flares in my chest, fear tangled with white-hot anger, but Chris speaks before I can get a word out. "Don't look at her." His voice is quiet. Too quiet. The kind of quiet that comes right before a door breaks or a bone snaps.

Scar-Eyebrow ignores him, steps closer, voice dropping. "Maybe she wants to be looked at. Plenty of Omegas do." His gaze lingers on my shoulder. "Bet she's sweet as honey when—"

Chris moves.

He doesn't lunge. Doesn't shout. He just steps back, placing more of his body between me and them, guiding me behind him with one smooth, controlled sweep of his arm. His shoulders square, legs bracing wide on the ice, the calm precision of someone who's taken down men like these a hundred times before.

"You're going to rethink everything you just said," Chris murmurs, low and lethal. "Right now."

Beard laughs, a harsh bark that grates on the air. "What? Touch a nerve?"

Chris's head tilts just a fraction. "I am going to give you one chance to walk away," he says quietly. "You should take it."

Scar taps his gloved fingers against his thigh, amused. "There it is. The lecture voice." His gaze drifts past Chris again, trying to find me. "Come on, man. Share a little holiday spirit. Let the Omega be with someone who knows how to treat her."

Beard laughs under his breath. "Yeah. We could show her a real good time."

My pulse spikes so hard I feel it in my throat. Heat flashes through my chest again, sharp and furious, but my feet might as well be nailed to the ice.

"Last warning," he growls. "Walk away."

They don't. Beard reaches, trying to get around him, fingers brushing the air close to my arm.

The rink lights flicker.

Once.

Twice.

Then the world snaps into darkness.

Music dies. Voices rise. Skates scrape in sudden stops. Shadows stretch and twist in my peripheral vision.

Chris's hand clamps on my hip, dragging me tight against his back. "Hannah?"

"I'm here," I manage.

"Don't move."

Then the stockier man lunges, arm swinging toward Chris's head in a wild arc. I see the punch coming, sharp against the dim glow of the distant streetlights. Dread consumes me.

Chris intercepts the punch mid-swing, forearm snapping up to block with a force that jolts through his body and into mine. The impact cracks through the air like a snapped branch. Beard jerks at the collision, pain twisting his face.

Before the man can recover, Chris rotates his stance, catches the front of Beard's jacket, and drives a controlled, vicious strike straight into the ribs. Not wild. Not sloppy. Perfectly placed. Beard folds, choking on a breath.

But Scar is already moving.

He steps wide around Chris, using the distraction to go for me. In the dimness, his outline is sharp enough to see his gloved hand stretching toward my arm.

"Come here, Omega," he hisses, his voice cutting through the muffled noise of the crowd. "Let me show you what a real man can offer you." He gropes himself.

My feet scramble backward on the slick ice, skates wobbling. My nails dig into the back of Chris's jacket. Every cell in my body screams at me to move, but fear punches deep and makes me slower than I should be.

Scar's fingertips are inches from me—

Then he's gone.

Two heavy shapes slam into him from opposite sides, appearing out of the shadows so fast I barely register them before the impact. Noel hits him low, driving his shoulder into Scar's hips with enough force to knock the air straight out of him. Kane strikes high, grabbing the front of Scar's coat and using that momentum to yank him upward and sideways.

The three bodies crash into the boards so hard the metal rattles. Scar's breath leaves him in a shocked, strangled sound as Noel drags him down to the ice, pinning him with ruthless anger, while Kane braces beside them, ready to break him in half if he tries anything.

The impact is brutal. Someone screams. The crowd surges away, bodies pressing back, skates scratching hard against the ice as people scramble to get clear.

Beard tries to push up again, fury flashing in his eyes.

Chris doesn't warn him, just moves. His fist snaps out in a brutal, perfectly timed strike that connects squarely with Beard's jaw. The sound is sickening, hard knuckles meeting bone with a crack that echoes across the ice.

Beard goes down like a felled tree, his whole body whipping backward before he slams flat onto the ice, arms sprawled, eyes glassy.

Chris stands over him, breathing steady, drawing me closer to him. "Stay down," he commands, voice low enough that only Beard and I can hear. "Try getting up again and I will put you right back through the ice."

Beard doesn't move. Not even a twitch.

Across from us, Noel has Scar facedown on the ice, one knee grinding between his shoulder blades, hand locked on the back of his neck. Kane braces at his side, free hand fisted in Scar's jacket, ready to drive him down again if he even breathes wrong.

The lights hum. There is a flicker, then a sudden blaze of harsh white as the system kicks back on. People wince, shielding their eyes.

"Sorry about that, folks! Little hiccup with the circuit breaker. Everything's fine again. Enjoy your night!" the rink attendant chirps over the speakers, blissfully unaware that the ice just hosted a small war.

Everyone else is very aware.

Skaters have frozen mid-glide. People stare openly at the men on the ground, seeing blood from their noses, their heads.

And in the center of all of it, Noel and Kane each grab one of the attackers and haul them upright like they weigh nothing. The men can barely stand, legs wobbling, breaths hitching. Noel has a fist in the back of Scar's jacket, dragging him like a misbehaving animal. Kane grips Beard by the collar, nudging him forward with sharp, uncompromising shoves of his skate blades.

They don't escort them off the rink; they *remove* them.

People scatter to give them space, parting like the Red Sea.

Only when the men are handed over to two wide-eyed rink security attendants does Chris turn back to me. His breathing is steady. Controlled. His hands come up immediately, sweeping over my waist, my arms, checking for bruises, checking for shaking, checking for anything out of place.

"You okay, gorgeous?" His voice is low, raw around the edges, like he hasn't fully come down from the adrenaline.

I swallow hard, nodding. "I-I think so." My voice comes out shaky despite the nod. "That was… terrifying. And also pretty damn impressive. You all took them down like it was nothing."

A slow grin curves his mouth, the dangerous kind. "You have no idea how brutal it was about to get if they didn't stay down." He leans in, presses a kiss to my brow, soft and grounding. "No one touches you. Ever."

His hands stay on my hips, holding me in place, steady and protective.

Behind him, Noel and Kane return across the ice with predatory calm, their blades slicing smooth arcs as if they didn't just slam two grown men into the boards. They shoot glances at me, assessing, making sure I'm unhurt, before melting back into flanking positions around us.

My heart still thunders. My palms are still damp. But something in me settles.

Not because the danger is gone.

But because I've never felt safer in my life.

"I think we should go," I whisper, because if we stay out here, I might cry, or kiss all three of them in front of an entire crowd of families and children recording us for TikTok.

Chris nods instantly, pulling me fully into his side. His arm wraps around my waist, firm and protective, like he's putting himself between me and the whole world. "Yeah," he murmurs, voice rough with lingering adrenaline.

The three of them guide me off the ice. The crowd parts without question, sensing the danger still crackling off them.

We return our rental skates in silence, and when the cold night air hits my lungs outside the rink, I finally breathe again. "Thank you," I say quietly, looking at each of them one by one. "For everything."

Noel studies my face like he's memorizing every detail. "We protect what's ours," he says softly.

Kane nods, jaw still tense. "No one gets near you while we're around. Ever."

Chris threads his fingers through mine, his grip warm and steady. "And you don't thank us for doing what we were made to do. Keeping you safe isn't a chore. It's the easiest promise I'll ever keep."

The words should overwhelm me. They should feel heavy or frightening or too much too soon. Instead, something inside me loosens, like a knot pulled free after being tight for years.

We walk through the snow-dusted street toward their truck. The night is quiet now, the echo of the rink far behind us, and the only warmth in the world seems to be radiating from the three men walking beside me.

Their presence steadies the tremble still lingering in my bones. My pulse finally slows, syncing to something calmer, deeper. And as Noel opens the truck door for me, and Chris settles a hand at my back to help me in, and Kane stands close enough behind me that I can feel the heat of him through my coat...

It hits me. Not like a lightning bolt or a dramatic realization. More like a quiet truth finally allowed to surface. These men aren't a threat to my independence or my identity. They're not here to cage me or consume me.

They're choosing me.

And for the first time in a long time, I feel the urge to choose someone back.

Not because I'm scent-matched. But because being with them feels like the most natural thing to do.

And maybe that's the beginning of something real that doesn't take anything away from me but gives me pieces I didn't know I was missing.

I glance at them as the truck door closes, my heart steady for the first time all night.

I'm not falling.

I'm finally landing.

CHAPTER EIGHTEEN

HANNAH

I'm lying in the huge bed in what I've started calling my nest, and I can't stop moving.

Every position feels wrong, uncomfortable. My body won't settle, relax, or let me rest even though exhaustion is pulling at my bones.

The room is dim, just moonlight streaming through the windows and casting silver patterns across the mountains of blankets and pillows I've arranged and rearranged at least a dozen times tonight. The soft glow illuminates the careful creation I've created—pillows stacked, blankets folded and layered, my clothes sorted and organized on the chair in the corner by color and fabric weight.

I've been doing this for the past hour. Nesting like my life depends on getting every single item positioned exactly right. Which, according to every Omega biology book I've ever reluctantly read, means my heat is close. Very, very close.

I drag another pillow closer and hug it to my chest, burying my face in the soft fabric and inhaling deeply. It smells like the laundry detergent the guys use, but underneath that is the faint trace of their scents that have permeated everything in this house.

I shut my eyes and try to will my body to calm down and let me sleep for just a few hours so I can function tomorrow for the parade.

But nothing works.

My heart is racing, pulse thundering in my ears like drums. There's this restlessness crawling under my skin, a buzzing energy that won't dissipate. My body temperature keeps fluctuating. One moment I'm throwing blankets off because I'm burning up, and the next I'm pulling them back because I'm inexplicably cold.

And I know exactly what's causing all of this.

Tonight at the ice rink. Watching Chris, Noel, and Kane protect me without hesitation. Seeing them take down those men, no fear, just pure lethal precision and deadly intent. That was hero protector stuff right there. The kind of thing you read about in romance novels and watch in action movies but never think you'll actually experience in real life.

And God help me, it's turning me on in ways I didn't know were possible.

I shouldn't find violence attractive. I know that logically, intellectually, violence is bad. Fighting is problematic. I should be disturbed or upset or traumatized by what I witnessed. But watching my Alphas defend me and seeing them go absolutely feral when those men threatened me, it did something to my body that I can't undo. Flipped some primal switch deep in my hind-brain that recognizes strong protectors and screams *Mine*.

Every time I close my eyes, I see it playing out again like a movie on repeat.

My thighs clench together involuntarily, seeking friction and relief from the ache that's been building steadily all evening and has now reached a fever pitch.

I toss the pillow aside in frustration and sit up, running both hands through my hair and tugging slightly, hoping the small sting will distract me. It doesn't work. This is getting completely out of control.

I have to calm down and get myself together because tomorrow is the parade. And I absolutely cannot go into full heat in the middle of downtown Whispering Grove while I'm supposed to be managing everything.

That cannot happen. I won't allow it. So I climb out of bed, my oversized sleep shirt falling to mid-thigh, and head toward my door. My legs are shaky, and there's a slight tremor in my hands when I reach for the doorknob.

The house is completely quiet, everyone else asleep. It has to be past midnight by now, maybe closer to one in the morning.

A cold drink will help shock my system. And the spa, yes, the jets and the warm water. That will relax me enough to sleep. Hot water always helps, right? Relaxes muscles, calms nerves, helps me think clearly.

I sneak down the hallway as quietly as possible, testing each floorboard before putting my full weight down, avoiding the particularly creaky one near the bathroom that sounds like a dying animal when you step on it. The living room is dark except for the dying embers in the stone fireplace casting a faint orange glow across the furniture. The Christmas tree lights are off, but moonlight streaming through the floor-to-ceiling windows illuminates the ornaments.

In the kitchen, I grab a cold Dr Pepper from the fridge and pop it open. The fizz is loud in the quiet house, and I wince, freezing for a moment to make sure I didn't wake anyone.

Nothing. No sounds from upstairs.

I take a long drink of the cold, sweet soda, even though logic says caffeine before bed is a terrible idea. Yet it tastes incredible.

Then I head to the spa room on this level, offering a silent thank-you to whoever designed this house for putting it down here instead of upstairs where I might wake the guys. The last thing I need is them sensing my pre-heat getting worse and trying to help when I need to control myself long enough to get through tomorrow. One more day of keeping it together. Of staying professional and focused and in control with absolutely no signs of pre-heat affecting my ability to do my job.

I push open the spa room door and flip on the low ambient lighting. The room is beautiful, something I haven't had much chance to appreciate since moving in. All natural stone and wood, carefully designed to feel like a luxurious mountain retreat. The large circular tub is sunk into the floor, surrounded by smooth stone tiles. There are small shelves built into the walls, holding candles—though I don't light them—and the frosted windows let in enough moonlight to create a peaceful atmosphere.

I turn on the faucet and adjust the temperature until it's perfect and hot enough to relax muscles but not so scalding that it's uncomfortable. The sound of rushing water fills the space, oddly soothing.

While the tub fills, I grab a fresh, fluffy towel from the built-in cupboard and set it on the wooden bench nearby where I can easily reach it later.

The tub is only half full, but I can't wait anymore. My body is practically vibrating with need and restlessness. I strip off my sleep shirt, pulling it over my head and tossing it aside. My underwear follows, landing in a small pile on the floor that I'll pick up later.

The air is cool against my overheated skin, and I shiver despite the warmth radiating from the filling tub. So I climb in carefully, testing the temperature with my toes first, then sliding down into the rising water.

Oh, it's perfect. The heat envelops me immediately, sinking into my muscles and loosening the tension I've been carrying in my shoulders and back all day. All week, really.

I lie back against the curved edge of the tub, letting the water rise around me, covering my legs, my hips, my stomach, my chest. I finally shut off the faucet when the water level reaches about three-quarters full.

I slide down until the water touches my chin, stretching my legs out, letting myself float, and for the first time in hours, I feel like I can breathe properly.

The tightness in my chest eases slightly. My heart rate slows from frantic to merely elevated.

This is helping.

I hit the button for the jets, and they sputter to life with way more force than I expected. I yelp quietly, then giggle at my own reaction. The jets are cool at first, just regular water from the pipes, but they heat up quickly as the system cycles through, and within seconds, they're pulsing hot water at various points around the tub.

This is absolute heaven.

I shift positions slightly, moving so one of the jets hits my lower back where I've been holding stress for days. The pulsing water works like magic on the tight muscles, and I groan softly in relief, my eyes closing.

But then those earlier tingles, the ones I've been desperately trying to ignore all night, the ones I've been pushing down and denying, come roaring back with a vengeance that steals my breath.

The ache between my thighs intensifies, becoming impossible to ignore or rationalize away.

My body knows what it needs, and it's not spa jets and cold soda. And suddenly I'm shifting again without conscious thought, my body moving on instinct. Lifting my hips, adjusting my position, maneuvering until the powerful thrust of water from one of the jets hits exactly between my legs.

Oh.

Oh God.

The sensation is incredible, pulsing pressure right against my most sensitive area, the water fluttering against my lips, teasing and relentless and perfect.

A moan escapes my throat before I can stop it, echoing off the tile walls.

I lean forward slightly, my hips start moving on their own, seeking the perfect angle, and I let the jet work me over.

"Oh, shit, that feels so good," I whisper to the empty room, my voice breathy and desperate.

This is what I've been reduced to. Using spa jets to get off when I have three extremely capable, devastatingly attractive Alphas sleeping just upstairs. Three men with enormous cocks—I've seen enough through tight jeans and boxer briefs to know—and I've even had one inside me already.

Kane's. God, Kane's cock was absolutely perfect that night. Thick and long and filling me so completely that I could barely form coherent thoughts, just sensation and pleasure and the overwhelming rightness of having him inside me.

Just the memory makes me clench around nothing, my inner walls squeezing, desperate for that feeling again. For the stretch and fullness and the way he moved inside me like he knew exactly what I needed.

My heart races faster, pounding so hard I hear it over the sound of the jets. My body temperature climbs despite being submerged in water. I'm moaning quietly, continuously now, my hips working in small circles to find the perfect angle, and I don't care about anything except chasing the release building inside me like a wave about to crest.

The pressure builds and builds, coiling tighter in my core.

I flop back against the submerged seating ledge, my hand dipping between my legs, fingers spreading myself open. I rub my clit in tight circles with two fingers, adding to the sensation of the water pulsing relentlessly against me.

My head falls back against the smooth tile edge, and small cries that I can't contain escape my throat. The water laps against my nipples, which just breach the surface, hardened into tight peaks, and the dual sensation is almost too much.

My free hand comes up to cup my breast, thumb brushing over my nipple, and that added stimulation pushes me closer to the edge.

When my orgasm finally hits, it's sharp and bright and all-consuming, sending pleasure radiating through every nerve ending in my body. I cry out, louder than I intended, my body shuddering and convulsing, my inner muscles clenching around nothing.

A smile curves my lips as the waves slowly ebb, leaving me floating in the afterglow.

I stay there for a long moment, catching my breath, feeling boneless and satisfied and finally, *finally*, relaxed.

Maybe now I can sleep.

Then I sense movement. A shift in the air. The feeling of being watched.

My gaze immediately lands on a figure in the doorway.

Noel.

He's leaning against the doorframe with one shoulder, arms crossed over his bare chest, wearing only low-slung gray pajama pants that hang dangerously from his hips. And there's a massive erection tenting the fabric, impossible to miss even in the dim lighting.

His hand drops to rub himself through the material, slowly and deliberately, and the expression on his face makes my breath catch all over again.

Pure primal hunger. Raw need. Savage desire barely held in check.

His blue eyes are locked on me with an intensity that feels physical.

"Noel!" The word comes out as a squeak. I instinctively pull back farther into the water, my legs slamming shut, arms crossing over my breasts even though he's already seen everything. "I didn't… How long have you been standing there?"

He doesn't answer immediately. Just strolls into the room with that predatory grace that makes him seem more animal than man, and every hair on my body stands up.

"Long enough to watch you come apart." He steps closer to the edge of the tub, towering over me, and I have to tilt my head back to maintain eye contact. "You're making this so much harder on yourself, sweetheart. Fighting what your body needs. What it's screaming for."

"I'm not—"

"You are." He crouches down so we're at eye level, and the movement has his pajama pants straining even more across his erection. "What you need is a huge Alpha cock inside you. Your body is calling for it, screaming for it, actually, from the pheromones you're putting out. And you're denying yourself what you desperately need." His eyes rake over what he can see of me through the water. "Even that beautiful orgasm I just watched you have? It's not going to satisfy you. Not really. You already feel it coming back, don't you?"

Heat floods my entire body, my face, my chest, spreading downward, but he's absolutely right, and we both know it.

The ache is already returning, the satisfaction from my orgasm fading faster than it should. My body is already ramping back up, demanding more than my fingers or water jets could ever provide.

And damn him for standing there looking so arrogant and correct, all corded muscle and masculine beauty, his long brown hair falling messily around his face and over his broad shoulders, those intense blue eyes that seem to see straight through every defense I've ever built.

The moonlight coming through the frosted window highlights the planes and valleys of his muscular torso, the intricate tattoos covering his arms and chest, the defined V of his hips disappearing into those pajama pants.

He's gorgeous. They all are. And my body knows exactly what it craves.

"So what do you suggest?" I ask, aiming for teasing and confident, but the words come out breathless and needy and desperate.

Noel's pupils dilate, swallowing the blue until just a ring remains.

That question, that surrender hidden in those five words, is all the invitation he needs.

He rises to his full height and goes to shut the door behind him with a soft click that sounds impossibly loud.

Then his hands go to the waistband of his pajama pants, thumbs hooking under the elastic, and he pushes them down his hips in one smooth, unhurried motion.

His cock springs free, and I actually gasp out loud.

His cock is thick and long, curving slightly upward, and a prominent vein runs down the entire length, visibly pulsing even from several feet away. The head is flushed dark red and slick with precum that's been leaking. His balls are heavy and pulled tight against his body, and his entire physique is absolutely spectacular, with muscles everywhere, broad shoulders that could carry the world, defined abs that flex with each breath, powerful thighs.

The tattoos covering his arms and chest seem to move and shift in the dim lighting, and I dream about tracing them with my tongue, desperate to explore every inch of him.

I shudder involuntarily. My entire body vibrates so intensely that it's almost painful.

Lily's voice echoes in my head—*You deserve tenderness, sis, to be loved so loudly it drowns out everything else. So let those guys adore you.*

I lean back against the tub's edge, forcing myself to meet his burning gaze despite how vulnerable I feel at being completely naked in this water with him looking at me like that.

"So are you getting in already, or what?" I say brazenly. My attempt at a sexy grin probably looks desperate, but honestly, I might actually cry from how badly I need him right now.

Noel doesn't hesitate for even a second.

He climbs into the tub in one fluid motion, water sloshing violently and spilling over the edges onto the tile floor. He sinks down into the water directly in front of me, and his hands immediately find my waist underwater, large and hot and possessive as they pull me closer through the water.

He steps between my legs, which automatically wrap around his hips, and suddenly we're pressed together with nothing between us.

His cock is trapped between our bodies, hard and hot even through the water, and I whimper.

Then his mouth descends on mine, and conscious thought evaporates.

The kiss is everything, fueled by an inferno I didn't

know existed inside me until this moment. His tongue sweeps into my mouth, claiming every inch, tasting me, and I surrender completely to the sensation.

One of his hands tangles in my wet hair, gripping firmly, angling my head exactly where he wants it. The other hand stays locked on my hip, holding me against him.

I can't breathe. Can't think. Can only feel his mouth on mine, his body against mine, his scent fogging my head.

He breaks the kiss, his breath mingling with mine. "Do you have any idea how perfect you are? How long I've been waiting for you to call me like this?"

"Noel—" My voice breaks on his name.

"Shh. Let me take care of you, princess. That's all I want." His hands tighten possessively on my waist, fingers digging into my flesh just enough to leave marks I'll feel tomorrow. "My good girl finally letting go. Finally accepting what she needs instead of fighting it."

Just hearing him call me *good girl* melts something fundamental inside me, some last wall of resistance crumbling to dust.

I exhale shakily, and the sound that escapes is somewhere between a cry and a moan.

"Perfect," he murmurs, satisfaction evident in his voice and on his face. "Your body responds so beautifully to me. Like you were made for this. Made for me."

Then he scoops one large hand under my ass, lifting me effortlessly through the water until I'm positioned exactly where he wants me. His erection finds my entrance easily, nudging against me, and he pushes just the tip inside.

The stretch begins immediately, and I gasp at the sensation.

He pauses there, holding still despite what I know must be incredible restraint, and his blue eyes bore into mine with a seriousness that steals whatever breath I have left.

"Are you ready for me?" His voice is strained, rough with need. "Because once I'm inside you, once I fuck you properly the way you deserve, I have no intention of ever letting you go. You understand that? You're mine, Hannah. Ours. Say you understand."

"Fuck, Noel, I understand so well," I breathe, the words barely audible. "I'm yours."

Noel's expression turns almost feral at my surrender, something primitive and possessive taking over his features. He holds me there, pinned against him in the water, and I lose all remaining control as my pheromones surge out of me in waves. The chemical response is involuntary, my body calling to his, begging for what it desires.

Then he pushes into me slowly, stretching me around his considerable girth, studying my face the entire time. "You are so beautiful."

I writhe against him, a sharp ache of yearning cutting through me as I cling desperately to his broad shoulders, my nails digging into his skin.

"I really need you." The confession tears out of me. "To be deep inside me. Please, Noel, please—"

That breaks whatever restraint he was holding on to. He thrusts fully into me in one powerful stroke that drives the air from my lungs.

I cry out at the strength, the stretch almost too much, the fullness overwhelming, the sharp sting of pain mixing with pleasure so acute that it borders on unbearable. He's huge, filling me completely, and is incredible and terrifying and absolutely right all at once.

"That's it," he growls against my neck, his teeth grazing my pulse point. "Take all of me. Every fucking inch." He starts to move, slowly at first, letting my body adjust to his size, then gradually builds in speed and intensity.

And I'm lost. Completely, utterly floating on the sensation, finally surrendering to what my body has been screaming for since the moment I met these men.

To him. To them. To this pack that's claimed me whether I was ready for it or not.

As the water sloshes around us, spilling over the edges of the tub with every powerful thrust, as Noel drives into me with increasing power, and as I cling to him like he's the only solid thing in my collapsing world, I finally stop fighting.

I finally let myself fall.

And trust that he'll catch me.

NOEL

. . .

*H*annah feels so fragile in my arms, and every primal instinct in my body roars with satisfaction at having her vulnerable, trusting, completely mine.

She cries out, her grip on my shoulders tightening desperately, those perfect legs wrapped around my waist like she's afraid I'll pull away. Like I'd ever stop giving her what she needs.

I kiss her while I move inside her, spearing deep, hungry for her to feel every single inch of me. I'm compelled to make her understand exactly what I can give her. What her body has been craving.

Her entire body shudders against mine, trembling, and I fucking love seeing her this way. No walls. No resistance. No overthinking. Just raw need and desperate surrender.

She draws her lower lip between her teeth, sucking on it as I slowly pull out before pushing back in. I start out measured, controlled, letting her adjust to my size. But the water moves around us with each thrust, and she's completely lost.

Exactly where I want her.

I kiss her again, hard, possessive, claiming, and I love how fucking sweet she tastes, how she kisses me back with a yearning. She clearly can't get enough.

When I draw back just enough to stare into her eyes, I say, "I don't want you to ever forget that you are mine. And I will take care of you. Always."

She stares at me with those wide brown eyes, pupils huge, and then a purr rolls over her throat, a genuine Omega sound that buzzes through her entire chest and straight into mine.

I laugh, dark and satisfied. "There's my girl. So fucking beautiful when you let go."

She clings to me, and I give her what she's begging for with her body, taking her harder, faster, the water creating resistance but also adding sensation. Her breasts bounce with the movement, disappearing under the waterline, then emerging again, nipples peaked and tight, and watching them is driving me absolutely feral.

She's so tight around me, squeezing my cock with every thrust, and my need bursts forward, consuming rational thought. She's clamping down around me, her inner walls fluttering, making me want to ruin her for anyone else.

"More," she begs against my neck, her voice wrecked. "Harder, Noel—"

Hearing her say my name like that, hearing her beg, destroys whatever control I'm clinging to.

But the water is limiting what I can give her. Slowing things down when my girl clearly wants my full force. Happy to oblige. I pull out completely, and she cries out in protest, trying to pull me back. "Noel, no, don't stop—"

"I'm not going anywhere," I promise against her mouth, kissing her hard. "I just want to give you what you need properly. Up on your feet with me."

She stands, the water reaching mid-thigh, and my

hands go immediately to her tiny waist. Her gorgeous body is on full display, water dripping down her curves, and I take a moment just to look.

Mine. All mine.

I turn her to face away from me, running one hand slowly down her spine, feeling her shiver under my touch. "Bend over for me and grab the edge of the tub. Hold on tight, princess."

My hands fall between her thighs and spread them wider, positioning her exactly where I want her.

And because I can't resist, I lean to the side to take in the full view of her bent over in front of me. Fuck, her pussy is glistening with her slick—wet, swollen, ready for me.

A groan tears from my throat at the sight. "So beautiful."

She's already grinding her hips, seeking friction, and I stand directly behind her, lining up my cock with her waiting pussy.

When I sink back into her from this angle, we both groan at the tightness. Then I slam into her hard, and her legs twitch, trembling, trying to hold her weight.

I can't stop. Won't stop. The depth I reach in this position is unbelievable. She's so small compared to me, and my length goes to places inside her that make her scream.

She's arching her back, crying out with every powerful thrust. "Oh God—"

"I am your god right now," I growl, leaning over her

back, my mouth near her ear. "The only one you worship. The only one who matters. Say it."

"You're—" She can barely form words. "You're the only one—"

"Good girl." I take her faster, harder, giving her all of me, driving into her with everything I have, gripping her hips.

When she cries out and shatters, shuddering all over, her inner walls clenching around my cock, constricting me, I hiss. And it triggers my own release.

I groan, shoving into her one last time, powerful and deep. My cum floods her sweet pussy, filling her, wave after violent wave, giving her everything I have.

She moans beneath me, her body quivering, both of us lost to each other.

My knot swells at the base of my cock, that sharp sensation of it enlarging rapidly, growing, and I'm pushing all of me into her, including the knot.

She moans at the sensation, the stretch probably intense, and I lean over her back. "You can take it. Take all of me."

I'm swelling inside her to the knot's full size, locking us together, keeping us connected in the most primal way possible. And I fucking love this.

It's only once we've both started coming down from the high that I help her stand carefully, supporting her weight. I turn us both around and sit on the submerged ledge inside the spa, her on my lap so she's sitting with her back pressed against my chest, me still buried deep inside her.

Her breath is coming in shallow, broken pulls, her body trembling against mine. I'm still buried inside her, still throbbing, still feeling those tight little aftershocks flutter around my length every few seconds. The air between us is thick with heat and adrenaline, both of us suspended in that sharp, perfect high.

My hands slide up her waist, gripping, savoring every inch of her. I press my mouth to the curve of her neck, tasting the thin sheen of sweat on her skin, letting instinct take the wheel. The need hits me fast and violently—the need to claim, to brand, to leave something behind that says she's mine.

I bite down.

Not gentle. Not tentative. Deep enough that I feel her entire body jolt, that I break skin and taste the coppery tang of her blood. Her breath catches on a gasp that melts into a moan. Her walls clamp down around my cock so hard that I hiss against her. She arches into me, not pulling away, not flinching, but leaning in. Offering herself. Her fingers dig into my forearms, trembling because her body likes it. Wants it.

Approves.

I groan into her skin, the taste of her driving me insane. Her pulse flutters against my tongue, and I lick over the new mark slowly, taking the few drops of blood she offers me, and feeling her melt back against my chest.

"Fuck, Hannah..." I say, still holding her tight, my cock pulsing inside her, her heat wrapped around me like she was made for this moment.

Only then do I ease the bite into a trail of softer kisses, still claiming but slower now, possessive in a different way. She's still shaking, still fluttering, still high.

"How was that?"

She tries to answer, but all she manages at first is a shiver and a sound that's half laugh, half moan. She shifts just enough to glance back at me, her lips parted, her cheeks flushed, her eyes soft with something that looks dangerously close to devotion.

"Absolutely incredible," she whispers, breath still uneven. "And you marked me."

I grin. "Now you will never doubt that you belong to me."

She grins. There's no fear, no anger, just acceptance. Fuck, I am so obsessed with her.

"Rest against me," I command gently. "Let your body settle with mine. I've got you." I press another kiss to her damp shoulder. "Once my knot goes down, I'll make you my famous omelet. Don't know about you, but sex makes me fucking hungry."

She laughs breathlessly. "That sounds amazing."

She lets her head fall back against my shoulder, breathing deeply, finally relaxing completely. I move one arm up to palm her breast, cupping the full weight of it, and I'm in fucking heaven holding her like this.

"You're a very good girl," I whisper in her ear.

She softens immediately and giggles. "Not sure why, but the way you say that does something to my body. Makes me calmer."

"It's the trigger of an Alpha over an Omega. Your body recognizes its Alpha's approval and responds accordingly." I squeeze her breast gently. "Your biology knows who you belong to now."

She's exhausted, soft and pliant against me, and her voice is quiet when she speaks. "Noel?"

"Yeah?"

"I love that you found me. That you fucked me like that. I really needed it."

Pride surges through me. "It'll get better. You'll see. This is just the beginning of what I can give you."

I adore having my Omega melt under my attention like this. Knowing I satisfied her and gave her exactly what her body was screaming for. There are so many things I want to do with her, to her body. So many ways I will make her fall apart. And I can't wait to show her all the pleasure I can bring to her.

She's starting to doze in my arms, her breathing evening out, becoming slower and deeper. Her body goes heavy against me, completely trusting.

I hold her carefully and let myself just exist in this moment.

I don't remember the last time I felt this content. This right. Like after everything I've been through, I've finally found the one person who grounds me.

Hannah shifts slightly in her sleep, mumbling something I don't catch, and I press a kiss to her temple.

Mine. Ours. Finally where she belongs.

And I'll destroy anyone who tries to take her from us.

CHAPTER NINETEEN

HANNAH

The parade is finally happening, and I'm trying desperately not to let my nerves show.

Main Street in Whispering Grove has been transformed into a winter wonderland for this event. The historic storefronts are decorated with garlands and lights, snow dusting the awnings, and enormous red bows attached to every lamppost. The street itself has been closed off for blocks, rope barriers keeping the massive crowd on the sidewalks while leaving the road clear for the parade floats.

And there are so many people. Way more than I anticipated.

Families with children bundled in winter coats line both sides of the street, standing three-deep trying to get a good view. Vendors are selling hot chocolate and roasted chestnuts from carts positioned at intervals.

I've been working on this parade for months, coordinating with float builders, securing permits, hiring support teams, arranging insurance, triple-checking safety protocols. Every detail has been meticulously planned and executed.

And I'm still worried something will go really wrong. But I'm also still humming from last night with Noel, my body pleasantly sore between my thighs, and I'm so grateful he helped with my pre-heat issues. The desperate ache has eased significantly, letting me focus on the event instead of climbing the nearest Alpha.

Though, deep down, I know it's just simmering. Like a volcano building pressure, waiting to erupt. But not today. Please, not today. Get this parade done without a hitch. That's all I need. Then next week, all focus shifts to the tree lighting celebration.

I'm exhausted but excited for today to be finished successfully.

Chris is standing beside me, so close our bodies are touching from shoulder to hip, and he leans in to whisper near my ear. "It's going amazing. Coming together so well. You should be proud."

I smile despite my nerves, some of the tension easing from my muscles. "I know, right? So far, everything's running on schedule."

He inhales deeply near my neck. "You smell so fucking good today. Can't get enough of your scent."

Heat floods my face, but I can't help the grin. "Careful, or I'll think you only keep me around for how I smell."

"Oh, there are many other reasons." His hand finds

the small of my back, steady and grounding. "But your scent is definitely a perk."

My phone buzzes with an incoming text, pulling my attention back to work.

Team Lead Alpha Unit: Float 3 released. Running smoothly. ETA Main Street viewing area 4 minutes.

I'm positioned at the optimal viewing spot about halfway down the parade route, earpiece in my ear connected to my coordination team, phone in hand constantly updating with reports. The system I've set up is working beautifully. Each float has a team leader who reports to me at checkpoints, ensuring everything stays on schedule and any issues are addressed immediately.

So far, everything is smooth. I breathe easier, allowing myself a moment to actually enjoy what I've created. The parade itself is spectacular. The first float that passed was a winter wonderland scene of ice sculptures, performers dressed as snowflakes dancing and waving. The crowd loved it, children screaming with delight.

The second float featured a giant sleigh pulled by mechanical reindeer, with performers throwing candy to the kids lining the streets. The next float has everyone dressed up in red and white pants and shirts, collecting donations from people in the crowd for the local food bank.

And now I hear the excitement building as another float rounds the corner into view.

A huge inflatable balloon character, some cartoon Christmas elf I vaguely recognize from a popular kids' show, bobs along above the float, handlers gripping guide ropes to keep it steady. The float itself is decorated to look like a toy workshop, with elves building toys and waving to the crowd.

After that, the parade settles into a steady, glittering rhythm. A high school marching band comes next, uniforms a little too big, brass blaring slightly offbeat as they stomp out "Jingle Bell Rock." Behind them is a choir from one of the churches, carolers in matching scarves, walking in a tight formation and harmonizing like this is their Olympic event.

More floats roll past in a blur of tinsel and themed clusters. The local hockey team rides in the back of a truck strung with fairy lights, tossing mini candy canes and acting like they're too cool to care while clearly loving every second. A basketball team jogs behind, dribbling balls, with "Merry X-mas" spelled out on the fronts of their jerseys. Then come the politicians in their shiny, decorative cars, convertibles crawling along at a snail's pace—the mayor, some council members, and a few hopeful candidates all doing the careful, vote-for-me wave.

Local businesses follow, each trying to out-festive the last. There's even a float for the Whispering Grove bookshop, stacked with oversized cardboard books and a grinning elf mascot perched on a throne of wrapped boxes.

Then the farmers take their turn. Tractors rumble down the street, polished within an inch of their lives and wound with strings of lights. One has a trailer full of hay bales and kids in flannel shirts; another drags a flatbed lined with potted fir trees. A pair of ponies with braided manes and red ribbons at their bridles clip-clop past, followed by a very unimpressed line of goats in tiny knitted sweaters and tinsel-wrapped collars, each being tugged along by a determined kid in snow boots.

Somewhere in the middle of all that, the Parade Queen arrives, the girl whom the town voted for at the fall fair. She's riding on a snow-globe-themed float, dressed as a snow princess in a white cloak trimmed with faux fur, tiara sparkling under the streetlights. Fake snow drifts around her from hidden blowers, and she gives that practiced royal wave like she's been training for this moment her entire life.

By the time another school band squeaks its way through and a final cluster of carolers trails past, my toes are numb, my cheeks ache from smiling, and a good fifty minutes have blurred by in a whirl of lights, music, and too much sugar from all the candy thrown from the floats.

The crowd is cheering, singing along, and the energy is electric.

This is working.

"See?" Chris says, squeezing my waist gently. "Told you it would be perfect."

"Don't jinx it."

He laughs. "Always the pessimist."

My earpiece crackles. "Next float is being released now. Your personal favorite."

I grin because I know exactly what's coming.

Around the corner, I hear the crowd's excitement spike, children squealing, adults laughing, and then I see them.

Kane and Noel, dressed in full elf costumes, walking four of their reindeer down the center of Main Street.

The costumes are ridiculous and perfect, green-and-red-striped tights, pointed shoes with bells, tunics with jingle bells sewn all over, pointed hats with more bells. Their faces are painted with rosy cheeks and exaggerated smiles.

But nothing can hide how absolutely built they are. The costumes strain across their muscular frames, and they move with that confident grace that screams "dangerous men pretending to be whimsical."

They're holding the reindeer by decorative red and green reins, walking ahead of them with elf-like prancing that makes the crowd roar with laughter.

The reindeer—not Corn Dog, because we all agreed he'd cause absolute chaos—are behaving beautifully, occasionally stopping to let children pet their noses over the rope barriers.

Kane spots me and winks outrageously, blowing me a kiss that makes several women near me sigh audibly. Noel catches my eye and smirks, then does an elf dance move that has the crowd screaming.

I'm laughing, some of my stress evaporating.

"Your elves are a hit," Chris observes, amusement clear in his voice.

"They'd better be. Took me an hour to convince them to wear those costumes again."

Around me, I don't miss how women are openly

ogling the elves, some making comments loud enough for me to hear. "I need those elves to visit my house this Christmas," one woman says to her friend, fanning herself dramatically.

"Forget Santa. And to hell with Elf on the Shelf. I want *that* elf to myself!" another agrees.

They wish. They're with me. All three of them.

As Kane and Noel pass my position, leading the reindeer toward the rest of the parade route, I hear people around me continuing to talk about how adorable and sexy the elf-reindeer combination was.

Good. That's excellent. Memorable moments are what make events successful. My phone buzzes again.

Team Lead Bravo Unit: Next float releasing. ETA 3 minutes.

The centerpiece of the entire parade. I crane my neck to see down the street where it should be appearing soon.

The crowd's excitement is building again, parents lifting children onto shoulders for a better view, everyone pressing closer to the barriers.

Then I see it rounding the corner several blocks away. An enormous float, a two-story workshop scene with Santa standing on an elevated platform at the top, waving to the crowd. The platform has a small guardrail around it for safety, accessed by stairs built into the structure. Someone is inside the float, operating the vehicle that moves it forward.

The whole thing is wrapped in thousands of

Christmas lights that were supposed to create a magical glow.

But the lights are flickering. On, off, on again, then a section goes dark completely before sputtering back to life.

My stomach drops.

I had all the floats inspected and triple-checked by licensed electricians. Every wire, every connection, every power source was verified as safe.

This shouldn't be happening.

Chris notices too, his body tensing beside me. "The lights on the Santa float—"

"I see it."

"Could just be a loose connection," he offers, but his voice lacks conviction.

I want to believe it's just a minor technical glitch that hopefully people won't notice too much. The float continues down Main Street, getting closer to our position, and Santa keeps waving enthusiastically like nothing is wrong.

The crowd doesn't seem to notice the flickering lights, too focused on Santa himself.

Maybe it'll be fine and it'll hold together for the next ten minutes until the float clears the route.

Then, as the float reaches a position maybe fifty feet from where Chris and I are standing, something sparks from the light rigging.

A bright flash, visible even in daylight.

The crowd gasps collectively. "Ooooh!" People pull back instinctively from the barriers.

And then flames erupt from the edge of the float where the lights are mounted. Orange and hungry, spreading fast across the decorative garland.

"Oh, fuck," I breathe.

My training kicks in immediately. I'm already pressing the button on my radio. "We have a fire on Santa's float. I need fire suppression at the Main Street and Fourth Avenue intersection NOW. Everyone, clear the area around the float immediately!"

I'm moving before I finish speaking, Chris right beside me as we duck under the rope barriers onto the street.

"Everyone, step back!" I'm shouting, waving my arms. "Move away from the float! Clear the area!"

The float has stopped moving, and I see the driver scrambling out of the cab, looking shocked and terrified.

Chris is already getting onto the float on the opposite side of the climbing flames, reaching for Santa on the elevated platform. Santa is frozen, staring at the flames spreading across the front of the float. Chris barks something at him, and that gets him moving. They are down the stairs in no time and safely onto the street just as the flames spread to engulf nearly half of the float's decorative exterior. Smoke rises into the sky, and I want to die from this happening now.

The crowd is backing up, some people screaming, parents clutching children, everyone pulling out phones to film. This is a disaster.

Two firefighters in full gear are running toward us,

carrying specialized backpack units with nozzles. Atlas, the fire station chief, I recognize immediately because I coordinated with him personally to have fire support stationed at strategic points along the route. Just in case.

Thank God I did.

Atlas is a very large man, easily six-three, built like the Greek god he's named after, with tanned skin and dark brown hair trimmed short at the sides. And he is captivating.

"Clear out!" he shouts with the kind of authority that makes people obey instantly. "Everyone, back!"

He and his partner move fast toward the burning float, aiming their nozzles at the flames.

Chris appears at my side, his hand on my elbow, drawing me back from the heat. "They've got it. Let them work."

I watch, my heart hammering so hard I feel it in my throat, as the two firefighters spray the flames with some kind of chemical foam that I assume they use for electrical fires. The flames resist at first, but within a couple of minutes, they're extinguished, leaving black char marks across half the float and smoke rising in plumes.

Santa and the driver are safe, standing at a distance, looking shaken.

Everyone is safe.

But the parade is completely stopped, and hundreds of people are watching, filming, posting to social media.

Fuck. Fuck, fuck, fuck.

Of course a fire happens on my parade. Of course.

"We need to get it off the route," I say to Chris, my voice shakier than I want. "The parade needs to continue. We can't just—"

"I'm on it."

He's already striding toward Atlas, and I watch as they exchange quick words. Then Atlas nods, and suddenly all three men, Chris, Atlas, and the other firefighter, are positioning themselves around the charred float and pushing.

The float is enormous and heavy, but they move it, steering it toward a side street.

I rush forward to maneuver people out of the way, unhooking the rope barriers and directing the crowd back. "Please step aside! Make room!"

A few bystanders jump in to help direct foot traffic, and I could kiss every single one of them for their assistance. The men get the float pushed completely off Main Street into the side alley, out of sight of the parade route.

I jog over to Santa. "Are you okay?" I ask, scanning him for injuries.

"Fine. Just scared the hell out of me." His voice is trembling. "One second everything was fine, and the next second it was on fire."

"I'm so glad you're safe." I grip his shoulder. "I need you to do me a favor. Start walking down the parade route, waving like everything's okay. Show everyone that Santa's fine. Can you do that?"

He nods, some color returning to his face. "Yeah. Yeah, I can do that."

"Thank you."

I turn to the driver. "Stay with the float. I'm sending someone to tow it back to the staging garages for a full inspection."

He nods mutely, still looking stunned, and then I put the call in with the team.

Atlas approaches, pulling off his helmet, and even stressed and covered in soot, the man is objectively gorgeous—strong jaw, dark eyes, the kind of presence that commands respect.

"Electrical fire," he says without preamble. "Likely a short in the wiring or a faulty connection that sparked when it shouldn't have. If everything was installed properly, this shouldn't have happened. Needs a full inspection to determine the exact cause."

"That's going to happen," I assure him. "I need to know how this could have occurred when everything was supposedly checked."

"I'll stay here and make sure there's nothing else that might reignite," Atlas offers. "You get back to your parade. You've got people waiting."

"Thank you. Seriously, thank you so much."

He nods and turns back to the charred float.

I make my way back to the viewing area where Chris is waiting, and I feel like I might throw up.

"Sometimes these things happen," Chris says gently, reading my expression. "You couldn't have predicted—"

"But it's on me." My voice cracks slightly. "All of this comes back on me. The safety, the inspection, every-thing. This is *my* event."

"And you handled it perfectly. No one was hurt. That's what matters."

"People are going to remember the parade where Santa's float caught fire."

"Actually, people are already talking about those adorable reindeer," he counters. "I heard at least five different conversations praising that addition."

I want to believe him, but the dread sitting heavily in my chest won't budge.

Slowly, the crowd returns its attention to the parade route and watching Santa.

Chris produces a bottle of water from somewhere and hands it to me. "Drink. You're pale."

I take it gratefully and gulp down half the bottle, the cold water helping to clear my head slightly.

"You're doing great," he says softly, tucking a strand of hair behind my ear. "I know you're stressed, but you handled an emergency with grace and efficiency."

I lean into his touch for just a moment, drawing strength from his solid presence.

My team is moving along Main Street, removing rope barriers, waving to the dispersing crowd, who all seem happy and satisfied despite the earlier fire.

The Santa float has already been towed away to the staging area, but I can't stop thinking about how much worse it could have been. If the flames had spread faster, if people had panicked and stampeded, if Santa had fallen from that platform...

My phone rings, and my stomach drops when I see that it's the council member we booked this event through, the head of the public events committee.

I answer with a shaking hand. "Hello, Margaret."

"Hannah, I heard about the fire on the Santa float. How did that happen?"

My stomach churns. "We're investigating the exact cause. The electrician who inspected everything certified it as safe, but clearly something went wrong. I've already ordered a full—"

"Look," Margaret interrupts, and her tone is firm but not unkind. "I know sometimes shit happens. Equipment fails, things go wrong despite our best efforts. Most people I've talked to are actually raving about your last-minute addition to the parade, those adorable reindeer. They saved you in a way."

Some of the tension eases from my shoulders. "I'm so glad people enjoyed them."

"But, Hannah, the tree lighting ceremony next week is even more important. Higher stakes, more visibility, more things that can go wrong. I need you to promise me it will go off without a hitch."

"I promise. I'll triple-check everything. Quadruple-check. I'll personally inspect every single element."

"Good. I'm counting on you. *The council* is counting on you."

She hangs up, and I stand there staring at my phone. The pressure is crushing. The tree lighting has to be perfect. Has to be. And suddenly my body temperature spikes dramatically. Heat floods through me, not embarrassment or stress, but actual physical heat that makes sweat break out across my skin.

No. Not now. God, not now.

"Chris, we need to go see what they found with the float," I say quickly, trying to ignore the growing ache between my thighs.

"Are you okay?" He's studying my face with concern. "You look flushed."

"I'm fine. I just need to know what happened. Please."

He takes my hand in his, squeezing gently. "Want me to carry you? You look unsteady."

Despite everything, I laugh. "No, it's okay. But I love that you asked."

"I adore you, you know that?" His voice goes soft, intimate. "And you're not working here alone. We have your back. Always."

I stop walking and look up at him, and something in my chest clenches painfully. Then I hug him tightly, burying my face against his chest. "I love that so much. Thank you."

He embraces me fully, his arms wrapping around me securely, and we kiss, softly at first, then deeper as I lose myself in the taste of him. When we break apart, he's studying my face again. "Your scent is becoming stronger. I think we should head home."

"Not yet," I insist, even as another wave of heat rolls through me. "Please, I have to make sure—" I groan at the tightness building within me, the ache intensifying. "Just quickly, please."

He nods reluctantly. "Quickly. Then we're leaving."

We hurry down the street toward the staging garages where the parade started, and the fast walk helps distract me from the fire building inside my body.

Atlas emerges from the garage as we arrive, wiping his hands on a rag.

"Hannah," he greets. "Got some news, and you're not going to like it."

My stomach drops. "What did you find?"

"We checked the wiring thoroughly. Some of the internal wires were partially cut—deliberately exposed like someone took wire cutters to them. This wasn't an equipment failure or faulty installation. This was done on purpose."

The world tilts slightly. "Like someone sabotaged the float? Intentionally?"

He shrugs, his expression grim. "That cut was clean and on purpose. Not accidental damage."

"But why would someone—"

He tucks the rag into his belt. "I gotta get back to the station, but I'll send you my full report within forty-eight hours. You'll want to file a police report about this."

"Right. Yes. Thank you, Atlas."

He nods and heads to his fire truck parked nearby.

I turn to Chris, feeling sick. "Why does it feel like this is somehow aimed at making my parade fail? Do you think Scot might be involved?"

His jaw tightens, lips pressing into a thin line. "I wouldn't put it past that bastard. But we need proof before we can accuse him of anything. However, I suspect he's got a hand in this."

"Maybe I got too distracted. I didn't make enough effort to ensure this didn't happen—"

"Stop." Chris cups my face with both hands, forcing me to meet his eyes. "Sometimes you can't prevent things. If someone really wants to do something malicious, it's nearly impossible to stop them. Assholes will do whatever they want. All you can do is prepare for it, and you did. You had firefighters ready. You had protocols in place. You handled the emergency perfectly. Hannah, I am so fucking proud of you and how today went."

But I'm breathing too quickly, dread sitting heavily in my chest because it could have been so much worse.

And my body is officially burning up. Heat is spreading through every nerve ending, and suddenly my panties are gushing with slick, soaking through to my jeans. Oh, hell!

I groan from an impossible ache so deep it feels like I might die if I don't get relief soon.

Chris catches me as I wobble, his arms steadying me. "Okay, not asking anymore. We're going. You're about to go into full heat."

He has me off my feet in seconds, cradling me against his chest, and he's barking orders to my team, who are still finishing the cleanup. "Hannah needs to leave. Medical emergency. She needs a complete list of everyone who had access to the Santa float over the past three days. Get it to her by tomorrow morning."

My main team leader nods, already pulling out her tablet.

Then we're moving, Chris carrying me toward where their truck is parked, and I know my team will handle everything. They'll close everything down properly. I coordinated it all, gave them clear instructions. But I still feel awful for leaving them.

Before I know it, I'm in the truck and we're driving through backstreets to avoid parade traffic. And I'm moaning, unable to stop myself, leaning toward Chris like I can't breathe without touching him.

"Sorry that my heat—"

"Don't ever apologize." His voice is rough, intense. "You are my world. You are all I care about right now. Everything else can wait."

My hand trails down to his pants without conscious thought, fumbling with his belt.

"Hannah," he warns, though his voice is strained. "I have very limited control here."

"I need you inside me now, or I will pass out," I beg, pulling at his belt and zipper with desperate fingers. "And you're driving, so—"

"Fuck, you're going to kill me."

He lifts his hips slightly while keeping one hand on the wheel, helping me tug open his pants and pull down his boxers.

His already huge cock bounces free, thick and hard and perfect. My greedy hand curls around him instantly, and he hisses through his teeth. I lean over his lap without thinking, driven purely by raw arousal, and push my lips over his erection.

"Oh, fuck—" The truck swerves as his hand jerks on the wheel.

I pull back slightly. "Get us home safely, please."

Then I take him deeper, hollowing my cheeks, using my tongue, losing myself in the taste and feel of him.

"Jesus Christ," he growls, one hand dropping to tangle in my hair while the other white-knuckles the steering wheel. "This might be the most difficult drive of my entire life. If we crash, I'm blaming you and your perfect mouth."

I would laugh if my mouth weren't full, so I just take him deeper instead and let the heat consume me.

CHAPTER TWENTY

CHRIS

I'm driving erratically, the truck swerving across lanes as Hannah's mouth works absolute magic over my cock, and my vision starts blurring at the edges.

"Fuck. Holy fuck, Hannah—" My hand tangles in her hair because I'm about to lose my mind completely.

I barely register turning onto our property, or what I think is our property, as my climax slams into me. Stars explode behind my eyes as I hiss through clenched teeth, my entire body going rigid.

I manage to throw the truck into park but don't even think about the handbrake because it's somewhere under Hannah and rational thought has completely abandoned me as I pulse into her mouth. I'm gripping the steering wheel in a death grip with my other hand.

She swallows everything, her throat working, and the sensation nearly stops my heart.

"Jesus Christ, you're incredible," I gasp, my head falling back against the seat. "Absolutely perfect."

She finally releases me and sits up, wiping her mouth with the back of her hand, and the satisfied smile on her face is pure sin.

I'm boneless, wrecked. "You could have killed us both."

"But we're not dead." She's moaning already, shifting restlessly, her thighs rubbing together. "And you have no idea how good that was for me. Tasting you, having you, is everything."

I reach over and yank up the handbrake, my hands still trembling. "Let's get you inside before you combust."

I climb out on unsteady legs and immediately step into the flower bed, nearly face-planting into a tree trunk.

Oh, fuck. I parked like a complete disaster, the truck at a diagonal across the front lawn, nowhere near the actual driveway, tire tracks through what's left of our landscaping.

Don't care. Can't care. Not even a little bit.

I do up my pants hastily, zip, belt, then rush around to Hannah's side and pull open her door.

She practically falls out, and I catch her against my chest.

"You're with me," I say, lifting her into my arms in one smooth motion.

She wraps her arms around my neck immediately, pressing her face against my throat, and I love how she fits perfectly against me. How soft she is. Her scent floods my senses, and her arousal is thick. I'm half hard again already.

"You are perfect, Hannah," I murmur against her hair as I carry her toward the house. "So beautiful and sexy. And all mine. All ours."

I take her straight upstairs to her room, the one we designed specifically for Omega heats back when finding our match was just desperate hoping.

The room is perfect for this. Enormous bed piled with soft blankets and pillows. Supplies stocked in built-in cabinets. Everything carefully considered.

At the center is a low, cushioned platform we had custom-built, surrounded by plush rugs. Low enough for comfort, high enough for access from any angle. Designed specifically for heat care.

I set her on the edge, and she's immediately panting, rubbing her thighs together frantically, seeking any friction.

I crouch in front of her, my thumb stroking her inner knee. "Tell me what you need, sweetheart."

She looks at me with those huge brown eyes, pupils so wide there's barely any color left. "I need—" She swallows hard. "Something to hold me still. I want to be tied up so I feel constantly held. I trust you, Chris. I trust all of you completely."

Everything in me goes very still.

She trusts us. Trusts us enough to be vulnerable, at our mercy during the most intense biological drive she'll ever experience.

Something primal and possessive roars to life in my chest.

I rise slowly, pressing a kiss to her forehead. "Don't move. I'll be right back."

I take the stairs three at a time, my mind racing through options. I need something soft enough not to hurt her skin but substantial enough to give her the restraint she's asking for.

In the living room, I spot the basket of holiday decorations we still haven't put away. On top is a coil of thick, plush tinsel, the expensive kind that's almost feathery, golden and luxurious.

Perfect.

My cock is fully hard just imagining it. Hannah wrapped up like the most precious gift, presented to us.

I grab the entire coil and sprint back upstairs, my pulse thundering in my ears.

When I push open her door, she's already completely naked, sitting on the platform, hugging her knees to her chest, rocking slightly. Energy radiates off her in waves.

Her gaze snaps to me the instant I enter, and she moans, her hands reaching out desperately. "Chris, please, I can't—"

"I'm here." I cross to her, dropping to my knees in front of the platform. "I've got you. Now stand up for me, beautiful."

I help her to her feet, and my gaze devours every inch of her body. Her breasts are full and perfect, nipples tight and begging for my mouth. The curve of her waist. The swell of her hips. The glistening evidence of her arousal already coating her inner thighs.

"Do you have any idea what you do to me? How much it turns me on thinking about you like this? Wrapped up. Unable to hide anything from me. Just mine to take however I want."

She giggles breathlessly, but it dissolves into a moan when I lift her wrists gently and start wrapping the soft tinsel around them, not tight enough to hurt, just enough to bind them together in front of her.

While I work, she leans against me, pressing her breasts against my chest, her mouth finding my neck. She licks and sucks at my pulse point, and having her desperate and shameless and completely uninhibited is everything I've ever fantasized about.

She whimpers against my skin. "It's torture not having you inside me. I don't know how much longer I can hold on without breaking apart."

Her bound hands lower between us and are already tugging at my shirt, trying to strip me.

I step back just enough to admire my work. "I'm not done with you yet. Not done admiring what's mine."

I trail the rest of the tinsel down her body deliberately. Wrapping it around her torso just above her breasts, then just below, framing them beautifully. Around her slim waist. Around her thighs in criss-crossing patterns that still allow her legs to part freely, creating perfect handles for us to grip.

When I step back to take in the full picture, my jaw clenches involuntarily.

She's trembling. Golden tinsel wrapped around her gorgeous body. Flushed skin. Desperate eyes. Completely at my mercy.

"You are the sexiest thing I've ever seen in my life," I growl, meaning every word.

"Chris—" She's begging, shifting helplessly, her bound hands reaching for me again. "Please, I need your cock inside me now."

She's all over me suddenly, tugging at my clothes again, even trying to use her teeth on my belt, and I finally give in.

I strip off my shirt, toe off my shoes and socks, but she's already fumbling with my belt buckle again.

"You beg so pretty," I tell her, catching her wrists gently to still them for a moment. "Say my name again."

"Chris," she breathes, and the urgency in her voice nearly undoes me. "Please, Chris."

She drops to her knees on the platform, her bound hands clasped in front of her, and the position presses her breasts together perfectly, nipples peaked and tight.

I can't resist.

I fall to my knees in front of her and take one nipple into my mouth, sucking hard, then move to the other. Her moans grow louder, more desperate, echoing off the walls.

She somehow manages to get my pants undone, reaching for my erection, and she's absolutely insatiable.

I'm completely here for it.

Suddenly, the front door opens downstairs with a bang. Boots hit the hardwood floor heavily.

"Chris!" Kane's voice carries up, laced with amusement and confusion. "What the hell kind of parking job is that? Looks like you drove home blackout drunk! Did you have some kind of emergency or—"

He cuts off abruptly, and then he and Noel thunder up the stairs. They burst through the bedroom door just as I pull back from Hannah's breasts, and both of them stop dead, their eyes bulging.

Hannah pushes herself up onto her knees from where she was leaning back on her heels, presenting herself to them deliberately. Legs spread wide, chest thrust forward, golden tinsel wrapped around her like decoration, and she's the most erotic thing any of us have ever witnessed.

Kane and Noel both nearly trip over their own feet trying to get farther into the room.

"Holy shit," Kane breathes, his eyes raking over every inch of her.

"I swear you're trying to destroy us," Noel says, his voice strained and dark. "Looking like the world's sweetest present just waiting to be unwrapped."

Hannah's smile is pure seduction and need. "Then get your clothes off if you want to unwrap your gift."

They're stripping in record time, shirts flying, belts hitting the floor with metallic clinks, jeans kicked aside carelessly.

Hannah's inner thighs are glistening with slick, her

hips moving in small unconscious circles, and she's barely holding herself together.

Her bound hands find my cock again, pulling it free from my boxers, and I hiss at the contact.

"Please, Chris. Cock," she begs, her voice wrecked. "I can't wait anymore."

I lower my hand between her thighs, finding her soaking wet and swollen, and tease her entrance with my fingers.

She moans so loud it's almost a scream, her hips bucking against my hand.

Noel steps closer, inhaling deeply, his chest expanding. "Holy fuck, her scent. It's intoxicating."

Kane moves behind her, dropping to his knees, his large palms sliding down her arms slowly, fingers brushing over the tinsel binding her wrists appreciatively. He presses a deliberate kiss to her shoulder, his teeth grazing her skin, then he stares at the bite mark already healed over on the curve of her neck, which I barely noticed.

He glares at Noel over Hannah's shoulder. "That's your handiwork. Heard you two last night, by the way. The whole damn house did."

"Her cries woke me up around two a.m., and sleep was completely impossible after that. Just lay there listening and suffering," I add.

Hannah giggles breathlessly, then moans. "I want one from each of you. I want you to mark me. Make it hurt. Make me scream for all the neighbors to hear miles away."

She whimpers, her thighs shaking violently, and the sound snaps the last threads of restraint in all three of us.

I push two fingers into her, and she cries out beautifully, her back arching.

Noel crosses to the door and shuts it firmly, then turns back to us, his eyes locked on the gold tinsel wrapped around her thighs. "You did good, Chris."

Hannah tries to reach for Noel with her bound hands, trembling all over. "I'm burning alive."

I pull my fingers out of her as she moans, and I strip off my pants and boxers slowly, deliberately, letting her watch every movement, and Hannah's entire body shakes at the sight of me fully naked.

"You're such a perfect gift, baby girl," Kane murmurs against her shoulder.

Noel's hand reaches for her breast, palming it roughly, his thumb brushing over her nipple and making her gasp.

I take a seat on the platform next to her, leaning against the cushions, and hold out my hand to her. "Come here, sweetheart. Climb on."

She moves eagerly, straddling my lap, and I line myself up with her entrance.

She's drenched as I slide in easily despite my size, and we both groan at the sensation of finally being connected. She has her breasts against my chest, her bound wrists between us.

"That's it," I encourage, my hands gripping her hips

and guiding her movements. "You're doing so well. Taking me so perfectly."

She starts to move faster, rising and falling on me, and I'm in absolute heaven watching her.

Kane and Noel are staring too, hands moving over her body, one on either side of her. That's when Kane maneuvers to kneel behind her, his broad chest pressing against her back, his mouth near her ear. "Are you ready for more, baby girl? Think you can handle both of us at the same time?"

His hands slide down to her ass, gripping and kneading the flesh, spreading her open. I sense her body tensing slightly. "Let me ease you into it."

"Yes," she gasps, riding me harder. "Please, yes, I like it when you touch me there."

"What about when I push a finger in?" Kane asks.

She moans so loudly that her pussy squeezes my cock, and I'm hissing.

Noel's palm cradles the back of her neck, thumb stroking slowly along her hairline. "Look at you," he murmurs against her temple, voice thick. "You're perfect like this." She shivers, the kind that rolls through her whole body, and presses closer to me as if her body is choosing instinctively.

"We're making you ours today," Noel states.

"It's exactly what I want," she breathes, and I feel every part of her melt at those words, like choosing us has freed her of something heavy she's been carrying for years.

I grip her hips more firmly. "Easy, gorgeous," I

murmur against her shoulder. "You're safe. We've got you."

Noel cups her jaw and turns her face toward him. Their mouths meet, deep, claiming, hungry, a kiss that draws a low sound out of me even though I'm not the one kissing her. She's beautiful like this. Untethered. Letting herself fall. Letting herself be held.

"Breathe for me, sweetheart," Kane says, shifting behind her, clearly moving his cock to her rear entrance.

She pauses riding me and exhales loudly. Her hands rest against my chest for balance, and I lean back on mine, giving the guys time to find their place. She trembles, and every breath she gives is another plea she can't put into words.

Noel kisses her again, slower this time, reverent. "Look at her," he says against her lips. "She's letting go."

"Read for me, baby girl?" Kane asks, and as she nods, he pushes into her. I can tell by how tense she is against me. Her breath hitches, her whole body going tight with anticipation, and I feel it in my own chest, like someone hooked a wire around my ribs and pulled.

"Fuck, you're so tight," Kane grunts, but there's no rush. We wait as he works his way into her ass, slow motions in and out, and she's purring again. Hell, I love when she makes those sounds. Then the three of us are moving, her riding me, me lifting my hips to meet her for each thrust.

Kane's hands slide higher, bracketing her ribs, steadying her when she sways. "Beautiful," he says, voice rough. "Every little sound you make drives us insane. And now we're going to fuck you, knot you until you're full. Then we'll start again."

She tries to speak, but it comes out as a soft cry, her hands reaching out for Noel's cock, as he's still standing alongside us. I wrap my arms around her waist. Every part of her is shaking from being so completely surrounded, so thoroughly wanted, so deeply claimed.

"Let it happen," I whisper into her hair. "We're right here. All of us. You're not alone."

Then Noel guides his cock into her opening mouth, his hand at the back of her head, fisting her hair, and moving in closer, until she perfectly has three erections inside her.

Her breath breaks into a whimper, her body bowing between us, and the three of us move in unspoken synchronization, bodies grinding, each of us fucking her in a protective, possessive way.

"She's incredible like this," Noel grunts.

Kane leans in, brushing her shoulder with his mouth. "Ours," he murmurs, voice shaking slightly. "She's ours."

"You're doing so well, sweetheart," I say.

Her entire body softens at that, every resistance melting out of her until she's nothing but need and surrender and pure Omega instinct.

Kane brushes her hair over one shoulder with slow deliberation, exposing the curve of her neck. "You let Noel mark you last night," he murmurs. "I bet you took it so sweetly." His hand slides around her breasts, holding her steady. "Now it's my turn."

She shudders, a full-body tremor that starts at her spine and ripples outward until she's trembling between us. Her bound hands are still against my chest, her scent blooming so intensely I can barely think.

Kane lowers his mouth to the unmarked side of her neck, and her whole body tightens in anticipation.

He kisses first, slow, warm, claiming kisses down the arch of her throat, and she melts, her hips rolling faster.

Then Kane opens his mouth and bites.

Her sound, God, it cuts right through me. A strangled, desperate moan, guttural and need-soaked, her pussy tightening, her body arching violently as instinct floods her.

Noel groans beside us, his hand gripping the back of her head, steadying her. Kane holds her as she shakes, as her breath catches, his mouth still latched onto her.

A single red bead wells at the edge of Kane's mark, slides down the line of her throat, gliding over her collarbone... lower... over the swell of her breast, catching the light before disappearing into the edge of her nipple.

"Mine," Kane growls against her skin. "You're mine now as well. Bound to me."

Her answering sound is broken, overwhelmed, hungry.

I tighten my jaw, grinding into her with my hips. Her entire body trembles. She's lost in the marking, beautifully lost.

I can barely breathe. Watching her be claimed, feeling her body respond with that wild, helpless surrender… it's almost too much. My mark will come last. She'll be mine when she's ready, not a moment before. And that restraint nearly destroys me as I watch her unravel between us.

We move with her. Her sounds change, rising, breaking, turning into something so raw it punches the air out of me. Her body suddenly bows, yielding, tightening with frantic need. She clings to me, shaking.

"Hannah," I whisper, my voice barely holding. "Sweetheart, let go. We've got you."

And she does.

Her whole body shudders in a long, unstoppable wave, her cry tearing out of her as she convulses between us, Noel's cock still deep in her mouth. Her breath stutters, her nails dig into my chest, her thighs tremble violently. She's beautiful like this, undone, unguarded, instinct taking the wheel and driving her straight into us.

She constricts my cock, and I'm not the only one hissing, but Kane is in heaven. Our little Omega is convulsing, floating on her orgasm.

It's in that moment that Noel stiffens beside her, his breath slicing out of him in a low, choked groan. "Fuck!" Then he unleashes, and I watch her swallow his seed, some of it seeping out from the corner of her mouth, but she's doing so well taking it all in.

Kane curses behind her, gripping her waist hard enough that his knuckles go white.

Her body's reaction pulls us into a cascade, a chain reaction, primal and unavoidable, the three of us caught in the gravity of her release, our bodies answering hers without hesitation or restraint.

And just as Kane comes undone and pumps into her, I lose my grip and it all comes gushing out. I thrust deep into her, my cock throbbing. I'm growling with my release as I flood her with my cum.

Her breath hitches, her whole body going tight with anticipation.

Something inside me tightens the way a storm gathers, slowly at first, then suddenly everywhere. That deep, primal pull hits low in my gut, a pressure that builds with every breath. It's heat meeting heat, instinct answering instinct, and it rolls through me with a force that wipes out thought. That's the sensation of my knot swelling inside her, pushing against her, keeping us locked in. It's overwhelming and perfect and terrifying in how right it feels, like a piece of me made to fit only her is finally snapping into place.

Kane has the same expression on his face as I'm feeling, as he's locked inside her as well. Noel withdraws from her mouth, gasping for air.

"Fuck, I could do that again," Noel murmurs, his voice a low, satisfied rumble.

Hannah lets out a soft, breathless laugh, her body still trembling faintly, her forehead resting back against Kane's shoulder as he holds her upright with gentle hands.

I push myself up from where I'd been bracing back

on my hands, leaning in until her flushed face is inches from mine. She looks dazed, glowing, wrecked in the most beautiful way.

Her fingers brush my jaw. "That was… incredible," she whispers, still struggling to catch her breath. "I feel like I'm floating. My head is still foggy."

"You won't float away," I murmur, cupping the side of her neck as Kane steadies her from behind. "I'm going to bring you back down to us."

Her gaze locks on mine.

I lower my mouth to her shoulder, kissing the curve where her skin is warm and soft. Slow kisses at first. Her breath hitches, and she tilts her head for me, exposing more of herself without hesitation.

Kane's hands slide over her waist, grounding her. Noel strokes her hair, murmuring soft praise.

I kiss my way to the place just beneath her collarbone, over her heart, where I can feel her pulse against my lips, and look up at her again.

She swallows, eyes bright. "Chris… please. Claim me."

The world narrows to that single plea. I hold her gaze as I lean in, giving her every chance to pull away. She doesn't. She lifts her chin and leans toward me.

I bite.

Not hard, just enough pressure for the bond to flare, bright and electric, lacing through both of us.

Hannah cries out softly, her whole body shuddering as she clings to me, to Kane, to Noel. Her pulse jumps under my teeth, her breath stuttering.

And inside me… it's like a door I've kept bolted for years blows open all at once. Not another presence. Not another instinct. Just *me*, finally allowed to feel everything I've been holding back.

A rush of emotions slams through me: devotion, protectiveness, something fierce and absolute. I can sense the rhythm of her heartbeat syncing with mine. The warmth of her body settles against me like she was always meant to fit there.

When I lift my mouth from her skin, she's breathing hard, blinking up at me like she can't quite process what just happened.

"Chris…" she whispers, voice shaking. "I feel like… like you're inside me. Not physically—just… everywhere. Just like Noel and Kane."

I press my forehead to hers, breathing her in. "That's because you're ours now," I say softly.

Kane's voice is a low murmur behind her. "She's glowing."

She looks lit from within, trembling, flushed, breath soft and uneven. She's wrapped in all of us and tinsel.

She's ours.

And now I finally feel like I'm hers.

She buries her face in my neck, breath warm against my skin. We're still holding her up.

"Can we do this again?" she whispers, voice small and needy and so full of longing that it nearly floors me.

I inhale sharply, because the moment she asks, I can feel her arousal already flickering back to life, a slow bloom of heat rolling through her body, her scent thick and sweet.

She's not done.

Not even close.

Kane chuckles softly against her shoulder. "Baby girl, you're already begging, and I love it."

Noel brushes a kiss against the side of her jaw. "You don't have to ask for more. We're not going anywhere."

I tilt her chin up with gentle fingers so she has to look at me. Her eyes are heavy-lidded, lips swollen. "We're yours," I tell her quietly, every word steady and certain. "For a day. For a week. However long your heat lasts."

Her breath catches.

"But right now," Kane adds, voice velvet-smooth, "we need to give our cocks a minute or twenty to settle."

"Then," I promise, brushing my thumb over her lower lip, "you won't see us coming."

She shivers, smiling beautifully.

Kane nuzzles the back of her neck, breath hot. "We're going to take you apart."

Noel kisses her temple. "Piece by piece."

"And put you back together," I finish, leaning in to press a slow kiss to her mouth, "exactly how we want you."

She melts into me with a soft sound, all warmth and surrender and trust.

And I swear to God, I've never seen anything more devastatingly beautiful.

CHAPTER TWENTY-ONE

HANNAH

My body feels as though I've decided to run a triathlon after spending three years on a couch eating bonbons.

Everything aches. Muscles I forgot existed are staging a full protest. Even my hair hurts, which shouldn't be anatomically possible. But it's the best kind of ache. I grin like an idiot every time I move and remember exactly how I earned these particular sore muscles.

Three days since my heat broke, and I'm still buzzing. My body still hums at a frequency only dogs and extremely satisfied Omegas can hear.

It's more than just the mind-blowing sex, though holy hell, that was extraordinary. It's the marking bites. Three of them now, one from each of my Alphas, strate-gically placed on my body like the world's sexiest hickeys.

The marks connect me to them like invisible threads running between us. I sense them even when they're not in the room, their presence always humming at the edge of my awareness.

It's weird. It's invasive. It's absolutely incredible.

The snow finally stopped overnight, and actual sunlight is pouring through the windows this morning as if the universe is personally apologizing for the weather. The sky is that impossible blue that challenges you to write poetry, or at least Instagram the hell out of it.

I'm in the backyard wearing Kane's jacket, which is oversized on me, with my jeans and sweater, hauling a bucket of food to the reindeer pen.

They spot me immediately and stampede toward the fence.

"All right, all right, don't trample each other," I call out, opening the gate and slipping inside. "There's plenty for everyone, you greedy bastards."

I dump handfuls of grain into the trough, and they descend on it like locusts. Except Corn Dog, who's ignoring the food completely and following me around like a lovesick puppy.

"You know the food is over there, right?" I tell him, scratching behind his ears. "With all your friends? Remember food? The thing you literally break into the house for?"

He bumps his nose against my hand insistently.

I've noticed lately that the second I step outside,

Corn Dog abandons whatever trouble he's creating and runs straight to me. The other reindeer are friendly enough, but Corn Dog has completely imprinted on me as though I'm his mother or his Omega or his personal food dispenser.

"You're seriously high-maintenance," I inform him, pulling out the bag of fancy moss that the guys special-order. "You know that? Like, next-level needy. We should get you a therapist."

He makes this little huffing sound that I swear is indignant. I hold out a handful of moss, and he takes it hungrily from my palm, chewing while maintaining intense eye contact.

"So listen, I have a proposition for you," I say conversationally, like I'm not talking to a reindeer. "The tree lighting ceremony is in two days, and I have this idea that could either be brilliant or get us both banned from public events forever."

Corn Dog keeps chewing, watching me.

"I need you to be on your absolute best behavior. No eating decorations. No headbutting people. No breaking into buildings or blocking doorways or any of your usual nonsense." I scratch under his chin. "Think you can handle being a professional for one evening?"

He leans into my touch, and I'm choosing to interpret that as agreement.

"Good. Because if you pull this off, I'll make sure you get moss every single day for a month. The expensive kind. Maybe I'll even let you sleep in the house again."

"You're negotiating with livestock now?" a deep male voice asks.

I spin around to find Kane leaning against the doorframe of the house, arms crossed, looking unfairly attractive in jeans and a thermal Henley that shows off every muscle.

His hair is combed off his face, and there's a smile playing at his lips, which I adore.

"He's family," I correct, giving Corn Dog one more scratch. "And clearly the best listener in this entire household."

"Ouch." Kane presses a hand to his chest. "Wounded."

"Truth hurts, *Candy Kane*." I grin.

He groans. "I knew that nickname would come back to haunt me."

I move to distribute food to the other reindeer, ensuring everyone gets their fair share.

"He's really attached to you," Kane observes, watching Corn Dog shadow my every move. "We've had these guys for years, and he's never been this affectionate with anyone. Usually, he just tolerates us between bouts of property destruction."

"Well, maybe I've just got that special touch." I dust off my hands and walk toward the fence where Kane is now waiting. "Or maybe I've taken to all of you, reindeer included, and apparently you can all sense it."

"It's your home too now." Kane's voice drops. "You know that, right? You're not a guest anymore. This is permanent. So if you want to change anything—redecorate, make us all move into your room, burn down the guest room and build a shoe closet, whatever—just say the word."

"A shoe closet?" I laugh. "Do I look like I have that many shoes?"

"You could. I'd support that dream."

"How generous of you." I'm grinning as I reach the fence. "And about the room situation. I haven't decided yet. I might just wander the house like a nomad, showing up in random beds at random times. Keep you all guessing."

"Spontaneity. I can work with that."

"Or maybe I will make you all move into my room. Really lean into this pack-bonding thing. Just one giant cuddle pile every night."

Kane's eyes heat. "Also not opposed to that option."

"Of course you're not." I lean against the fence, staring up at him. "Speaking of the pack, I have an idea for the tree lighting ceremony. Something that'll make it unforgettable."

"Yeah?" He straightens slightly, interest clear on his face. "What is it?"

"Not sharing until I work out all the logistics." I shoot him a smile. "But it involves Corn Dog, so prepare yourself."

Kane actually laughs out loud. "You're planning to put Corn Dog in a public event? That will be interesting."

"That's exactly why I've been bonding with him. He trusts me."

"Yeah, to give him moss and scratch his ears. That's not the same as trusting you to get him to behave at a formal town event."

"Ye of little faith." I push off the fence. "Just wait. It's going to be amazing."

"I'm equally terrified and impressed." Kane opens the gate for me. "Also, I made breakfast. Eggs, hash browns, the works. Figured you'd be hungry."

My stomach growls so loudly it startles a reindeer.

"I'll take that as a yes." Kane grins.

I give Corn Dog one last handful of moss. "Be good. I'll be back later to work on your training."

As I pass through the gate, Kane catches my waist and pulls me flush against him, stealing a kiss.

"Morning, baby girl," he murmurs against my lips.

"Smooth talker." But I'm kissing him back because he's mine.

We head indoors together, and the warmth of the house immediately thaws my frozen fingers and nose. The kitchen smells divine.

Chris is at the stove, and Noel is at the counter with his laptop, scowling at whatever he's reading while drinking coffee from a mug the size of a soup bowl.

They both look up when we enter.

"The reindeer queen returns," Chris announces, abandoning his pan to pull me into a hug that lifts me slightly off the ground. "How are your subjects?"

"Fed and plotting my overthrow, probably." I squeeze him back. "Corn Dog is being clingy again."

"He's obsessed with you," Noel says, still scowling at his laptop.

I laugh and extract myself from Chris to grab an empty plate and turn to Noel. "What are you researching that's making you look like you want to fight your computer?"

"Scot's associates. Building a timeline. Anything I can find." His jaw tightens. "Still waiting on that list of who had access to the Santa float." Something my parade team was meant to supply by now. "But Atlas's report came through," he adds. "Confirming the cut wires were intentional and it wasn't an accident."

My good mood deflates slightly. "Right. The sabotage."

"We'll figure it out." Chris brings over the pan and slides a perfect omelet onto my plate. "And when we do, there will be consequences."

"The parade went fine overall," I explain, trying to redirect to something less stressful. "People loved the reindeer. Margaret from the council even said they saved the event."

"See? Crisis averted by cute animals." Kane loads hash browns next to my omelet. "Marketing gold."

"What time do you need to be there for the lighting setup?" Chris asks.

"Probably in the morning to set things up and triple-check everything." I look between the three of them, loving how much they care for me.

"Remember that you're actually helping, not just lurking menacingly in the background," I tease and sit down at the table with my breakfast, grabbing one of the forks.

"We can do both," Kane says cheerfully.

I take a bite of the omelet and nearly moan. "Okay, fine, if you keep cooking like this."

"Bribery accepted," Chris says with a grin.

And sitting here in this kitchen, surrounded by my Alphas, I realize I have a pack now of my own. A home. People who will stand between me and anything that threatens me. I can't remember the last time I felt so content.

KANE

"That guy yesterday was the dumbest fucking target we've caught in months," I groan, shaking my head as Chris drives us back toward the house. "Seriously. Who hides in their own mother's basement and then orders pizza to that exact address using their real name?"

Chris snorts, one hand draped casually over the steering wheel. "The same idiot who posted on Facebook about skipping bail. With location tags turned on."

"I mean, we appreciate the dedication to making our jobs easier, but Jesus Christ." I'm grinning despite myself, remembering the look on the guy's face when we showed up. "We didn't even have to do surveillance. Just walked right up, knocked on the door, and his mom answered and pointed downstairs like she was directing us to the bathroom."

"She was beyond pissed," Chris agrees, taking the turn onto the highway. "But yeah, his face when he saw us coming down those stairs, though. And tried to hide behind a water heater like we wouldn't see his fat ass sticking out."

"But what about those fucking Cheetos-stained fingers. Dude was leaving orange fingerprints on everything like he was marking his territory."

I stretch in the passenger seat, my back popping audibly. "Though I'm ready for tonight to be over so Hannah can actually relax. She's been stressed to absolute hell about this tree lighting ceremony."

"Can't blame her after what happened at the parade." Chris's expression hardens slightly. "That fire was deliberate sabotage and still no list from the team there, but we all know it was some dodgy shit. She's terrified something else is going to go horribly wrong tonight and destroy her reputation."

"Which is exactly why we're sticking close. All three of us. No way Scot gets another shot at ruining her event." I drum my fingers on my knee, restless energy building. "I just want this done so she can enjoy Christmas without this massive weight hanging over her. It's only a few days away, and we haven't even talked about what we're doing."

"Something special," Chris says. "She's had nothing but stress since moving here. She deserves a proper celebration."

"What about throwing a party at the house?" The idea forms as I speak. "Invite Lily and her Alphas, Ruby and hers, maybe some other people from town that Hannah's gotten close to. Make it a real social thing so she doesn't feel like her entire life changed overnight and she lost all her connections outside of us."

Chris glances at me, considering. "That's actually a solid idea. She mentioned missing her friends the other day. Said she felt guilty for being so wrapped up in work and us that she hasn't had time to see them."

"Exactly. Big Christmas feast, all the trimmings, proper celebration. Turkey, ham, all the sides, enough alcohol to stock a bar." I'm warming to the idea. "Make it memorable. Let her see that being with us doesn't mean giving up her life—it means expanding it."

"Fuck, I'm getting hungry just thinking about it." Chris grins. "Which means tomorrow we're going on a big shopping trip and praying to God everything isn't already sold out."

"You think stores still have turkeys available two days before Christmas?"

"Probably not the good ones. We might be fighting some grandmother for the last decent bird."

"If not, we're hunting one ourselves. I'm not serving our Omega chicken nuggets for Christmas dinner," I add.

"Could go full mountain man. Hunt a turkey, catch some fish, forage for vegetables."

We're both still chuckling as Chris pulls onto our property, the truck rumbling over the gravel, and I'm half listening to him talk about how many chairs we'll need for this so-called Christmas party. I'm already thinking about food, drinks, and whether we can guilt Noel into baking something, but Lily is a master of her craft, so maybe we'll just order from the bakery in town. Then something shifts in the corner of my vision, and every part of me goes still.

The front gate is wide open.

Not drifting open from the wind. Not unlatched. Wide. And crooked. Hanging at an angle that tells me someone put their hands on it and didn't give a single fuck about the hardware we set up.

My pulse spikes. "Who the fuck broke in?" I yank out my phone and tap into our surveillance app, flicking through feeds. The gate camera doesn't load at all. It's just a dead black screen. "Gate feed's out," I mutter, already knowing that's a bad sign.

Chris kills the engine so hard that gravel sprays across the yard like shrapnel. We're both unbuckling before the truck even fully stops, boots hitting the ground in the same breath. Adrenaline floods my system, sharp and clean, pushing me forward. Chris doesn't ask questions, just shoulders past me toward the front door, ready to go through it if it doesn't open.

The door is closed. Locked. Perfectly intact.

"Watch this," I say, stopping short when one of the

front yard house feeds finally loads. I angle the phone toward Chris as he comes to a halt next to me.

The front yard camera shows a white van with a trailer and no license plate rolling up our driveway an hour ago. No hesitation. No attempt at hiding. Just a slow, confident pull to a stop right in front of our house.

Four men pile out. All black clothing, hoods up, gloves on. They move quickly, knowing exactly what they're after.

"Fuck me," Chris murmurs, leaning in. "Play it back."

I scrub backward a few seconds. We watch again, four men, heading straight for the side of the house. Not the front door. Not even checking the windows. Straight to the back.

"Hell," I growl.

"Keep going," Chris says tightly.

I tap the next camera, the one covering the southwest side of the house. It flickers, static crawling over the screen, then shows the men reaching the back corner.

Then a hand appears, grabbing the lens.

The feed goes white.

Then dead.

"Back cameras are gone," I say, my teeth grinding. "They found them and destroyed them."

Chris curses under his breath. "You're telling me four masked fuckers came onto our property in broad daylight, cut our cameras, and no one noticed?"

"Someone noticed," I say, thinking of the missing reindeer. "Us."

He doesn't argue. We both break into a run, circling around the house toward the rear where the last cameras died. The air feels colder back here, heavier somehow. My instincts are pounding in my ribs like war drums.

Then I see that the gate to the reindeer pen is wide open like someone ripped away the locks and walked straight through without looking back. And there are no reindeer in sight.

My stomach drops. I sprint to the barn, sliding on the frost-hardened dirt, grab the door, and yank it open, already knowing what I'll see. Nothing.

Empty stalls. Fresh hay. The faint smell of feed. Not a single antler in sight. "Fuck!" The sound rips out of my throat, raw and loud enough to echo. I shove out of the barn, breath turning a sharp white in the cold.

Chris tried the back door of the house. "No one went inside!"

"They didn't need to." I point toward the empty pasture, my voice dropping to a lethal growl. "They took our reindeer."

Chris's expression goes dead cold.

I stop at the gate, fingers brushing the metal, and the second I see the damage up close, a blast of ice shoots through my bloodstream. "The bastards cut the locks."

Chris reaches me a moment later, and the second his eyes land on the severed metal, his whole expression turns murderous. He runs a thumb over the edge, jaw tightening. "Assholes." He rolls his shoulders as though he's warming up for a fight. "They cut the lock, moved fast, and took every single one of our animals. But why?"

We lock eyes, and his eyebrow rises as the answer slams into me. A red-hot anger burns in my veins. "What if that bastard, Scot, found out what Hannah planned for tonight with the reindeer?"

Chris's jaw goes tight enough to crack. "Corn Dog is supposed to be the star." His voice drops to something dark. "That's from Scot's playbook—to sabotage."

"Whoever did this knew Hannah's plans."

Chris drags a hand over his face, furious and thinking fast. "She only told the council team. And us. You don't think someone in the council—"

"Leaked it?" My laugh is sharp and humorless. "What's the bet that Scot paid one of those fuckers to give him insider information?"

My phone is in my hand before I consciously grab it. I dial Noel. He answers on the first ring. "Kane? What happened?"

"They're gone," I say.

A beat. "Who?"

"Our reindeer."

Chris steps close so Noel can hear him. "Four assholes broke onto the property and took every one of them. Corn Dog included."

"Are you fucking kidding me?" Noel growls. "I mean, the show can still go on, but Hannah has promised a reindeer show to the council, who all agreed and are attending to view Corn Dog. They are about to start advertising the magical reindeer on the radio to get more attendees tonight."

There's a moment of heavy, deadly silence. "Shit!" I mutter.

"Look, Hannah is going to absolutely freak when she finds out," Noel adds.

"Tell her we're working on a solution, that we're handling it, but try to keep her calm if you can. We're almost certain Scot has something to do with this." I say.

"That fucking bastard." Noel's voice goes cold and lethal in a way I've only heard a handful of times, usually right before someone ends up in the hospital. "We still don't know where the hell he's actually living, or I'd go wring his neck right now. I'd bet every dollar I have that we'd find our reindeer tied up in his backyard."

Chris suddenly grabs my arm hard enough to leave bruises, his eyes lighting up with realization. He's pulling out his phone, scrolling frantically through something with his other hand.

What? I mouth at him.

He snatches my phone right out of my hand and puts it on speaker, still scrolling through his photo gallery on his phone. "Hey, Noel, I'm sending you a photo right fucking now. You know the mountain areas around Whispering Grove way better than Kane and me. Do you recognize this cabin or anything about the location in this picture?"

There's the sound of his phone buzzing on the other

end, then silence as Noel examines the photo Chris sent him of Scot with his two criminal buddies.

"I've never seen that specific cabin before. It's not anywhere I've been personally," Noel answers after a long pause. "But wait, hold on… that waterfall in the background. It's not super clear in the photo, but the shape of it, the way it comes down the rock face in two tiers… that looks familiar. I can't place it exactly, but it's definitely triggering something in my memory."

"Think you can find it if we come get you right now?" I ask, hope sparking despite the urgency and stress of the situation.

"Yeah, I can try. If I'm thinking of the right spot, and I'm like seventy percent sure I am, it's deeper into the dense woods on the eastern side of the mountain. Probably a solid thirty-minute drive from town."

"Okay, good. Perfect. We're coming right now to grab you," I say and am already moving toward the truck. "Hang tight and update Hannah for us. Tell her—fuck, I don't know what to tell her that won't make her completely panic."

"I'll handle it," Noel says, and I hear the determination in his voice.

"On our way." We hang up. "Keys," I bark at Chris as we both sprint toward the truck. He doesn't question it, just yanks them from his pocket and throws them. I snatch them out of the air with one hand, and we dive into the cab, the doors slamming shut hard enough to rattle the frame.

The instant my seat belt clicks, I'm reversing so fast

that gravel sprays across the yard like shrapnel. The truck fishtails slightly before gripping, and then we're flying down the road.

I need this speed to pour all my violent energy into before it explodes out of me.

"If Scot hurt those reindeer, I'm going to kill him." My hands are welded to the steering wheel, tendons tight, knuckles bone white. "Slowly. Painfully. I'll make it last for days."

"Get in line," Chris adds. "Those animals are family. He didn't just steal livestock. He stole from our pack. And he did it to punish Hannah. To humiliate her. To make her look incompetent in front of the entire damn town."

My teeth grind. A fresh surge of fury spikes hard through me. "I'm done. We're done. No more waiting for the proper channels to deal with him."

"We end this today." Chris's voice is flat, a lethal certainty to it. "Whatever it takes. He crossed every line. Hannah is ours to protect, and we've let him get away with too much already."

"Completely fucking agreed."

We're flying down rural roads at a speed that would get me arrested anywhere else. I take a turn hard enough that the tires squeal in protest. I don't care. I'd drive through buildings if I had to.

The sun paints the mountains in gold and fire. Beautiful, but I barely register it. All I can think about is Corn Dog, the others, and Hannah, tonight, waiting for a moment that's supposed to be hers.

Three hours to find our stolen reindeer, destroy the prick who took them, and give Hannah the opening she deserves.

No pressure.

"Failure is not on the table. Hannah is counting on us. We track, we retrieve, and we deliver Corn Dog before that ceremony starts. End of discussion," I state.

"And Scot gets exactly what he deserves for fucking with our Omega," Chris barks, cracking his neck.

Bring it on.

Kane is driving through the mountain like a man possessed, the truck bouncing violently over snow-covered ruts and rocks on these barely maintained dirt roads, and I'm in the passenger seat, gripping the handle above the door, staring out at the dense forest, trying to recognize anything familiar.

"Left at that fallen pine," I say, pointing to a massive tree that's split down the middle, probably from lightning.

Kane jerks the wheel hard without slowing down, and we slide sideways on the snow-packed road before the tires catch again with a spray of ice and gravel.

"Chris looked so fucking pissed when he drew the short straw," I say, grinning despite the tension coiling in my gut. "Man wants to beat the shit out of Scot as much as we do. Might have actually cried a little when he lost."

Kane barks a laugh, and it's dark. "We'll tell him all about it when we get back. Give him every bloody detail so he can live vicariously through us. Maybe even take photos."

"This is a damn long shot, though," I admit after a moment, scanning the increasingly dense trees. The forest is pressing in from both sides now, branches reaching across the narrow road like skeletal fingers. "Might not even be where Scot actually lives. Could be some random cabin he visited once for a weekend, and then we're back at square one with no reindeer, no time, and Hannah's event completely fucked."

"Don't say that shit," Kane snaps, his knuckles bone white on the steering wheel. "Don't even think it. I mean, where the fuck else would he be hiding eight stolen reindeer? He's not keeping them in a damn apartment in town. He's not boarding them at some public stable. This has to be it."

"You're right." I go back to scanning the landscape. "Just nervous as hell. Hannah's counting on us."

"Which is exactly why we're not failing."

The road narrows even more as we climb higher into the mountains, trees pressing in from both sides, their snow-laden branches scraping against the truck with sounds like fingernails on metal. Then, through a gap in the trees maybe thirty yards ahead, I spot something that doesn't belong.

Metal. Geometric shapes. Human construction in the middle of wilderness.

"There," I say, pointing through the windshield. "Slow the fuck down."

Kane eases off the gas, and we both lean forward instinctively to get a better look through the trees.

A cabin sits in a small clearing carved out of the forest, and far behind it is a thin waterfall, completely frozen to ice. But the place is not exactly what I expected. The entire property is surrounded by a high steel fence, seven feet at a minimum. The fence is rusted in places, orange stains bleeding down from the posts, but it's still formidable as hell. The front gates give us an easy view of the side of the home. More than that, there are security cameras mounted at each corner of the fence line, professional-looking equipment with weatherproof housings.

This isn't some rustic mountain retreat where you go to disconnect from civilization. It's a damn compound, secured like someone is expecting an assault.

"What the actual fuck is this place?" Kane mutters, pulling the truck off the road and into the tree line where we won't be immediately visible. He kills the engine.

I'm watching those cameras carefully, studying their positioning. "Something's off. Those cameras should be rotating on their mounts. You see those motors underneath? They're pan-tilt models. But they're completely stationary. Haven't moved once."

"And the whole place is too quiet," Kane observes. "No generator running, no sounds of activity, no smoke from the chimney even though it's freezing. Place looks abandoned except for that fence."

We both climb out, easing the doors closed as quietly as possible, and approach through the dense tree cover.

The fence is definitely bizarre for a place this remote. Who needs this level of security out here in the middle of nowhere, miles from the nearest neighbor, unless they're hiding something serious? Something illegal?

I grab my metal keys and toss them at the electric wires lining the fence from about ten feet away.

It hits the metal with a clatter, then drops. Nothing. No sparks, no electrical buzz, no alarm shrieking. Complete silence except for wind howling and trees rustling through the forest. I go and pick up my keys and pocket them.

Kane moves closer, watching the cabin windows for any signs of movement, then presses his palm directly against the metal fence.

He holds it there for several long seconds, testing, then looks back at me and shakes his head. "Cold. No current running through it at all. No vibration, no heat, nothing."

As we creep closer to the front gate, moving from tree to tree for cover, staying low, I catch movement near the cabin's front porch.

Big burly guy dressed in dark pants and a jacket. He appears bored as absolute hell, looking at his phone, posture completely lazy and relaxed, clearly not expecting anyone to actually show up out here in the wilderness.

"We're not walking through that front gate," Kane whispers.

"Side wall. Around back. Stay quiet and low." We slip deeper into the trees, circling the property and moving along the perimeter fence until we find a small area where the camera angles create a natural blind spot. The security system might be down, but there's no point in taking stupid chances if someone is monitoring on backup power or battery.

I grip the top bars of the fence, testing my weight distribution, then swing myself up and over in one fluid motion. My boots hit the ground on the other side with barely a whisper. Kane follows, but the metal groans slightly under his heavier weight and bulk.

We both freeze completely, not even breathing, listening for any indication that we've been heard.

Nothing. The guard on the porch is still absorbed in his phone.

Kane deliberately steps on a dry branch half buried in the snow, snapping it with a crack that sounds like a gunshot in the quiet.

The guard's head jerks up immediately, phone forgotten. He straightens from his lazy slouch and turns, scanning the yard with suddenly alert eyes in our direction. "Who's out there? This is private property!"

He starts walking toward our position around the side of the cabin.

We let him get close until he rounds the corner of the cabin, and we're right there.

The moment his silhouette clears the cabin wall, Kane explodes forward, all brute momentum. He slams a fist into the guard's face with enough force to knock the air out of him in one sharp burst.

The guard's eyes go wide. His mouth opens to groan. I've already moved behind him, and I hook my arm across his throat, my other hand locking on the back of his head, forearm cutting across his carotids. His windpipe stays clear, but the blood flow to his brain stops instantly.

He jerks hard, trying to elbow backward, but Kane traps his arms and pins them in place.

"Easy," Kane mutters. "Time for a nap."

I tighten the hold.

Three seconds.

Two.

One.

The fight drains out of his body. His knees buckle. I lower him to the ground.

Kane crouches, pats him down—no weapons, no radio, just a cheap burner phone. "Amateur," he mutters, crushing the phone under his boot.

I drag the unconscious guard into the shadows behind a stack of firewood and check his pulse out of habit. Steady. He'll be out for a while. Then I zip-tie his wrists and ankles.

We approach the main house, and the door opens effortlessly. The structure is dark inside, no lights visible, no power humming, no electronic sounds at all. Weird for a winter day in the mountains when you'd expect heat running constantly.

We slip inside, greeted with the stench of stale sweat and unwashed bodies, old beer and cigarette smoke. The living room is shabby but appears lived-in recently. Empty beer bottles scattered across a coffee table. Pizza boxes stacked in a corner, grease stains spreading across the cardboard. A couch with suspicious stains that look like dried blood.

This isn't some weekend hunting cabin. People are living here full-time, and living rough.

From the kitchen area deeper in the house, I hear a distinct creak, that specific sound of someone stepping on a loose floorboard trying to be quiet. A man steps out and freezes completely when he finds us standing there.

I recognize him instantly, and shock jolts through me. "Holy shit. That's Carl Brenner," I murmur. Carl is a bail jumper we've been actively hunting for three months. Skipped on armed robbery charges totaling fifty grand in bail. Disappeared completely off the grid, no credit card usage, no family contacts, no known associates turning up anything.

And he's standing right fucking here in this random mountain cabin.

Carl's eyes widen in response, and he bolts immediately back toward the kitchen.

I'm faster.

I tackle him before he makes it three steps, driving

my shoulder into his lower back and taking us both down hard onto the floor. The impact drives the air from his lungs in a whoosh. We've gotten used to taking down assholes without guns or blades if we can help it… then we don't get sued.

I grab his wrist, twist it at an angle behind his back, and he bucks in agony, then I slam his head into the floor once, hard enough to daze him. He goes limp.

Kane zip-ties his wrists behind his back, then does his ankles, pulling the plastic tight enough to leave marks.

We shove him behind the couch, out of sight from the hallway.

From deeper in the house, voices carry. "Why the hell are all the systems still down? I thought you said it was just a breaker."

"The grid blew, man. Whole electrical panel is fucked. What the hell is the boss doing about it? We've been sitting in the dark freezing our asses off for over an hour."

"Should've stayed in the city. At least there we had heat and running water."

Two men step out of the hallway into the main room, still talking, not paying attention, then they see us and everything changes. They're big fuckers.

The first one, bald head, scar on his face running from temple to jaw, easily two-fifty of solid muscle, assesses the situation in a split second. "Who the fuck are you?"

The second, with long dark hair pulled back, shifts his weight into a fighting stance.

"Your fairy godmothers," Kane growls.

Then all hell breaks loose.

The bald guard moves first, grabbing a heavy metal flashlight from a side table and swinging it at Kane's head with brutal force. Kane ducks smoothly, and the flashlight whistles through empty air where his skull was a heartbeat ago.

He drives his elbow up and into the guy's ribs with enough force that I actually hear something crack, ribs breaking or cartilage separating.

The guard grunts in pain but doesn't go down, swinging a backhand fist that catches Kane's shoulder with a meaty thud.

Meanwhile, the dark-haired man charges at me like a linebacker with a death wish, head down, arms wide, trying to drive me straight through the wall. I pivot hard to the side, but not fast enough, as his shoulder clips my ribs with the force of a battering ram. I stumble, pain lancing through my side, and I grunt, staggering another step, breath knocked tight in my chest.

He doesn't get off clean either. He crashes into the wall, and that throws off his balance as plaster cracks under the impact, a spray of crumbled drywall raining down around him.

I turn on instinct, riding the burn in my ribs, and grab his jacket before he can fully push off the wall. My knee drives into his kidney once. Twice. A third time. Fast and vicious.

He lets out a strangled howl, more animal than human, spine buckling as he tries to twist toward me.

I grab him and use his own momentum against him, throwing him across the room into the opposite wall. His head bounces off the drywall with a sickening thud, and he slides down, leaving a visible dent and a smear of blood.

But he's not out. He shakes his head like a dog shedding water and starts to push himself up. Fuck!

The bald guard is still trading blows with Kane. The man grabs a kitchen knife from a side table near a couch.

"Really?" Kane sounds almost amused despite breathing hard. "You're bringing a knife to this kind of fight? That's your play?"

The guard doesn't waste breath responding. He lunges with the blade in a surprisingly skilled thrust aimed at Kane's gut. This guy has knife training, knows what he's doing.

My guy is getting back up, blood running from his nose and a cut above his eye, and there's murder in his expression. He comes at me again with a roar, just raw fury.

I let him get close, then I drop low, hook my arms around both his legs, and drive forward, sweeping his feet out from under him. He slams onto his back before he even realizes what hit him. I dart to his back and get him in a rear naked choke, my forearm across his throat, needing him to join his friend outside and pass out. He thrusts, throwing punches at my head… fucking ass, but he's weakening fast.

Kane leaps back from a swishing blade, but the edge catches his jacket and probably cuts into flesh. He doesn't even flinch. He counters immediately with two brutal punches delivered in rapid succession, one to the throat and a second to the jaw. The guard makes a horrible choking sound, then his knees buckle and he drops like someone cut his strings, the knife clattering away across the tile.

I release my guy, who's gone limp in my arms, and I drop him.

"You good?" Kane asks, breathing hard and holding his forearm where the knife cut him. Blood is seeping between his fingers, but it doesn't look arterial.

"I'm upright," I gasp, my ribs screaming where that first charge connected. "You?"

"Same. Cut's not deep."

Before we can catch our breath properly or assess our injuries, I hear more footsteps from the back of the house, heavy boots on hardwood, moving fast.

Someone is approaching, probably heard the fight.

"Fuck!" I pull my Taser from my belt, hands shaking slightly from adrenaline, and the second he rounds the corner from the hallway, I hit him center mass without hesitation.

The probes catch him in the chest, and he convulses, every muscle locking up, then drops to the floor, twitching.

"Fuck, I don't have the energy for another fistfight right now," I mutter, changing the cartridge on the Taser with fumbling fingers.

"You and me both."

We drag all four unconscious bodies into the kitchen —they're heavy as hell, dead weight—and zip-tie them together in a pile against the cabinets.

Kane is checking the criminals' faces carefully now, pulling out his phone with his uninjured hand and opening our current active bounty list. He flips through photos methodically, comparing faces to the men we just took down.

His expression changes, eyes going wide. "Noel… they're not random guys living here."

"What do you mean?"

"They're on our list." He holds up his phone so I can see the screen. "Carl Brenner, fifty-grand bail on armed robbery. That bald guy is wanted for aggravated assault and attempted murder, seventy-five grand. The one with the black hair is wanted for drug trafficking, hundred grand. And this new one I'm sure is on the list too."

I lean over to verify, and he's absolutely right. They match our active cases. "Why the fuck would wanted criminals all be hiding in the same location? That's the opposite of good strategy."

Kane's eyes go hard with understanding. "This house is collecting them. Someone's gathering wanted criminals in one place on purpose."

"A goddamn safe house for fugitives," I breathe, the full picture becoming clear.

"Someone who benefits from having wanted criminals in their pocket," Kane adds. "People who owe them everything, have nowhere else to go, and will do whatever they're told because the alternative is prison."

We search the rest of the house quickly and quietly, moving through rooms and finding no one else.

Bedrooms with mattresses thrown directly on bare floors. Minimal furniture, just what's absolutely necessary. Empty food containers and trash piled in corners. The whole place smells like too many people living in too small a space without enough hygiene.

At the back of the house, there's a door standing slightly ajar, cold air flowing through the gap.

We exchange a look, then carefully slip through to a backyard veranda. Outside, in a small corral maybe thirty feet from the back of the house, surrounded by a hastily constructed fence made of scrap lumber and wire, are our reindeer. They are pressed together nervously, stomping and shifting restlessly, but alive. Thank fuck we found them.

"We're at the right fucking place," Kane whispers.

A loud bang echoes from inside the house, the sound of something heavy crashing and metal scraping.

"What the hell was that?" We sprint inside, moving through the house, following the noise to another room on the opposite side from where we entered.

I push down the handle, and the door swings open.

Corn Dog proudly stands in the room in the shattered remains of what used to be a filing cabinet, surrounded by debris.

"What in the world?" I mutter.

It looks like he chewed enthusiastically on electrical wires hanging from a destroyed breaker panel mounted on the wall. Half the panel is torn completely open, sparking components exposed and dead, explaining why the whole property has no power.

Papers are scattered everywhere, the same ones he's been shredding with his teeth. And in his mouth right now is a thick ledger book, pages torn and soaked with reindeer saliva.

"Oh God," Kane groans.

"Fucking hero," I add, starting to laugh softly despite everything—the pain in my ribs, the blood on my face, the absolute insanity of this situation.

Kane lunges forward and snatches the ledger from Corn Dog's mouth. Pages fall open as Kane holds it, and we both lean in to read it.

Neat columns of numbers. Names, some I recognize as the criminals we just encountered, others I don't. Payment schedules with dates and amounts.

Professional. Detailed. Meticulous.

Corn Dog is at my side, and I pat him. "Good boy, destroying their power." I lift my gaze. "What the fuck's going on here?"

Kane gives me the book as he goes to haul open drawers and cupboards in the room now, his movements frantic. There are stacks of cash wrapped in paper bands. Hundred-dollar bills, some still in bank wrappers.

"This is easily seven figures just sitting here," Kane states, his voice tight. "Maybe more. Who keeps this much cash on hand?"

"Someone running a serious criminal enterprise. Money laundering fits the bill. Pun intended." I grin.

"You think that's what's going on here?" Kane asks. "Using these criminals he's hiding. Laundering massive amounts of money through them, making them look like legitimate workers with paychecks. So that book is a complete money-laundering ledger. Fuck!"

"If this is Scot's doing, he wasn't just sabotaging Hannah's events for petty revenge," I whisper, understanding crystallizing. "Scot was sabotaging everything for money."

Footsteps sound somewhere in the house. Our heads snap up simultaneously to the door. Before we can move, the door swings open. And fucking Scot steps into the doorway, flanked by two more guards with guns already drawn and pointed directly at us.

Of course he's in charge. Fuck!

For a frozen moment, nobody moves. Scot's eyes are taking in the scene: Corn Dog standing by the destroyed electrical panel, the ledger in my hand, the cash visible in open drawers.

His face twists into fury. "You two sons of bitches just can't mind your own goddamn business, can you?" His voice is venomous, dripping with hatred. "Had to stick your noses where they don't belong. Had to play hero for that ungrateful bitch."

The guards' guns are steady, professional grips, fingers on triggers. These aren't amateurs.

We're outgunned and we know it.

"On the floor. Now!" one guard orders.

Kane and I exchange a glance. We could try to fight, but one of us, if not both, would get shot before we reached them.

We get to our knees.

"Smart choice," Scot says, stepping into the room properly while his guards pat us down and take our phones, blades, and Tasers. "I'd hate to get blood all over my half-destroyed ledger there. That's important documentation." He comes over and snatches it from my grasp. "Fucking reindeer wrecked this room."

I grin, adoring Corn Dog for being such a devious little reindeer.

"You're running a criminal network," Kane states flatly, not making it a question. "Using fugitives as your personal army. Keeping them hidden from law enforcement in exchange for their loyalty and labor."

Scot smiles, and it's ugly. "Someone's been doing their homework. Not that it matters anymore. You won't be sharing your discoveries with anyone."

"Laundering money," I add, trying to keep him talking.

"It's actually quite elegant when you think about it," Scot replies, sounding almost proud. "These people are desperate. They'll do anything to avoid prison. Work for nothing, ask no questions, disappear when told. And if they cause problems?" He shrugs. "Plenty more where they came from."

"And sabotaging Hannah's events?" Kane asks, his voice dangerous despite our situation.

Scot's face twists with pure hatred, all pretense of civilization vanishing. His lips curl back from his teeth. "I helped Giuseppe grow that business. Me. Not some fucking Omega who showed up batting her eyelashes and playing helpless. She was just the pretty face I brought in to charm clients and look good in photos."

"That's complete bullshit and you know it," I say. "You're just a jealous, bitter prick who couldn't handle the fact that she rejected you."

His jaw clenches. "It's all mine now. The business, the contracts, the reputation, everything. And soon? Hannah herself will be mine too."

The way he says her name has me tensing as fury burns through my veins.

Kane's laugh is cruel and mocking. "She would rather sleep in a sewer filled with rats and diseases than let you touch her. You disgust her."

Scot's eyes go dead cold, and I see something break behind them, whatever thin veneer of sanity he was maintaining.

"Who gives a fuck what she wants?" he snaps. "With you two and that other pet Alpha of hers out of the way, she'll have nowhere to turn. No protection. No support system. She'll be vulnerable and alone, and I'll be there to pick up the pieces. To comfort and console her. She'll learn to appreciate what I can give her."

"Fuck you," Kane growls.

Scot laughs like a hyena. "Shit timing, though, for you. We have a delivery we're supposed to meet in twenty minutes, important clients, can't reschedule. Don't need this complication right now."

He shoots a glare at the guards flanking him, both still aiming at us. "Take them out back, deep into the woods where the ground is soft enough to dig. Finish them there, make it clean, then bury the bodies where no one will ever find them. Take all the damn reindeer too."

Corn Dog bleats angrily from across the room, stamping his hooves like he understands exactly what's being said.

Then we all hear it, a loud car horn beeping repeatedly outside, insistent and annoying.

"The fuck?" Scot's head snaps toward the door, irritation clear on his face.

"They're early." He points at the guards. "Both of you, tie up these assholes now. Fast."

The guards move immediately. Zip ties bite into our wrists before we can twist away, then our ankles, rough hands forcing us onto our stomachs. Cold floorboards press into my cheek as they cinch everything brutally tight.

"Good, now come with me!" Scot turns away with the guards on his heels and closes the door behind them.

"Fuck," Kane hisses.

"We need a plan. Fast."

We're both staring around frantically for anything useful, seeing that the room is a mess.

Then I feel it, a warm huff of air against my arm. I lift my head just enough to see Corn Dog standing over Kane, staring down with those unsettlingly intelligent eyes, his little reindeer nostrils flaring as he sniffs along the line of the zip tie digging into his wrist.

Kane notices too. "Hey, buddy..." His voice is low. "If you *want* to chew on something, you can chew on that tie."

Corn Dog blinks once. Twice. Then he lowers his head and very deliberately takes the plastic tie between his teeth.

"Oh, shit," I whisper. "He's actually doing it."

A sharp yank. Kane jerks. "Christ, I definitely feel teeth. Easy, bud, don't take the hand with it—"

Corn Dog shifts, finds better purchase, then bites down with determined little crunches. Plastic strains. Groans. Then—*snap.*

Kane's wrists come free.

"Holy fuck yes," he breathes, swinging his arms forward to rub his raw skin. Then Corn Dog trots around behind him.

He's on his feet instantly, hopping to the desk in the room, rifling through drawers until he finds a pair of old scissors. He slices through the ties around his ankles. Once free, he comes over and frees me.

The second I'm loose, blood rushes back into my

hands with a painful sting. I grunt and rub at the circulation returning as I get to my feet. We're moving to the door.

Kane crouches and pats Corn Dog. "No, buddy. You stay here. We'll be right back." He nudges the door closed before the reindeer can escape with us.

We don't wait. We're already moving, fast and silent, slipping out of the room like shadows hunting something that never should've touched what's ours. Every step is loaded with murder.

The hallway opens into the living room, dim and stale, and that's when Kane taps my arm and points.

Our weapons, dumped stupidly on a side table by the couch.

Phones. Blades. Tasers.

Like Christmas morning for pissed-off bounty hunters. Fucking idiots.

We grab everything. Kane checks the charge on his Taser like he's itching to use it. We crouch low and slip toward the front door, keeping to the shadows.

Through the partially open doorway, we spot Scot on the front porch, staring after a black van pulling down the snow-covered dirt road. Two guards stand in the yard, backs fully turned, relaxed, unaware that we're right behind them.

Perfect.

I lift my hand, fingers counting silently—three… two…

On "one," Kane moves first.

Fast. Deadly. Beautiful.

We step outside from behind the doorframe, blades flicking through the air in matching arcs.

Thunk.

We bury both blades cleanly in the guards' backs, angled to drop them fast. The men jerk forward with startled cries before collapsing face-first into the snow, twitching and gasping. They're down—not dead, but very much done.

Scot hears the sound and whips around, already reaching into his coat. I see the outline of a gun, see his hand curling around it, starting to pull it free—

I fire the Taser.

The prongs hit dead center, right in the groin.

The effect is instant and goddamn glorious.

Scot's eyes go huge, bulging in disbelief, before the electricity tears through him. His knees buckle, his spine bows, and he lets out a strangled, high-pitched sound that is somewhere between a dying ostrich and a man being force-fed regret.

The gun slips out of his hand. Clatters on the wooden boards.

His whole body seizes, jerking violently as he falls flat on his back, twitching hard enough that snow stirs around him.

Kane bursts out laughing. I might be laughing too. Hard to tell over the screaming.

When the current stops, Scot just lies there, whimpering in a pathetic puddle of sweat and pain. We don't have time to savor it.

"We're running out of minutes," Kane mutters, scanning the tree line. "We need Corn Dog back at the town square now."

"Yeah." I grab Scot by the collar and drag him across the porch like trash. "But this asshole isn't going anywhere."

We haul him into the yard toward the pine tree near the house. He tries to scramble, kicking weakly.

"You can't—fuck—you can't do this," he wheezes.

Kane slams him face-first against the trunk.

"I can," Kane says. "And I will."

Scot sputters as we spin him, yank his arms back, and zip-tie his wrists tightly around the rough bark, securing him to the tree. He jerks against the restraints, skin scraping raw, but he's not going anywhere.

He's still crying from the Taser, and now he's cursing through the tears.

"You're dead—you're both dead—you think you can—"

Kane punches him in the kidney hard enough to fold him.

"That's for hurting Hannah," he growls.

Scot chokes. "You—fucking—psychos—"

I hit him once across the jaw. Controlled. Precise. Enough to shut him up, not enough to knock him out.

"And that," I say coldly, "is for trying to ruin her career."

Scot hangs there panting, drooling onto the pine roots, still twitching from the aftershocks.

I pull out my phone and dial 911 while Kane deals with the two muscleheads who are trying to get up.

He zip-ties them and pulls our blades free. A dispatcher answers immediately. "Emergency services—"

"This is Noel Saxon," I say, voice clipped and professional. "Bounty hunter license 4728. I'm reporting a criminal hideout at these coordinates—" I rattle them off using the GPS on my phone. "Multiple fugitives with active warrants. Illegal confinement. Money laundering. Armed suspects subdued. Primary target, Scot Giordano, is restrained on-site."

The dispatcher sounds stunned. "Sir, can you remain at the location—"

"No," I cut in. "We have a critical, time-sensitive obligation. The suspects are secured and will not be leaving. Send the sheriff and every deputy available."

I hang up before she can argue.

"You bring the truck around," Kane says. "I'll get Corn Dog. The rest are too damn big to cram in the back."

"Yeah," I agree, chest still heaving. "We leave them here. They're safe enough in the pen until the sheriff shows. I'll call it in, tell them that the animals belong to us and we're coming back after we get Corn Dog to Hannah."

"They'll want our statements anyway." Kane is already gone, cutting across the yard.

I sprint toward the front gate, boots slamming against the snowy ground, the adrenaline still running hot. By the time I get the truck nosed down the driveway toward the house, Kane bursts out of the cabin with Corn Dog in his arms, carrying him like a toddler throwing a tantrum.

I pull up fast.

Kane yanks open the back door and shoves the reindeer inside. Corn Dog immediately turns in three frantic circles on the seat, hooves thumping against upholstery like we're launching him into space.

He gets in and slams the door shut.

"We good?" I ask.

"Go," Kane says. "Before he kicks through the damn window."

Corn Dog is already climbing across the back seat, nose pressed between the headrests, breath fogging my neck. He shoves his face against my cheek like he's trying to merge our skulls together.

"Buddy—hey—personal space," I mutter, pushing his snout back gently. "You're adorable, but I need to see the road."

Corn Dog responds by licking my ear.

Kane laughs under his breath. "He's excited."

"He's a beast," I shoot back, gripping the wheel. "Buckle him down."

Kane reaches into the back, grappling with him, then sighs. "Not going to happen." He slumps back into his seat. "He rides loose. Just drive." Then he grabs the first aid kit from the glove compartment and wraps gauze around his forearm where he was cut with that asshole's knife.

I throw one last look toward the yard where Scot is still zip-tied to the tree, squirming like a giant pissed-off earthworm, shouting curses, and I love that I lit up his groin with a Taser.

He sees us backing out and yells something muffled and furious. Something about revenge. Something about lawyers.

I don't care, and I peel out fast.

Corn Dog's hooves skid on the seat, and he lets out a startled bark of a sound before he happily plants both front legs on the center console like he's the damn copilot.

"We're saving Christmas, buddy," I tell him, eyes on the road, heart pounding. "Try not to break the truck before we get there."

Kane reaches back to steady him. "Hannah's gonna lose her mind when she sees us."

"She'd better," I mutter, flooring it. "We're coming in hot."

My phone buzzes. Chris. I hit speaker and try to shove Corn Dog's muzzle away from my shoulder. "Yeah?"

"Where the actual fuck are you two? Did you find them? Is everyone alive? Hannah's about to start hyperventilating and pacing holes in the ground. Talk to me."

"We found them," I say, taking a sharp turn. "We're heading back right now. All reindeer accounted for and alive."

"Thank fuck. And Scot?"

"Gift-wrapped for the sheriff with a bow on top. There's a whole thing involving money laundering, a safe house full of fugitives, and Corn Dog chewing through their wiring. Long story. We'll explain when we —Corn Dog, stop chewing my shirt right now."

The reindeer gets a solid grip on my collar and yanks. Hard. I practically fold backward over the middle seat. We swerve for a moment.

He only lets go so he can headbutt the phone in my hand, which triggers God knows how many settings at once. My screen lights up, then swipes, then opens five apps in a row like it's possessed. Then the phone sends a text and hangs up on Chris.

Asjkdfh help reindeerlkjsdf CORN fuck sdkjfhksjdf TRUCK ksjdhf. A full, nonsensical voice-to-text horror show.

"Fuck, give me the phone," Kane states, snatching it from my hand. Chris calls back instantly.

"Did you have a stroke?" Chris barks.

"That wasn't me," I say, prying his hooves off the middle console, stopping Corn Dog from fully climbing onto it before he can stomp the gear shift. "That was Corn Dog. He texted you. With his face."

Kane laughs under his breath, shaking his head. "He's smart, but not in a useful way."

The back passenger window lowers in a smooth, cheerful hum, and suddenly his head is hanging out of the truck like a very large, very enthusiastic golden retriever.

"Noel, close his window. Shut it," Kane groans, while trying to grab Corn Dog and not get kicked in the teeth.

"Hell, this reindeer," Kane grumbles, and I'm

pressing every button except the right one. "Why are there so many switches on this damn door?"

Wind blasts into the cab. Corn Dog's ears flap wildly. His tongue is lolling out like he's never been happier in his life.

Chris is still on speaker. "What's happening? Did your reindeer jump out of the truck?"

"He's not jumping," I snap—then immediately second-guess myself as Corn Dog shifts forward like he might absolutely jump. Kane finally gets him inside, and I hit the button for the back window. Thank fuck.

Corn Dog licks the top of my ear in protest. I swear my soul leaves my body for a second.

"Chris," I say, steadying myself while Corn Dog tries to put his front hooves on my shoulders like a toddler, "how much time do we have?"

"Twenty minutes until the ceremony starts," Chris replies. "Maybe less. Hannah is pretending she's fine, but she has the same look you get right before you beat the shit out of a suspect."

I exhale through my teeth. Twenty minutes. We barely have time to breathe, and we're in a truck with a reindeer currently trying to make us crash.

"We'll make it," Kane mutters.

"We have to," I say, tightening my grip on the wheel. "And if Corn Dog destroys this truck, we'll deal with that later."

Corn Dog honks loudly behind us, then nose-dives into a pile of jackets like he's burrowing for winter.

The truck swerves a little.

And we keep driving like lunatics toward town, our lights piercing through the dark, praying we're not too late to save Hannah's entire event.

Corn Dog suddenly dives forward, bumps my elbow, and we're swerving all over the road.

"Stop moving," Kane states, shoving him into the back.

I'm laughing despite everything—the pain in my ribs and the absolute insanity of driving down a mountain road with a lunatic reindeer in our truck.

CHAPTER TWENTY-THREE

HANNAH

The town square is absolutely packed, and I'm about thirty seconds from losing my mind completely.

Families crowd every available inch of space in front of the enormous Christmas tree, children perched on parents' shoulders, couples pressed together sharing body heat. The choir is singing carols to fill the awkward waiting time, their voices rising into the crisp night air, and the sky above is black and absolutely dripping with stars.

It's perfect. The decorations I spent weeks coordinating. The atmosphere and crowd are exactly what I wanted.

Except my reindeer isn't here.

My star attraction that I promised the council would blow everyone's minds—currently missing somewhere between a mountain cabin and this town square.

I'm going to throw up. Or pass out. Or both, in some order I haven't determined yet.

"They're on their way," Chris says quietly, his arm wrapped around my shoulders, his solid warmth the only thing keeping me from falling apart. "Won't be long now."

That slight tension threading through his voice tells me he's just as worried as I am but doing a better job of hiding it than me.

I check my phone for what has to be the hundredth time. No new messages. The last text from Kane just said "Driving fast" with about seventeen exclamation points and what I think was supposed to be a reindeer emoji but came out as a horse wearing a party hat.

Margaret, the councilwoman who's been alternating between being my biggest champion and my harshest critic throughout this entire process, is approaching with that tight-lipped smile that means bad news is coming wrapped in professional politeness.

My stomach clenches.

"Hannah." She checks her watch. "We really need to start. The schedule called for the lighting to begin ten minutes ago. We can't keep everyone waiting much longer. Parents have children who need to get to bed, the elderly are getting cold, and frankly, people are starting to get restless."

I straighten my spine and force every ounce of confidence I don't actually possess into my voice. "Just a few more minutes. I promise. We're starting very soon."

"You said that five minutes ago."

"And now we're five minutes closer to it being true."

Her eyebrow arches, but I hold my ground, keeping my expression pleasant and professional even though my insides are staging a full rebellion.

"Trust me," I add, because apparently I've lost all sense of self-preservation. "It will be worth the wait."

Margaret's expression says she's not remotely convinced, but she nods curtly and retreats to where the other council members are clustered together like a flock of judgmental birds, all checking their watches and exchanging meaningful glances.

The second she's out of earshot, I deflate against Chris. "I'm dying. This is what dying feels like."

"You're going to be okay."

"My organs are liquefying from stress. I can feel it happening."

He chuckles. "That's not how organs work."

I check my phone again. Still nothing. "What if they don't make it? What if something happened? What if Scot did something else and they're hurt or—"

"Hey." Chris turns me to face him, his hands on my shoulders. "They're coming. Kane and Noel are the best at what they do. If anyone can pull off a miracle, it's them."

I force myself to actually stare out at the crowd instead of just seeing a blur of anxiety-inducing faces. Children are laughing, pointing at the decorations, their eyes wide with wonder. Couples are swaying to the choir music. People are smiling, genuinely happy to be here.

I did this. I coordinated all of this. Whatever happens with the reindeer, this moment exists because of my work.

It helps. A little.

"Thank you," I whisper. "I really needed to hear that."

"I know." He presses a kiss to my temple.

My eyes keep drifting to the street at the edge of the square, scanning desperately for any sign of a familiar truck, faces, or a certain troublemaking reindeer who'd better appreciate everything I've gone through for him.

Then I see them.

Kane and Noel, sprinting down the street toward the square like demons are chasing them.

And Noel is carrying Corn Dog in his arms. The animal's legs dangle awkwardly, his head bobbing with each of Noel's powerful strides.

Relief rushes through me. I give Margaret a thumbs-up with probably way too much enthusiasm, and I see her signal to someone near the sound system. The choir music begins to shift, transitioning into the processional piece we rehearsed.

"They made it," Chris breathes.

Noel reaches the edge of the crowd, panting hard, sweat on his face despite the freezing temperature, and sets Corn Dog down on the ground—

And Corn Dog immediately bolts.

My heart plummets. "No, no, no—"

The reindeer takes off running, weaving between startled audience members who jump out of his way with surprised yelps and nervous laughter.

Chris is already moving, ready to chase him down, except—

Wait.

Corn Dog is running directly toward me.

Not away into the crowd to wreak havoc or to the food vendors or the shiny decorations. Straight toward where I'm standing near the stage like I'm a beacon calling him home.

People are pointing at him, phones appearing everywhere to capture the moment. Children are squealing with delight, calling out, "Rudolph! Rudolph!" even though he doesn't have a red nose.

I step forward, dropping to one knee on the cold cobblestones. "Come here, buddy! Come on!"

He rushes to me like I'm the only person in the entire world who matters, his hooves clattering on the snow-cleared stones, and I barely have time to brace myself before he's there. He almost bowls me over completely, his momentum carrying us both backward, but I manage to stay upright and wrap my arms around his neck.

He licks my face with his rough tongue, and I'm laughing. "Oh, I missed you too, you ridiculous creature. I'm so glad you could make it."

He unleashes that happy bleating sound, nuzzling against me like we've been separated for years instead of hours, and I swear on everything I own that this reindeer is smiling.

Cameras are flashing everywhere. Everyone is

watching and filming, and for once, the attention doesn't make me want to crawl into a hole.

"Okay, superstar," I whisper in his ear. "Ready to do your thing? Don't make me look bad."

I stand and walk him up the small ramp to the stage, moving slowly so he follows without resistance. He's being remarkably well behaved, probably exhausted from whatever insane adventure he's been on today. I'll get the full story later, and something tells me it's going to be wild.

At the side of the enormous tree—which seems to stretch forever into the night sky, decorated with thousands of ornaments and wrapped in lights that are currently dark and waiting—sits the prop we set up earlier. A beautiful red carriage styled to look like Santa's sleigh.

I pick up the leather reins with bells attached and the decorative harness, carefully securing it around Corn Dog's body so it looks like he's drawing the sleigh. The bells jingle softly with his movements, and the crowd coos appreciatively.

"Look at him!" someone calls out. "He's adorable!"

"Mommy, is that really one of Santa's reindeer?"

Corn Dog seems to understand he's being admired, because he stands taller and lifts his head regally. Of course he loves being the center of attention. That's peak Corn Dog energy right there.

He starts sniffing the tree with intense focus, his nose working overtime, and I gently redirect his attention before he can try to eat any ornaments. "Not tonight, buddy. We've come too far for you to ruin it by snacking on decorations," I whisper.

Chris winks at me from his position on the far side of the tree. He's holding the lighting controller, ready to work his magic on my signal.

The festive music fades to silence.

My heart hammers so hard I hear it in my ears. I stand up straighter in my red dress, a fitted number with a sweetheart neckline, and adjust my stance in my red heels. My hair is loose around my face, curled softly, and I'm suddenly very aware of how many people are staring at me.

Hundreds of faces. Families. Children. The council members with their judging eyes. My Alphas watching with pride.

I activate the small microphone clipped to my neckline.

"Good evening, everyone, and welcome to Whispering Grove's annual tree lighting ceremony!"

The crowd cheers, and something settles in my chest. I can do this. I was born to do this. "For those of you who don't know me, I'm Hannah Parker, and I've had the incredible honor of coordinating this year's holiday celebrations. And what fun they've been."

More cheers. My shoulders relax a fraction.

"Whispering Grove is a special place. A beautiful community where I've experienced more kindness, more warmth, and more genuine holiday spirit than I ever imagined possible."

I glance at Kane and Noel in the audience, then at Chris by the tree, my heart fluttering.

"Christmas is a time to remember the people we love and celebrate how much they mean to us. It's a time for family, whether that's the family we were born into or the family we've chosen along the way. It's a time for gratitude, for hope, and for believing that magic is real."

The crowd has gone quiet, listening, and unexpected tears prick at my eyes.

"This year, I found my family. I found my home. And I found magic in the most unexpected places."

Corn Dog perks up at the sound of my voice and nudges me.

"Speaking of which, we're incredibly lucky tonight to have a very special guest. One of Santa's own reindeer has traveled all the way from the North Pole to help us with our tree lighting."

The children in the audience start bouncing with excitement. "He is still in training, and his name is Corn Dog. So, he's going to do us the honor of turning on our lights this year. Everyone, please give him a warm Whispering Grove welcome!"

I gesture to him with a flourish, and he lifts his head as if he knows exactly what's happening.

The crowd erupts, kids calling him by his name.

Corn Dog turns to look at them and makes a loud, proud bleating sound that echoes across the square.

The children completely lose their minds.

I move to stand with him in front of the Christmas tree at the edge of the stage so everyone has a clear view. I position myself on his far side so he's between me and the audience. Tonight he's the star, not me.

"Are you all ready?" I call out.

"YES!"

The music starts again, softer now, a gentle instrumental holiday song.

"Let's count down together! Starting at three!"

The crowd joins in immediately, hundreds of voices in unison.

"THREE!" I urge Corn Dog forward, guiding him closer to the tree with a hand on his harness.

"TWO!" I slip a small treat from my pocket, the moss he loves, and hold it near a special ornament we placed at his eye level. It's a large, sparkly bauble that glitters more than any other, designed specifically to catch his attention.

"ONE!" I show him the treat right against the bauble, and Corn Dog, bless his food-motivated heart, pushes his muzzle hard against my hand and directly into the ornament.

The moment he makes contact, the lights explode to life.

They start at the bottom of the tree and climb upward in a wave of brilliance, thousands of lights in warm white and gold racing toward the sky, spiraling around the massive trunk, illuminating every branch until the entire tree is blazing with magic.

The star at the very top bursts into light last, a beacon that I'm sure is visible for miles.

I glance at Chris, who winks at me and subtly

pockets the controller. The crowd erupts into the loudest cheering I've ever heard.

Applause, screaming children, the choir launching into a triumphant carol. People are hugging each other, taking photos, pointing at the magnificent tree with wonder on their faces.

I pat Corn Dog's neck, tears streaming down my face now. "Good boy. Such a good boy."

He nuzzles me, probably looking for more treats, and I give him another piece of moss because he absolutely earned it.

"Everyone, have a very merry Christmas!" I say into the microphone, and the crowd responds with another wave of cheers.

I switch off the microphone, and suddenly the official part is over and I can breathe again.

Chris appears at my side immediately, pulling me into a hug. "You were incredible. Absolutely knocked it out of the park."

"I couldn't have done it without—"

"Hannah."

I turn to see Margaret from the council approaching, and my stomach tightens with fresh nerves. So I quickly step off the stage to meet her.

"You surprised me tonight, Hannah." Her voice is measured, giving nothing away. "I was genuinely worried there for a bit. When the ceremony was delayed, when we weren't sure what was happening... I thought you might let us all down."

I swallow hard. "I understand. There were some unexpected complications."

"But you handled them with grace." A small, genuine smile appears on her face. "That moment with the reindeer was superb. The children will be talking about this Christmas for years. Well done. Truly."

Relief floods through me. "Thank you. That means everything to me."

"Merry Christmas, Hannah." She gives me a brief nod, then turns and walks back toward the other council members.

I can't be certain if that means we'll get the five-year contract, but right now, in this moment, I did my absolute best. That's all anyone can do.

Kane and Noel materialize at my side, and before I can say anything, they're both kissing me, Kane on my lips, lingering and warm, Noel on my neck, just below my ear, in a way that makes me shiver.

"That was the sexiest thing I've ever watched," Kane murmurs against my mouth. "You commanding that stage and the crowd... I'm going to be thinking about it for weeks."

"Couldn't take my eyes off you," Noel adds. "Every person in this square was completely captivated."

My cheeks flush. "I couldn't have done any of it without you two. Whatever you went through to get Corn Dog here..."

They trade one of those loaded looks that tells me *whatever* they went through was probably illegal, violent, or deeply stupid.

"We'll tell you everything," Kane promises. "But it requires alcohol."

"I can't wait," I say, and I mean it.

We stand there for a few minutes, all four of us tucked close to the edge of the square. The choir has moved into the softer carols now, voices floating up with the snow, families clustered under the glow of the tree. Kids are still lined up for photos with the tree and Corn Dog on the stage, who is posing, seeming to love the attention. Chris is close by, keeping an eye on him.

And for the first time in weeks, my chest doesn't feel like it is being crushed.

The rest of the evening goes smoothly. The crowd lingers, enjoying hot cocoa and surrounding stalls, and soon enough, the team handles the breakdown exactly as I trained them to.

Eventually, the line thins out, and Corn Dog is officially off duty. Chris comes down from the little stage, hand on Corn Dog's halter, the reindeer trotting proudly beside him like he just won an award. "We should probably get him home before he decides to break something," he says, stopping beside me. "He's got that look."

"He always has that murder look," Noel mutters.

"Okay," I say, breathing out as the crowd starts thinning and the choir packs up their sheet music. "Everything went very well. I'm exhausted. Let's go home."

Chris nods. "Yeah. Let's load Corn Dog and get moving."

Kane and Noel fall into step beside us as we head toward the truck.

"All four of us in the truck with him," Kane says, shaking his head with a laugh. "This is going to be a fun ride."

Noel snorts. "*Fun* is one word for it."

I narrow my eyes at both of them. "Why are you talking like that?"

Kane lifts his hands. "Nothing. Just… prepare yourself."

"For what?" I look between them, baffled. "It's a reindeer, not a demon."

Both men chuckle.

Corn Dog suddenly shoves his nose into my hip like he wants attention immediately.

Kane laughs harder. "Yeah. Good luck with that."

Both men just start climbing into the front of the truck, while Chris opens the back door for me. I jump in, and he goes on the other side with Corn Dog, shoving him in alongside me, then he gets in.

"Yeah," Noel calls from the passenger seat, "and we really do wish you luck."

Corn Dog lets out a loud, proud grunt, like he absolutely agrees.

I glance at Chris.

He shrugs helplessly. "We'll figure it out."

"You two ready back there?" Kane asks from the driver's seat, grinning into the rearview mirror.

"Ready for what?" I ask, slightly worried.

"The wildest ride of your life."

The truck pulls away from the curb. For about thirty seconds, everything is fine.

Then Kane takes the first turn, and Corn Dog doesn't just lurch; he *launches* sideways into me, hooves scrambling across the seat like he's trying to scale a cliff.

I shriek. "What the—Corn Dog, sit! Or... whatever the reindeer equivalent of 'sit' is!"

He ignores every sound coming out of my mouth and tries to climb over me, his surprisingly strong body shoving me flat against my seat. His tail, which should not be that powerful, starts smacking Chris straight in the jaw.

He's groaning and trying to shove him down.

"This is what we dealt with on the rescue run!" Noel yells from the front, laughing so hard he can barely breathe. "Welcome to the circus!"

Corn Dog decides the window looks like the most interesting part of the truck and wedges his head between Kane and Noel, his front hooves scraping against the center console. Kane swears as Corn Dog's nose nearly lands in his ear.

"Back seat!" Chris is trying to haul him by the harness. "Stay. Back. Seat!"

Corn Dog doesn't care. He now licks Noel's neck with a wet enthusiasm, which I'm fine with him doing as long as he's not climbing on me.

"Get your reindeer under control!" Noel snaps, pushing him away.

"He's *not* my reindeer!" Chris snaps back, trying to

peel Corn Dog off him like he's a toddler on a sugar high.

That's when Corn Dog abandons the front altogether and collapses *directly* onto Chris's lap. "Off!" he gasps. "Get off! You absolute beast!"

He just settles more firmly, like Chris is his personal throne. His chin rests on his chest.

Then Kane hits another modest turn—but apparently even *that* is too much—and Corn Dog slides sideways, dragging Chris with him, pinning me against him.

"Drive straighter!" I demand, muffled under a reindeer.

"I *am* driving straight!" Kane shouts with laughter.

Noel is laughing so hard he has one hand clutching his stomach and the other braced on the seat. "Stop— stop talking—you're all killing me."

Corn Dog chooses that moment to grab the bottom hem of Chris's flannel shirt in his teeth and *pull*. Hard.

Chris jerks forward, half strangled by his own clothing. "Let GO! I need that shirt! Hey—HEY!"

Corn Dog gives the shirt one last yank, rips off a button, and then immediately loses interest like a furry criminal.

Noel twists around just in time to film Corn Dog trying to nudge open the rear window with his nose, fogging the glass with dramatic huffs.

"Oh, this is gold," Noel says, cackling. "Christmas miracle. I am making a montage."

"I hate all of you," I wheeze, trying to shove a reindeer thigh off my rib cage. "Every single one."

Chris sputters. "Can you—Hannah—tell him to stop hitting me with his ass?"

I glare at him. "Yes, let me just reason with the wild forest creature currently using me as a mattress."

Kane catches my gaze in the rearview mirror, eyes warm and amused. "Welcome to pack life, beautiful."

And somehow, despite everything—the reindeer squishing us, Chris covered in fur and a slobbered shirt, Noel filming like this is the most fun he's ever had, and Kane trying to control the truck while snickering—I feel something settle inside me.

Something warm and steady.

My life is never going to be boring again.

And honestly? With these men?

I wouldn't trade it for anything.

CHAPTER TWENTY-FOUR

HANNAH

Christmas Day, and I'm standing at the living room window, watching fat snowflakes drift down like a winter wonderland snow globe, and I'm smiling so hard my face might actually crack.

This is my life now. This cozy, slightly chaotic life. The house is fully decorated, and I mean fully. Garlands wrapped around every single railing. Lights twinkling in every window because apparently the guys don't believe in subtlety. Christmas music plays softly through the speakers.

Then there's the smell. Oh my God. The entire place smells absolutely divine from the roasts the guys have been working on. I made batches of snowflake- and reindeer-shaped shortbread cookies earlier, and they're cooling on racks in the kitchen, dusted with powdered sugar and looking almost too pretty to eat.

Almost. I've already eaten three. Quality control is important.

Everything feels stupidly perfect. Cozy in a way that makes me suspicious the universe is setting me up for something terrible to balance it out. But I'm choosing to ignore my pessimistic tendencies and just enjoy this moment.

I'm officially moved in now. Fully, completely, all-my-stuff-is-here moved in with my three Alphas. I have my own room for now until we work out the best sleeping arrangements, as I know the guys love it when we're all together for the big sex marathons, but having those one-on-one moments with each of them is unforgettable.

And it feels so right that it's actually terrifying, which is probably something I should discuss with a therapist, except I'm too busy being deliriously happy. I'm also still riding this incredible high from yesterday's phone call.

Giuseppe finally called after days of me checking my phone every five minutes like some kind of obsessed teenager waiting for a text from her crush. And he delivered news so good I literally screamed and scared Corn Dog, who was standing outside the window at the time.

The council was so impressed with the tree lighting ceremony that they offered him the five-year contract. Not just offered it, but specifically requested that I be the one coordinating all their major events going forward.

Little do they know I'm taking over the entire business.

So here I am, soon-to-be official owner of Confetti & Meatballs Event Planning. The lawyers still need to finalize paperwork after the holidays because apparently even good news requires bureaucracy, but it's happening.

It's really, actually, pinch-me-I-must-be-dreaming happening.

Meanwhile, Scot is drowning in so much legal trouble that he probably won't be seeing Whispering Grove for a long time. Money laundering. Harboring fugitives. Operating a criminal safe house. And about a dozen other charges I can't even remember because the list was so long.

And because he's a coward as well as a criminal, he panicked the second things got serious and tried to buy himself leniency by spilling which council member tipped him off about using the reindeer in the tree lighting ceremony. Turned out to be some new recruit on the council, way out of his depth. Scot figured rolling over on him would save his own skin.

It didn't. The recruit got fired on the spot and might be facing charges of his own.

Plus, when we finally got the complete list of everyone who had access to those parade floats, guess whose name was right there at the top?

That's right. Scot's.

So add sabotage and reckless endangerment to his growing collection of felonies. The council is pursuing its own criminal charges too, for breach of contract and public endangerment.

Karma isn't just real; she's thorough and apparently holds grudges.

I turn away from the window and take in my three Alphas scattered throughout the kitchen and dining room, and something warm and ridiculous blooms in my chest.

Chris is at the stove, basting what has to be a twenty-pound turkey with the kind of focused concentration usually reserved for defusing bombs. Kane is setting the dining table with an absurd number of plates and decorations. And Noel is chopping vegetables at the counter.

These men. My men. My world. My everything.

God, I've become one of those sickeningly in-love people I used to mock. Past Hannah would be so disappointed in Present Hannah.

But Present Hannah doesn't care even a little bit. I can't imagine my life without them now.

I walk over to the kitchen, weaving between them. "Okay, what can I do to help? I'm feeling completely useless just standing around admiring the view."

All three of them immediately stop what they're doing and converge on me like I've activated some kind of Alpha homing beacon. It's flattering how synchronized they are sometimes.

Chris wipes his hands on a towel and pulls me against his chest. Kane wraps around me from behind, his arms circling my waist. Noel moves in from the side, and suddenly I'm completely surrounded by heat and muscle and the intoxicating mix of their scents.

I might be slightly obsessed with being surrounded like this. I feel safe and cherished and absolutely adored in ways I never experienced before them.

"Just take it easy," Chris murmurs against my hair. "You've been working nonstop for weeks. Let us handle everything for once."

"But I want to help—"

"You can help by relaxing," Kane interrupts, pressing a kiss to my neck. "Revolutionary concept for you, I know."

"We adore you," Chris says, pressing a kiss to my forehead. "But you need to learn to sit still occasionally."

"Sitting still is for people who don't have anxiety and perfectionist tendencies," I inform him. "I'm an event coordinator. We don't do still."

"Today you do."

I'm about to argue more when I realize I actually like standing here in their arms, surrounded by them, listening to Christmas music and smelling the amazing food they're cooking for our friends and family.

Fine. I can relax. For a few minutes. Maybe.

"Actually," I say, my voice coming out softer than intended. "Since you're all here and I have your attention… I want to tell you something."

They all go still immediately, giving me their undivided attention. "I'm definitely, completely, stupidly, head-over-heels in love with all three of you." The words tumble out in a rush. "Like, so much that I might actually cry right now thinking about it, which is embarrassing because I'm not a crier. I don't know exactly when it happened, maybe gradually, maybe all at once like some kind of emotional ambush, but I'm so ridiculously in love with you that I get legitimately angry that we didn't meet earlier so I could have had this amazing life sooner."

Silence for about three seconds.

Then Chris tilts my face up and kisses me so thoroughly that my knees actually wobble and I have to grab his shirt to stay upright. When he breaks away, he says, "I love you too. So much it actually scares me sometimes. Like, I didn't know I was capable of feeling this much for another person until you showed up and turned my entire world upside down."

"I'm completely gone for you," Kane adds. "Never thought I'd find that all-consuming, can't-live-without-you love. But then you crashed into our lives."

Noel cups my face with both hands. "You're my everything. My love. My soul. My oxygen. The person I didn't even know I was searching for until you were standing right in front of me. I love you more than I have words for, and I'm really good with words."

Now I'm crying, tears streaming down my face while I'm grinning like a complete idiot.

"Actually," Kane interrupts, exchanging loaded glances with the other two that immediately make me suspicious. "Since we're declaring our love and getting all emotional and sappy, we want to give you your Christmas gift."

I brighten immediately, my tears forgotten. "Oh! Yes! I'm excited and extremely curious. Also slightly scared, based on the way you're all looking at each other like you're planning something."

"Close your eyes," Kane instructs.

I narrow my eyes at them. "What did you do?"

"Just do it, baby girl. Trust us."

I shut my eyes, mostly because the curiosity is killing me. Hands guide me—one Alpha on each side, one behind me, steering gently. I hear doors opening, footsteps on different surfaces, and then there's this shift in temperature and air quality.

"Are we in the garage?"

"No peeking," Chris warns.

"I'm not! My eyes are closed! I'm just using basic deductive reasoning and common sense!"

"Too smart for your own good," Kane mutters, but I hear the smile in his voice.

"It's one of my most charming qualities."

We stop moving, and I feel all three men positioning themselves around me.

"Okay," Noel states, and his hands are on my shoulders, steadying me. "Open your eyes."

I follow their instructions, and my mouth falls open.

Sitting in the garage, gleaming under the overhead lights like something from a car commercial, is a gorgeous red Jeep Wrangler. Not just any red, but a deep, rich, candy-apple red. Black wheels and trim that make the red pop even more. Tinted windows. And a huge red bow perched on the hood like something from a Christmas movie.

"Oh my God," I breathe, my voice coming out

embarrassingly squeaky. "What is that? Did you steal it? Are we about to be arrested?"

All three of them are grinning like they've just won the lottery.

"It's your new car," Chris says simply, like he's announcing that we're having pizza for dinner instead of gifting me an amazing new car. "You need something reliable if you're living out here in the mountains. That Honda had to go."

"In fact, we already got rid of it," Kane adds way too cheerfully.

I spin around to stare at them, my mouth hanging open.

"Traded it in," Noel says, completely unrepentant. "Got you this instead." He holds up a set of keys, dangling them in front of me. "Merry Christmas."

I'm frozen, shocked, smiling like crazy. "This is so perfect."

Then all three of them pull me into a group hug that nearly lifts me off my feet, and I'm crying again. Evidently, that's just what I do now.

"Can I see what it's like inside before I have a complete emotional breakdown?" My voice comes out embarrassingly squeaky.

They practically carry me over to it, and Chris opens the driver's door with a dramatic flourish like he's presenting me to royalty.

The interior is absolutely stunning. Black leather seats. A modern dashboard with all the tech features I could possibly want and several I didn't know existed.

That new car smell that I love. I climb into the driver's seat, running my hands over the steering wheel, and all three of them crowd around the open door, watching me with identical expressions of satisfaction.

"This is incredible," I whisper, because apparently I've lost the ability to speak at a normal volume. "Thank you. All of you. This is the best gift I've ever received in my entire life, and I'm including the Easy-Bake Oven I got when I was seven."

"We have plenty of space for Corn Dog in the back," I point out, gesturing to the rear seats.

"NO!" all three of them say in perfect unison.

I burst out laughing.

That's when the doorbell rings from inside the house, cutting through our moment. "Guests are arriving," Chris murmurs. "Time to be social humans instead of people having emotional breakdowns in garages over cars."

I get out of the Jeep, and we head back inside through the connecting door. I'm still slightly dazed from the gift as I practically sprint to the front entrance and swing it open.

Lily stands there with platters of baked goods stacked so high in her arms that I'm amazed she can see over them. And next to her is Dad, grinning.

"So good to finally see your new home, Hannah," Dad says.

"So good you've arrived." I throw myself at him for a hug, nearly knocking the platters out of Lily's arms in the process. "Come in!"

Behind Lily are her three Alphas, Archer, James, and Hunter. Archer has a baby bag and toys in his hand, while James and Hunter are each carrying their gorgeous little twins in handheld carriages.

"We brought half the bakery," Lily announces, handing platters to whoever has free hands.

Everyone is talking and laughing at once, moving into the kitchen to set things down, and I'm gushing over Sage and Blake, who are making the cutest baby sounds. They are the most precious little things. Sage has tiny reindeer antlers on, while Blake wears a gingerbread suit. My entire heart just folds in on itself.

"Oh my God, come here," I whisper, scooping Blake from his carrier while Hunter hands Sage to Chris. Blake stares up at me with those big, sleepy eyes, then lets out this soft coo that absolutely destroys me. "You two are illegal levels of adorable," I tell them, kissing Blake's warm forehead and wiggling Sage's foot until she kicks happily.

James and Hunter step in behind me, loaded with diaper bags and assorted baby gear.

"Where can we set up the play mat?" James asks.

"I cleared space near the couches," I say, shifting Blake to my hip and pointing with my free hand. "Right over there with a perfect view of the tree."

Hunter huffs a laugh and starts unrolling the play mat. I kneel to help him, still bouncing Blake gently on my hip as Sage babbles from Chris's arms. The whole house feels different now, warmer, fuller, alive in a way

I didn't realize it had been missing until this exact moment.

I finally hand Blake over to James, smoothing the front of his tiny onesie before letting go. When I stand, my gaze catches on Chris nearby. He's cradling Sage effortlessly, one big hand supporting her small back, his expression soft in a way that punches all the air straight out of my lungs.

He looks *good* with a baby.

Dangerously good.

His eyes slide to mine, slow and knowing, heat simmering under the sweetness. "You getting those feelings, gorgeous?" he murmurs.

My face flames instantly. I laugh it off—at least, I pretend to—but inside, something warm and terrifying and *right* unfurls in my chest.

God.

Maybe.

I get up and go see who else needs my help before I drag Chris upstairs and say we need to get more practice for baby making. Time passes in that weird way it does at parties, where you look up and suddenly two hours have gone by. More friends arrive, Ruby with her three Alphas, who immediately get recruited to help Kane set up extra chairs. Some other people from town I've gotten friendly with during event planning, and my men's friends.

The house fills with voices and laughter. People scatter throughout, some crowded around the dining table, others claiming the couches, groups standing in the kitchen, sampling appetizers, while the guys work on the finishing touches for the feast.

The doorbell rings again, and I'm closest, so I go to answer it, expecting maybe more neighbors or someone's plus-one who got lost.

Instead, a woman I've never seen before stands on the porch, and my brain completely stutters trying to process her. She's... stunning. Like, offensively gorgeous in that effortless way that has me wanting to check my hair and wondering if I have food in my teeth.

Strawberry-blonde hair flows to her waist in soft waves. The greenest eyes I've ever seen, like actual emeralds. Dramatic, dark eyeshadow, long lashes, and glossy lipstick that's the perfect shade. A black leather choker around her neck that manages to look elegant instead of edgy.

She's wearing a short crop top under a thick white coat that's hanging open despite the freezing temperature. Deep blue jeans sit low on her hips, and there's a belly button ring glinting.

She looks like she walked off a runway and decided to slum it with us normal people for the day.

"Hey there," I manage, trying not to sound as intimidated as I feel. "Are you here for the party?"

She laughs, and it's a genuine sound. "You must be Hannah, right?"

I blink, thrown off. "That's me. Do we know each other? Did I plan an event for you? I'm terrible with faces when people aren't yelling at me about decorations."

She steps inside without waiting for an invitation and pulls me into a hug. She smells like expensive perfume and something minty.

I stand there, awkwardly patting her back, completely confused but also extremely curious about who this gorgeous stranger hugging me is.

"I'm Adelaide," she finally says, drawing back with a grin. "Chris's sister."

"Oh." My brain processes this information. "OH! Hello! Wow! Come in properly! I just—he never mentioned you. Like, not even once. I didn't know he had a sister."

She laughs again, shrugging out of her coat to reveal even more of that crop top situation. "Yeah, Chris isn't exactly great at the whole sharing-personal-information thing. But I did tell all three of the guys I was coming. From what Noel said, Chris has been a little preoccupied with his new Omega to remember to mention me." She grins. "Can't say I blame him. You're exactly as gorgeous as Noel described."

I can't stop smiling. "Oh, you and Noel chat often?" I'm trying really hard not to sound jealous. Why would I be jealous? She's just absurdly stunning and apparently talks to one of my Alphas regularly, and I've read enough romance novels to know that guys always harbor secret crushes on their best friend's hot sisters.

But I'm being ridiculous. Totally ridiculous.

Adelaide must catch something in my tone—or my face, which has never been good at hiding my emotions —because she nudges me playfully with her elbow.

"Don't worry. Noel has always been like an annoying older brother to me. Nothing more, never will be, and frankly, the thought makes me want to gag." She makes an exaggerated disgusted face. "I sometimes run things past him when I need advice, because he has way more patience than Chris and is slightly less likely to punch first and ask questions later."

Relief floods through me so fast I feel lightheaded. "Oh, good. I mean—not that I was worried. Because I wasn't. I'm very secure and confident and not at all prone to overthinking—"

"You were totally jealous," Adelaide interrupts, grinning wider. "It's cute. Chris's family is your family now, which means I'm your family too. Whether you want me or not."

Something comforting blooms in my chest. "I definitely want you. Welcome to the crazy house."

Adelaide's expression softens. "Thank you. That actually means a lot. It feels really good knowing he finally found someone who brings him happiness. Chris has been lost for so long, you know? Drifting. But I can see why he's completely smitten with you."

Before I can respond, Chris appears in the hallway.

"Adelaide?" His voice is surprised but genuinely happy. "You actually came. I thought you weren't since you never called back or answered any of my fifteen messages."

Adelaide raises an eyebrow. "Someone's needy."

"Someone was worried about his sister."

"Well, here I am." She spreads her arms dramatically. "In the flesh. Surprise?"

He crosses the room in three long strides and sweeps her into a hug so tight her boots lift an inch off the floor. Adelaide lets out a soft laugh against his chest, wrapping her arms around him with the kind of relief that only comes from seeing someone you haven't in too long.

"No way," Noel says as he rounds the corner from the kitchen, a beer in hand. "You didn't warn us you were showing up tonight."

Kane appears right behind him, wiping his hands on a dish towel. "Adelaide," he crows, pulling her into a second hug the moment Chris lets her breathe. "Jesus, you always pick the nights with the most going on."

She snorts. "I like to make an entrance."

"You like to make a mess," Noel counters, kissing the top of her head affectionately before tugging one of her curls. "You still dating that asshole from Denver?"

Adelaide rolls her eyes so hard they practically clatter to the floor. "Please. That ended months ago."

"Thank God," Kane says. "I never liked his face."

"You never met him," she fires back.

"Didn't need to. His face offended me in theory."

She laughs while Chris studies her closely, eyes narrowing at the exhaustion she tries to hide. She gives him a look that says *Not here, not yet,* and he squeezes her shoulder once, silently promising he won't push.

Kane loops an arm around her neck, dragging her

into his side. "Welcome. There's loads of food, and we need to eat it before Corn Dog tries to devour all of it."

Adelaide groans. "Please tell me you're joking."

"Nope," Noel states.

Her laugh is brighter this time, but there's still a tension beneath it.

Chris says, "Come on, sis, let me take your bags up to the spare room."

"I don't have much," Adelaide says with a casual shrug that seems slightly forced. "Not staying long, you know how I am. Got places to go, people to meet, adventures to have."

Chris's expression tightens. "Right. Of course."

They disappear upstairs, and I immediately turn to Noel and Kane. "Okay, what is the deal with those two? Because that was weird and awkward and I need the full story."

Noel sighs, running a hand through his long hair. "Chris basically protected her growing up from lots of bullying she used to experience."

"But then Chris needed to build his own life," Kane continues. "And Adelaide wanted independence. So she went her way, and Chris went his. Now there's this weird tension between them where you can tell they love each other but neither knows how to bridge the gap."

My heart actually hurts at hearing this. "That's awful."

"They just need to talk," Noel adds. "Really talk, not

surface-level how-are-you stuff. But neither of them will take that first step."

"Well, if she's staying here, maybe I can help," I say, already forming plans. "Get to know her, earn her trust, figure out what's really going on."

Both of them stare at me with so much affection that my cheeks heat up.

"This is why we love you," Kane murmurs, pressing a kiss to my mouth. "You immediately want to fix things and help people."

"Probably unhealthy but we're working with what we've got," I reply.

We rejoin the party, and soon Chris and Adelaide come back downstairs. She immediately gravitates toward Lily and Ruby, and within minutes, all three women are laughing like they've known each other for years.

Noel starts carving the turkey at the dining table, and everyone gathers around to watch and cheer him on like it's some kind of sporting event. It's chaotic and loud and absolutely perfect.

Later, after we've eaten enough food to feed a small army and everyone is lounging around in food comas, I grab Lily to show her my new Jeep.

"You have to see this gift," I tell her, practically dragging her toward the garage. "It's insane. Like, completely insane."

We're walking through the hallway when we hear Adelaide's voice coming from one of the side rooms—

the study, I think. She's on the phone, her voice low but carrying in the quiet hallway.

Lily and I both freeze, exchanging glances.

"Yeah, I'm here. I'm safe. Would you stop worrying so much?" Adelaide's tone is affectionate but exasperated. "I won't be here long enough for anything to happen. I'll do what I came to do, and then I'll be gone."

She pauses, listening to whoever is on the other end.

"I know. I keep my word. When have I not? Chris knows nothing about any of this, and I'm going to keep it that way. It's better if he doesn't know."

Another pause.

"Okay, I heard you the first fifty times. Yes, I'm being careful. Yes, I understand the risks. Yes, I know—"

Silence while the other person talks.

"I know what's at stake here." Her voice drops even lower, almost a whisper. "I'm not stupid. I know exactly what will happen if this goes wrong. But it won't. I'll be careful."

More silence.

"I have to go." Her voice softens. "I love you too." The call ends.

Lily and I stare at each other with wide, shocked eyes and immediately scramble toward the garage before Adelaide can catch us eavesdropping like creeps. We burst through the garage door and close it behind us, both of us breathing hard.

"What the hell was that about?" Lily whispers, even though we're alone now.

"Something's going on," I whisper back. "She sounded kinda scared."

"Are you going to tell Chris?"

I bite my lip, thinking. "I don't know yet. I need to figure out what's going on first. If I tell him now with no context, it might just push Adelaide away, and then we'll never find out what kind of trouble she's in."

"You think she's in trouble?"

"Did you hear that conversation? She's definitely in some kind of trouble."

Lily nods slowly. "Okay. So what's the plan?"

"I'm going to get to know her. Earn her trust. Figure out what she's hiding and whether I need to tell Chris or if I can help her handle it quietly. She's family now, which means she's my responsibility too."

"Good plan."

I take a breath, pushing Adelaide's mysterious phone call to the back of my mind for now. "Okay, enough about potentially dangerous secrets. Let me show you this absolutely ridiculous gift that's making your men look bad by comparison."

I hit the lights dramatically, and the Jeep gleams under the fluorescent bulbs.

Lily actually squeals. "Oh, hell, Hannah! Are you serious right now? This is gorgeous!"

We're both climbing all over it like excited kids, and I'm showing her all the features when the garage door opens and my three men appear, clearly looking for us.

"Secret party in the garage?" Kane asks with a grin.

"Just showing off the best Christmas gift ever," I say, unable to stop smiling. "Also making Lily's Alphas look bad, which is an added bonus."

Lily spins to face them, hands on her hips. "You guys are setting an impossibly high bar here. What are you going to get her for her birthday at this rate? A private island? A palace? A small country?"

They all laugh, and I fall into their waiting arms, letting them surround me again.

"I gotta go tell my men they need to seriously lift their game," Lily says, still grinning as she heads back inside.

When she's gone and it's just the four of us in the quiet garage, I glance up at all three of them, who are staring at me with so much love and pride and happiness that I might cry again.

"This is our first Christmas as a family," Chris says.

I melt against them, and we stand there for a long moment, just holding each other while snow continues to fall heavily outside and muffled music and laughter drift from the house.

This is home and family. Not the building, not the location, but these people. This feeling. And whatever challenge comes next, I know I can handle it because I'm not alone anymore.

I have them. They have me. And together, we're unstoppable.

Even if that means dealing with mysterious family secrets and reindeer with destructive tendencies. But that's a problem for tomorrow. Today is for celebrating everything we've built together.

And it's absolutely, perfectly, wonderfully imperfect.

Just like us.

EPILOGUE

HANNAH

One month later, and I'm standing in Sweden with absolutely no clue what's happening.

Well, that's not entirely accurate. I know we're in Sweden because I saw my plane ticket. And we've been traveling for a long time through flights, layovers, another flight, and then a car ride through increasingly snowy wilderness that looked like something out of a Nordic noir film.

But beyond those basic geographical facts, I'm completely in the dark.

My three Alphas have been infuriatingly tight-lipped the entire journey. Every time I asked where we were going, they exchanged those smug looks and said, "You'll see."

Every. Single. Time.

So here I am, climbing out of an Uber in front of what appears to be some kind of hotel entrance, snow falling softly around us in fat, lazy flakes, the air so cold it burns my lungs in the most refreshing way possible.

It's dark, but there are lights ahead of us. Warm golden glows spilling from windows, lanterns lining snow-packed pathways, everything sparkling and twinkling against the pristine white landscape.

My heart is already racing with anticipation. Whatever this is, wherever they've brought me, I can feel in my bones that it's going to be special.

In front of us stands this large arch-like structure that appears to be made of snow and ice, illuminated from within so it glows pale blue against the night sky. Like a portal to another world.

"Walk through," Chris says, his breath forming clouds in the freezing air. His eyes are bright with barely contained excitement. "Keep going straight ahead, gorgeous."

The guys are pulling our luggage behind them, and I'm too mesmerized to do anything except obey. I step through the arch and onto a snowy path, and immediately I feel like I've entered a fairy tale.

Buildings flank us on either side, restaurants with frost-covered windows, where people inside are laughing over meals, candlelight flickering on their tables. A small shop with handcrafted items displayed in the window, everything looking cozy and inviting. Cabin-like structures that glow with warmth, smoke curling from chimneys.

Everything has this magical, otherworldly quality as

though we've stepped into a snow globe or a storybook illustration come to life.

But we're not stopping at any of these places.

"Keep going," Kane encourages from behind me. "Straight ahead, baby girl."

My boots crunch on the pristine snow, my breath coming faster with each step as anticipation builds in my chest.

A structure rises ahead of us. The front of the building curves outward like a dome, and the entire thing appears to be made of snow and ice. Not decorated to look like snow and ice—but actually constructed from it. The structure spreads outward in organic curves, low and wide rather than tall, hugging the landscape like it grew there naturally. Soft blue light emanates from within, making the whole thing glow ethereally against the dark sky.

Large double doors mark the entrance, simple and elegant, and I can see people going in and out, their breath creating clouds as they move between the frozen exterior and whatever lies within.

My heart is pounding so hard I can feel it in my throat.

"Oh my God," I whisper, and my voice comes out shaky, turning to the guys. "Is this… are we…?"

I can't even finish the sentence because my brain is struggling with hope and disbelief and overwhelming joy.

"Keep going," Noel says softly, his hand finding the small of my back. "It gets better inside."

I'm shaking as we approach the doors. With every step, the reality of where I am sinks deeper into my bones, and tears prick at my eyes.

Chris and Kane each grab a door handle and pull them open, stepping aside so I can enter first.

I walk through, and I completely lose the ability to breathe. The foyer stretches before me, and every single surface is carved from ice.

The walls rise up in a smooth, crystalline bluish white that catches the carefully placed lighting and throws it back in a thousand directions. The ceiling arches overhead, and my breath forms clouds that drift upward into the frozen space. The floor beneath my feet is ice too, textured for traction but unmistakably frozen water.

Massive pillars run in two rows down the length of the entrance hall, each one a work of art. One is covered in delicate snowflake patterns so intricate they look like lacework. Another has climbing vines frozen in eternal bloom. A third depicts what look like the northern lights in flowing, undulating waves.

I walk deeper in, turning in slow circles, trying to take everything in at once and failing completely because there's too much beauty to absorb.

There are other guests here, people wandering through with the same awed expressions I must be wearing, staff members in warm parkas directing traffic with practiced ease. A reception desk ahead is carved from ice, with actual humans standing behind it like this is all perfectly normal.

Which, for them, I suppose it is.

But for me…

I turn to face my men, and something breaks open in my chest. All the emotions I've been holding back—the anticipation of the journey, the trust I placed in them to bring me somewhere special, the overwhelming reality of where I'm actually standing—crash over me at once.

My eyes are burning. My throat is tight. My hands are shaking.

"We're at the ice hotel," I manage, and my voice cracks on every word. "We're actually at the ice hotel in Sweden."

They're all grinning, huge, satisfied, proud grins that make them look like boys who just pulled off the world's greatest surprise.

"Surprise," they say together, and then they're surrounding me, pulling me into a warming hug.

I'm crying now with happiness, and I don't even care that I probably look like a mess in front of all these strangers.

"You once told me," Kane murmurs against my hair, his arms tight around me, "what your dream event would be to coordinate. Do you remember what you said?"

I nod and glance up at him. I'd rambled for probably twenty minutes about ice sculptures and live orchestras and champagne fountains and venues so elaborate they took your breath away.

"We decided to bring you to your first ice event as a

guest," Kane continues. "So you can experience the magic before you create your own version of it."

I'm crying even more now, which is probably dangerous, given the subzero temperatures, but I physically cannot stop. "I'm so emotional," I gasp, laughing because the alternative is full-on sobbing. "I love you all so much. This is everything I ever dreamed about and more. I don't have the words for what this means to me."

Chris wipes my tears with his thumbs, his touch gentle. "We wanted to give you something you'd never forget."

"Mission accomplished." I hiccup, which is very attractive. "I can't believe you actually brought me here. I would never have done this for myself. I would have said it was too expensive or too impractical or we should save the money for something sensible, and I would have just kept dreaming about it forever instead of actually experiencing it."

"That's exactly why we did it," Noel says, pressing a kiss to my forehead. "Because you deserve to have your dreams become real. Not someday. Not eventually. Now."

"You three are going to ruin me," I manage. "I'm going to become one of those spoiled Omegas who expect elaborate international surprises on a regular basis."

"Good," Kane says firmly. "That's the goal."

I cry a little more, because apparently that's just who

I am now—a person who weeps at grand romantic gestures.

Kane eventually excuses himself to handle the check-in, while Chris and Noel stay with me, letting me wander around the foyer and gawk at everything. I touch the walls, feeling the cold seep through my gloves. I examine the pillars up close, marveling at the craftsmanship. I watch other guests having the same overwhelmed reactions.

"How did they even build this?" I ask, running my hand along a carved column. "How is this structurally possible? This defies everything I know about architecture and physics."

"They rebuild it every year," Chris explains, his arm around my waist. "Fresh construction each winter with new designs. When spring comes, it melts back into the river it came from."

"That's the most beautiful and devastating thing I've ever heard. All this work and artistry, and it just... disappears?"

"Makes it more precious," Noel says. "Knowing it won't last forever."

Kane returns with key cards and a staff member in a warm parka who introduces herself as Elsa, which I desperately want to make a *Frozen* joke about but manage to restrain myself.

We follow her through hallways carved entirely from ice, passing more guests and doors leading to other suites. The walls in this section are decorated with nature scenes. One area has ocean waves frozen mid-crash, and another has a forest scene with trees and animals.

"First time at an ice hotel?" Elsa asks, clearly noticing my inability to stop touching everything and gasping at random intervals.

"Is it that obvious?"

"You have the look." She says it kindly, with the patience of someone who's guided thousands of awestruck tourists. "Everyone has that expression their first time. You never quite believe it's real until you're standing in it."

"I still don't believe it. Part of my brain keeps insisting that this is an elaborate dream and I'm going to wake up any second."

"You won't," she assures me. "But I understand the feeling."

We reach our suite, and Elsa opens the door. I step inside, and my knees actually go weak.

The entry area has benches carved from ice with thick fur throws for sitting, a small ice table, and carved alcoves where we can store our clothes and belongings. There's even a door leading to what Elsa explains is a heated bathroom.

But the masterpiece is at the back of the room.

An arched entrance carved from ice leads into what can only be described as a sleeping alcove. The arch is flanked by two stunning sculptures. A wolf on one side, fierce and beautiful with every hair seemingly carved in detail, and a bird on the other, with wings tucked elegantly against its body, head turned as if watching over whoever enters.

And beyond that arch is an enormous bed, easily big enough for four people to sleep comfortably, covered in so many fur blankets and throws that it looks like a cloud made of luxury. Soft blue lighting makes everything glow like we're sleeping inside a precious gem.

"The sleeping bags are in the wardrobe here," Elsa is explaining, showing us a carved alcove with specialized thermal sleeping equipment. "The room stays around twenty-three degrees Fahrenheit, so you'll want to follow the layering instructions carefully. The bathroom through that door is heated to normal temperatures, and you can warm up there whenever needed."

I'm barely listening. I'm too busy walking through the space, touching the wolf sculpture, running my fingers along the carved arch, staring at the bed that looks like something from a winter fairy tale.

The bathroom is visible through a doorway, and I peek inside to find more ice artistry—walls with decorative carvings of wolves and forest animals that match the theme of our room, and what appears to be an ice structure surrounding a normal heated tub.

When Elsa finally leaves after explaining approximately fifty things I'll never remember, I turn to my Alphas.

"I love this room," I announce, my voice echoing slightly off the frozen walls. "I love this hotel. I love Sweden. I love ice as a building material. I love everything about this moment, and I will carry it with me for the rest of my life. And I love you three so much."

They're watching me with those soft expressions that leave my heart fluttering.

"We're glad you approve," Kane adds with a sinful grin.

"Approve? I'm going to write poetry about this room. Bad poetry. Rhyming poetry. That's how much I approve."

"Please don't," Noel says. "Your creative talents lie elsewhere."

I laugh. "Rude. But fair."

Chris has disappeared into the bathroom area, and when he emerges, he's carrying the most beautiful dress I have ever seen in my entire life. It's ice blue—of course it is, because these men understand themes—with long sleeves and a high neckline trimmed with soft white faux fur. The fabric shimmers like it's woven from starlight and frost crystals, catching the ambient glow of the room and throwing it back in tiny sparkles with every movement.

In his other hand is a matching mask, decorated with crystals and small white feathers, clearly designed for something formal and magical.

"Is that for me?" My voice comes out barely above a whisper.

"We're booked for a masquerade ball in the ice bar tonight," Chris says, and there's this satisfied smile on his face that tells me he's been waiting to reveal this part. "They're hosting a special event, and we have tickets. After cocktails, we're having dinner, and then there's dancing."

I make a sound that's somewhere between a squeal and a sob.

"Is this actually my life?"

"It sure is," Kane confirms and steals a kiss.

"We should get ready," Noel adds, also leaning in to kiss me. "It starts in an hour."

I'm already moving toward Chris, reaching for the dress. "Why are you only telling me this now? I need time! I need to do my hair! I need to figure out makeup that works with this mask! I need to have a moment to process the fact that I'm living inside a romance novel!"

The three of them are chuckling at me.

I clutch the dress to my chest, overwhelmed all over again. "I honestly don't know how I can ever repay you for this," I whisper. "This is… everything I never thought I'd get to have. I didn't even let myself *want* something like this. And you just—" My voice catches. "You gave it to me."

Noel steps in first like he's approaching something sacred. He frames my face with those big, calloused hands, angling me up into his gaze. "You don't repay us," he says quietly. "That's not how this works. We choose you. We keep choosing you. And giving you the things you never thought you deserved?" His thumb strokes my cheek. "That's our privilege, Hannah."

My heart flips. God, he means it.

Then he kisses me, slow, lingering, a promise

pressed directly into my mouth. The kind of kiss that has me trembling when he pulls away.

Chris is there and brushes a kiss along my jaw, warm breath trailing after it. "You have no idea," he murmurs, "how easy it is to give to you. How good it feels." His hand skims down my arm, fingers tangling briefly with mine. "Let us spoil you a little, sweetheart."

Then Kane's palms settle at my hips, drawing me into the heat of his chest. He presses his mouth to the side of my head, a slow drag of lips that makes my spine melt. "You think this is a lot?" he rumbles against my skin. "Just wait. We haven't even warmed up yet."

A laugh slips out of me, half breathless, half desperate to keep standing under all this attention.

They're surrounding me—touching me, claiming me without needing to mark a single inch.

It's dizzying. It's perfect.

Kane nuzzles my temple. "Go on, beautiful," he says, voice dipping low. "Get dressed."

Chris's hand pats my ass. "We've got a ball to attend," he adds, smirking. "And trust me... we plan on being the ones who get to unwrap you later."

My whole body lights up. And for the first time in my life, I don't feel like someone who's being given a gift. But like *I'm* the gift they can't wait to cherish.

I float into the bathroom on a cloud of happiness. "Can you believe this is happening?" I ask the carved wolf as I blend eyeshadow. "Because I can't."

The dress fits perfectly. My hair goes into soft curls

that cascade over my shoulders and down my chest, a few tendrils framing my face.

When I finally position the mask and look at myself in the mirror, my breath catches.

I might as well be an ice princess. Someone who belongs in ballrooms and palaces. With a deep breath, I adjust my mask one final time and step out of the bathroom.

My three Alphas are waiting, and I nearly fall over.

They're all in formal suits, perfectly tailored to emphasize their broad shoulders and powerful builds. Chris in deep charcoal that makes his green eyes pop. Kane in midnight blue that somehow makes him look even more dangerous than usual. Noel in classic black with his long dark hair pulled back, looking like a fallen angel.

Each of them wears a black masquerade mask over his eyes, and the effect is absolutely devastating. They look like secret agents. Like villains from a Gothic romance. Like every fantasy I've ever had made flesh.

"Your Majesty," Noel says, dropping to one knee in front of me. "You honor us poor mortals with your presence."

I laugh, the sound echoing off the ice walls. He takes my hand and presses a kiss to my knuckles before rising gracefully.

Chris and Kane move in like they planned it, but I know they didn't. They just... orbit me. Big hands skim over whatever skin they can reach. Chris's lips brush my bare shoulder where the neckline has slipped.

Kane's mouth finds the curve of my neck. Fingers trail along my waist, slow and appreciative.

"You're so beautiful," Chris murmurs against my skin, his breath warm and distracting.

A shiver rolls down my spine.

He continues, "This dress was the right call. I worried the blue would be too on the nose, given the venue, but…" His palm slides down the fabric over my hip, slow enough to make me inhale sharply. "It's perfect. You're perfect."

I smirk. Chris kisses my shoulder again. Kane's hands tighten on my waist as he says, "We should get you to this ball before we mess up your hair and your dress and your very carefully applied makeup."

"Ruining my makeup seems inevitable," I shoot back, my cheeks heating.

Noel opens the long white coat they must have brought for me. Faux fur collar. Cuffs looking as soft as clouds. He drapes it over my shoulders. I snuggle into it, moaning at the warmth.

"You really thought of everything," I murmur.

"We tried," Chris says, offering me his arm. There's a subtle, devastating pride in his voice. "Come with us."

I take his arm. Kane offers his other arm with a wicked little tilt of his mouth. Noel falls into step behind us, his palm warm and possessive at the small of my back.

We make our way through the ice corridors like we're royalty processing to a state event. Other guests pass us—some in formal wear, clearly headed to the same destination, others in casual clothes, exploring the hotel—and every single one of them turns to look.

We must make quite a picture. The three massive Alphas in their dark suits and masks, and me in my shimmering ice-blue gown, looking like I escaped from a winter fairy tale.

I've never felt more beautiful. More cherished. More like I belong exactly where I am.

The ice bar is in a separate section of the hotel, and when we step through the entrance, I have to stop and just breathe because it's too much to process at once.

The entire space is carved from ice—walls, seats, bar, glasses, everything—but it's been decorated for the masquerade with incredible artistry. Ice sculptures of dancers frozen mid-waltz are positioned throughout the room, so detailed that I can see the expressions on their faces, the movement in their gowns and coattails. The bar itself is a huge ice structure with soft blue lighting embedded within, bottles of spirits chilling in carved alcoves that glow like treasure.

"Starting with drinks," Noel says, already in mission mode. "Because we're in an ice bar and it would be borderline offensive not to." He gestures at a menu. "They use cloudberries and lingonberries and aquavit. I'm committed."

He disappears toward the bar.

Chris, Kane, and I find a table near an enormous ice sculpture of a snow fox. It's so intricately carved that I swear it's watching us. I run my fingers over the table's frozen surface, still marveling at how this entire place is made of water and cold and magic. Temporary magic.

Noel returns, carrying four drinks in ice-glasses shaped like faceted gemstones. Mine holds a deep plum-colored cocktail that glows slightly under the lights, garnished with frozen berries and a shard of crystallized mint. The men's drinks are amber and rich, swirling with herbs trapped in ice like prehistoric specimens.

Chris lifts his glass with a slow smile that hits me somewhere low in my stomach. "To Hannah. Who trusted three bounty hunters enough to get on a plane without knowing where she would end up."

Kane grins. "To us. For surviving the interrogation she put us through. I still have bruises on my ego."

Noel raises his glass last. "To all the places we'll go after this. Because this is only the beginning."

I lift mine, cold seeping through my gloves. "To my three Alphas, who somehow made a surprise trip across the world feel like the most thoughtful thing anyone has ever done for me. Whatever you were trying to accomplish... you succeeded."

They laugh, and when we drink, the taste is unreal. Sweet. Tart. Warming in a way that feels like it unfurls inside my ribs and makes room for something new.

Chris slides his arm along the back of my chair, fingers ghosting over my shoulder. "This is what your life looks like now," he says softly.

Kane shifts closer, his palm trailing down my spine

with gentle possession. "We're here. All the way. No fear. No hesitation. You're ours, and we're yours."

Noel grins from across the table. "You're stuck with us. Permanently. We checked the contract and everything."

I laugh. The sound rings bright and clear, bouncing off the ice walls and mixing with the soft music drifting through the space. It feels like the ice itself is carrying the sound upward and scattering it around us.

For a moment, everything fades. The world, the past, the uncertainty. All I feel is their heat pressed against my sides, their attention resting fully and completely on me, the surreal beauty of the glowing ice palace, and the knowledge blooming slowly inside me.

Happiness doesn't feel the way I thought it would. It's not loud or dramatic. It's not something fragile I have to hold tightly before it slips through my fingers.

It's warmth inside a frozen world, being held even when I'm scared. This love that melts everything I thought I knew about my life.

I turn to them, heart full, and whisper, "I'm all in for the long haul."

Chris's breath catches. Kane goes still. Noel's smile is captivating. And they close in around me, our glasses clinking softly like a promise forming in the cold.

For the first time in my life, I'm not afraid to keep something wonderful.

And I'm never letting it go.

BONUS SCENE

HANNAH

Three months back from Sweden, and my life has transformed into something I barely recognize.

The kind where I wake up every morning sandwiched between warm Alpha bodies and wonder what I did in a past life to deserve this level of happiness.

Confetti & Meatballs Event Planning has absolutely exploded. Word spread about the tree lighting ceremony, then about the parade recovery, and then about how I handled every crisis Scot threw at me with grace and professionalism—okay, maybe not grace, but definitely stubborn determination that people seem to respect.

Now I'm booked solid for the next eighteen months.

So solid, in fact, that I had to hire help. Three Alphas, more specifically, now work with me while still doing bounty hunting on the side. Turns out that men who can track criminals and negotiate with dangerous fugitives are also excellent at wrangling difficult vendors and managing impossible timelines.

Who knew?

I love having them around more. Seeing Kane sweet-talk a florist into a last-minute delivery. Watching Chris intimidate a catering company into honoring their original quote. Noel charming venue managers into giving us better rates.

We make an incredible team.

Now, I'm standing in the most gorgeous wedding venue I've ever seen, watching the final preparations come together for my friend Emma's wedding.

Emma is a hugely successful romance author who lives locally in Whispering Grove. She writes these sweeping love stories, and now she's living her own happily-ever-after with her three Alphas, Atlas, the fire chief, and River and Levi.

When they proposed, Emma knew exactly what she wanted. A proper, full-scale, no-expense-spared wedding that would rival anything she'd ever written in her books.

And she wanted it at Savor Functions. The brand-new event venue operated by the same guys who run the Savor restaurant in town—easily the most popular and critically acclaimed dining establishment in the entire region. The new venue is booked solid two years in advance, with a waiting list that stretches even further.

Getting Emma in here seemed impossible.

But I don't believe in the impossible anymore.

Lily knows Cindy, the Omega to the men who run the Savor empire, and she pulled some strings. Called in favors. Worked whatever sisterly magic she possesses. And somehow, miraculously, we found a weekend that worked.

I would do anything for my clients, and when Emma asked for this specific venue—the grounds at the base of the mountains, landscape stretching out as far as the eye could see, and world-class catering from Arrow himself —I made it happen.

So, standing here watching everything come together, I feel a swell of pride so intense it almost brings tears to my eyes. The venue is spectacular. In the distance stands Cindy and her Alphas' mansion, a sprawling estate that looks like something from an architectural magazine. But we're farther out on the grounds now, in a section that's been transformed into a wedding paradise.

The ceremony space is set up beneath an enormous oak tree, its branches spreading wide like nature's own cathedral. Spring has brought everything to life, blossoms covering nearby trees in clouds of pink and white, birds singing from hidden perches, the air sweet with the scent of flowers and new growth.

The sun is beginning its slow descent toward the mountains, throwing off colors that no photographer could fully capture—golds and roses and soft lavenders that paint the landscape like a watercolor. And the one Emma hired is crazily clicking photos now of the men waiting for their bride with the celebrant.

White chairs are arranged in rows on either side of a cobblestone aisle, each one dressed with ribbons in soft ivory and sage green that flutter gently in the breeze. The aisle itself is lined with arrangements of spring flowers—peonies and roses and trailing greenery that spill from tall glass vases.

At the end of the aisle, beneath the oak tree, an arch has been constructed from twisted branches and woven with more flowers, a frame for the moment when Emma will finally marry her men.

And speaking of her men, Atlas, River, and Levi are already in position, standing tall and devastatingly handsome in their tailored suits. Atlas with his massive frame and tanned skin, looking every bit the protective hero. River with his longer dark blond hair and easy smile. Levi with his sharp features and intense gaze. And the chairs are filled with guests.

I'm so incredibly happy for them.

Soft music plays from hidden speakers, and everything is perfect. Every detail is exactly as Emma envisioned, precisely as we planned.

I do a final sweep with my gaze, checking for anything out of place, but there's nothing. Just beauty and anticipation and the promise of love about to be celebrated.

Time to get the bride... or at least wait for her arrival.

I turn and head across the lawn toward the driveway, my heels clicking on the stone path. My dress for today is a soft pink that catches the fading sunlight, fitted through the bodice with a corset-style top, then flowing into a skirt that flutters around my knees with every step. The sleeves are long and sheer, adding elegance without overwhelming, and my hair is swept up with a few tendrils escaping to frame my face.

I feel beautiful. Which is saying something, because today isn't about me at all.

Nearby, the enormous function hall sits with its front doors open, ready for the reception. It's a stunning building designed solely for events like this, complete with a full commercial kitchen, every amenity you could dream of, accommodations upstairs, all first-class everything.

The price tag made my eyes water when I first saw it, but Emma and her Alphas didn't even blink. When you're a bestselling author with three successful partners, apparently budget concerns become somewhat irrelevant.

As I approach the driveway area, I spot Arrow, owner of Savor, standing near the entrance, clearly handling some last-minute coordination. He's in tailored dark pants and a crisp white button-up shirt that does absolutely nothing to hide the muscles underneath—and there are a lot of them. The man is built like a Greek statue, with dark blond hair worn longer and loose around his face.

His brown eyes find me as I approach, and that easy grin spreads across his handsome face.

"There she is," he says, his voice deep and warm. "The woman who made all this happen."

"I had a lot of help," I reply, though I'm smiling. "Your team has been incredible. Honestly, working with Savor has been the easiest vendor relationship I've ever had."

"We aim to please." He gives a small bow, arms crossed, looking every inch the dangerous Alpha he probably was before going legitimate. There's something about him, about all of Cindy's men, actually, that reminds me of my own Alphas. That edge. That sense that they've seen things, done things, survived things.

Ex-bikers, Lily told me. The dangerous kind. They came with baggage and rough edges and complicated pasts.

Just like my three men.

Maybe that's why we all get along so well.

"Everything's ready to go," Arrow continues. "Cindy's got the music handled with the DJ, kitchen's prepped for the reception, bar's stocked. We're ready to roll whenever the bride shows up."

"She's about fifteen minutes out," I confirm, checking my phone. "Her driver just texted."

"I gotta say, Hannah, working with you has been refreshing. Most event coordinators are nightmares. Demanding, micromanaging, calling at three in the morning about napkin colors."

"Oh, I've definitely called people at three in the morning about napkin colors," I admit. "Just not you. Yet. Give it time."

He laughs, and the sound is deep and rich and genuinely amused. "I believe it."

A pair of arms wraps around me from behind, and I don't even startle because I know that scent, that touch, that presence.

Noel.

"Bonding without me?" he murmurs against my ear, and there's a teasing possessiveness in his voice that makes me shiver.

"Just discussing the event," I say innocently.

"Mmm." He doesn't sound convinced. His arms tighten around my waist. "Just remember who you're going home with tonight," he teases.

I twist slightly to look up at him, grinning. "Is that jealousy I detect?"

Noel chuckles and winks at Arrow, who laughs out loud.

"On that note…" Arrow adds. "I should get inside and make sure the kitchen staff isn't having any last-minute crises. Good luck with the ceremony, Hannah. And, Noel"—he nods at my Alpha with a knowing smile —"try not to distract her too much. She's got a bride to manage."

"No promises," Noel calls after him as Arrow disappears into the function hall.

I turn fully in Noel's arms, taking in the sight of him. He's dressed impeccably—a dark suit that fits his tall frame and a white shirt open at the collar because he refuses to wear ties unless someone's life depends on it. His hair is pulled back, and those captivating blue eyes are focused entirely on me.

"Have I told you how gorgeous you are today?" he asks, his hands sliding down to rest on my hips.

"You have. Only about seven times, actually. Way below your usual quota."

"Seven?" He looks genuinely distressed. "That's unacceptable. I'm slipping."

"It's been a busy day. I'll forgive you."

"No, no. This needs to be rectified immediately." He dips his head to press a kiss to my neck, just below my ear. "Gorgeous." Another kiss to my jaw. "Stunning." Another to the corner of my mouth. "Absolutely breathtaking."

"We have a wedding to run," I remind him, though I'm tilting my head to give him better access because apparently I have no self-control. "The bride is almost here."

"*Almost* being the key word." His lips find that spot on my neck, and my knees soften. "I was just inside chatting with Cindy's other two men, Holt and Luke. Did you know they're thinking about expanding the events side of the business? They want to discuss potential partnerships with us."

That gets my attention. "Really? A partnership with Savor?"

"Joint events. Cross-promotion. Using our planning expertise with their venue and catering excellence." He's still kissing my neck between words, which is very distracting. "Could be huge for the business."

"That would be incredible. Their reputation alone would bring in so many new clients."

"See? I'm not just seriously handsome. I'm also networking on your behalf."

"My hero."

He pulls back to look at me, and there's heat in his eyes now. "Come with me."

"Noel—"

"Just for a few minutes." He's already tugging me toward the function hall.

"For what?"

The grin he gives me is pure wickedness. "For you to properly thank me for that networking."

"Noel!" I'm laughing as he hauls me through the doors of the function hall, past the elegant reception setup, and toward the stairs that lead to the upper level. "We don't have time for this!"

"We absolutely do. I calculated it very carefully."

"You did?"

"I'm very good at math when properly motivated."

We're rushing now, me trying to keep up in my heels, both of us grinning like teenagers sneaking off at prom. He leads me to one of the accommodation rooms on the upper floor that we booked specifically for quick outfit changes and emergency situations.

I suppose this counts as an emergency situation. A Noel-created emergency, but still.

The moment the door closes behind us, his mouth is on mine. The kiss is magnificent. Deep and consuming and absolutely compelling. I'm drowning in his scent, my fingers clutching his shirt, pulling him closer even though there's no space left between us.

My body responds embarrassingly fast. Three months of this, and I still react to my Alphas like I'm starved for their touch. Maybe I always will.

He walks me backward until I'm pressed against the window, heavy lace curtains covering the glass, and then he spins me gently, pulling my hips back.

"Keep watch," he murmurs against my ear as my gaze lifts to the driveway in the distance. "Let me know when the bride's car appears."

"You're impossible."

"You love it."

I do. God help me, I really do.

His hands are everywhere. My dress shifts, his lips trail down my spine, and I grip the window frame to stay upright.

"We could wait until after the ceremony," I manage, though my voice comes out breathless.

"We'll do that too." His voice is rough with desire. "But I have zero patience when it comes to you. Never have. Never will."

"That's going to be a problem when we're old and gray."

"I'll still be chasing you around when we're ninety. You'll just have to move slower so I can catch you."

I laugh, but it turns into a gasp when his hand comes down on my ass, firm, claiming. Heat shoots through me so fast my head spins. He takes advantage immediately, lifting the back of my dress to my waist and dragging my panties down slowly. The cool air hits my skin, and then his mouth is on me, his lips brushing the back of my thigh as I step out of the fabric.

His hands slide up between my thighs, and I melt, spine arching as he spreads my legs open with a touch that borders on sinful. The world drops away. My breath stutters. The faint sound of music from the backyard filters through the window, but it's meaningless compared to the hot glide of his fingers and the rough scrape of his jaw against my hip.

"You're going to kill me," I murmur, half laugh, half moan, as he presses closer.

He takes a mock bite of my ass, and I squeal as he stands up behind me. "I just want to make you scream for me," he says, low and dangerous, and the sound of his zipper sliding down behind me sends a tremor straight through my core.

Down below, Kane and Chris linger casually at the edge of the driveway, chatting, looking incredibly handsome in their suits and completely unaware of the way Noel is about to wreck me above their heads.

Noel curves his hand around my hip, steadily guiding me forward until my palms brace against the window frame. "Good girl," he murmurs. "Always so easy to worship."

The words alone have me trembling, while his fingers trail higher, finding my fire. He slides his fingers between my lips, where I'm soaking wet. He groans as he pushes two fingers into me, and I cry out.

"Is this how you like it?" he teases, pumping them in and out of me quickly.

I can't find my voice, as I'm completely falling apart. It doesn't take him long to remove his fingers and push his huge cock into me. There's no ceremony, no pause, just fast claims, and I'm here for it.

"Hold on," he demands while his grasp tightens around my hips. And he's fucking me wildly, thrusting without pause, breathing heavily.

Rocking back and forth, I'm purring under him, loving how deep he goes, how far he stretches me. And there's no slowing down, just a faster pace.

"Fuck," he growls. "When Kane and Chris find out I fucked you, they are going to go insane. It's going to be so good."

"Y-you don't need t-to tell them."

He laughs like I asked for the utterly impossible.

Through the haze of my climbing arousal, I keep my gaze on the driveway. Watching for the limousine. Trying to remember that I have responsibilities. That there's a bride counting on me. That I'm supposed to be a professional.

But Noel makes it very difficult to remember anything except how well he fucks.

And then I see the sleek white car turning onto the driveway, approaching the venue.

"The bride is—" The words break in my throat as the pleasure steals my breath and pulls every thought straight out of my head. It starts low, a tight coil that snaps loose all at once, heat spiraling up my spine until my whole body arches. My fingers clamp down around the window frame, my thighs shake, and I can't stop the helpless, choked moan that rips out of me.

His hands steady me through every second of it, holding me up, grounding me as the aftershocks keep rolling, little flickers that dissolve me into nothing but sensation.

By the time it finally eases, I'm limp, panting, with my pulse racing. My skin still tingles everywhere he touches, and I swear I can feel the echo of it still thrumming inside me.

Noel holds me steady, his arms wrapped around me, drawing me upright as he slips his cock out of me. Then his lips find my neck.

"How was that? Later, we'll continue so I can fill you with all my cum."

I laugh, still breathless, still floating. Below, I spot Kane and Chris moving toward the car, ready to help the bride and her party.

We have maybe two minutes before I need to be down there.

"We need to go," I say, though I make no move to leave his arms.

"We do." He doesn't move either.

"The bride—"

"Can wait thirty more seconds while I hold you."

I lean back against his chest when Noel brushes his lips against my ear. "Do you want that too? A wedding. With us."

The question blindsides me. Of all the things I

thought he might say after what we just did, *that* was not on the list.

My breath stalls in my lungs. Weddings aren't expected for scent-matched packs. Marks, bites—instinct binds us. Ceremonies are optional, pretty, symbolic, unnecessary.

I'd never really let myself imagine it. But the second he asks… a picture flashes into my mind so fast and so vivid that I'm smiling.

Lights strung overhead. The three of them in suits. Me in something soft and shimmering and *lovely.* Their hands on me. Their vows. A celebration of us.

My chest warms, too much, too fast. Noel wraps an arm fully around my waist, pulling me tight to him.

"You do want it," he murmurs. Not a question. A knowing.

"Maybe," I whisper, cheeks burning. "I… haven't let myself think about it. But now I am. And it… feels good."

His answering sound is a soft, satisfied growl against the back of my neck. "Then one day, sweetheart, we'll give you whatever version of that dream you want. All three of us standing beside you. That's a promise."

My heart does an actual somersault. I slip from his arms before I combust, grabbing my panties from the floor and stepping into them, still tingling everywhere. He tucks himself away and watches me with that slow, possessive smile that always softens me.

"I really have to go," I say, leaning up for a quick peck.

He kisses me back—deep, slow, claiming. "Let's make this wedding perfect," he murmurs against my lips. He takes my hand as we rush toward the stairs, giving my fingers a final squeeze before letting go. "We'll talk more later, with Chris and Kane too," he says quietly.

And as I hurry down to the ceremony, cheeks flushed, dress perfect, heart pounding with something that feels suspiciously like joy, one thought blooms bright and unstoppable…

I used to dream small because I thought that was all I deserved.

Now… with them?

I get to want everything.

And for the first time in my life, I think I just might get it.

LILY'S BROWNIES

Bake Lily's brownies and you'll understand exactly what all the fuss is about.

<u>Ingredients:</u>

¾ Cup Salted Butter, softened

2-60% Cacao Dark Chocolate Baking Bricks/ (227 g) Dark Cooking Chocolate

¾ Cup Granulated Sugar

¾ Cup Packed Brown Sugar

1 Rounded tsp Espresso Powder

2 tsp vanilla extract

2 Eggs + 1 Yolk (at room temp.)

⅓ Cup Cocoa Powder

1 Cup All Purpose Flour

¼ - ½ Cup Dark Chocolate Chunks or Chips.

<u>Directions:</u>

In a microwave safe bowl melt your butter and
chocolate bricks together. Heat in 30 second
increments to prevent chocolate from burning, mixing
each time.

While the chocolate and butter are melting, in a
separate bowl add in your sugars, espresso powder,
vanilla, eggs, and cocoa powder. Give it a mix to
combine everything.

Pour in the melted butter and chocolate into your bowl
of other ingredients. Mix until combined. Add in your
flour and mix.

Lastly add in your chocolate chunks and mix until
incorporated in your brownie batter. The batter will be
a little thick. Pour into your prepped baking dish and
spread until evenly distributed.

Bake for 30-35 minutes. The inside will be fudgy so if a
tooth pick is inserted it will likely not come out clean.
Let rest for 30 minutes before cutting and serving.

ABOUT HARLEY KNIGHT

Hi, I'm Harley Knight! I'm a romance author who's absolutely obsessed with books, writing, and happily-ever-afters. I love creating stories filled with emotion, passion, and unforgettable characters that stick with you long after the last page. When I'm not writing, you'll find me lost in a good book or dreaming up my next big adventure. For me, there's nothing better than crafting love stories that remind us all why love is worth fighting for.

*Contact: **knightharleyus@gmail.com***

www.ingramcontent.com/pod-product-compliance
Lightning Source LLC
Chambersburg PA
CBHW062311200726
48292CB00006BA/1972